THE SPLIT

The Sixth Kelly Turnbull Novel

THE SPLIT

By

Kurt Schlichter

Kindle Paperback ISBN: 978-1-7341993-3-8
The Split - Kurt Schlichter - Paperback - Final - 071821 – v79

For Irina

ACKNOWLEDGMENTS

I usually write this part first. Seems weird that I know who is going to help me with each book, but after a half-dozen Kelly Turnbull adventures I kind of have it down. I'll just add the ones I did not foresee as I write *The Split* over the next six months.

Now, you need to understand that these books would not be possible without the help and support of a bunch of people, and I want to name all of them and the biggest stress point of the writing process is that I miss crediting someone deserving.

Always first in my acknowledgments and in my heart (aahhhh...sentimental Kurt is the most disconcerting Kurt) is, of course, my hot wife, Irina Moises. She is always there every step of the way, from initial ideas to final product, reading and critiquing the drafts and always demanding yet another read to purge them of typos. She also helped with the crocodile stuff.

Many other folks contributed to this in various ways, some obvious and others not so obvious. I can't list them all, but I'll try to name several in no particular order: Cam Edwards, Robert O'Brien, Matthew Betley, Larry O'Connor, Glenn Reynolds, Chris Stigall, Seb Gorka, Tom Sauer, Hugh Hewitt, Tim Young, Jim Geraghty, WarrenPeas64, Big Pete, Austin Peterson, Terry Maxwell, and Pat O'Brien, and many more.

I want to give a special thanks to our good friend and the Official Kelly Turnbull Series Sommelier, Drew Matich. I would text him "I need a really expensive red," and he'd tell me one after quizzing me on the circumstances. Cheers!

I want to thank my father-in-law, US Army vet Ed "Mundi" Alvarez for his help with some Cuban phrases. I hope he gets a kick out of it.

Bill and Joyce Wilson remain my gun gurus, and they have answered all my questions about their mighty Wilson Combat pistols. Ned Ryun helped out too – I had the chance to read an early edition of his excellent Bunker Hill novel *The Adversaries*, which saved me significant research on that battle.

I also want to thank Adam Kissel for his tireless work on the manuscript. He just seems to love it, and I'm not going to stand in his way. My favorite thing is when he suggests corrections to words in other languages. How many languages does this guy speak?

My cover artist J.R. Hawthorne, *aka* Salty Hollywood, has continued his winning streak with this cover. It's pretty awesome, huh? I dig the crocs.

And a special thanks to all my Townhall and Twitter supporters, and everyone who has embraced the Kelly Turnbull novels. I love hearing how much you enjoy them!

And, finally, I always thank Andrew Breitbart. He was a visionary who recognized the power of culture and how important it was to our fight. Thanks, Andrew!

KAS

PREFACE

This is the sixth novel in the Kelly Turnbull series.

Let's get the timing squared away here – *The Split* is a close follow-on to *Crisis*, taking place a few months after those events in which America formally divides into red and blue nations.

The series skips around, mostly because my mind does. The chronological sequence is:

Crisis
The Split
Indian Country
People's Republic
Wildfire
Collapse

Collapse told the story of how America might come back together, and Book No. 7 may well follow that one. But I can't think that far ahead.

There are now a half-dozen of these books, and the real-life timeline is starting to get close to the one in the books. Maybe I will prepare a new edition that corrects the canon, *a lá* George Lucas. Or maybe I won't, which is probably how George Lucas should have gone.

Until then, I recommend you suspend disbelief and not be too picky about whether something in *The Split* is perfectly consistent with something in an earlier book. Relax, have a bourbon. Chill, and enjoy the ride.

I began this during the disputed post-2020 election period and through the early part of the Biden* administration – that desiccated old weirdo gets a perpetual asterisk from me. I wrote this one during and after the pandemic and the George Floyd riots. And, of course, there was the bogus "insurrection" panic, which resulted in dozens of people calling me "Nostradamus" over the eerie semi-parallels to *Crisis*.

I did foresee a mob attacking Congress in the last volume, but I did not foresee a guy in Viking drag leading it.

So, my challenge since I started writing these, and even more with *The Split*, has been to try to keep the insane events from overcoming my speculation, and it's hard. I would write something ridiculous and – boom! – suddenly it's happening.

Now, since you are not dumb, you understand that these books are a warning signal, not a wish list. I don't want any of this to happen. However, I cannot and will not pretend that it never could happen, and I am going to write these warnings disguised as novels hoping that, in some small way, I can help inspire others to stop the madness of hateful division that the left is inflicting upon us.

The Split is a cautionary tale, but one that I hope you find to be a fun read.

Do what needs to be done to ensure that it never comes true.

And David enquired at the Lord, saying, Shall I pursue after this troop? shall I overtake them? And he answered him, Pursue: for thou shalt surely overtake them, and without fail recover all.

1 Samuel 30:8

BOOK ONE

1.

"I kill communists for fun."

Edmundo "Mundi" Vega considered this a sufficient explanation for his action. But now, after Kelly Turnbull had just shaken his head in response, the wiry operator seemed a little hurt while standing over the corpse of the Cuban private and holding his Ka-Bar knife as crimson drops fell onto the sand.

"I thought we were supposed to be covert," Turnbull growled in a whisper. Mundi shrugged.

Turnbull had wanted to make the infiltration in from the warm Caribbean waters quietly. They wore black fatigues to blend into the darkness. This mission was supposed to be, at least initially, all about the stealth and the subtlety. But entering Cuba unnoticed was out of the question now. Turnbull opened his mouth to respond to his partner but there was movement in the darkness.

Someone else was there.

"*¿Qué carajo paso aquí? ¿Quiénes son estos dos tipos?*" shouted a sergeant in rumpled green fatigues as he appeared out of the darkness. The soldier was about ten meters up the beach, and having spotted the two men and his deceased buddy on the sand, he was fumbling with the sling of his AKM, the slightly improved but still obsolete update of the AK-47.

Turnbull's Wilson Combat .45 was out in an instant, the suppressor screwed onto the special threaded barrel he had bought for just this mission. He pulled the trigger twice, deploying a pair of Federal 230-grain Hydra-Shok rounds into the soldier's sternum. The sergeant was not a big man – his skinny carcass was a tribute to the bounty of socialism – and he was lying dead on his back on the sand before Turnbull could deliver the final headshot to complete the Mozambique Drill.

Turnbull and Mundi paused, with Mundi sliding his blade back into its scabbard and bringing his short HK416A5 assault rifle up to the low ready position in case there were more interlopers. Turnbull left his rifle on the sand, holding his 1911A1 ready. They stood-to for at least 60 seconds as the low waves rolled in, listening in case there was someone else.

"See," Mundi said, relaxing just a bit when the minute was up. "It's fun to kill communists."

"Yeah," admitted Turnbull. "Of course, now we have to deal with these two."

"We could bury them in the sand?"

"I thought you were trying to keep us from running into people," began Turnbull, "when you picked our entry point as a freaking alligator preserve...."

They stared at each other for a moment, and then Mundi began to laugh.

"Grab his boot," Turnbull said, reaching down to the private's foot. Mundi took hold of the other one and they dragged him up the beach toward the swamp.

"Watch out," Mundi said, holding the left foot. "*Caimanes cubanos* are very emotional creatures, the females especially. They can turn vicious in an instant."

"So, basically, they're like all Cuban women," Turnbull said. The sole of the dead soldier's scuffed leather combat boot was coming off.

"*Sí*," Mundi replied as they left the beach and entered the swamp. They were no longer on sand but on dirt, moist and slippery. Enough moonlight dappled through the leaves that they could see without flashlights. They dragged the body inside the tree line about 30 yards until they came to a large pond. Turnbull tossed the man's AKM into the water first.

"*Adiós*, communist *puta*," Mundi said as they toppled the corpse into the water. The body floated there for a moment. Nothing happened.

"Maybe they're taking a siesta," Turnbull said, staring at the still, dark water. "Let's go get his buddy."

They made their way back to the beach and, ensuring the coast was clear, dragged the other dead man back to the pond. The first body was gone, except for one boot that was floating forlornly.

"At least someone in this country is eating well," Turnbull observed.

Turnbull tossed the second man's rifle into the pool and together with Mundi swung the body in as well. This time, as soon as the splash settled, a black shape burst out of the water and grabbed the floating soldier between its jaws. A thick, muscular saurian body twisted out of the water and over onto its side, dragging the carcass under the surface. But then a second crocodile appeared and lunged for the prize hanging out of the other's mouth.

Turnbull and Mundi watched as the two huge creatures battled over the dead communist, tearing it to bits even as they wrestled with each other. It went on for several minutes as they stared, silent.

"Holy shit," Mundi said, eyes wide, when they were both gone into the pond. "You see that, Kelly?"

"Yeah," Turnbull said, still staring, fascinated. "Two crocs, one swamp. That's a recipe for conflict, at least until one does in the other."

He glanced at his watch. 0124 hours.

"We need to get our stuff and go," Turnbull said.

Mundi nodded and they headed back toward the sand where they had left their gear. Like Turnbull, he had been personally recruited by Clay Deeds, the shadowy US operative responsible for undertaking missions that didn't officially exist. Before joining up with Task Force Zulu, Mundi had been in Marine recon, and he was an expert at getting in and out of places via the ocean. It was his plan to have the sub come up close to the coast and have a couple Navy special warfare combatant-craft crewmen drop them off at the beach in a muffled, lo-vis Zodiac. He picked the landing spot at the alligator preserve, wrongly assuming that it would be deserted. The guards were more likely there to protect the reptiles from hungry poachers than to stop Yankee infiltrators, particularly since half the Yankees were now bestest buddies with the Cuban communist regime.

It had been less than six months since the Treaty of St. Louis had split the United States in two, and the People's Republic of North America had not spared a second in sucking up to every America-hating dictatorship around the globe. Of course, Cuba was at the top of the People's Republic's to-do list. Besides the natural affinity of the Marxist rulers of each country, having the doddering PR president palling around with the doddering Cuban dictator Raúl Castro – who had retaken the reins of power again after temporarily giving them up – was certain to enrage the new United States.

The operators gathered up their backpacks and rifles and moved off toward the access road they had seen on the Google Earth photos they used to plan the mission. The imagery was good enough, and except for some covert interviews with people with first-hand knowledge of the key geography, Clay Deeds had sought to avoid requesting intel from sources outside TF Zulu. That included from within the new United States government. Trusting no one had gotten Deeds and his team this far, and of all the things Turnbull had learned from his handler, trusting no one was perhaps the most important.

The dirt road led from the beach about a kilometer inland to a yellow traffic gate off an east-west two-lane road. The gate was festooned with signs that, though he could not read Spanish, clearly warned people away from the domain of the 'gators. One pictogram featured a most unhappy stick figure in the maw of one of the beasts, and Turnbull wondered if Castro's vaunted literacy program was all it was cracked up to be.

He checked his watch again.

0206 hours.

Mundi gestured to a dense copse of trees with a good view of the road in both directions. To the north, the terrain rose, with scattered trees over grasslands. It was dead quiet. They set up under cover. Mundi offered to take the watch.

"Wake me when he gets here," Turnbull said, leaning his head against his pack. "And look out for alligators."

Mundi nodded.

It seemed that no time at all had passed when Mundi nudged him awake. Turnbull gripped his HK416A5 rifle just in case there was a threat. But there was only a pair of dim lights in the distance. It was a vehicle, coming from the west along the road.

"It's him," Mundi said.

Turnbull watched as the lights came closer, and he noted one was conspicuously less bright than the other. He also heard the engine from afar, loud and indicating the need for a valve job. There was a shot – at least that was what Turnbull first took it as – but it was a backfire, and the men relaxed a bit. Still, if the vehicle, which was now identifiable as an ancient Russian-made white cargo van of some sort, got out of line, they would instantly dump a pair of 30-round mags of 5.56mm ammo into it and its occupant.

Mundi was correct, as the van confirmed when it slowed as it neared the gate. They did not move; instead, they waited for the van to pull to a stop. In fading red paint on the side were the words "*Servicio Veterinario Del Pueblo Provincial*," and the rear cargo area had no windows. The driver waited a few moments, then cautiously stepped out and came around the front of the idling van, looking down the dirt road south beyond the gate. He was in his fifties, or maybe in his thirties and he just looked older thanks to the hard miles of communist living. He also seemed scared, which probably demonstrated common sense.

After observing the driver for a few moments and being satisfied that it was kosher, Turnbull looked to Mundi and nodded. Mundi broke cover and greeted the visitor in Spanish as Turnbull covered him with the rifle. Turnbull's Spanish was limited to ordering carne asada burritos and bottles of Dos Equis, his last training in the language having been a nearly forgotten class in sixth grade. The pair conversed in Spanish for about a minute as Turnbull kept watch, then Mundi turned and motioned his partner to come forward.

"This is Alberto. He's a veterinarian. If he is stopped, he'll say he was out at a collective farm working on a sick cow all night."

"*Hola*, Alberto," Turnbull said, wondering if he had gotten it right.

Alberto seemed terrified, and with good reason. The life expectancy within the Cuban underground was pretty short, and getting the call out of the blue to drive a couple of heavily armed gringos from an alligator preserve into the city of Guantánamo at oh-dark thirty was probably not one he ever wanted to receive. But he hated communists as only one who had to live under them could.

The trip was uneventful. Through the windshield, in the moonlight, Turnbull could glimpse the grasslands and farms lining the road. The poverty was evident everywhere – not a building in town or out in the country was anything except dilapidated. It was as if a malaise had settled on the country. It was simply decaying, and no one was lifting a finger to stop it. Why would they? No one owned any of it. The whole island was a living example of the tragedy of the commons.

The only things that seemed to be taken care of were the propaganda signs. They were everywhere. "*Viva el Socialismo!*" was popular, and on another the Cuban flag was crossed with a several-months-old iteration of the People's Republic of North America flag (this old version had a brown band across the top while the latest had a pink one), and the sign bore the legend *"¡El pueblo cubano se une en solidaridad con sus hermanos del Norte contra el racismo yanqui!"*

Guantánamo had probably been a prosperous town back better than a half-century before when the locals could still work for good wages on the nearby United States Navy base at Guantánamo Bay. Castro, his pride stung by this American foothold in his worker's paradise, had killed the golden goose. The economy stagnated and the people suffered, but the ruling clique got to congratulate itself on its fearless resistance to the imperialist oppressors. None of its members ever had to worry about missing a meal.

After the Split, the Americans left the naval base to the south and the People's Republic Navy had taken over, but the new landlords had not been hiring. Nor were the Chinese, who would be accepting the assignment of base lease from the PRNA for the next 99 years in the coming week. They were bringing their own work force with them. The Cuban communists did not much care about that – merely having a Chinese naval base in position to seal off access to the Caribbean from the new US's ports along the Gulf of Mexico was exactly the sort of stick they yearned to poke into the Yankees' eye.

Through the windshield, Turnbull got a good look at Guantánamo. Most of its buildings were low and dirty, with the bright pastel colors they had been painted some time ago faded and peeling. Half were quaint and delightful Spanish-style buildings, or had been back in the 1950s, while the rest were the kind of grey slab brutalist monstrosities that socialists around the world seemed to love. Bare powerlines hung across the streets in no rational pattern. Though it was late, a few shirtless men in shorts still shuffled along the sidewalks. There were some soldiers as well, but few vehicles. The town had a vibe similar to the dirty, decaying cities of the Middle East.

"It's like Baghdad with mojitos," Turnbull said, impressed by the power of socialism to make even a people as industrious and talented as the Cubans poor.

"No, mojitos are only for the tourists," Mundi replied. "These people get shitty rum they make themselves with stolen sugar cane." In fact, at one time his family had owned a sugar cane farm. It was expropriated in the Revolution. His immediate family had come over to Florida in the 1980s and he had joined the Marines, earning enough of a reputation in Force Recon to be visited by Clay Deeds one evening at a base in Djibouti that was running covert ops into Somalia. Deeds offered the newly-promoted gunnery sergeant a red pill trip down the rabbit hole.

Alberto pulled the van to the side of the road in front of a row of two-story apartment buildings with peeling white façades. He turned and spoke to Mundi, with Turnbull catching only a couple words of the quick Cuban cadence – "*sí*"and "*no.*"

"We need to get inside quickly. The spies are always watching." Mundi meant the local informers of the *Comités de Defensa de la Revolución*, the Committees for the Defense of the Revolution that functioned as a fascist neighborhood watch. There were spies on every block, Fidel Castro's brainstorm being to outsource his secret policing to neighborhood busybodies and gossips. Hopefully none of them would be awake at four in the morning.

They sprinted out of the van into a doorway and up the rickety stairs, dodging one step that was broken in half and held together with a 2" x 4" nailed over it. The walls were covered with dirty, peeling wallpaper, and the hallway reeked of unwashed bodies. Soap was a luxury, and if you obtained it, you would often trade it away for an absolute necessity like bread.

It was hot as well, and all the windows were open. On the second floor there was a room with a single ancient bed. Apparently, Alberto had moved the three or four people living in it out to make room for the Americans for the night. Turnbull got a look at them, peeking from the doorway at the end of the hall.

A couple were pretty young women. Alberto left the Americans alone inside, shutting the door behind them.

They worked by moonlight, opening their packs and removing smaller day packs suitable for tourists. They broke down their HK416s and put them inside the day packs next to their six 30-round mags and their radios, covering it all with sweaters they would never need in the stifling heat. Their pistols they kept out for the evening; they would carry those in the front pockets of the day packs. Finally, one at a time, they changed into their American tourist gear – cargo shorts, billowy floral shirts, and tennis shoes with ankle socks.

"We look like assholes," Mundi observed.

"Then we should fit right in with the PR tourists," Turnbull said. "Is Alberto getting rid of our fatigues and boots?"

"He'll use them for his underground cell, except two of his men could fit into one of our uniforms."

"I'll take the watch," Turnbull said. His Timex read "0402." They had a few hours.

The terrified private had just handed Major Luis Jesús Gomez the combat boot with the snapped-off stumps of a tibia and fibula poking out of the foot stuck inside just as the sergeant next to him shouted and fired off a burst of 7.62x39mm rounds into the murky pond.

"Stop it, you idiot!" the major shrieked in Spanish.

"But, but the *caimanes* were coming!" the senior sergeant pleaded.

"¡*Tonto*!" the major spat, handing the horrified senior sergeant the boot.

The sun was rising, and its rays were peeking through the trees in the swamp. Hours before, the senior sergeant had come to change the guard and found his subordinates gone. He had assumed, not without reason, that the men were off sleeping in the swamp. Why someone would do so in an alligator preserve escaped him, but Pedro was a junior sergeant in charge of a shift at the preserve for the first time, and who knew if he would take his duties seriously? The senior sergeant had gone through the swamp looking for his men, and had come to the pool and found the combat boot floating by the bank. He had called headquarters, and now here was the major from the military police.

The major was the region's senior military police officer for the *Fuerzas Armadas Revolucionarias*, the Cuban Revolutionary Armed Forces, and his natural suspicion, which sometimes bordered on paranoia, regarding those posing a threat to the communist regime had accelerated his career past his peers in the FAR. Ironically in light of his middle name (which Gomez, a devout Marxist atheist, detested), he had recently overseen the arrest of a dozen members of a secret Bible study group within one of the local barracks, and he had been selected to lecture visiting members of the People's Republic Army's own military police on the subject of rooting out subversion in the ranks. But considering the pre-Split American military's political purges, the PR exchange officers had plenty of ideas of their own to share with their Cuban comrades.

Now Major Gomez considered the possibilities. Most likely these two fools had decided to share a bottle in the swamp instead of walking their post and had slipped into the water and become a snack for the vicious alligators. The beasts were known to be territorial, and the skinny hides of the two FAR soldiers would make a tasty meal.

That was the most likely explanation, but not the only one. The naval base was so close, and the turnover to the Chinese so critical to the nation, that any anomaly had to be fully investigated. Perhaps poachers had come across the soldiers and did them in, but the poachers would have at best crude spears – Castro's disarmament of the population was something their new fraternal allies in the People's Republic of North America were studying with great interest. Fools or not, both soldiers had automatic rifles, and as the senior sergeant had just demonstrated, the conscripts were not hesitant to use them. There was a possibility, a remote one, that this was something more, something perhaps related to the build-up of United States naval forces in the region over the last week.

It simply had to be investigated.

He walked out of the swamp and across the beach to the dirt road, where his driver was sitting at the wheel of the elderly American Army surplus jeep with "FAR" painted in white on the side that had brought him here.

"Guantánamo," he said. It took a full minute for the driver to convince the Willys engine to turn over.

"Here you go," Mundi said, handing Turnbull a half-empty miniature bottle of Bacardi brown rum. Turnbull took it and poured a bit into his hand, put down the bottle, then rubbed his paws together and patted them around his face and neck. Then he took a swig and looked for a place to spit it out.

"Don't you dare," Mundi said. Turnbull swallowed it, then assessed the two of them.

"We smell like a distillery," he announced.

"*Perfecto*," Mundi replied. They had the smell, and now they needed to complete the look. "Muss up your hair."

Turnbull did. He had not cut it for a while for this very reason.

"Just two PR assholes out on the town," he said, gazing at himself in the mirror on the old bureau that sat against the wall. There were pictures in frames, all black and white, of happy people doing happy things in pre-Castro Cuba.

"Alberto could probably get arrested for those," Turnbull observed, placing his Wilson Combat pistol in the front pocket of his day pack.

"Not probably," Mundi replied, slipping his own pistol and Ka-Bar into his pack's front pocket.

"Better get going. Hope the narcs are up."

"Oh, those *brujas* are already up and watching," Mundi said. "We need to give them a show."

There was no hiding this time; instead, the Americans sought to be seen pouring out of the apartment building, laughing, high-fiving, and staggering down the street. Turnbull was fully aware of the impression they were giving, the impression Alberto had allowed them to give – that they had spent the night partying with Alberto's attractive female family members, no doubt for money. He grimaced at the shame of it, and that it would be so readily believed and accepted that a couple of boorish Yankees had used the local talent so cavalierly only reiterated the degradation of the communist system. That the girls would be seen by many of their fellow serfs as lucky to have hooked up with some tourists only made it worse.

There were many eyes on them as they walked along the route they had scouted on the map in preparation for their mission.

"We counted sixteen vehicles on the road last night after midnight," the FAR lieutenant told Major Gomez. "Five were military."

"The rest?"

"Some delivery vans, a veterinarian, an ambulance. Oh, and a commissar from Santiago in his official sedan."

"Does the commissar have a *novia* in Guantánamo?" Gomez asked. The lieutenant smiled.

"I checked with the *Dirección de Inteligencia* and they confirmed three. He has three girlfriends. And he's reliable."

"The other drivers, what about them?"

"None of the drivers assigned the vehicles are unreliable, or at least there is no record of it. I can contact the *Comités de Defensa* in their *barrios* and enquire further."

Major Gomez's natural suspicion was in full effect. He thought for a moment, and then issued his order.

"Do it. Start with this veterinarian."

The Hotel Washington in downtown Guantánamo had clearly not gotten the word that George Washington, whose name was initially preserved only because of his own revolutionary credentials, was now *persona non grata*. It was an ugly construction of cement blocks and rusting metal located on what passed for a busy street near the center of town, just a 15-minute walk from Alberto's flat. The tour group from New York City had experienced no hesitation in lecturing the baffled and bewildered staff on the perfidy of the first president of the former United States.

"I don't understand how a country as progressive and enlightened as Cuba could allow this honor for a racist slaveholder," spat a wizened crone in a $600 designer black t-shirt with white lettering that read "DON'T ASSUME I AM A WOMAN." She was disclaiming to a perplexed young lady at the front desk. The hostess was wearing the same threadbare maroon and teal uniform she had worn every day for the last two weeks.

"You should be ashamed of yourself!" the crone informed her.

"*No hablo inglés*," the girl lied. She was actually fluent, and had competed against hundreds of others for the chance to cater to rich, bitter PR tourists.

"Racists are everywhere," the crone sputtered as she stomped off. "And this hotel is filthy!"

"*Puta*," whispered one of her male coworkers, and the girl giggled.

The tourists were gathered in the lobby, sitting on the worn chairs and standing on the dirty linoleum floor, mostly complaining about the socialist paradise they idolized. Turnbull and Mundi wandered in the front, past the security guard assigned to keep out curious and/or desperate locals as well as unapproved hookers. Turnbull and Mundi were not the only tourists staggering back to the tour group after a night on the town; the majority of the males treated Cuba as a Caribbean Bangkok, and the locals' poverty provided all sorts of unseemly opportunities for those so inclined, including those tending toward the more exotic and appalling tastes.

The pair did not stand out from the rest of the PR citizens in their floral shirts and with their day packs. They fit in both in terms of their tackiness and in their reek of alcohol-fueled debauchery.

The complaining was not limited to picking on the hapless employees of the hotel. One woman with a nose stud and a $700 purse was berating her unshaven husband, telling him, "I don't care if you interact with sex workers, but do you have to be so tragically cis?"

"We could just open fire now," Mundi whispered.

"Don't tempt me," Turnbull replied.

"*Hola* comrades! Time to get on the bus!" said a chipper Tourist Bureau woman. She was very pretty, and several of the women standing near Turnbull complained that they could not understand "how a progressive socialist system could perpetuate traditional male gaze versions of beauty."

Another hefty PR citizen added, "Would it kill them to have a fat guide as a repudiation of fatphobia?" She was oblivious to the fact that there were no fat people under socialism – at least not down at the tourist guide level of the *nomenklatura*.

Turnbull and Mundi lingered a bit, then slid into the middle of the pack as it flowed out the front door to where a wheezing red and blue bus manufactured by some obscure Yugoslavian factory in the 1970s idled uneasily, belching fumes into the blue sky.

"It's like they never even heard of climate change," grumbled the middle-aged man in a Harvard t-shirt ahead of Turnbull, seemingly forgetting that he not only flew to Cuba but that he was stepping onto the offending bus.

"That's probably why it's so hot and humid here," the man's life partner replied. "But we can't really blame Third World people for not knowing these things."

"It's 'Formerly Colonialized and Oppressed World' people who don't know these things," the Harvard shirt man said. The life partner gazed downward, chastened.

They all got in the bus and the tourist guide seemed to be taking a count. She finished and frowned. Then she looked at her clipboard, and back at the people. After a moment, she put the clipboard down.

"*¡Atención, atención!*" she cried.

Turnbull smiled. Undoubtedly, she had come up with an overcount and decided to go with it. A missing tourist – that could be a problem for her. An extra one? That was a problem for someone else down the line. Everyone in the bus was obviously from the PR – tackily dressed and complaining – so she did what everyone in a socialist dictatorship did to survive and went with the flow.

"We will now travel to the liberated Guantánamo Bay Naval Base," she said. "You will see the truth of the oppression and torture carried out there at the Museum of Resistance to Fascism, and then tour the old prison buildings. Best of all, you will see the flags of Cuba and the People's Republic of North America flying together!"

The bus erupted in cheers. Turnbull noted that she ignored the real news – that in a few weeks the PR and Cuba would be handing the base over to China.

The crowd settled down and the bus haltingly lurched forward, gasping and gears grinding as it moved down the road. Behind them, one of the PR tourists was explaining how Cuba did not look like this before Donald Trump. "It was a paradise," she explained. A horse and cart passed to the left of the bus as it headed south.

The trip was under ten miles but took a half-hour. A '57 Chevy had broken down on a narrow bridge and stopped traffic until a dozen men got out of their vehicles and pushed.

"Why don't they let the women help push?" one of the tourists wondered aloud from her seat. "Latin macho culture is extremely problematic."

What was apparently her husband, also from his seat, added, "It's actually toxic." The woman patted her husband on the hand.

The gate was personned by both PR and Cuban soldiers, and, as promised, both the Cuban and the PR flags flew from the pole. Turnbull noted it was the wrong flag, the banner having been altered only a week before to recognize "the impactful resistance and journey of Pacific Islander and Micronesian two-spirit peoples." With the addition of the mauve banner representing Samoan transexuals, the flag of the People's Republic now sported a total of 26 stripes.

Transiting the gate was a mere formality. The tourist guide spoke briefly to a Cuban officer and then the bus lumbered inside the fence line and on down the road. The base itself was well-kept, with six months of PR control not having completely destroyed it. There were many new signs, most of them touting the shared destiny of the PR and Cuba, as well as warnings to "Beware of Racist Spies." The picture of the burning stars and stripes on the billboard made clear who the racists were supposed to be.

They drove through main post, and there was a shuttered McDonald's restaurant. The chain had been the subject of much criticism in the PR for "appropriating Scottish imagery and nomenclature," and when that charge itself was deemed problematic, since one could not be racist against the Scots, the brand was accused of racism for selling Big Macs, which someone found offensive somehow.

"Our first stop will be the Museum of Resistance to Fascism," the guide announced. "And then we will take a trip to the former detention facility for our tour."

The Museum of Resistance to Fascism was built in a warehouse along Marti Road. Out front was a recently-dedicated statue of Bernie Sanders with his foot on a supine Mitch

McConnell and a longsword in his hand. Sadly, Sanders had perished in a fire a few months before when he dropped his bong into a pile of old copies of *Socialist Worker* and the fire trucks mistakenly responded to the Sanders mansion in downtown Burlington instead of the burning Sanders mansion on the shore of Lake Champlain.

The bus pulled to a halt and the tourists filed out into the heat, which they began to complain about at length. The heat they chalked up to climate change; they were unclear about the culprit for the drenching tropical humidity, so they took it out on their tour guide, complaining incessantly about it. Unable to pretend not to speak English, she simply smiled, uttered something about "enemies *de la Revolución*," and motioned for her dripping charges to follow her inside.

Turnbull and Mundi waited as the moist, grumbling tourists entered the building and immediately began walking east across a large, empty parking lot toward the office complex at the terminus of Administration Road. There were some civilian vehicles in the lot, and a row of Chevy SUVs painted white with "MILITARY POLICE" on their sides was near the building.

Outside the entrance was a wooden sign, painted brown, that read, in yellow letters cut into the boards, "525th Military Police Detention Battalion." The old unit symbol, a crest showing a knight's helmet, crossed knives, and an angry dog, had been pried off and replaced by a new one. It had an orange background with a stylized raised fist, no doubt challenging oppression, and each finger was a different color. It had six fingers, plus a thumb, to accommodate all the requisite hues.

Turnbull and Mundi paused behind the eight-foot-high sign to silently take their pistols out of their daypacks and screw on their suppressors. The weapons went under their billowy floral shirts. Then they came around and went through the door.

It was a fairly ordinary orderly room of the kind each had seen a thousand times before. A long counter created a foyer, and beyond it were desks, most of them obviously not in use, and beyond them offices next to each other for the commander and command sergeant major. A stairway led upwards off to the right.

A single staff sergeant in camo, maybe 5'7" and 180 pounds, was working one of the desks – actually, he was on the internet perusing a site that involved women and their many friends interacting, secure that the People's Republic's military's "Freedom from Judgment" policy would protect him from persecution for watching porn on-the-job. Sure, his cis tastes were a bit iffy, but diversity was important in the PR Army.

The sexy cable TV repair man had just joined the sexy plumber and the sexy pest control technician at the buxom blonde's apartment when the orderly room door opened. The PR soldier was baffled at the pair of tourists walking into his space. The sergeant stood up, revealing two horizontal tapes, sewn on his rumpled uniform just above nipple level, reading "PR ARMY" and "SWAN (HE/HIM)." He was unarmed, which did not stop Turnbull.

"Hey, you can't be...," he got out before Turnbull's .45 round emptied his brainpan out the back. SSG Swan dropped to the floor as if his bones had all turned to jelly, leaving nothing but the clink of the brass shell bouncing around the foyer's dingy linoleum. Mundi secured the front door. Turnbull leapt the counter and, leading with his Wilson, checked the two offices.

"Clear," he said, but he kept his suppressed pistol handy.

Mundi was already at the counter, pulling the pieces of his HK416 out of his daypack and assembling them. When he was done, he took up the watch as Turnbull reassembled his own weapon. Both attached suppressors to their assault rifles; they would remove them when they left the building, as the weapons looked enough like M4s, even with Aimpoint CompM4 optics, to not draw suspicion from a distance, and silencers would give it away.

"I can't fit in that," Turnbull said, nodding to the twitching body. "You try it."

Mundi nodded and hopped the counter. He knelt by the dead man as Turnbull stood guard.

"You didn't get any mess on the uniform," Mundi said, undressing the corpse. "Nice shooting."

"You see the key lock box back there?"

"Yeah," Mundi said, pointing, and he continued stripping the dead man. Turnbull went around to the lock box, which was locked.

"Pockets, keys," Turnbull grunted. Mundi fished around in the trousers and then tossed Turnbull a key ring. Turnbull used one of the keys to open the lock box and select an SUV remote from the several hanging inside on hooks.

It took a couple minutes for Mundi to change into the staff sergeant's uniform. In the meantime, Turnbull reassembled his own HK416A5, and then dragged the dead man into the CO's office. He used the battalion colors to sop up the blood.

"How do I look?" Mundi asked after he finished. The uniform and boots fit, sort of.

"Did you iron those camos with a rake?" Turnbull asked.

"Standards sure went to shit fast in the blue," Mundi said. "Why do they gotta look so 'ed up all the time?"

"To ask that is to answer it," Turnbull replied. He gestured to the stairs. "You first."

Mundi went upwards, the HK416 ready. Turnbull followed, his own up and ready with its suppressor in place. At the top of the stairs, Mundi turned a corner and cautiously approached a closed door with "GUARDROOM" painted on it. There were muffled noises inside. Mundi placed his hand on the handle, and looked to Turnbull. He nodded and Mundi pushed it open. Turnbull rushed in.

It was a locker room, with three soldiers in various states of undress. They were armed, their weapons lying nearby, but they never got to them. Turnbull fired six shots, and they all fell. Mundi got the door.

Selecting the uniform of the largest, Turnbull changed into it as Mundi kept watch. When he was finished, they each liberated an MP brassard and a utility belt, installing their own pistols inside the holsters. They also took the key cards and IDs the soldiers wore around their necks. Their radios went on the utility belts. Their spare mags went into their cargo pockets.

"You look good, Lieutenant Palmer," Mundi said, reading the nametapes on Turnbull's requisitioned People's Republic Army uniform. "Did you know your pronouns are 'XI/XIR'?"

"Come on," Turnbull growled. They made their way back downstairs and, after removing their suppressors, walked outside into the tropical sauna that was Cuba in the spring and headed to their SUV.

Major Gomez rolled down the street in his elderly FAR jeep, looking for something that would provide a hint as to where the two tourists had gone after leaving the veterinarian's flat that morning. His lieutenant had driven over to see Comrade Hidalgo, an elderly woman who was the block's senior member of the *Comité de Defensa* but had made the mistake of parking his own ancient jeep out front. By the time he had been informed about how two Yankees had been seen stumbling out of the veterinarian's house that morning, the flat was empty and the traitors were gone.

Major Gomez knew they could not go far – where in Cuba could they go? – but right now he needed to find those tourists. Obviously, they were not tourists at all, but what would they be doing in a remote city like Guantánamo?

Then his driver turned the corner and his eyes settled on the ugly concrete façade of the Hotel Washington. One of his prior jobs had been surveillance of tourists, though that was back in the days before the colossus of *del Norte* split in two. The visitors from the People's Republic were deemed so ideologically reliable that they rated only minimal observation.

This would be where the infiltrators were going, but why? The shabby lodge could not possibly be their final destination.

His driver pulled up in front and Major Gomez got out and rushed inside.

"I was here once before on a training mission," Mundi said as he drove up into the hills on a decaying blacktop road. Weeds were poking out of cracks, and the downsized of the PR military presence at Gitmo – just 100 personnel – left no one to pick weeds or paint rocks.

Turnbull had not been there before, but had studied the imagery and spoken to a couple of reds who had been serving there at the time of the Split, so he had an idea where they were going.

Their destination was Camp Alpha-7, the secret detention camp. No signs explained what it was, only informing those approaching, in both English and Spanish, to keep out.

The compound was at the top of a hill, with a magnificent view of the base and its two airfields, as well as the bay itself. There was a double chain-link fence surrounding the 75 meters by 75 meters square that was Camp Alpha-7. The fence was 18' high and topped with concertina. Inside the compound was a large, two-story pre-fab steel building with no windows. The gate was locked with a padlock.

Turnbull pulled down his soft cap. Hopefully whoever was on the monitors was paying attention to porn and not to what appeared to be the guard shift relief that had just shown up a bit early at about 1145 hours.

He got out of the now idling SUV – the gate key was on the ring with the remote and the vehicle's ignition was pushbutton – then walked to a scanner on a post off to the side of the road. He waved his stolen key card past it, then walked over to unlock the padlock, head low and the brim of his soft cap hiding his face. He had noted the cameras, installed high on the main building to the left and right.

The padlock opened and he pulled the chain out and motioned Mundi forward. Mundi pulled in and parked in the "GUARDPEOPLE VEHICLES" space by the building entrance as Turnbull locked up the gate behind him.

Mundi got out with two rifles and handed Turnbull his weapon. They walked over to the entrance as if they had done it a hundred times before, as if they were dreading yet another long, stultifying shift.

There was a metal door with a sign in big red letters with florid language explaining how entry was forbidden except to the authorized, and then explaining how this was not intended to further marginalize members of historically excluded demographics. Next to the door was another keypad. A camera loomed above.

"Ready?" Mundi said under his breath.

Turnbull didn't answer. He swept the card by the keypad and there was a click. Mundi grabbed the door handle and pulled it open hard, revealing a long hallway. It was empty and they entered.

They walked down the hall toward the metal door at the far end, about 30 feet. A red flasher that looked like it was lifted from a 1970s fire truck was mounted above the door.

"That's their signal," Mundi said.

"Better not let them activate it or we've come a long way for nothing," Turnbull replied.

They moved down the hall towards the door.

Major Gomez's jeep and his convoy of three old, OD green Russian-made ZiL-131 trucks carrying troops under their canvas barely slowed down at the base's front gate. He had his phone to his ear as his subordinate reported on the corpses discovered in the 525th's headquarters.

He hung up, then shouted at his driver to take a left. He knew where the intruders were headed because he, as the head of military police intelligence in this military region, knew what almost no one else did.

He knew that Camp Alpha-7 was here on the base, low-key, with a tiny footprint, hiding itself and its secrets in plain sight. It had been the subject of much laughter, the sheer irony of doing this thing here at Guantánamo Bay of all places. But someone had found out. And now that tiny PR security footprint, designed to deceive outside observers, had become a liability instead of an asset.

Mundi pulled open the next door, and it opened into another hall, except to the immediate right was a door and then a glass window taking up half of the wall. Behind the glass was a control station, with consoles, monitors, and government issue desk chairs on rollers. A rack of M4s hung on the wall, mags in. A bored sergeant sat at the console facing the hallway. At the far end was another door, with a red block lettered sign reading "CELLBLOCK," and another flasher was mounted on top.

"You guys – uh, persons – are early." The sergeant hit the buzzer to open the control station door before he even looked up at his relief. Mundi was already pushing the door open and bringing up his rifle as the guard realized these two persons weren't from his unit.

The cellblock door opened, and an armed MP stepped inside the hallway. Turnbull pivoted as the soldier went for his Beretta. Turnbull blew off a half-dozen 5.56mm rounds into his chest, sending him sprawling, falling back and blocking the door open.

The sergeant at the console slammed a red button with his fist before Mundi shot him twice in the face, leaving his own ears ringing and the blue's brains splattered on several of the screens.

"Kelly, go!" Mundi yelled, as a horn sounded and the red light began spinning and flashing.

Turnbull powered forward, pushing open the door and stepping over the body. Beyond it was a two-story cellblock, the doors solid but with a sliding metal window four feet up that was big enough to slip in a tray. Red flashers on each of the four walls were going off, and a horn sounded a blast each second.

Rounds slammed into the door as he came through. One MP was firing from the upper left walkway. Another had his Beretta in his hand and was pulling open the sliding window on the ground floor cell at the far-right end of the block. Activating the flashing red lights and the booming horn had meant one thing.

Kill all the prisoners.

Turnbull engaged the prisoner culler as he ran, firing a long burst that walked a series of sparking impacts across the steel cell door and into his target's pelvis. The soldier twisted and fell. His buddy on the second tier was still firing, with Turnbull counting on the 30-meter distance and the fact he was moving as his best protection from the pistol fire. Turnbull pivoted the HK416 up and unleashed two bursts. Sparks erupted as some of the bullets hit the metal railing, but at least two rounds hit the shooter, who staggered. Turnbull fired again, and the man went down.

A round slammed into the radio at his hip, knocking Turnbull to the concrete floor. The wounded guard on the ground floor was firing, and if not for the now-deceased Motorola, Turnbull would have had a 9mm ball round through his hip joint's acetabulum. He rolled into position and brought the rifle up as the wounded soldier kept firing ever more desperately and inaccurately. He should have done as Turnbull did and taken his time. Turnbull peered through the optic, placing the red dot on the shooter's forehead and exhaling before gently squeezing the trigger. The 5.56mm round struck home, and the shooter's head jerked and his face fell to the floor.

The red flashing lights ceased, as did the horn. There was a clank, and Mundi was inside the cellblock, rifle at the ready, as Turnbull got himself to his feet.

"You hit, Kelly?" Mundi asked, still scanning for targets.

"Right in the radio," Turnbull replied. They split up and each went to the stairway at the end of each side's cellblock and made their way up. Turnbull limped a bit going up the stairs; he would have a nice bruise. No one else was on Turnbull's side. Mundi cleared the second floor of the side with the shooter, and there was one shot before Mundi descended and announced, "Clear!"

"Clear," Turnbull echoed.

They moved to the cells. Some of the prisoners were pushing open their own unlocked doors. Others were too scared to move. They had to be coaxed out.

Turnbull and Mundi instructed the prisoners, each a somewhat familiar face, to move to the center of the cellblock and stand there. In cell number three, the pale prisoner sat on his bed shivering. He was unshaven, but his hair was perfect.

"Did you have to shoot them?" he asked.

"Yeah," Turnbull said. "Now get up." The prisoner did not move, less from defiance than fear.

"Fine, you stay here," Turnbull said, slamming the door shut.

There were now 15 prisoners standing in the block – not all of the 20 cells were occupied – and they seemed a bit disoriented. They were wearing orange jumpsuits with black numbers. The orange jumpsuits were a deliberate choice that had given the PR authorities endless jollies, just like the choice of venue.

Mundi trotted back to the control room to keep watch on the monitors. It was unclear whether anyone outside of Camp Alpha-7 was notified when the breach alarm was activated.

Turnbull checked his watch. 1150 hours. Not long now.

"Okay," he said to the assembled prisoners. "We're Americans. We're getting you out of here. We just need to hold on in this location for a little bit longer."

"Are you a SEAL?" one of the prisoners asked.

"I'm not a SEAL," snapped Turnbull. "Now, is there anyone else other than these dead schmucks in this compound? Maybe a cook?"

"They feed us MREs," said a very large, moon-faced prisoner with a Jersey accent. Still, because of the involuntary diet, his

Size XXXL jumpsuit hung off him like a muumuu. "You guys bring any real food?"

"Governor, focus. Any other PR personnel here?"

"None that I'm aware of," answered another familiar face, adding, "You sure you're not SEALs?"

"Senator Cruz, I'm not a SEAL," Turnbull replied. "Look, we need to hold on here just a bit longer before we extract you. You're safe in here. Now, I need someone to look after your pal Mitt. As much as I'd like to leave him behind, I can't."

"Why not?" asked one of the prisoners. "He was always telling the guards on us." There was a murmur of agreement.

Turnbull looked at the dozen-plus faces and settled on one, then pointed.

"Your file said you worked with him in 2012, Ambassador O'Brien," Turnbull said. "So, he's your problem now." The Romney duty delegee sighed and nodded.

"Kelly!" shouted Mundi from the control room. "Company."

"How many?" Turnbull shouted.

"Like I said, a fricken company!"

"Shit," Turnbull hissed. He turned back to the prisoners. "Okay, I'm going to need to go hold off these guys until the cavalry comes. I want you all on the floor and don't go anywhere. I won't have time to wrangle you all up again when it's time to go."

"I can help," offered a strikingly good-looking prisoner. "I'm a hunter and I can handle a weapon." Turnbull knew that was correct from the man's file. In his case, PR Special Forces had kidnapped him on a safari in Tanganyika.

"Okay, there's a rack of M4s in the control room. Take a couple extra mags." The man nodded and started to move.

"Hey," Turnbull said. The man paused. Like all the rest, the prisoner had vanished under mysterious circumstances, and his family had refused to accept his loss. Due to its special status, it was the only family briefed on the fact there was a rescue planned, and it had asked that the operators pass on a message.

Turnbull complied, telling him, "Your family sends its love. Oh, and since you disappeared, Barron dropped out of Duke and volunteered to join the Rangers and get his citizenship."

The man smiled. "You gotta come to Florida and meet my dad and the family."

"Unlikely," Turnbull said. "I don't like other people. Now move!"

"I can help too," boomed a loud, bottomlessly deep and vaguely accented voice from a tall man with a goatee. "I was in the British Territorial Army." Turnbull knew this prisoner had shot one of his kidnappers with a Kahr handgun before being struck with a non-lethal shotgun beanbag round and pulled unconscious from his Mustang.

"Okay, Doc, pick up a weapon," Turnbull said. "The rest of you, on the floor."

Turnbull trotted back to the control room and the remaining prisoners grabbed some concrete. Mundi pointed at the monitors. A small convoy of Cuban FAR vehicles was hauling ass up the road toward Camp Alpha-7.

"They're maybe two minutes out," Turnbull said. "We take them at the gate if I can't talk us out of a firefight. Come on."

They went outside through the entry hallway, propping open the doors so they could fall back fast if need be. Mundi was speaking quickly into his Motorola as they went.

Turnbull pointed toward the SUV parked out front. "Doc, I want you on the ground right behind the front driver's tire. Your sector of fire is from the gate right to the north corner of the fence. Junior, same with you, only down behind the front passenger tire from the gate to the south corner. If we have to fall back, we take up by the control room and hold them in the entry hallway. Stay out of sight until it goes down, and don't fire 'til I do, but then kill any commie bastard in your sector. Clear?"

They assented and took up their positions, weapons up, concealed behind the vehicle. Mundi went to the south corner of the building, a good position to provide enfilading fire on the gate and the area to its immediate front. He was still talking into his radio.

Turnbull walked calmly toward the gate, in the open, rifle hanging off his right shoulder, as the rumble of the approaching vehicles got louder.

Major Gomez crested the hill and the jeep was now on the approximately fifty meters of flat ground to the immediate front of Camp Alpha-7. His driver slowed as the three trucks behind them caught up. Gomez surveyed the complex. As the senior MP for the FAR in the region, he had received the alert on his phone, but the compound looked peaceful. In fact, one of the PR guards was walking toward the gate, carrying what looked like an ordinary M4, as if nothing had happened.

"*Alto aquí*," the major told his driver, who pulled to a stop. The truck stopped in a column behind them, idling. He got out of his ride as the PR lieutenant approached casually from the other side of the padlocked gate.

Gomez had decided to leave his AKM in the vehicle. He still had his Makarov pistol in his flapped leather holster.

"Hey, what's up?" asked the big second lieutenant, his sand-colored combat boots clomping across the blacktop as he approached the gate from the inside. "You speak *inglés*?"

"Yes, I speak English," Gomez said. "Is everything under control here? We received an alarm."

"Oh, right, that," Turnbull said. "That was a false alarm. Wiring issue, you know? Everything's good."

Gomez looked the big man over – the major was much smaller, having grown up eating the inevitably inadequate diet of a worker's paradise. The communist officer's natural suspicion was tingling. He had not seen this Yankee before, but then that was not unusual. There was something about him, though, that was not quite right.

"Are you sure?" Gomez asked. The lieutenant seemed a bit old to be an O-1, but he might have been a sergeant before and gotten a commission somewhat older than usual. He knew the Americans sometimes did that.

"Oh yeah, everything is A-OK," the lieutenant reassured him, adding. "That means fine."

This explanation annoyed Gomez, since he had made it a professional goal for years to fully understand his enemy, and this continued even after his enemy split and half became *amigos*. He understood their language, including their colloquialisms. He also understood their uniforms, and the lieutenant's uniform was correct. And he understood their weapons.

"I need to come inside the camp and confirm that everything is in order," Gomez announced.

"No can do," Turnbull replied. "Orders. No one is allowed in."

"I am the chief military police officer for the *Fuerzas Armadas Revolucionarias* in this region and our agreement with the People's Republic of North America gives me the right to enter, lieutenant."

"Tell you what. You go back down the hill and get my colonel's permission and then you can come back up here and look around to your heart's content," Turnbull said. "But you're not coming in here now."

Gomez considered the situation. The lieutenant stood expressionless before him through the chain link fence. What was stoking his suspicions, Gomez wondered. What was off? His eyes dropped to look at the man's weapon. It *sort of* looked like an M4, but as he looked at it, he realized that it was not quite an Army-issue M4. And the optic was non-standard.

Gomez raised his eyes to meet the eyes of the lieutenant, who smiled.

"*Soldados!*" Gomez yelled as he turned to run and as Turnbull unlimbered his HK416.

Gomez dived behind the jeep just a moment before Turnbull unleashed a burst through the windscreen into the chest of his driver. Men in their olive drab green fatigues with AKMs were now leaping out of the covered backs of the trucks onto the blacktop. There was loud, confused shouting in Spanish.

Turnbull took aim at a pair of the communists, the two he instantly assessed as closest to getting their AKMs up into position to effectively return fire. The red dot danced on the chest of the first, and Turnbull squeezed, then he shifted the dot slightly to the other and squeezed again. Both went down with three 5.56mm rounds stitched across each of their rib cages.

Mundi was firing now, with well-aimed single shots that found communists' heads at 50 meters, and the ex-prisoners joined in, each dropping several FAR soldiers who crossed into their sectors of fire.

Turnbull pivoted to a sergeant who was motioning his men forward and killed him with three rounds to the neck, chin and nose. After spraying the remainder of his rounds to suppress and scatter the attackers, he hit the mag release and the Magpul magazine clattered on the parking lot as he rammed in another and the bolt slammed closed.

There was a roar, and Turnbull saw that the driver of the first ZiL truck in the line had had the presence of mind to seize the initiative and hit the gas.

The ancient vehicle lurched forward, troops spilling out of its canvas-covered rear, and made straight for the gate. Turnbull was distracted by a soldier taking cover behind the jeep who put a 7.62x39mm round past his ear; Turnbull's red dot found his face and then a single shot slammed through his top front teeth, his uvula and out the back through his C1 vertebra. The dead man dropped into Major Gomez's lap.

Throughout the fight, Major Gomez had sat down behind the jeep, Makarov in hand, waiting. Eventually his men would take down the infiltrators, and once they did, he would be there to claim the credit. He pushed the bloody carcass off him and squatted with his pistol out. While it did seem that a lot of his troops were dropping around him, he knew he had a lot more. It was just a matter of time.

Turnbull pivoted back just as the ZiL-131 cargo truck smashed through the gate and, brakes squeaking, stopped a few feet from him, rear tires tangled in the collapsed chain link gate. Turnbull leapt upward with his foot landing on the broad front bumper. He leaned forward and rested his arms on the metal hood, pointing the HK416 at the terrified driver. Turnbull flipped the selector back to auto and fired. The driver disappeared in a cloud of broken glass and pink mist. Turnbull emptied the mag, swinging the weapon left and right to spray through the cab into the cargo area back beyond it. From the shouts and moans, there had still been some FAR soldiers left back there.

Still standing on the bumper, he dropped the dry mag and replaced it with a freshie from his cargo pocket, mentally noting that he had just three remaining. A Cuban soldier ran through the open gate on his left and was bringing his AKM up to shoot Turnbull off the front end when a round from Mundi went in his right temple and out his left. Turnbull sent his rifle's bolt forward then jumped backwards off the bumper, executing a flawless PLF – a parachute landing fall – where his legs and his fourth point of contact, his ass, absorbed the energy of the impact.

Now on his rear below the chassis level of the trucks, Turnbull could see dozens of pairs of legs running to and fro. He sprayed on full auto from right to left, emptying out the mag into the lower extremities of the FAR troops. He had no idea how many he hit – it was a fair number – and he reloaded again even as the enemy's return fire began, for the first time in the firefight, to top the volume of fire from the defenders.

One more mag after this one, and then it was him against a couple dozen soldiers with his Wilson Combat CQB.

The odds could be worse, he told himself as he took down an advancing communist lieutenant with a burst to the pancreas.

The rear truck exploded, the detonation lifting it off its wheels and depositing it on the north side of the road. The battle seemed to pause as everyone took in this unexpected development – everyone except Mundi, who had called in the Hellfire missile strike from the approaching pair of United States Navy Sikorsky MH–60S Seahawk combat search and rescue helicopters, each painted sea foam gray and bristling with armament.

Now Mundi advised the choppers to engage the danger close enemy with their devastating GAU-21 .50 caliber machine guns, which were mounted to the sides of each aircraft. Looking much like the time-tested Browning M2 "Ma Deuce" machine gun that had smoked everything from Nazis to *jihadis* over its storied history, the GAU-21 did not just strike the scattering communist fighters. The heavy rounds obliterated them and the remaining untouched truck as well.

Major Gomez was still staring at the burning wreckage of the third truck when the .50 caliber rounds began to impact. The jeep shuttered and lurched as one round struck the engine block, then another went through the front passenger seat, and another went through the rear seat, then another went through the cargo space in back, and then one went into the ground right beside Major Gomez. This struck the officer as odd, since the ground was now all red and chunky. His left arm tickled, and he turned his head and saw that he had no left shoulder, only a gaping hole. But before his brain could process that image, the last round of the burst vaporized Major Luis Jesús Gomez from the shoulders up, sending him to meet his namesake. He would have a lot of explaining to do.

Seeing the air support, and wanting to get away from the impact zone of the gunfire, Turnbull got up and sprinted back to his comrades by the building even as the truck he had stopped was shredded by the choppers. The white MP SUV was already pocked with bullet holes and the rear window was shot out.

He turned back around and sought targets, but there were none. The road and the lot around the gate were a Hieronymus Bosch tableau of jagged metal, smoking hulks, and chunks of socialist lackeys. Even with his ears ringing – it was only now that, as they landed at the other end of the parking lot, that Turnbull actually heard the Seahawks – Turnbull could hear Mundi laughing uproariously at the sight.

The twin rotor washes kicked up a cloud of swirling brownish dust that rapidly dissipated. When it did, Turnbull could make out a dozen Task Force Zulu operators being disgorged. Their lethal cargo deployed, the choppers lifted off again to circle around Camp Alpha-7 to provide air support – and to hunt down any Cuban troops who thought they had gotten away by taking off running through the scrub brush that covered the hill.

Joe Schiller and Casey Warner, fully kitted out – in Casey's case, including a weird patch velcroed over his chest plate that mashed up The Punisher and Hello Kitty – trotted over to him as the rest of the team assumed defensive positions around the perimeter.

"Any of you hit?" Schiller asked. He carried an FN SCAR while Casey packed a tricked-out M4.

"No, we're good," Turnbull said. Even as they landed, he had looked over his rescuees to ensure none of them were damaged in the battle.

"All the packages accounted for?" Schiller asked. The two prisoners and Mundi had joined them, still holding their weapons.

"Yeah, these two are good to go and the rest are inside."

Casey was looking at them both, apparently starstruck.

"Hey Doctor, I loved your radio show," he said to the taller one.

"Thank you," the host replied in his booming bass, his rifle cradled in his arms.

The other prisoner was beaming. "Gentlemen, after I get settled in, all of you are invited to Mar-a-Lago. I'm going to show you the time of your lives."

Casey was beaming. "Can we golf with the Pres–?"

Turnbull grabbed Casey by the web gear. "Hey, focus! You need to get inside and get the prisoners ready to evac before their ride gets here." The plan was that a big Navy CH-53 Sea Stallion would come in after the insertion of the operators and take the rescued hostages out and back to the U.S.S. *Gerald R. Ford.* The U.S. Navy's newest nuclear aircraft carrier was currently steaming towards the base with the rest of the fleet just over the southern horizon.

"But I want to meet Kimberly!" whined Casey.

"Go! And you're in charge of Romney!"

"Why me? He's a pain in the ass."

"Exactly, you're perfect for the mission. Move!"

Casey went inside dejectedly as Schiller took over responsibility for the two men in orange outside.

Overhead, one of the Seahawks lit up something – someone – below on the hillside with its .50 cal. Mundi smiled broadly.

"One down, a few hundred thousand to go, and then Cuba *libre*," he said, beaming.

From their hilltop vantage point, they could look down on the base. There were two airfields, the unused one on their side of the bay and the active one across the waterway that split the base in two. A flock of C-17s were disgorging battalions from the 82nd Airborne Division over each one to join the Rangers who had dropped in first a few minutes before, unnoticed by the two Task Force Zulu infiltrators because of the firefight. A nearly 2,000-man Marine Expeditionary Unit embarked on the U.S.S. *Iwo Jima* as part of the *Ford* task force was inbound to reinforce the paratroopers. Unseen from their vantage point, F-22s and F-35s flying from bases in Florida had already swept the sky of the ramshackle Cuban Air Force. But they could see some airstrikes in Cuba proper as F/A-18 Super Hornets flying from the *Ford* leveled the local military facilities that housed forces that could be used to counterattack.

The United States of America was back in charge of Guantánamo Bay Naval Base, as it had been, except for the last six months, since 1903. The Chinese People's Liberation Army

Navy would not be getting its foothold in America's backyard after all.

"We go out with the packages on the Sea Stallion," Turnbull said. "Should be in-bound now."

"Nah, not me, Kelly." Mundi replied, reloading.

"What do you mean?"

"Well," Mundi began. "I made a deal with Clay Deeds. I'd use my cousins to help us if I could go get them out afterwards. And he said okay. So, off to the rendezvous out by our family's old sugar cane plantation. Then I bring them back here and then back to the States. Shouldn't take me too long."

"Oh yeah?" Turnbull said. "You need any help?"

"What, from a big Yankee who sticks out like a sore thumb?"

"Hey, I can speak Spanish. *¿Frutas, frutas, quién quiere frutas? Tengo muchas frutas,*" he said, trying to remember a Spanish lesson from long ago in junior high.

"You suck," Mundi said, laughing. The he turned serious. "It might have to get kinetic, *amigo.*"

Turnbull scoffed.

"You know what I always say," Turnbull said. "I kill communists for fun."

2.

"Do you suppose they are all drunk yet?" asked Merrick Crane III. He was in the backseat of his parked Mercedes S560 sedan, a Gauloises cigarette between his fingers in his right hand. These French smokes were illegal to import, but the law did not apply to special people, and though he rarely popped his head up from the underground, Crane was most definitely special.

He took a drag and awaited an answer from Wayne Gruber, who was leaning nonchalantly into his window. The big man was a little too close for Crane's liking, and Crane could smell the lesser cigarette brand on his man's breath. Gruber was muscular with a craggy face and a close-cropped goatee. His hair was long and a bit greasy, but pulled up into a manbun. Unlike the late Mr. Soto, Gruber spoke, both often and cryptically, and Crane accepted this as part of the total package. Gruber drawled as well, but it was less the accent of the South than the institutional accents of the military and the prison system, and he had spent time in both.

Like his boss, Gruber wore a suit, but his was from something called Suits 4 Less and Merrick's was from a niche tailor in Manhattan. He wore no tie, and the grip of the .50 caliber aluminum Desert Eagle pistol he carried showed from his shoulder rig under his coat. Gruber would, of course, carry the biggest gun available, Crane noted. That was the attitude that was needed for the man overseeing the four dozen thugs –

talented thugs, but thugs nonetheless – of the Special Investigations Section of the Department of People's Justice.

Crane's allies had, upon his insistence, allowed him to deputize a band of followers and to operate under the color of law, such as there was law in the People's Republic. It was very useful to have his own operatives with badges and access at his beck and call. The People's Militia was a nice blunt instrument, but the SIS was for when he needed a scalpel. After all, he had many enemies, some inside the government, such as Senator Harrington, and others outside it. And he had some in his own organizations. Most did not yet realize they were his enemies.

Gruber considered his boss's question for a moment, smiling serenely. Gruber's habit of taking a moment before responding, as if his response was some profundity worth waiting for, was another of Gruber's habits that grated on the Wall Street heir turned communist kingmaker. But Gruber's other qualities – a certain animal cunning, utter ruthlessness, and a giddy sadism that indicated what others would call a very disturbed mind – more than made up for his quirks.

"Oh yes, boss," said Gruber. The words hung in the air and Crane had to stop himself from leaning forward for more. Gruber continued. "By now they are mighty drunk. I made sure their party was well-stocked, yes sir. Tequila, vodka, whiskey, beer. And dope. Plenty of kush. I told them to kick up their heels, and our guards – I have my boys providing security – tell me that's just what they are doing."

"Then it's time to go crash their party, Mr. Gruber," Crane said. Gruber smiled, and shouted to the other dozen men.

"Mount up, boys. You know the plan. Hummingbird is a go!"

The other men, many with long weapons, complied, and Gruber slid into the passenger seat of the Mercedes and shut the door. The nervous driver, likewise in a suit, started the car. Gruber made his right hand into a gun and pointed ahead, and the driver hit the gas and went that way. Behind them, the little convoy followed along.

It was drizzling slightly as they drove on the winding Washington road leading into the woods from the town of Snoqualmie. They occasionally passed a mansion, or rather, a private road leading to a mansion situated back in the forest. Some, those belonging to rich and loyal blues, were untouched by the changes. But several had been requisitioned to serve "the needs of the people," mostly the ones abandoned when their owners skipped out to the red after the Split. "The needs of the people" turned out to be "the desires of the powerful," and the elite divvied up these estates to use as getaways.

An omnigendered Seattle communist congressbeing – xe not only refused to be defined by fixed concepts of gender but by fixed concepts of species either – had happily arranged for Crane to convene a council of key People's Militia leaders from around the country in a particularly large estate once owned by a libertarian tycoon who got rich with a dating app designed to bring together herpetic singles – called "Vir♡Us" – and blew town pronto post-Split.

The pine trees passed beyond his rain-streaked side window, and Crane reflected on how, once again, Adolf Hitler provided him with valuable leadership lessons.

"Do you have the final guest list?" he asked Gruber.

Gruber took his time in pulling a folded piece of white paper from his jacket and handed it back. It was a printed list of invitees with check marks next to most of the names. Crane reviewed it, noting those marked absent. Martin Rios-Parkinson had not shown up, of course – that cunning bastard could smell a trap a mile away. He had somehow managed to lose the Battle of Cajon Pass and still not get put up against a wall. His time would come.

Crane handed back the paper.

"It is sufficient," he said, turning to once again watch the pine trees pass by his window.

There was a gate and two of Gruber's SIS men were there. There were no women in his unit. In a perfect world, Crane would have insisted on diversity of gender identities, but one female-identifying person had been enlisted and three weeks later she was found dead, and not prettily. When Crane asked what happened, Gruber simply replied, "Well boss, seems she had the devil inside her, and you can't have two devils on one dance card." The matter was dropped, though Crane insisted that Gruber himself dispose of the mess.

The qualities that made Wayne Gruber excellent for operations like this one, which Crane insisted be referred to as "Hummingbird," more than made up for his quirks.

The two guards, with M4s and suits, waved the convoy past, they shut the gate behind it. Like all the SIS men, they had the required rough edges – almost all had done time – but also something more. Most had some college and many had graduated. Others possessed the kind of animal cunning Gruber displayed, if not to the same extent. The capacity for wet work was necessary but not sufficient for membership; they had to be able to think and investigate as well. "Smart thugs," is how Crane had explained what he was looking for to populate his own personal government law enforcement body to the few trusted members of the People's Militia he had chosen as the seed of the SIS. Then he had found Gruber, and Gruber was a natural as its head.

There were several cars and a dozen SIS guards out in front of the mansion, which had a wide, circular driveway built of imported paving stones. The building was enormous, three stories, as if Downton Abbey had been Americanized and transported to the moist woods of Washington State.

Crane stepped out, his Walther at his hip, and told his driver to wait for him. There was some sort of loud electronic music coming from inside, and apparently the gathering of People's Militia leaders had not noticed the arrival of the platoon of SIS personnel and its, and their, leader.

"Time for the rodeo, boss," Gruber said. Unlike the others, he had no long weapon. They moved toward the front door, where a pair of SIS men stood with their M4s, flanking Dworkin, Gruber's deputy. Others followed, and still others went around back.

"Everything's ready," Dworkin said.

It was almost sad, Crane reflected, but all good things must end. The People's Militia was, by its nature, a revolutionary organization. That made the organization a wild card in a country where the revolution – or, at least this tepid version of the *real* revolution that Crane sought – had been installed as the government. Some of the individual People's Militia leaders, like Rios-Parkinson in Southern California, had seen the writing on the wall and understood how they could end up lined up against it. He and a few others, most of whom were not invited to the council, were already integrating their People's Militia units with the new PR government, though that had not been enough to keep Crane from inviting the ambitious Rios-Parkinson. Crane simply neither liked nor trusted him. Rios-Parkinson, his senses tingling, sent his regrets.

The hardcore Militia leaders at the party called those submitting to the government's control "sell-outs." Crane noted wistfully that they simply did not realize that the time for militias was over. Antifa had been absorbed into the People's Militia structure previously, and the tiresome strain of anarchy it embodied only made the organization as currently constituted less convenient. The People's Militia was a wild card, outside the government, and with a mind of its own. It was intolerable. Crane's allies in the government were clear that the situation had to be resolved, once and for all. And tonight, it would be.

Gruber went through the door first, smiling his disconcerting smile. Crane followed and saw that the entire first floor had been turned into a rave, with multicolored lights mounted on stands and a DJ on a raised dais with his left hand on his earphones pressing one muff to the side of his skull while spinning an uncomfortably loud tune.

Various men and women, and several others who were not part of the male/female dynamic, were staggering by. The scent of weed was in the air, and there were bottles and cups left on most flat surfaces. He recognized many of the partygoers as names on his list. Others, mostly very young and of all genders, or none, were there for entertainment value. Crane frowned, not because he disapproved of sexual debauchery – the only sexual preference he despised was traditional cis man/woman monogamy – but that all these extra bodies complicated Hummingbird's logistics.

A skinny male, his arm around a woman who seemed likely to have been a woman, stopped and blinked. Peter Skelly was the head of the 20,000-strong Detroit People's Militia, and one of the more prominent national figures in the movement. He was a familiar face on the news before and after the Split, and had recently taken to threatening the Michigan PR government for its failure to go far enough down the road to radicalism.

"Merrick?" he said, swaying a bit. "You weren't supposed to get here until the meeting tomorrow." The woman stood there, equally unsteady.

Crane stepped forward and his men flowed around him into the other rooms on the first floor and up the wide staircase to his front. Gruber stayed by his side, with two other SIS men.

"Seems like a fun party," Crane said.

Skelly smiled. "Great party," he replied.

"You were going to have it all cleaned up before I got here tomorrow morning? All of you will be bright-eyed and bushy-tailed for our meeting after this bacchanalia?"

Skelly went pale, his jaw moving but no words coming out.

Crane broke into a warm smile. "I'm just kidding, Pete," he said.

Pete exhaled and laughed with relief. "Hey, you want something? We got everything. Wine, whiskey? Maybe a partner?" Pete kept his query generic because he would never make any presumption about another's erotic preference.

"I'm fine," Crane replied. "Can you have the DJ turn off the music? And get the lights?"

"Go tell him," Pete told the woman, who staggered off. Crane smiled beatifically for the sixty seconds it took to turn off the music and the strobe lights. Gruber then flicked on the house lights with the switch by the door.

There was noise, confused yelling and some crashing, coming from the other rooms.

"Why are you here?" Skelly asked, his mouth dry.

"It's time to make some changes," Crane said. "And sometimes, changes are hard."

There was a shot upstairs, then several more. Pete looked around. SIS men were hustling in the others from other rooms on the ground floor. There were more shots upstairs, and now a couple from outside. Apparently, a few guests had decided to take their chances in the woods and learned that Hummingbird anticipated that contingency.

"What are you doing?" Skelly shouted, making the error of stepping forward toward Crane. Even before Crane could flinch, Gruber was there, his meaty fist slamming into Skelly's face. Skelly went down on his back, and Gruber knelt down and continued pounding his face, which was by now a bloody mess.

The other guests, maybe three dozen of them, were crying or moaning as they watched. Gruber went on until Skelly was still, then got up.

"You have blood on your suit, Mr. Gruber," Crane observed.

"Expected that, boss," Gruber replied after a pause. "That's why I wore my favorite suit. And I'm expecting more."

He smiled his smile.

"I don't understand," cried Venus DiPaulo, who headed the Boston branch. Xir – that was her pronoun – extrajudicial hangings of some traitors and racists last month had been quite the embarrassment and greatly upset his government contacts, though Crane appreciated xir sentiment.

"You have betrayed the revolution," Crane announced in a loud, flat voice. "Your treachery demands accountability."

"I am committed to revolutionizing society!" DiPaulo shrieked. An SIS man slammed xir to xir knees onto the white marble floor with the butt of his M4.

"I know you are," Crane said with a frisson of consolation in his voice. "But that doesn't matter." He looked at the terrified, assembled group. More shots echoed from upstairs. Then he spoke to them all.

"The revolution is a hard thing, and there must be sacrifices," he said. "Know that this is yours."

The guests erupted in screaming and pleading. Crane turned an about face toward the door. Gruber was there, smiling benignly, twirling a thin black Fairbairn-Sykes stiletto in his hand.

"Taking the idea of the night of the long knives literally, I see," Crane said as Gruber grinned his odd grin.

"Carl will get you to the airport, boss," Gruber said. "I'll see you in Manhattan tomorrow night."

"Make our point, and make it memorable," he said. "They just all need to be dead by sunup."

Those in the front of the crowd that heard him speak screamed even louder, pleading their loyalty to him and the cause, but Crane walked past the nodding Gruber and out the door.

The screaming only got louder as he walked to the idling Mercedes, but that did not stop Merrick Crane III from smiling at how smoothly Hummingbird had worked out, and at the thought of Gruber's long knife.

3.

Turnbull walked across the plaza and admired the American flag flapping in the hot Texas breeze, though it now had just 27 stars. He thought they seemed a little lonely.

There were no homeless sprawled out on the pavement like you would have seen before the Split, or could still find (in greater numbers) in the blue. In the new United States, bums were not allowed. They had the option of shipping off to the blue, or shipping off to jail, and then to be shipped off to the blue. Or they could work and support themselves like everyone else.

Turnbull made his way across the broiling pavement, noting the scores of mask-free men and women walking through their lives with their eyes glued to their iPhones and their free hands clasping cups of Starburns coffee – Starbucks having refused to do business in "the racist states that promulgate hate" and a right-wing tycoon improbably named Monty Burns having bought up the corporation's infrastructure in the red states for a song. Now, each of the ubiquitous latte stations had a big sign out front reading "FIREARMS ENCOURAGED." The Enya and El Salvadorian folk music were banished from the store's sound systems, while Interior Secretary Ted Nugent's tuneage got plenty of airplay.

The coffee was better too; it no longer tasted like steeped charcoal.

Many of these people had served in some paramilitary capacity during the Split, and thus earned their citizenship. Some were armed now. Yet most were not committed warriors. Turnbull was. These people, the ones he protected, had no idea that there was a shark walking among them. But then, part of his job was not to be noticed. His ability to keep his head down had been a big asset during his multiple post-Split runs into the People's Republic of North America. The cold war between the two erstwhile sibling nations was, more accurately, a lukewarm war.

Turnbull went inside one of the four nearly identical buildings that surrounded the plaza, the air conditioning inside making him feel like he stepped into a walk-in freezer like the one at the Jack in the Box in Woodland Hills he had worked at as a teenager. That gig terminated when he punched his 24-year-old manager for grabbing the tush of a young lady working the cash register. She was even madder at him than the mashed masher. It turned out she was Romero's Juliet, and Turnbull's view of chivalry had been a bit jaded ever since.

There was no armed security in the lobby. Instead, a good number of people were open carrying, and certainly more were carrying concealed. A middle-aged woman who looked like she had a dozen cats and who wore tennis shoes with her dress had an AR-15 slung over her back. One of the first acts of the new United States Congress was to re-ratify the Constitution, but this time they took the Second Amendment seriously. Now, no one paid an armed citizen any mind. And everyone was really polite.

Turnbull's Wilson Combat .45 was at his hip. He'd have sooner left home – he had a tidy condo not far away that he rarely stayed in – without his pants than without his gun.

He got into the elevator, and hit the button for the second highest floor, the 15th. The button for the 16th floor, where he was going, would not have worked. The security for the two floors of the organization was right off the elevator bank on the 15th. His ride complete, he stepped out and two gentlemen with

M4s confirmed his ID and gave him a visitor badge to wear around his neck like a cowbell.

There was no sign informing visitors of the identity of the tenant. Clay Deeds was awaiting him on the other side of the double doors.

"Welcome back to Dallas," he said.

Turnbull grunted.

"Well, you look tan," Deeds observed.

Turnbull shrugged.

They began walking past the cubicles toward the internal stairway up to the 16th floor.

"That was quite a little adventure after the Camp Alpha-7 mission," Clay continued. "Next time, can you run it by me before you decide to go off and raise ad hoc hell in a foreign country?"

"I got your prisoners out. I just took a leave of absence afterwards with my buddy. Sightseeing. It worked out okay, though."

"The less said about it, the better," Deeds replied. "It's all classified now, by the way."

"What is?"

"Perfect."

"So, Clay, who are all these people and what are they doing in a Dallas office building?"

"I don't know the answer to either question, actually," Deeds said. "We're starting a country from scratch and this is some kind of intel organization in the process of establishing itself. I'm just using the space."

"Are we now official?" Turnbull asked. He would not speak the name "Task Force Zulu" among a sea of cubicles.

Deeds reached the foot of the stairs. "We'll never be official, Kelly," he said. "Come on up to my office where we can talk."

They climbed the steps and made their way to a corner office which was guarded by a severe looking secretary whose old-school Browning Hi-power automatic was lying on her desk. She scowled as they went inside Deeds' office and closed the door.

"What's with Mrs. Moneypenny?" asked Turnbull.

"I think she's here less to assist me than to watch me," Deeds replied. The corner office door had had no nameplate on it – if you did not know who Clay Deeds was, you had no business knocking.

Now Deeds walked to the windows, which provided a very nice view of the rapidly expanding new American capital city, and activated the dampener system attached to the glass. That way no one outside could use a laser to scan the vibrations to read their speech and eavesdrop on them that way. Of course, the techs swept the place for bugs daily.

The office itself had a western motif. There was a pair of horns on a plaque mounted on the wall.

"That came with the office," Deeds said, having noticed Turnbull eyeing it. "This was all here when I got here."

Turnbull sat in one of the dark leather chairs. "I never had you pegged as a buckaroo. Now, I guess we can share interior design hints – by the way, Sunday I went to Target and got this rug that really ties my room together – or you can tell me what MacGuffin I'm chasing this time."

Deeds sighed and shook his head. "Kelly, I can't call up one of my top operatives and just chat and share our feelings?"

"No."

"You're a very angry man, Kelly." Turnbull frowned.

"Now I'm *one* of your top operatives?" asked Turnbull.

"Oh, I love all my misfit toys equally," Deeds said.

"I'm the squirt gun that shoots jelly."

"You shoot anything that moves."

Deeds sat behind his desk, which was totally empty except for a monitor and keyboard. In all the time Turnbull had worked with Clay Deeds, he had never seen the man use a computer.

"Your MacGuffin is a Harvard professor," Deeds said.

"I have a feeling Boston is next on my hit parade," Turnbull replied.

"It's more than a feeling."

"More than a feeling?" Turnbull asked.

"Okay, Kelly, we are not doing this," Deeds replied. Turnbull found it amusing, as his dad loved his FM radio classic rock to the point of insisting on referring to "October" as "Rocktober" without irony.

Deed continued. "He's got a Nobel Prize for integrating math and computer science, not some woke nonsense, and you're bringing him out."

"Why would we want a professor from Harvard?" Turnbull asked. "Didn't we just split away from the PR so we'd have *fewer* professors?"

"Dr. Kenneth Strickland is the exception," Deeds said. "He's best thought of as an anarcho-libertarian-royalist, if his politics matter. And they do only to the extent that he's a bad fit for the new country he has found himself in and he's ready to bolt."

"So, why doesn't he just leave? The border's not closed, at least not yet."

"He thinks they are watching him. He may be right. But he thought people were watching him long before the Split."

"Sounds like a nut."

"Oh, he is," Deeds said. "Seriously. He's got grave mental issues, OCD being the least of them. But he's a brilliant computer scientist and mathematician. The election of 2020 got him really riled up."

"He's not the only one."

But he's the only one with a Nobel Prize who decided he would mathematically analyze the election and create his own computer program utilizing the data he gathered to mimic the vote manipulation he believed went on in 2020."

"I'm lost," Turnbull said. Deeds sighed.

"On Tuesday August 1st, the People's Republic of North America holds its first presidential election to replace Joe Biden. Strickland wrote a program to prove the 2020 election could have been stolen, in the process creating a program that may be able to steal this future one. They're changing a lot of their procedures under their new election law, so this won't work after the August election. But Stickland's program is the key to the PR election happening in about five weeks."

"And you would like to have some input into who wins?" Turnbull said.

"Not me. The powers that be do. Picking the winner of the PR's election by hacking their election system is echelons above Clay Deeds. But if we can have input in who they pick next month, maybe we can put off the inevitable for a least a few years."

"The inevitable?"

"You can't have two big dogs in one kennel and not have them fight for dominance."

"Or two crocodiles in one pond."

"That was oddly specific."

"I'm oddly specific."

"Their election is already primed for chaos because it was not like they could just stop on a dime with mail-in votes, early votes, and reparations supplemental voting for traditionally oppressed peoples. With the PR's weird ranked voting system, you have a bunch of candidates and any of them could win. Buttigieg, De Blasio, the fake Indian, someone else."

"Choosing between them is like choosing between syphilis and gonorrhea," Turnbull observed. "And genital warts."

"I don't need to know which is which," Deeds said. "They're all bad in their own way, but our leaders are looking for a win by the least worst."

"I'd have to say De Blasio is probably gonorrhea, if I had to choose."

Deeds sighed and Turnbull leaned forward.

"And what makes you think what we do matters, that their ruling clique hasn't already picked the winner?" he asked.

"That's the thing," Deeds said. "All of them would gleefully cheat their way into the White House – which the PR is busy renaming something less triggering – if they could, but that kind of means none of them can. They are all watching each other and looking for the other ones to pull a fast one. I can't say if this is one person, one vote, one time or not, but our analysis is that none of them will be able to stuff boxes or harvest enough ballots to win by fraud."

"And we can," Turnbull said. "If this guy's high-speed, low-drag computer program –"

"It's called 'Kraken,'" Deeds said.

"Of course it's called Kraken," Turnbull replied. "So, if this program works, then our preferred PR presidential candidate wins by fraud next month?"

"Yes," Deeds said. "That's about the size of it."

"Great, I'm in, because the hell with those blue bastards," Turnbull said.

"That's certainly the attitude in the New White House and Congress. Half the people want nothing to do with the blue, and the other half want to invade it. Did you see how Senator Searcy has started ending every speech with 'The People's Republic must be destroyed'? They voted on National Peanut Day yesterday and he got up and said that. Some of these guys make even your pal General Karl Martin Scott look like Neville Chamberlain."

"I don't like politics or generals."

"The fact is we are in a cold war with hot flashes. You guys capped a couple dozen of them taking back Guantánamo, and there have been some border clashes too. It's only a matter of time before they seal the border. The Treaty of St. Louis requires free travel, but too many of the useful blues are packing up and heading to the US, while our losers and welfare bums are heading to the PR, especially since we've ended welfare. And it did not endear the PR to our leadership when their special forces kidnapped a dozen or so prominent Americans and locked them up in Gitmo."

"That did work out poorly for them."

"You've seen it yourself – the economy is already falling apart up there. And there are insurgents too."

"Sounds great," Turnbull said glumly. "When do I leave?"

"Tonight. You go in via Montreal. Upstate New York is unstable. Guerillas. Apparently, they are rallying around a leader named 'T.'"

"Is he related to Q?" Turnbull asked.

Deeds snorted "Of all the weird things that happened over the last decade, Ben Sasse turning out to be Q might have been the weirdest."

"The weirdest was when he opened his shirt up in the Senate and had Trump's face tattooed on his chest," Turnbull said. "Or maybe it was releasing that sex tape."

Deeds sighed and unlocked, then opened up, a drawer and took out a piece of paper, a manila envelope, and an iPhone 14, then pushed envelope and phone across the desk. He kept the paper. "We thought about you just driving in from Kentucky, but that's how you'll come out."

"And you never go out how you came in," Turnbull said. He took the envelope, tore it open and began rifling through the contents as Deeds continued. It was wads of US and People's Republic dollars, various pocket litter, and a set of fake ID.

"Cristobal Ruben Sanchez?" Turnbull said. His New York driver's license read "VALUED IMMIGRANT."

"The remaining cops and the People's Security Force are less likely to screw with you if they think you're an immigrant. The FBI is still a thing, as you know. They're getting more political."

"*More* political?"

"Hard to believe, right? But some agents are resisting, wanting to focus on real crime. That's why there are several new internal security agencies, politically-focused but controlled by different political actors. Some sit around all day accusing each other of privilege. Some are dangerous as hell. So be careful."

"Speaking of political actors, any word on the location of my boy Merrick Crane III?" Turnbull asked.

Deeds paused. "This can't be personal, Kelly."

"It's not personal. I'm just going to waste that piece of shit."

"He's active, consolidating power. He's got tentacles into the security forces. But he's keeping under the surface, for the most part. We know he had tight links to the People's Militia, and that someone killed most of its leadership all in one night a few weeks ago, while you were gone. Crane was notably not among the dead – their media claimed it was a house fire, but they did not try to suppress the rumors that the dead did not go pleasantly."

"I take it that it was not us," Turnbull said.

"No, it wasn't us."

"What a shame," Turnbull said calmly. "So, there's trouble in the worker's paradise?"

"The progressives are now the centrists, and they are currently in charge. The radicals want to take power."

"Maybe we should let them fight."

"The Militia became a loose cannon, particularly after it sucked up the Antifa crowd. It's allied with the radicals. We know that the government was getting nervous with large groups of armed radicals running around out of their control."

"So, they capped them. Like Hitler did with the SA when it stopped being handy having brownshirts running around in the streets."

"Yes. We assess that Crane was behind it, that he did it to mollify the nervous politicians who wanted the Militia under control. And, lo and behold, the new leadership is integrating it into the security infrastructure."

"I guess the Militia suckers served their purpose," Turnbull said. "Oh well. So where is Crane now?"

"We have not been able to track him, and we don't know where he is."

"Would you tell me if you did?"

Deeds paused again. "No, because you might go off mission to put him down and I need you focused on this job."

"Not 'might.' If I get the opportunity, I'm going to do him," Turnbull said calmly. "But I guess that will have to wait. What's the rest of it? Because there's always a complication."

"And there's one here, too," Deeds said. "As we discussed, Strickland is straight up nuts. Paranoid, obsessive. Lots of quirks. That's, of course, part of what makes him brilliant. But it also makes him a wild card."

"Well, at least he's not on the bad guys' radar."

Deeds sighed.

"They're looking for him?" Turnbull asked.

Deeds sighed again. "Maybe. We've been communicating with him via code embedded in Facebook, which we have to spoof as coming from the PR since Facebook cut off the red a couple months ago."

"Throw us in the briar patch, Zuck," Turnbull said.

"He told us he believes one or more of his grad students is, well, his exact words were," Deeds began, reading off the paper he had taken from his desk. "'A Deep State operative collaborating with the Trilateral Commission to stop my work.' In other words, he thinks one of his assistants is informing on him, and if you peel back the layers of insanity, that could be true. So, we need you to bring him out. With his election program."

"The border is still technically open. I get us a car in Boston and head south and you got your genius lunatic and I take a vacation. Unless it all goes to hell, which it undoubtedly will," Turnbull said, glumly.

"Remember, it would be nice to have him, but the main MacGuffin is the program disc. There's only one copy. Professor Strickland in the flesh is a nice bonus, but let's be clear – if it's him or the disc, get the disc. Now, he told us he is keeping the program disc off-site and gave us some clues where it is in case he's...," Deed read from the paper again. "'Sent by the Freemason rendition teams to GITMO.'"

"Maybe he's not totally nuts."

"I know, right?" Deeds said. "He also says that he 'deposited it somewhere safe,' but he won't say where."

"It's in a safe deposit box."

"Obviously," Deeds said. "The second part is a little more esoteric. He says, 'The key to the puzzle is my loving defiance of the Georgia Satellites.'"

Turnbull sat staring at Deeds for a moment, then blinked. "What the hell?"

"So, he hid the key somewhere and that's the clue. But our smartest guys are baffled about the rest. We thought that was some sort of minor league baseball team but our Oogle search came up with a rock band from the 1980s. We even spoofed Google so it would work from a red IP address and it came back the same way."

"I remember hearing them in my dad's car as a kid," Turnbull said. "They had one big song, and I forget the name, but it was less about being defiant than horny."

"According to both Oogle and Google, the biggest hit for the Georgia Satellites was 'Keep Your Hands to Yourself.'"

"So, if I don't get there before they grab him and get him to retrieve the disc from his safe deposit box, our mission depends on us decoding the puzzle of a crackpot with a taste for one-hit wonders?"

Deeds nodded. "Then get there fast, get him, and have him take you to the bank and get the disc. That's Plan A."

"What's Plan B?"

"Plan B is 'Do whatever you have to do to get it and bring it out,'" Deeds said. "Plan B is the Full Kelly."

Turnbull stared at his boss.

"You should never go full Kelly."

4.

"All clear on my end." It was Sean McGowan's voice on the Motorola. Danny Doyle cupped his hand over his earpiece – because Tommy O'Meara was running his mouth again inside the cramped panel van – and listened.

"Me too," Mikey said. "All clear on this end."

Doyle had placed a man at each end of the block, and now they were giving him the thumbs-up to roll. But he was still on edge, not that being alert was bad, but this was the first score they would be taking with Tommy O'Meara, and so far, Doyle was distinctly unimpressed. O'Meara had just gotten out of People's Correctional Institute Norfolk after serving three years of a seven-year stretch. The PR was letting go inmates, or as they were known, "Justice System Involved Individuals," both because the old justice system was inherently oppressive, and because the PR needed the space for gun owners, racists, and other newly-minted categories of criminals.

Tommy had gotten pinched for splitting the skull of another Charlestown local with a pool cue. If a couple of cops, back when Boston cops were Boston cops instead of those People's Security Force mutts, had not been walking in the door to roust the habituates of O'Dowd's, and if Tommy hadn't started swinging at them, the event would have been just another unreported instance of mick-on-mick mayhem. It was Charlestown, and no one would have talked, including the lad who had just got his bell rung.

Tommy was replacing Nicky O'Shea, who had gotten himself shot to death by a couple of PSF officers coming out of a liquor store he just robbed to get the money he needed to feed his habit. At least he went down shooting, getting a round off from his .38 before they gunned him down. If he had shouted out that he was fighting oppression by looting the place instead of going for his gat, they might not have popped him and instead given him a medal.

Nicky was no genius, but he did as he was told. Doyle missed him. Doyle had known guys like Tommy from the neighborhood, and from the service, and if the plan had not called for seven bodies, Tommy wouldn't be the newest member of the Leprechauns.

But the plan did call for seven, including Jimmy O'Connor their driver, and with Nicky on a slab they had to find a replacement. Tommy grew up twelve blocks away from the rest of the crew, who all grew up within 100 yards of each other, and that might as well have been across the continent in Los Angeles. But Jimmy Sullivan had shared a cell with him for a while, and when word got out that Tommy was telling anyone he could pigeonhole that he was "looking for anything heavy," Doyle reluctantly agreed to give him a try on the Diversity Savings job.

There wasn't much choice. Torrey Sullivan – no relation to Jimmy but the brother of Mikey – had already accessed the alarms system and had it set to go down. Doyle didn't care much for politics, but he was thrilled that when the People's Republic came into being, a lot of the security companies just shut their doors and their owners fled to the red. No one was looking for intrusions, and Torrey – a trained electrician and security system installer – was usually able to cut in unnoticed.

Plus, they needed this score – bad. Most of the guys were deep into the Shylocks and/or bookies – that brand of capitalism was undisturbed by the political changes. And Doyle could use a few bucks himself. The Leprechauns talked it over, while drinking, and after an hour, a lot of yelling, and one fight between the Sullivans, they decided to give Tommy O'Meara a trial run. But Doyle still had his doubts.

The van picked up speed. O'Meara was telling Jimmy Sullivan about a guy he stuck in the gut with a shiv at Norfolk. "He was eye-ballin' me, the bitch. He never eye-balled me again!" O'Meara was smiling broadly.

"You remember your mission?" Doyle asked, leaning forward toward Tommy. Tommy kept smiling, but pulled out the ancient Auto-Ordnance M1911A1 .45 automatic Doyle had issued him.

"Damn straight," he said. "Guard the front door. Nobody's getting inside." He lifted the pistol. "But I could sure use another couple mags, you know, in case shit goes down."

"Your job is to make sure no shit goes down," Doyle said, and not kindly. "You stand by the door and keep the civvies from coming in. That's it. We need three minutes fifteen seconds. Can you watch the door with no drama for three minutes fifteen seconds?"

"Sure," Tommy said. "No problem. But just saying, if we gotta rock, I am ready."

Doyle sat back, his sawed-off Remington 870 shotgun on his lap. The stock was cut down too, and the weapon would fit under his jacket nicely.

"Tommy, this is all about getting in and out smooth and clean."

"I know," Tommy said. "I'm cool. Cool as ice."

"Mask up," Doyle ordered. COVID-23 meant about half the people at any one time were wearing masks, even though only one in five thousand people died from it. It was basically the flu, but masks remained ubiquitous – something very convenient for men in their profession.

"Okay, ready?" Jimmy O'Connor said from the driver's seat over his right shoulder. They had stolen the panel van from a roofing contractor's lot last night. It had no windows in back, so only Jimmy O'Connor could see that they were just about in front of the bank.

"Okay Jimmy, once we bail go around the block!" Doyle said. "Everyone, time!"

Torrey Sullivan, Jimmy Sullivan and Tommy O'Meara all lifted their watches for the time hack. The van stopped, its brakes squealing.

"Go!" Doyle shouted, hitting his stopwatch and popping open the rear doors. The day was sunny, and he was looking out at a downtown street with many storefronts, about half boarded up. Every few yards, a "housing deficited individual" lay sprawled on the sidewalk, usually nearby a bottle or a reeking pile of last night's processed dinner. The street itself was relatively free of traffic – the $10 per gallon climate change carbon assessment made cars prohibitively expensive – and there were only a few passersby.

Doyle was out onto the street first, with Torrey, Jimmy, and Tommy behind him. Tommy slammed the rear doors shut and Jimmy O'Connor took off as the first three went into the branch of Diversity Savings, careful to conceal their shotguns. Tommy took up his position at the front door, his hand under his jacket wrapped around the grip of the .45.

Jimmy Sullivan casually walked up behind the guard, a slight man in his fifties, and savagely clocked him on the back of the head with the short butt of his shotgun. The guard went down in a heap. Jimmy pulled the man's Beretta out of his holster and kept it.

"Everyone down! Down!" Doyle yelled, his sawed-off 12-gauge out and pointing. There were maybe a dozen customers of all varieties in the bank, plus the six bank personnel they expected from the recons Katie McGowan had made for them.

Step One was to establish dominance. They were all shouting, swearing, threatening, pointing their shotguns. It worked – people hit the ground. Jimmy found the manager, got his keys, and he and Torrey left Doyle to shepherd the sheep and ran to the back with their duffel bags. They had several locks to open before they reached the dollars.

"Cell phones! I want them out!" Doyle yelled. "I said out! Now! Toss them over here!" He pointed to the counter.

The terrorized civilians were slowly pulling out their phones and throwing them over. Cells were his true bane – the alarm system was down, but a cell call to 9-1-1 could bring the PSF down on them in force. The only good thing was that the PR forced callers to go through an electronic operator that asked them to push "One" for a hate crime, and "Two" for "All other emergencies."

He glanced at his digital Timex. It was on the stopwatch feature and it clicked over to one minute.

The people were cooperating. That was good. Doyle hated heroes. He looked around the lobby. A banner hung over the teller windows apologizing for the bank's legacy of having been built on slavery. He ignored it. The people were still cowed.

So far so good.

Tommy O'Meara stood fidgeting in front of the bank's front doors, and he spotted the woman coming towards him with a determined look. Her hair was short and brown, and she wore a t-shirt that read "Queer and Here." In fact, Abigail Chalmers was completely heterosexual, a condition that caused her no end of personal grief and self-loathing. And that morning she needed to get cash for her therapist, who demanded payment in US dollars instead of PR scrip, even though doing so was technically illegal.

"Bank's closed, lady," Tommy said as Abigail reached for the door. He stepped in front of her and expected her to back off.

"Who are you calling a lady?" Abigail said. She felt a tinge of excitement rising – she was being victimized by this cis male in a leather jacket and this was her chance to fight back.

"Lady, move on!" Tommy snapped.

"You sexist cis piece of shit!" she yelled.

Tommy looked at her hard. "Lady, you better step off."

"This is word rape!" she screamed. People walking on the street turned and looked.

"I said shut your mouth, bitch!" Tommy yelled back.

"Get out of my way!" Abigail said and grabbed at his jacket. Tommy pushed her back, and Abigail was momentarily stunned that he put his hands on her. Then her fury peaked and she charged him, uttering a guttural howl.

Tommy drew the .45 and shot her in the face. The shot echoed down the street and amongst the buildings as Abigail, her eyes wide in shock, stood unsteadily for a moment before realizing she was dead and slumping to the sidewalk.

Doyle heard the shot and was heading toward the door even as Sean was in his earpiece yelling that "Tommy just shot some lady, Danny!"

He burst out the door, and saw the wide-eyed Abigail lying still on the sidewalk, with Tommy standing, .45 in hand.

"She made a move, man," he said. Doyle saw that the civilians on the street were all on their phones.

Doyle went back inside, yelling "Abort! Abort!" A few moments later Torrey came out of the back, confused.

"We're almost there!"

"Abort! Now!"

"The money...!"

"We're pulling out!"

Torrey swore and rushed back to get Jimmy, who was about to open the last lock guarding the stash of US dollars. The PR cash they would have left untouched.

"Card?" Mikey said, holding a playing card in one hand and a 12-gauge in the other.

"No card," Doyle said.

"Hey, man," pleaded Tommy, making no effort to hide his Remington. "I had no choice!"

"Shut up," Doyle snapped, his eyes searching the street for the van. Jimmy O'Connor was on the same freq and knew they were aborting. He just needed to finish coming around the block.

"Company!" Sean yelled. A blue and white PSF cruiser – a repurposed Boston Police Ford – turned the corner where Sean was standing post and accelerated down the block toward the bank. The pair of officers had gotten the call of a hate crime in progress.

The cruiser skidded to a stop in the right lane as Doyle raised his shotgun and fired a blast of buckshot at the window, then another, then another that tore a gash in the hood. Torrey and Jimmy burst out and they too immediately unloaded on the patrol car. The windshield was shattered under the volley of buckshot, but the officers rolled out and took up positions behind their doors with their Berettas. Maybe they had been actual cops and stayed on – most of the cops left or were fired - but they at least had the tactical sense to return fire, if not accurately.

Jimmy and Torrey were firing away until Doyle ordered them to cease fire.

Sean trotted down from the end of the block with his .357 Smith & Wesson and carefully shot the driver in the back. The passenger stood and turned to meet this new threat, and now Doyle fired again, hitting the PSF officer in the back of the head. He fell to the asphalt.

Sean assessed the passenger as clearly dead. He stepped around to the driver, who was crawling on the blacktop, a red stain on his right scapula. Sean looked up at Doyle.

Doyle considered, and nodded. Sean shot the driver through the head.

The van appeared, skidding to a stop. The crew piled in and Mikey, having come from his position on the corner, pulled the doors shut as the van accelerated.

"What the hell happened?" Sean shouted as he settled onto a bench.

"This idiot happened," Doyle said, reaching forward and snatching the pistol from Tommy's hand.

"The bitch came at me!" Tommy pleaded. "I had no choice."

The van made a turn. They were ten minutes from Charlestown.

"What the hell now, Danny?" Sean asked Doyle.

"We dump and burn out the van like we planned," he said. "And Jimmy takes the guns to his uncle and gets rid of them." Jimmy's uncle captained a fishing boat in Gloucester. Uncle Jimmy would never ask his nephew Jimmy about what the lad was dumping into the Atlantic.

The van turned again, picking up speed.

"Danny, we had a wicked hard time getting these pieces," Sean said. The PR gun bans had made the always tricky task of getting firearms exponentially more difficult, and expensive.

"We can't keep them," Doyle said. "Because of this dipshit, we're good for three murders. Do you want to give the FBI ballistic matches to your and this dumbass's pieces, and striker matches on the shells with our sawed-offs?"

Sean didn't push it. Doyle was always careful, always meticulous in his planning, and disciplined enough not to compromise what he called "OPSEC." The Army had taught Doyle well, before it put him in prison.

Doyle never left loose ends.

"Open the door," Doyle said to Mikey. Mikey began to comply.

"What the hell, man?" Tommy said, an edge of panic in his voice. "What are you doing?"

"Trying not to go deaf," Doyle said, and he brought up the twelve gauge and fired a load of buckshot into Tommy's chest.

Their ears were ringing even with the open back door, but Doyle shouted so they could hear him.

"Throw this bum out of my van," he said. The smell of cordite bit at their nostrils. Mikey and Torrey each took an arm and, after Tommy spilled out onto North Washington Road, they pulled the doors shut again.

Johnny Ross surveyed the torn-up PSF cruiser and, behind the open front doors, the two tarp-draped bodies. Thin rivers of scarlet twisted from under each to the gutter.

His partner Paul Sorenson exhaled.

"Freakin' cowboys," he observed.

Ross stepped over to the apparently female medical examiner, who was near the dead driver, arguing with a PSF sergeant about not touching the bodies.

"Don't mansplain at me about my job or I'll complain so fast it'll make that cis head of yours spin," she snapped.

"Are you saying I'm cis?" asked the sergeant angrily.

"Excuse me," Ross said, his ID hanging from his hand at shoulder level. "Special Agents Ross and Sorenson, FBI."

The bickering pair stopped bickering.

"These stiffs are my guys," the sergeant said, before correcting himself. "My persons. It's my investigation."

"No," Ross said firmly. "This is a bank robbery, and that makes it federal." Technically, the correct term for a crime against the People's Republic would be a 'republican' crime, but for obvious reasons the anachronism remained in use. "That means the FBI has jurisdiction over all of it."

"I want to know who killed my...persons," the sergeant sputtered.

"We do too," Ross assured him. "Let us do our thing."

The sergeant turned and stalked off. Ross and Sorenson came around to the dead driver. The medical examiner looked them over.

"You federal boys gonna high hat me too?"

"Agent Ross is considering transition," Sorenson said deadpan. "So, the term 'boys' is offensive."

The medical examiner looked crestfallen. "I'm sorry."

"It's okay," Ross said, not correcting his partner. His gender identity was rigorously conventional, though if you got a few drinks in Sorenson it was anyone's guess how the night might turn out. Regardless, Ross was not one to fail to press even a tiny social advantage. "Can you walk us through what you know?"

Relieved that her faux pas had apparently been so readily forgiven, the medical examiner switched into professional mode.

"PSF Officer Jeff Daley, former Boston PD," she said, pulling back the sheet on the facedown corpse. "Hit upper back at range with a large caliber handgun. Then finished at close range with the same weapon, I'll wager, in the back of the head. The other PSF officer was initially firing forward with his Beretta, because there's brass on the sidewalk, and he must have turned toward the rear and then was hit back of the head with a 12-gauge. Do yourself a favor and don't look."

"Crossfire, front and back," Sorenson said.

"They had security on the corners," Ross said. "The PSF rolled in on a hate crime call, and got engaged when our suspects came out of the bank. Then their security came in from the back, bang, bang, two cops down."

"And they executed this one."

"The lady and the other cop were dead, so why leave a witness alive?" Ross said, deep in thought. They had already walked through the bank itself, talked briefly to the customers, and examined the corpse of Abigail Chalmers. They had looked for, but not found, a playing card with a picture of the Celtics mascot, Lucky the Leprechaun.

"They planned this down to the last detail," Ross said. "Their actions in the bank were totally professional. They were tactically proficient. When Chalmers got killed, they had the discipline to leave the money and walk. And when they were confronted, they fought without a second's hesitation."

"Seems like the Leprechauns, but they don't usually get bloody and there was no card, Johnny. They always leave a card."

"Maybe didn't want to take credit for this fiasco."

"Maybe," Sorenson said. "But whoever it is, it's not your usual crew of drunken mick bank robbers."

"The word 'mick' is racist against the Irish," the medical examiner snapped.

"The Irish aren't a race," Sorenson snapped back. "Stop appropriating grievances."

"Hey!" Ross shouted. The pair ceased their argument. He continued speaking. "This crew is very good and very dangerous. But I still don't get why they killed Chalmers."

"A screw up?" said Sorenson. His phone rang, and he pulled it out and answered it as Ross turned back to the cruiser. It looked like a sieve. These guys would go from DEFCON 4 to DEFCON 1 in a flash.

"Johnny," Sorenson said. "They found a male body with a 12-gauge hole in the chest dumped on North Washington Road."

"That's on the way to Charlestown," the medical examiner said.

"I bet we just found the guy who screwed up," Ross said. "Let's get back to the office and get the facial rec going on the surveillance video. Someone scouted it out within the last couple days. And we need to upload the info into JFCID and see what comes back." The Joint Federal Criminal Investigation Database was a program federal law enforcement embraced just before the Split that compared details of crimes with a database of other crimes and criminals. It was not perfect, but sometimes it made solid connections between cases that otherwise appeared unrelated, or linked to an individual who was not currently a suspect. Regardless, it was mandatory to use it; Ross suspected that higher ups used it to keep an eye on the status of ongoing investigations.

"And then what?" Sorenson asked.

"Then we start looking for our bad guys in Charlestown. And I know where to start."

"Nothing?" Katie McGowan said. "All that work, three murder raps, and not one damn cent?"

"That's how it goes sometimes," Danny Doyle replied. They were in her house. He hadn't wanted to come over, especially tonight, but she demanded it. Katie never listened to anyone, not to her brother Sean, not to Danny, no one.

"You got rid of everything?" she asked. Katie's German shepherd Clover wagged her tail as Danny pet her.

"The van, the guns, all gone. And Tommy too."

"I told you he was a psycho piece of shit," she said, and she had. "You should have let me come."

"You did the recon," Danny said. "They had your face on video."

"In a mask."

"They'll still probably be coming around to talk to you."

"I was just cashing my paycheck. And the whole staff at the diner can tell them I was waitressing when the robbery went down. But next time, I'm coming."

"Too risky," Danny declared.

"I thought Army guys liked risks."

"Well, I'm not in the Army anymore. And I don't take any risks I don't have to," he said. "I meant it when I said it, Katie. I am never going back inside. Not ever."

"We just need a big hit, Danny. One big hit and we can get the hell out of here. Maybe go to New Mexico."

Danny laughed. "New Mexico? What the hell do you know about New Mexico?"

"I know it's not Charlestown."

5.

One of the manifestations of enmity between the left-wing government of Canada and the right-wing government of the United States was that after the Split, citizens of the People's Republic were allowed entry without clearing customs while US citizens still had to. It did not matter to Turnbull, who was flying as Cristobal Ruben Sanchez, PR citizen. It just made him a bit annoyed that the maple-mongers would pull that petty garbage. But then, the US had been tacitly supporting the Albertan resistance, which was conducting an extremely polite, low-key insurgency against the arrogant left-wing establishment in the East. Quebec, which itself had flirted with separatism fifty years before, was the staunchest opponent of freedom for the interior. Turnbull noted Royal Canadian Mounted Police with submachine guns patrolling the terminals of Montréal-Pierre Elliott Trudeau International Airport.

He had not cleared security in Dallas – he was escorted past the screeners – and his Wilson Combat .45 and eight mags were under the false bottom of his carry-on bag. Now he held up his passport and walked past the line of waiting US citizens. The uniformed Canuck at the desk smiled as he passed, but did a tugging gesture at his face. Turnbull had wanted to keep his mask on to avoid the mounted cameras, but that was out the window. He tugged the mask down as he walked through.

He picked up a Hertz Ford Fusion with New York plates and had gone through the border without stopping, as borders were racist. Apparently, the Canadians had not accepted this notion; a long line of cars, most packed with families and their possessions, was waiting to go north. Tweaking the US by making its citizens stew while letting PR tourists waltz right through airport customs was one thing; allowing a mass migration of Yankees intending to stay for good was quite another. The Canadians had finally found one kind of immigrant they didn't want.

Fat drops of water landed on the windshield when Turnbull was a few miles south of Plattsburgh, New York, headed southbound on Interstate 87. He had avoided the slightly shorter route through Vermont because activists had attacked and burned the vast majority of gas stations as a response to the threat of global warming.

Not that upstate New York seemed particularly prosperous. It was late afternoon, but there were few vehicles on the road, and little economic activity was apparent. He had caught glimpses of Lake Champlain off in the distance to the east, but there were no boats on it even though it was early summer. Most of the time, the freeway was hemmed in by low green trees on each side, with a wide green turf median between the north and southbound lanes.

But there were signs. "DIVERSITY IS THE FREEDOM TO BE UNIFIED" read one. Another announced "NEW YORK APOLOGIZES HUMBLY FOR ITS COMPLICITY IN SYSTEMIC RACISM." There was also one reading "HONOR THE VICTIMS OF OPPRESSION ON CELEBRATION OF INDEPENDENCE FROM RACIST OPPRESSION DAY JULY 4TH." A sub-script added "Celebrating racist Independence Day is a hate crime." There was a red circle and slash over an exploding firecracker.

He figured it was four or five hours to Boston. He had a hotel reservation lined up. The next morning, he would go get the professor, visit the First National Bank of Wherever, put him in the car, and drive down to Kentucky and cross the border. Easy. Done by the weekend. Home well in time to celebrate the Fourth of July with a Shiner Bock and a ribeye for one.

Unless the Freemasons intervened. Or the Trilateral Commission. Or the Lizard People from Space.

Brake lights ahead.

It looked like a traffic jam, out there in the midst of the woods. Turnbull slowed down the Fusion. There were several big rigs and a dozen or so smaller vehicles stopped ahead. Past them, a sheriff's SUV was parked across the freeway, perpendicular and lights flashing. The PSF had not taken over many of the rural departments yet, so that figured.

Turnbull had taken out and loaded his Wilson Combat .45, and it now rested between his thighs. He did not want trouble, and he was cautiously optimistic that this was some sort of routine road stoppage. Maybe someone had hit a deer and run off the road ahead. This certainly did not seem to be a police roadblock.

He slowed and stopped 20 meters behind the Dodge Caravan to his front. One bumper sticker read, "A WOMXN OF COLOR FOR PRESIDENT – WARREN," and the other read, "My Child Is Special. My Child Is Not Constrained By Myths Of Gender." There was a pictogram of a boy in a dress, smiling. Turnbull suspected the child would be constrained by the need for years of therapy.

He waited. Several more cars pulled up and stopped behind him, as well as a couple of big rigs. No one was getting out of their vehicles, and no one seemed particularly upset by the delay. At least the rain had stopped.

A pack of pick-up trucks appeared fast out of barely visible dirt roads breaking off into the forest. They took up positions behind the idling cars, to the side and the front, about eight of them, full of armed men and some women in civilian clothes.

"Shit," Turnbull said. Someone in civilian clothes with a shotgun was getting out of what had to be a stolen squad car. Was this a highway robbery?

Most of the raiders were scruffy, some bearded, others not. They carried a variety of weapons, some modern semiautomatics, some hunting rifles, all highly illegal, as a sign every ten miles or so had warned. A large, bearded bear-like man in a brown jacket was walking down the line of cars to his rear, knocking on windows saying something, then moving on. Next in line was Turnbull's Fusion.

He needed to make a call.

Turnbull slid his .45 between the seat and the center console.

The bearlike gentleman, with a scoped Remington 700 rifle over his shoulder, tapped on the glass. Turnbull slowly moved his hand to hit the window button, dropping the glass six inches.

"Okay," the bear-man said. "We need you to stay in your vehicle. We're not here for you. We're here to make a point about tyranny."

"I'm against tyranny," Turnbull said.

"Yeah, well you should do something about it. Follow T. You look hard enough on the dark web and you'll find him and he'll show you the way."

"T, huh?"

"Yeah, T."

"Okay, thanks for the T tip," Turnbull said. The bear walked to the SUV and promptly got into a screaming match with the occupant, who likely was less receptive to the suggestion to research the thoughts of whatever the hell T was.

Just some locals playing guerilla, Turnbull decided, and all he needed to do was wait them out. They were swarming on the big rigs, opening the back doors and climbing in. Probably raiding to collect some supplies, and also to make a point about who owned the countryside.

"Rock on, patriots," he said to himself as he relaxed.

The two People's Militia vehicles appeared from the rear, roaring down the freeway. They were hummers, military-style but painted black. Apparently, the militia was professionalizing, at least somewhat. One hummer had a machine gun up top, an

M240. It appeared, from the shooting that erupted, other forces were coming from the front.

"Shit," hissed Turnbull.

A burst of machine gun fire ripped overhead. Turnbull's weapon was in his hand. The guerillas, who seemed to outnumber the approaching militia, were scrambling for cover. A random round pinged into his trunk.

He evaluated his options.

The guerillas were taking cover and returning fire, but the ones he could see were uncoordinated and unled. Luckily, the militia types were equally uncoordinated. If this was a planned trap, and since they were coming both ways it had to be, they should have had overwhelming force. The ambush was poorly coordinated. Likely there were a bunch more blues coming, meaning the guerillas better get out of dodge fast.

His rear window caught a round, spraying glass into the backseat. Ahead, the bear was firing his rifle from behind the front of the minivan belonging to the family with the kid with gender issues.

There was a lot of shooting noise.

Turnbull completed his review of his potential courses of action. If he stayed put, the victorious People's Militia would check him out and probably roll him up – at the very least he'd be delayed. Maybe killed, he thought, as another machine gun round hit his windshield.

Or he could intervene.

The hummer with the turret pulled up ahead of him on the left. From behind, several more individual militiamen, in black uniforms, were advancing, all with AK family rifles.

The minivan hit the gas and pulled out of line, exposing the bear, but the machine gunner chose to ventilate the vehicle instead. In his side mirror, Turnbull saw a militiaman running fast down the line of cars, spraying and praying. The rounds went right past his window.

"Shit," Turnbull said again, throwing open his driver's side door. The running militiaman slammed into it and bounced back. Turnbull was out on the freeway, firing twice into the man's sternum and then engaging the man's battle buddy a few feet behind with a shot to the neck and the face. The targets dropped and Turnbull took up the door jammer's AK-74 – a brand new but cheap Norinco imported from Shanghai – along with a hand grenade latched to the man's web gear.

The machine gunner was trying to stitch the bear, who was weaving through the line of cars. Engaged to the front, the hummer's occupants did not notice Turnbull trot up from the rear. He pulled the pin on the liberated grenade and tugged open the rear passenger door. There was a female militia fighter in the backseat whose eyes got as big as saucers when Turnbull lobbed the pineapple inside and slammed the door shut. There were shouts and, too late, the gunner tried to traverse to engage the attacker, but he could not get a low enough angle.

Turnbull stepped off and turned away. The doors contained the explosion, so the force went out the top, chucking the gunner into the sky. He landed on his head and was still, the angle of his neck something unspeakable.

A round pinged off the armor of the hummer and Turnbull sprinted around to the front. The bear and another guerilla, a young man with way too much gear bought from some online store before the Split, approached. The young man had an AR-15. Another round pinged off the armor – there were a couple militia left, firing from the other hummer 50 meters to the rear.

"You two!" Turnbull yelled. "You flank, I'll suppress!"

They looked at him blankly.

"I'll shoot at them and you go hit them from the side!"

The bear nodded and he grabbed his partner by the plate carrier and they moved out, staying behind the line of cars and their cowering occupants. Turnbull clambered up onto the hood and stepped back to the machine gun mount. It was unharmed, and there was nothing but smoke and silence down inside the hummer. He swung the machine gun around to the rear and opened up on the two militiamen still fighting. He got one who stayed out of cover too long trying to take an aimed shot, and he pinned the other one behind an abandoned Mazda. After a few seconds there was more firing, from the bear and the guy with the AR-15 advancing from the flank, and the last militiaman at the rear was done.

At least for the moment. There had to be more militiamen coming.

Turnbull leapt down and ran toward the front of the column with his AK. There was still shooting up there – someone was firing admirably controlled bursts.

It was about 100 yards up to the front of the column. Most of the civilians were wisely still cowering in their cars. A couple who had gotten out were dead on the road, and a few others were making for the tree line unmolested. Ahead, a dozen guerillas were shooting it out with the remaining militiamen among a line of three hummers. One guerilla, short and wearing gear that looked lived in, was engaging fast and hard.

"Good technique," Turnbull thought as he watched the fighter drop a mag, reload his M4, and immediately re-engage.

Far ahead, a militiaman fell, and then it was quiet.

The man with the M4 took charge. "Sweep them," he yelled to some of his guerillas. "Get their weapons. Move!"

He turned to see Turnbull, who tossed down his Norinco.

"Who are you?" the man said, weapon on the stranger. The guerilla seemed vaguely familiar, as did his voice.

"I'm the guy who's going to make that M4 into a suppository if you keep pointing it at me," Turnbull said. Some more guerillas gathered and the bear came up from behind.

"He was fighting for us, T," the bear said. "He got out and whacked a bunch of them."

T lowered his weapon, most of the way. "I asked you who you were," he said.

"Call me Chris. You better get your asses out of here. There have got to be more coming."

"I can lead my own unit, Chris."

"Really? Because somehow the blues knew you were throwing this party. You're compromised."

"More enemy in-bound, about a mile out!" one of the guerillas said, staring down the straight freeway.

"They'll be coming from both sides," Turnbull said. "What's your call, Mr. T? Or is that a different T?"

"You don't know who I am, do you?"

Turnbull shrugged.

"Didn't you listen to talk radio before the Split?" asked the bear.

"You're Ben Shapiro?" Turnbull asked.

"No!" the leader snapped. "I'm Teddy King!"

Turnbull shrugged again. Then he spoke.

"I'd ask you how you got all 'Nam and stuff, but maybe you can write me a novella about your journey from microphone loudmouth to guerilla warlord later, since they're coming and all."

"Load up!" King shouted. The guerillas scrambled for their pick-ups. A female stayed behind.

"What about the wounded?" she asked.

"Bring ours," King said.

"What about theirs?" Turnbull asked.

King stared hard at Turnbull, and seemed about to speak when the woman spoke first.

"There aren't any of theirs," she said.

"Saved you a tough call, Teddy," Turnbull said.

"I'd have made it," King said, then rushed away to join his troops.

Turnbull looked back down the row of cars. His own ride was shot to bits – it was not going to get far without drawing unwanted attention, assuming it would even start again. He sighed.

"Hey," he yelled to the bear, who was getting into the back of a blue Ford F-150. "I'm coming too."

"We're made," Johnny Ross told Paul Sorenson as they glided down the street. Hard eyes from the sidewalks and the porches glared.

"It's the car, right?"

"And us. This is the Town, Paul. These people survived for centuries by being paranoid about outsiders. And these particular paranoids have always had enemies."

"What I don't get is how they can't get it through their thick Irish heads that we're trying to liberate them from their real enemies, the mobsters and scumbags right here in Charlestown. We're the good guys."

"No, not to them," Ross replied as he pulled into an open space along the dirty sidewalk. "Everybody who isn't one of them is a bad guy."

"You're a bad guy and you're one of them, Johnny."

"My mom was. Her family never liked my dad. Thought he had airs because he was a doctor. And every time I came to visit the relatives, I spent the whole time fighting. Got the crap kicked out of me I don't know how many times. Marine Corps boot camp was a resort after my summers in Charlestown."

"Kiss my ass, feds," a dirty blonde – the adjective accurate as to both her hair color and her hygiene – shouted as she walked past on the sidewalk.

"Nice," observed Sorenson.

"Let's go," Ross replied.

A couple doors down was the Tangier, a bar at the northeast quadrant of the busy corner. The sign was right out of 1966; no one remembered who thought it was a great idea to name a saloon catering to sullen micks after an exotic Middle Eastern destination, but things here didn't change fast and the name stuck. Even after the Split, Charlestown – particularly the ungentrified part they were currently walking through – was still what it had always been, an ethnic enclave whose diversity was limited to different kinds of Irish stereotypes. Dark haired and ginger, freckled and lightly freckled, drunk and drunker.

A couple louts stood at the door smoking, eye-balling the approaching agents.

"Where's Seamus?" Ross called out pleasantly.

"Do I look like his doorman?" the bigger one said, taking a puff.

"You look like you're on parole and maybe I should call your PO, tell him you're not cooperating," Sorenson said. Both louts chuckled.

"Hey, you ain't heard? Parole is canceled. I'm a victim of the patriarchy, or something. I'm getting ten grand in reparations for my false imprisonment. So, you can kiss my ass, fed."

"How about we kick it instead?" asked Sorenson. The louts dropped their butts and fronted up.

"Hey, boyos, no need for this," Ross said calmly. "We just want to talk to Seamus, real civilized. Respectfully."

"Your friend's got a big mouth," the lout pouted.

"Where's the man?"

The lout considered. "Inside," he said.

"Thank you," Ross replied.

"You guys have a good afternoon," Sorenson added as they went through the worn wooden doors.

The interior, like the name, seemed like something out of another time. Stale smoke hung in the air – apparently the two louts outside were sentries, since this establishment opted out of the law against smoking inside. The décor was a mix of fanciful early Sinbad, rickety stools and tables of various mismatched types, and sports memorabilia from before the fabled Boston teams were ordered to admit women and fat people in the name of diversity. All of the sports photos predated 2010.

There were a couple rummies at the weathered bar, heads hanging low over their whiskey. A pair of thugs sat at a rear table, and Ross noted that their positioning gave them a solid field of fire toward the door. No need to roust them – they were certainly packing.

An older man, late-fifties most likely, though men aged hard in the Town, sat on a stool away and alone at the far corner end of the bar, an iPad on a stand and a bottle of Jameson's plus a glass with a bit of the old peat before him. He looked up, his hard eyes on the feds as they approached him slowly and making no sudden moves.

"Hello, Seamus," Ross said.

"Been a while, Johnny," Seamus McCloskey replied. "What brings you to my establishment today?"

"Thought we ought to catch up."

"Well, I'd ask you and your running buddy there to join me for a taste of Jameson's, but it would hurt my brand to be seen drinking with the feds."

"I don't drink with criminals, so…," began Sorenson.

"Hey Paul," Ross said. "Maybe you go watch the door."

Sorenson sullenly stepped away, taking a seat opposite the thugs and initiating a staring contest with them.

"Your friend is disrespectful," McCloskey observed. "You know how to behave, even though you're a fed. But these outsiders, they can't help pissing people off. And since the Split, it's gotten worse. Apparently, we've been privileged all along and didn't know it."

"I'm here to talk about the Diversity Bank job."

"Never heard of it."

"Three dead, one a civilian, two PSF."

"Do the People's Security Force even count as cops?"

"They count as corpses when they get gunned down. Look, someone from the Town hit that bank and screwed up royally. Now, all kinds of heat is going to come down and it's going to be right on your head since you're the big man around here."

"Never heard of the Diversity Bank," Seamus said, taking a sip.

"How about Leprechauns? Heard of them?"

"Nope. They're like a, what? A myth? Like elves."

"Seamus, everything changed after the Split. We could work together in the old days, come to an understanding, but now you guys are persona non grata, and all the folks in the municipality who used to be your pals, taking money? Gone. They're all college punks running things now, true believers, and if you want to see what 'no respect' looks like, just wait until they get you in their crosshairs."

"I still don't know about any leprechauns."

"Nothing that big happens in the Town without you having your fingers in it, Seamus. Getting the guns, the financing, even just getting your cut because you're the big blarney stone around here, you know who pulled this off. They have to go down."

"That's what the English used to say about my great-great-great-great-great-grandfather. But no one would give him up. And he kept on killing Englishmen."

"Until the day they caught him and killed him?"

"No, he got away and came here."

"And started doing crime in the New World. That's a proud legacy, Seamus."

"I like you, Johnny, because of your mom's family, but I'm not helping you. No one here will."

"The heat won't come from me, Seamus. But it will come."

"We've survived Cromwell and the Potato Famine by sticking together," Seamus said.

"But will you survive woke?"

"We'll take our chances."

Ross nodded, and Seamus took another sip. Ross turned and walked out, joined by Sorenson.

"He knows," Sorenson said.

"Of course he does. He may have even set up the score in the first place. But he won't say shit to us. These people – stubborn. They never give in."

"And you're one of them."

"Only half," Ross said, reaching the car. There was a huge loogie someone had hucked onto the windshield right in front of the driver's seat. "Let's get back to the office, get our report into the JFCID, and get ourselves a drink."

The guerillas' rally point was by a lake a few miles back in the wooded hills east of the interstate. Turnbull said little but listened intently to the guerillas in the back of the pick-up as they drove. They were skittish – this was their first real firefight. They seemed quite happy to have a former conservative talk show host as their leader. Turnbull wondered where Teddy King's weapons skills had come from.

The vehicles parked facing outward for a quick dispersal – a good sign. There were maybe fifteen of them, and except for a couple of fighters pulling security, they all gathered near the shore where Teddy King, rifle hanging from its sling, waited to address them. Turnbull walked over and King's eyes met his – it had not occurred to King that this stranger would be joining them. He turned his attention back to his troops.

"Good work today," he said. "A lot to improve on, though. But we've made a first strike for freedom. We've announced that we're here, and that we're ready to fight!"

The guerillas cheered.

"No retreat, no surrender!" he added.

"And now for a word from our sponsor," Turnbull muttered.

The group broke up and King came over to him.

"We're not looking for new members."

"I'm not looking to join," Turnbull said. "Especially a unit that's got a traitor. Or traitors."

"You don't know that."

"You think they just stumbled onto you from two directions? If they weren't amateurs too, they'd have come heavier, with air support, and you would all be lying under tarps back there."

"Why are you even here?"

"That's my business, and since you got my last ride shot to pieces, I'm going to need another."

"Do I look like a used car dealer?"

"No, you look like a guy who picked up some skills along the way and thinks he can run a real-life Robin Sage out in the Adirondacks."

"Robin Sage is a Green Beret exercise. This is real life."

"Yeah, it is, and in real life those blues are going to hunt you down since they own at least one of your people."

"My people are solid."

"You think about that," Turnbull said. "It isn't my problem, because I'm getting a car and getting gone. Now, I have a call to make to my people."

"Who are your people, Chris?"

"Let's just say I'm a foreigner here. Now. As of six months ago."

"You're from the red."

"I sure as hell ain't from here. Think about how we get me a car. And about who in your little platoon might have sold you out."

Turnbull walked off into the trees and drew his iPhone 14 from his pocket. It was loaded down with spoofing software that would hide his cellular info and route his calls to Canada, Japan, and back to the United States. Its encryption protocols would keep anyone who did manage to listen from being able to understand, at least as long as he was terse. At least that's what the quartermasters had told him.

He dialed a number from memory.

It rang, then picked up. A stopwatch appeared on the screen – 120 seconds. More than that increased the risk of detection.

"How's your trip?" asked Clay Deeds.

"Got interrupted an hour south of Plattsburgh. Got caught up in a firefight between some PMs in military vehicles, and some guerillas led by that right-wing radio guy, Teddy King. Someone ran him through a Special Forces mini-Q course, because he's at least marginally competent in a fight."

"Wait, I heard Teddy King on the radio here in Dallas just this morning."

"No, that was Ben Shapiro. This is a different one."

"Wait," Deeds said, and the line went silent for nearly a minute. Turnbull looked around, impatient. The guerillas were relaxing before getting back to work.

Deed returned to the line. "Kelly, bring him out with you."

"What?"

"Teddy King. Take him with you and bring him out."

"I already have a mission."

"And now you have a supplementary one."

"What's so important about this guy?"

"Great question. None of your business. Just bring him and the professor both out."

"And what if Teddy King doesn't want to come?"

"Persuade him."

Turnbull sighed, and noted that the stopwatch was at 110 seconds. "Gotta go."

"See you soon," Deeds said before Turnbull hung up. He put the iPhone back in his pocket and walked over toward King.

"Figure out your snitch yet?" Turnbull asked.

"I trust these people," King said.

"Yeah, you got some tactical training somehow, but learning how to truly not trust anyone takes on the job experience."

Turnbull looked at the guerillas, scowled, then turned back to King.

"Is that guy texting?" The guy from the firefight with way too much gear was sitting on a log hunched over his phone pressing buttons.

"Shit," King said. "They know no cell phones on an op!"

Turnbull stepped over and put his Wilson Combat to the back of the young man's head.

The man froze in mid keystroke.

"What are you texting?" asked Turnbull pleasantly, pushing the barrel against the man's scalp.

"Nothing," the young man said, his voice quivering as he felt the steel on his skull.

"Gimme your phone."

The young man passed it up and Turnbull took it. In the text box, waiting to be sent, were two images.

"What is it?" King asked.

"Two little cartoon pictures," Turnbull said.

"They're emojis," the young man said.

"Shut up," Turnbull snapped. He squinted. "Okay, what does an eggplant and a smiley face with a big grin mean?"

"Nothing," said the young man.

"Tim, I need the truth," King said. "Are you sending codes to a handler?"

"No!" Tim said emphatically, turning around. "It's to my girlfriend!"

"You're sending an eggplant and a smiley face to your girlfriend?" Turnbull asked.

"It's a sex thing," Tim whispered. The other guerillas laughed. Turnbull tossed him back his phone.

"A real narc would have a less embarrassing alibi," Turnbull said. "So, who else knew the whole plan?"

"Everyone. I briefed everyone right before we moved."

"But who knew about it before then?"

"Just me and...." King stopped and looked at the bear. "Bob."

Bob swallowed, and his hand twitched near his rifle, but his twitching stopped when Turnbull pointed the .45 at his bearded face.

"Well, Bob?" Turnbull asked.

"I didn't..."

"Give us your phone, Bob," Turnbull said. "Carefully."

Bob slowly pulled out an iPhone and tossed it over to King. It was unlocked, and King took a moment to go through it as Turnbull patiently held his pistol on the bear.

"It's clean. No weird calls, no weird texts," King said.

"No, there wouldn't be," Turnbull said. "Bob, give up your other phone. The one your handler gave you."

"I don't have one," Bob said, pleading.

"So, when we search you and we find one, Bob, I can shoot you?" Turnbull said. "Because if you make me search you and I find it, I will cap you just for inconveniencing me."

"If you did something, Bob, we need to know," King said.

"They had my balls in a vice, T," Bob said. He pulled a phone out of his pocket. "I had no choice."

"Oh Bob," King said. "What did you tell them?"

"When and where. And, some names."

"Your little guerilla war just went poof," Turnbull said. "And I noticed a bunch of these folks turning off their cells while we were quizzing Romeo about his texts to Juliet. The blues know your phones, and now they know you know they know."

"They'll be coming," King said loudly to his troops. "We need to scatter. Now. Don't go home. Don't go to work. Just go. You're all blown, thanks to this piece of shit."

Bob started blubbering. "I'm sorry," he moaned.

The guerillas started scattering to the trucks.

"What about him?" Turnbull said. "He knows a lot."

"Right," King said, lifting his rifle and shooting Bob in the chest. The big man fell on the ground, writhing. King shot him again and he stopped moving.

Turnbull looked down at the dead man, and then at King.

"He's not my first. I'm not just some radio bigmouth anymore."

"We need to go," Turnbull said.

"You can go your own way, Chris, whoever you are. I've got to rebuild this movement."

"Those guys I work for? They want you in Texas."

"I don't understand."

"Orders. They want you to come out of the blue with me."

One of the pick-ups, loaded with guerillas, pulled away.

King looked at Turnbull. "Why would I do that?"

"The fact the bad guys are swooping in as we speak is one reason. But mostly because I'm supposed to bring you out."

Another truck took off.

"I guess I am kind of high profile," King said. "I can see how they'd want me in the red."

"Yeah, you'll be a big help," sniffed Turnbull. "And since your guerilla army just vaporized, maybe we can get moving?"

"They want to help me start up another insurrection, don't they?"

"Sure," Turnbull said. "That's got to be it. You're like Che, only shorter and not a communist."

"Che got killed."

"Yep. I love a happy ending. Let's move."

King nodded, and smiled.

"They must have heard of T back in Texas," he said.

"Oh yeah. T's got epic street cred. Come on." They walked to the last truck.

"So, we go south or north?" King asked.

"East."

"East?"

"We got a stop to make in Boston."

"What's in Boston?"

"Harvard, your alma mater."

"That's Ben Shapiro. I went to Berkeley."

"Whatever," Turnbull replied. "Let's go."

6.

"Simply put, bearing children is a crime against nature, and we should seriously consider making it a crime under the People's Justice Code!" Senator Richard Harrington said into the microphone. "At least for persons of oppression."

The room was packed with skinny people who were probably male, and many others who likely identified as women, none particularly attractive, and all set with similarly grim visages even as they enthusiastically applauded him.

"All the while the reds breed indiscriminately, careless of the environmental catastrophe every one of their squealing brats represents, and apparently just because Jesus told them to...," he declaimed, pausing for effect. This was a laugh line inserted by his speechwriter, and it took the audience a moment to realize they were supposed to respond. Instead of laughter, most nodded and muttered their affirmation. There were only a few chuckles. The members of the Connecticut Anti-Natalist League were not a jolly bunch. The audiences in the People's Republic's approved comedy clubs mostly responded similarly to the sets by the government-licensed comics.

"We must take a responsible approach to population in light of the Earth crimes that are the legacy of the old United States," he continued. "Obviously, abortion delivery remains a key component, including strongly advocating and providing it free to all men and women who are pregnant. Our new Constitution enshrines that! And we must welcome refugees and other immigrants! We reject walls. And we reject locking children in cages!"

The audience clapped politely. Senator Harrington nodded solemnly in acknowledgment of their recognition. He did not mention that the abortion programs had been a huge success, especially in persuading the reluctant to partake. And the number of immigrants had declined sharply over the last year as the economy tanked under President Biden before the Split, and it had positively cratered afterwards. The People's Republic was suffering a net loss in population, with many of the former middle and working class embarking for the red, while the only people coming to the blue arrived with their hands out, eager to cash in on the recently doubled social welfare payments decreed by the new PR government. Even Mexico had complained about the tide of refugees heading south from California. There was growing talk that it might build its own wall.

And, while there were no immigrant children in locked cages, there were native children locked in cages whose parents had been arrested for any of the many new crimes enacted into law. Racism. Climate catastrophe denial. Gun ownership. Unlawful memes.

"Human beings, in general, are a blight upon the Earth," Harrington concluded. "Our population must be smaller, more sensitive, and above all, more aware of the racism, transphobia, and earthism" – this was the crime of denying the rights of the Earth – "that are the legacy of human hixtory!"

He pronounced the "x," and none of the audience as much as blinked.

Mx. Drysdale – she also pronounced that "x" – met him at the foot of the steps up to the podium. Xe was channeling maleness today, sort of, wearing a grey men's suit, a white shirt, and a skinny black tie. Xir hair was close-cropped to xis head, and there was a black stud through xis nose. Drysdale was competent, and acted as the Senator's right hand being, though he would never use that term. It was ableist, in that some beings had no right hand, and it further otherized those who were left-dominant, or ambidextrous. Or neither.

"A triumph," Drysdale said, xir voice deeper than usual. The gender Drysdale embraced on any particular day was a crap shoot, and xir voice changed to mirror the gender xe had chosen.

"I could not agree more with their underlying proposition," Harrington said as they walked off to the sound of the applause petering out. Drysdale was unsure exactly what xir principal meant, which was not unusual. Did he agree with the idea that humanity must peter out to save the Earth, or that it should die off because it was largely composed of fools. Xe knew enough not to seek clarification.

For his part, Harrington kept to himself his uncharitable observation that the people most against human reproduction were clearly those least likely to be asked to engage in it. But he was happy to show them his solidarity, as the Anti-Natalist League punched far above its weight in terms of political power. Its members had nothing else to focus their lives on but activism, since their time was not taken up with children or love.

The two made their way outside, shadowed by a pair of hulking security officers in suits. Harrington was all for diversity in theory, but when it came to keeping his ass in one piece, he insisted on the opposite. His four security men were, in fact, men, each with military training and experience, and each carrying concealed weapons that would cause a regular comrade of the People's Republic to be locked away for the better part of the next century. He had no intention of repeating his experience in St. Louis during the Split negotiations, where he had almost been killed in the crossfire between a frighteningly aggressive red operative he knew only as "Chris" and that bastard Merrick Crane III.

They got in the rear of the black Chevrolet Suburban, indifferent to the irony of riding in a gasoline powered V8 engine. In the hierarchy of needs in the context of the climate crisis, his prerogatives were at the top. While the regular comrades must be weaned from their vehicles – he was a strong advocate of the new gas tax – those with responsibilities, like

Senator Richard Harrington, required exemptions from the general sacrifices necessary to appease Gaia. And the fact that traffic was much, much lighter since fewer could afford to drive was a fringe benefit.

"Is my dinner still on?" he asked Drysdale, relaxing in his spacious seat. Drysdale was flicking through xir iPad.

"Yes, at six. Mayor Portnoy is a vegan, both food and verbal, so you must be careful to avoid animal-related terms and analogies."

Harrington nodded without looking up as he looked through his emails. Nothing of particular interest. Just more election gossip, none of it very intriguing or even new. He prided himself on knowing everything, and strove to be the source of gossip as well as the recipient.

"There was a major gunfight in upstate New York," Drysdale said. Harrington did not react, remaining intent on his phone. Xe continued: "People's Militia against white supremacists and racists. The Militia lost."

Now Harrington looked up, smiling.

"Oh really?"

Drysdale nodded. "About a dozen dead PM. The racists scattered before reinforcements arrived. No dead, no prisoners. 'T' supporters, it appears. Obviously, the media is barred from reporting it."

"But *we* all know," Harrington said, his mood bright. "Crane's militia fails again. I expect this can't help but accelerate the takeover of the militia by the People's Security Force. Poor Merrick is losing his power base, even after sacrificing all his friends."

"These 'T' criminals are outrageous. They stopped traffic on an interstate," xe said, staring at the pictures in the report. Harrington glanced at some of the photos on xir screen and got very serious.

"Give me that," he said, taking the device out of xir surprisingly strong hands. There were several screen captures from a People's Militia Humvee's dashcam. Harrington used his fingers to enlarge one.

"What is it?" Drysdale said, staring at the blurred image of a large man in civilian clothes shooting a big handgun on the freeway.

"I've met this man before," Harrington said.

"It's blurry," Drysdale observed. "You can't make out the face."

"It's him all right," Harrington said.

"Are you sure they identify as male?"

Harrington ignored xir. "It looks like someone I met in St. Louis," he said. "And I definitely recognize the gun."

"Should we report it?"

"No," Harrington said. "No, let's keep this to ourselves." His mind was roiling with options and possibilities. Why was Chris back in the blue? What did he have to do with this 'T' person? Was Chris there to gin up a guerilla war, or something else? And how could Harrington play it to his advantage?

"There is another thing related to Merrick. I'm not sure if it's important," Drysdale said.

"Do tell."

"We monitor the JFCID, the Joint Federal Criminal Investigation Database. It's a program federal law enforcement uses."

"I know what it is."

"Well, a routine political unreliability report came in on a Harvard professor. Cis male not of color," xe said. "Dr. Kenneth Strickland."

"Another privileged academic. So?"

"Dr. Strickland is a Nobel Prize winner in mathematics and computer science. The report was by a grad student of his – his pronouns are 'he' and 'his' – and it was pretty typical. You know, racism, classism, merit privilege, denial, the usual."

"Again, so?" The PR was packed with such criminals, at least for now.

"The key word that came up was 'election.' It appears from the report that Professor Strickland was obsessed with demonstrating that the 2020 election was a fraud."

"Denying President Biden's election is a felony, but that is hardly of interest to me."

"True, the prisons are full of deniers. But two things stand out. The first is that this informer – excuse me, 'information-providing individual' – claimed that Dr. Strickland's work had gone beyond simply validating election results. The information-providing individual claimed that Dr. Strickland had created a computer program that could be used to manipulate the results of a national election."

Now Harrington was very interested.

"And the second thing?"

"After the report was posted to JFCID, the SIS requested further information on Dr. Strickland's location."

"Crane's thugs," Harrington said.

"Yes," Drysdale replied.

"Who do we have in Boston?" he asked. "I mean in the security services?"

"Obviously, we know most of the political structure, but not much of the new law enforcement leadership. The People's Security Force will not be helpful."

"That leaves the old security structure," Harrington said, pulling out his phone. "And we do know the head of the FBI."

Wayne Gruber shrugged and smiled his enigmatic smile.

"Again," Merrick Crane III asked, his anger bubbling up. "Why is he dead?"

"He was," Gruber replied, pausing for a long time before finishing his thought. "Delicate."

"He wouldn't talk and you ended up killing him?"

"When you dance with the devil, the devil picks the tune."

"It was a simple request," Crane said. "Pick him up and find out if he could really do what his student said he could do."

"Well, he did tell me that," Gruber said. "He was very definitive that he had a program that could work all sorts of magic." What Gruber chose to leave out is that after saying his program could do everything Gruber's boss would ever want it to do, Strickland had spit out the teeth that were tumbling about in his ruined mouth and told Gruber there was no way he was ever going to tell him where it was hidden. And this defiance had pushed Gruber too far. The interrogator had really thought his prisoner's cervical spine would be hardier.

"So, the ability to control the election is out there, and now we don't know where to find it."

"Everything that is, is somewhere," Gruber said, and then he stood there grinning to let the profundity roll over his boss. The tech guys had searched Strickland's Harvard office and home computers. They found bits and fragments of programs, enough to show that it had once been there, but the whole enchilada was *adios*. The informer had mentioned that Strickland was old school in that he liked physical media – "You send things over the web and the spiders catch them," he had told his acolytes. The program would be on a thumb drive. But they tossed the office and his house and no luck.

"Do you even have a clue where this somewhere is?" Merrick Crane III sputtered impatiently.

"I have clues," Gruber drawled. "Good ones."

Crane waited a moment. Nothing.

"Okay, what clues?" Crane demanded, impatiently.

Gruber grinned again. "He sent some messages over the interwebs. Our boys got a pretty good sense of things. They think he was playing footsie with the reds. And they think he's parked his disc in a safe deposit box."

"You buried the lede," Crane snapped. "He was talking to the reds?"

"Yep."

"That kind of changes the situation," Crane said. Time was even more of the essence now.

"I don't suppose he told you which bank before you killed him."

"Nope," Gruber said.

"And did your crew of geniuses figure out which bank?"

"Not yet."

"Well, you better, because there have to be a hundred banks in Boston with safe deposit boxes."

"We open 'em all up," Gruber said. It seemed like the obvious solution.

"Has it occurred to you why safe deposit boxes are still legal?" asked Crane. "Because powerful people still want them to be legal, and they will not take kindly to us exposing all their secrets. There's no way we can just open them all up to find a thumb drive, even one that would let me pick the winner of this election."

Gruber laughed a small, ugly laugh. "Yeah, them powers that be, they're a bitch."

"Search his house again," Crane said. "And his office. He has a key to the box somewhere. Find it."

Gruber winked enigmatically and walked out the door.

Paul Sorenson hung up the phone and looked over at Johnny Ross.

"We're wanted on the seventh floor," he said.

Ross's computer screen was filled with pictures of bank robbers. He had looked at hundreds of them, and he felt it pretty certain his targets were among them. Figuring out which were Leprechauns was the hard part.

"Why?" Ross asked.

"Well Johnny, the boss did not see fit to tell me."

The boss weighed in at three hundred pounds, and his pronouns were "he" and "him." Part of the "Fat is Fit" program launched within the federal bureaucracy immediately post-Split, Leonard Colby lolled in what appeared to be a comically small leather chair parked behind his desk. When Ross had gotten assigned to Boston five years before, coming from the Dallas field office, Colby had been merely chubby. The removal of all of the biased barriers to hefty civil servants had been a green light. A bag of Cornie's Corn Chips – they had been Fritos brand, but the term was racists for some reason so they changed it a few months before – lay opened on the oak desk next to a syringe and a vial of insulin.

"Sit down," Special Agent in Charge Colby said, gesturing to a pair of chairs before his desk. The effort started him sweating.

They sat.

"No suspects yet," Ross said.

"I don't care about the Diversity Bank robbery right now," Colby said. Ross raised an eyebrow.

"We have three dead, including a civilian and two PSF."

"You can chase your bank robbers again once you finish this new assignment. I got a call right from the top, so it's a no-shit, five-alarm priority. And I don't need the aggravation. I'm already swamped with the work this damn name change is going to require." The FBI would soon be renamed the PBI – the People's Bureau of Investigation. And the paperwork was going to be a nightmare.

"What's the case, boss?" asked Sorenson.

"Some dipshit professor at Harvard. The info is in that file there. He's got some sort of computer program that we want."

"Send the PSF," Ross said. "Or some newbie."

"No, Special Agent Ross, I'm sending you, because I know you won't screw it up."

Colby paused, and everyone in the room understood that he was wondering if he had gone too far. The FBI had lost over half its agents after the Split, with many of the competent ones departing for the red, leaving mostly time servers and a few good agents who just did not want to leave. The new hires for the last few years were likewise mostly shaky – the continent of origin of their great-grandparents and the manner in which they peed were prioritized over things like "competence." In fact, the

FBI (like the entire federal government) had expressly rejected the use of the false and oppressive construct of "merit" in personnel decision-making.

"It's not hard," Colby continued. "Go to Cambridge, I mean Floyd – excuse me – hook him up, and bring back his computer program."

"What program is that?" asked Ross.

"Well, the Director did not bother to tell me that, Johnny. But I assume that if the FBI shows up at his office, this Professor Strickland will have a pretty good idea why. So, ask him. But bring it back. The bigwigs want it."

"Is this political?" Ross asked. "You know I don't do political. Remember when they tried to get me on a political case before the Split?"

"Yeah, I do. You almost ended up unemployed."

"I catch crooks. I leave the politics to the hacks."

"Jeez, Johnny," Colby said, quieter. "You gotta be careful. You need to be on board with how things are. Or they'll throw you overboard."

"We got this," Sorenson said, standing. "Right, Johnny?"

Ross grunted.

What the hell was going on?

Seamus McCloskey stared into Danny Doyle's eyes, and Doyle did not flinch. That was unusual, and McCloskey immediately began to wonder which of the two types of people who were not terrified of Seamus McCloskey Danny Doyle was. Was he stupid, or was he himself extremely dangerous?

He decided that Danny Doyle was dangerous. But not so dangerous as to cause the criminal overlord of Charlestown to back down.

"The feds were here," Seamus said.

"If they had anything to go on, I'd be hooked-up and in stir," Doyle said. It never occurred to him that Seamus would have told the FBI anything but where to stuff their questions.

"You and your boys owe me money, Danny," McCloskey said. "I subsidized the score and I'm owed."

"It went south," Doyle said.

"Not my problem."

"It kind of is your problem, Seamus, since we have no money to pay you off."

"I like you, Danny, but people who talk to me like that usually end up floating face down."

"I like you too, Seamus. I always respected you, the way you keep order here and how you keep these People's Republic fake cops off everyone's back. But if you're going to make a move, make it now."

Seamus had two of his gunsels parked at a nearby table watching the proceedings, one with an MP5 and the other cradling a sawed-off 12-gauge. He could nod and this kid would be all over. The only question was whether Seamus McCloskey would be all over before his men could act.

"Danny, we need to stick together now more than ever," McCloskey said kindly, moving past the unpleasantness. "We're under siege here in the Town. The old feds, they understood the game. We do crime, they come catch us if they can. But these blues, they aren't like that. They hate us and they hate our people. We're privileged, they say. I don't know where they got that idea, but it's in their heads. They see us as throwbacks. They hate us, our faith, our family life, everything. We're stubborn, we won't play along. My point is we need to stick together. And part of that is honoring our own rules."

"I will get you the money my crew owes you," Doyle said. "You know my word is good."

"That's really all we have in the end, our word," McCloskey said. "What do you have lined up next?"

"You'll know when I show up here at the Tangier one day with a big bag of cash."

"See, that's smart," Seamus said. "Keep things close. That's how we survived the English, and then the old FBI, and how we'll survive the blues."

"In the Army, we called it OPSEC."

McCloskey smiled. "You want a shot of Jameson?" He turned to the barkeep. "Lonny, a shot of Jameson for Danny here!"

"No thanks," Danny said.

"What, too early for you?" It was 11:25 a.m.

"No, Seamus," Danny said. "I owe you enough already."

7.

At a farm outside of the town of Mineville, New York, Turnbull paid the neighbor of one of the guerillas $2,000 in U.S. cash for a battered 2011 Taurus.

"Anything for T," the man had said.

Turnbull made King put his M4 in the trunk, but King kept his Smith & Wesson SD40 pistol in his waistband. They drove back out to I-87, and a convoy of People's Militia passed by them heading into the woods.

"I hope your folks listened when you told them to scatter," Turnbull said.

"Doubt it. They're locals. They followed me because most knew me from before, when I was on the radio, and because I knew how to organize. I was T, a legend. They'll stay in the area. They can't imagine going anywhere else. Most will just hide out in the hills."

"The blues will retaliate against their families."

"Good. Then they'll find out the hard way that this is prime guerilla country. And more locals will join," said King.

"You were looking to provoke the blues," Turnbull said.

"Not this much this soon, but yeah. That's classic insurgency strategy."

"Well, you were T, after all," Turnbull said.

King scowled. "I didn't count on an informer who gave up all the fighters' names. But yeah, the I-87 op was designed to get a reaction. What I was really wanting was for them to try the gun confiscation sweeps they've done in the suburbs. That was going to piss these folks off, and then I'd have had a giant army."

"And when the blues overreacted to you, you'd get even more soldiers."

"That's how it works," King said. "Poke the tyrants, make them strike back, and pretty soon no one can just sit on the sidelines. But the blues infiltrated us too fast. I never had a chance to really build up my cadre."

"Great marketing though, T. It's very catchy."

"People need a symbol of resistance. Too bad we had a setback."

"Sorry your guerilla war fell through."

"Me too. But I'll just come back and start another, except with some help from the red this time."

"Sounds like you hate the blues almost as much as I do."

"More," King said, without emotion.

"We need to eat," King said as they entered Massachusetts. Turnbull grunted. Not long after, Turnbull and King sat at the lunch counter of a sparsely-attended diner outside Springfield. There was a chalkboard posted next to the menu listing the items that were currently not available.

"No white bread?" Turnbull mused. "How do you not have white bread?"

"Maybe it's racist," King suggested. "Everything else is."

There was a TV monitor hanging off the wall and tuned to CNN. The chyron read "EXCLUSIVE: Brian Stelter Shares His Feelings Upon Convictions of Hate Criminals." CNN's journalism license number was displayed in the lower left-hand corner of the screen.

"How are you feeling today, Brian?" Alisyn Camerota asked. They were facing each other across the anchor desk, and she took his trembling hands in hers.

"It's gratifying to see justice finally done," Stelter said. "I know I am not the only one suffering this kind of terrorism."

"Brian," the anchoress said softly. "What went through your mind when these people would tweet that you were a potato?"

Stelter swallowed. "Fear. It was actual violence, Alisyn. I felt unsafe. And it wasn't just online. One of the right-wing extremists convicted today saw me in a restaurant ordering French fries and..."

He paused, pulling himself together.

"Please, go on," urged Camerota.

"He shouted at me that I was a 'cannibal,'" Stelter said, struggling to get the words out. "They even bullied my son in college. The terrorists would call him 'Chip.'"

"You're so brave," she reassured him. He sat up tall.

"I am going to take back the word 'Tater,' Alisyn. It's *my* word, and when I own it, I strip away its power to cause harm."

"Can you turn that off?" Turnbull asked the waitress behind the counter.

She shook her head. "They check," she said.

Turnbull sighed. "Then give me a coffee and a cheeseburger, if you have meat and buns."

"We do, for now. Side?"

"An order of French-fried Brian Stelters."

"The same," King said, and the poker-faced waitress walked off. He turned to Kelly. "You think you're funny, but you don't get it. When the country split, it really split. It's different now here, and all this nonsense, this PC bullshit, it's real. You can laugh at it, but I've been here the whole time since the Split. People have to live in this world."

"They can leave," Turnbull said.

"Or fight," replied King, keeping his voice down. "But most people don't want to do either. They just want to live. And thanks to the Split, nobody gets to just live. Nobody gets left alone. Everyone has to play along, all the time, no matter what. The ones who don't get crushed."

"And the red states are going the other way, hard," Turnbull said after ensuring there were no prying ears listening in.

"Yeah, how can two totally opposite countries next to each other on the same continent get along?"

"They can't," Turnbull said, thinking back to his recent visit to the tropics. "Two big crocodiles, one small pond."

They drove in toward Boston, past more billboards demanding unity against "Racists, Wreckers and Fatphobes," among other undesirables.

"Their greatest crime is not using the Oxford comma," King observed.

"You and your fancy book learning," Turnbull said. "I don't get this whole T thing. On the radio, you kind of came off as a..."

"Wimp?" King asked.

"I was going to say something else, but yeah. Not exactly an aspiring guerilla leader."

"Hard times make hard men."

"I know you disappeared. What happened?"

"Moderately long story. The spoiler is that I'd just like to get back to my calling."

"Fighting blues?"

"That's right."

"We're going to stop here in Cambridge, pick up a passenger, and the three of us are going to have a nice drive back to the US of A. And after that, you can work out your future plans with the reds."

"The town's called 'Floyd' now, after George Floyd. His birthday's a national holiday, too. Anyway, what's at Harvard?"

"A professor, name of Strickland."

"The math guy?"

"Yeah. You know him?"

"Of him. He won a Nobel Prize in math or something. That's a real Nobel Prize, not like Obama and Ben Rhodes getting a Peace Prize, or the new Social Justice Prize."

"It was embarrassing when Biden wet himself accepting it."

"You know it's now a felony to point out Biden's dementia?" King said.

"I just assume everything here is a crime," Turnbull said.

They approached the Harvard Fauci Science Center building from the west across what had been Cambridge Common until the faculty and students successfully demanded the town be renamed for George Floyd, who had been named the "Male Birthing Person of the People's Republic" by a unanimous Congressional enactment. At the signing of the law, President Biden had referred to the PR's premier martyr as "George Foreman" and opined on his contributions to the sweet science. The ceremony was carried live on all networks, but this tangent drew no comment by the anchors. In all, since the Split, no fewer than sixty-seven public schools had been named for him across the new country.

The route Turnbull selected turned out to be a mistake, since the area was packed with tents, shanties, and lean-tos. A large sign announced, "HARVARD IS DECOLONIALIZING ITS HIXTORY OF OPPRESSIONING," and the students – who rarely went to classes – had invited "the community" into the campus to live. This meant the school was swamped with a tsunami of hobos, bums, and drug-addled derelicts, all of whom showed up at the various campus dining facilities and demanded free food. These meals were paid for by the university's rapidly declining endowment.

Students were scarce, partly because it was summer and partly because there was no real need to attend classes. It was illegal for a college to fail a student, as the enforcement of standards was a form of oppression. An "A" was the default grade, though it sort of had been for a couple decades.

Regardless, the young students admitted to the People's Republic's most prestigious academy were effectively graduates and credential-holders upon receipt of their acceptance emails. Many spent the next four years going through the motions of "distance learning," which was okay with the university. It had found during the COVID-19 panic that it could pretend to teach and the students would pretend to be taught. And now that charging tuition was illegal, it could simply not teach at all and still be subsidized by the government.

The transient colony generally ignored the two relatively normal men walking through the chaos. There were a few shouted offers of drugs or unsavory love to the passing pair, which Turnbull and King ignored. The advantage of crossing through the encampment, which reminded Turnbull of San Francisco, was that it avoided any kind of security checks. There was no wall between the campus and the teeming abscess to its west, walls being bad in this and most other cases, though not in the case of surrounding government buildings.

The Fauci Science Building had a new statue of its namesake out front, the elfin epidemiologist pointing to the cloudy sky and wearing a surgical mask. The plaque read, "YOU MUST COVER YOUR FACE." A bum was urinating on the base, and it was apparently not a new idea. The surrounding pavement was an open sewer, which was probably why this was the only statue on campus that had not yet been torn down.

The Science Building itself was an angular, modernist construction of nine stories. The exterior of the lower two floors was all covered by plywood, which was itself painted over with graffiti and sprayed with other even less appealing markings. There was a banner hanging above announcing the school's "Celebration of Independence from Racist Oppression Day" festivities set for July 4th.

A group of students in black tights with covered faces was performing an interpretive dance out front to an atonal soundtrack coming from speakers hooked up to an iPad. The dozen or so students danced a jerky, uncoordinated routine under the guidance of a professor. A sign propped up next to them read, "Respect this space and validate our expression. Advanced Trigonometry 201."

As Turnbull and King passed by the gawking hobos, they overheard two people, probably faculty members, discussing the performance and praising "how Dr. Zaremba refuses to accept the male idea of mathematics as involving only numbers and not bodily movement." At that moment, the math class began a series of poorly synchronized pelvic thrusts followed by a collective twerk.

Turnbull was first through the door and inside the Center. King followed – like Turnbull, he carried only his handgun, and it was under his jacket. Inside the lobby was a collection of apparent students and faculty, along with apparent homeless catching some z's on the floor. A banner across the wall read, "DEPALLOR SCIENCE" and another read, "SCIENCE THAT DOES NOT SUPPORT SOCIAL JUSTICE IS NOT TRUE SCIENCE – Dr. Julius Freen (Xe/Xir)."

There were several dozen pictures framed on the wall under letters reading "GREAT SCIENTISTS," none of whom Turnbull or King recognized. Most seemed to have been taken during the 2020 or later riots. None of the subjects were doing science things, unless tossing a Molotov cocktail counted as a chemistry experiment.

Another sign warned, "WARNING: ON JULY 4 FIREWORKS ARE ILLEGAL AND RACIST BECAUSE THEY TRIGGER OPPRESSED PEOPLES."

Turnbull found a directory on the wall, but all the names were scratched out. He turned and looked around for someone in authority. A derelict in a tutu began to scream, and no one noticed.

There was a woman with red hair who was trying to talk a homeless man out of taking a dump in the corner. He was calling her a racist, but she was very polite and he pulled up his pants and went outside. Turnbull approached.

"Excuse me," he said. "I'm looking for Professor Strickland."

"You're late," she said. "Frankly, it was about time."

"I don't understand."

"Your comrades were here before and they took him. About time. He was clearly a racist."

"Yes, we're very much against his racism," Turnbull said.

"They searched his office for a long time. Are you going to keep searching? They didn't seem to find what they wanted."

"How do you know?"

"Because they said so. And their gaze made some of the students unsafe. Do you all have to be so cis to enforce the law?"

"Oh," King interjected. "This one's pronouns are definitely not 'he' and 'him.'"

"What are they?" asked the woman.

"Uh," Turnbull growled. "'Zip' and 'zap.'"

"Oh," the woman replied. "I admire your courage. Even with the red scum being expelled, this society is still built on the hatred of those with alternative sexual identities."

"It's been a struggle," Turnbull said. "Where is Dr. Strickland's office?"

"Seventh floor, number 720. The power is on today so the elevators work." She hit the call button.

"Thank you," Turnbull mumbled. The elevator doors opened and he stepped inside.

"No," she said. "Thank you for protecting us from these hate criminals. And for your example as a sexual minority thriving in the hostile environment of law enforcement."

"Zip inspires me every single day," King said, stepping into the car.

The doors shut behind them.

"You do that again," Turnbull hissed. "And I'll beat your brains out."

"Hey, I won us an ally. When in Rome, do as the Romans do."

"What, vomit, have orgies, and stage gladiator fights?"

"Sounds like college back in the good old days."

A bell dinged.

"Our floor."

The doors opened. The hallway was dirty, but at least it was not soaked in urine. There was some graffiti and a great number of handwritten posters decrying this -ism or that -phobia. The doors of the professors' offices each had a whiteboard and each of them seemed to be attempting to outdo each other in the hysterical political correctness of what they wrote on them. All except the one outside Room 702, which said only "MATH IS MATH." There were plenty of responses about how that was offensive, oppressive, and literally violent.

The door was ajar.

Using his left hand – his right was under his jacket wrapped around his .45 – Turnbull pushed open the portal. The room had been tossed, and hard. The bookshelves screwed into the wall were empty, the books scattered across the floor. The desk drawers hung open, and lengths of black wires hung where the computer had been before it was confiscated.

The pair went inside and shut the door behind them.

"They went through it pretty freaking thoroughly," King said. "What were they looking for?"

"A safe deposit box key," Turnbull replied.

"My guess is they beat the location out of our professor. Maybe we need to call this off and get driving south."

"Where would you be if you were a safe deposit box key?" Turnbull asked, looking around the office.

"Key ring, desk drawer," King said. "But they hit all the obvious places."

"And if you were owned by an OCD nut?"

"So, Strickland's Rain Man?"

"Not quite, just a weirdo. But he does love him some eighties rock."

"I was born in 1996, so…"

"You ever heard a Georgia Satellites song?"

"I could call my dad if you want. Except he's dead. Why are we talking about some old band for fossils?"

"Because Strickland left a clue. He told us 'The key to the puzzle is my loving defiance of the Georgia Satellites.'"

"I'm baffled," King admitted.

"Me too. But it's supposed to be a clue. He wanted us to find it."

"Maybe you should start with their lyrics."

Turnbull grunted and pulled out his cell phone. He used his spoofer app to sign into the Harvard student Wi-Fi system. Then he brought up Google and typed in a search.

"Sheesh," he said.

"What?" asked King.

Turnbull showed him the screen. "HARVARD ACADEMIC FREEDOM CONTROL COMMITTEE WARNING: THESE SONG LYRICS IMPOSE A CIS-BASED SEXUALITY THAT DENIES THE EXISTENCE OF NON-TRADITIONAL IDENTITIES AND LOVES. ONLY ADULTS USING THIS FOR SCIENTIFIC OR HISTORICAL PURPOSES AND WHO ARE CAPABLE OF IDENTIFYING HATE THOUGHT ARE AUTHORIZED TO PROCEED."

"You need to check that box to confirm you are sufficiently woke," King observed, pointing.

"It's probably going to draw a herd of campus cops," Turnbull said. He checked the box and hit the "PROCEED" button.

The lyrics to the song came up. They both read.

"So basically, the singer's got to marry her before she puts out," King said. "I'm not sure how this relates to our current dilemma."

"Well, it does, somehow."

"How?"

"I don't know. I'm usually good at hiding things, but unlike Professor Strickland, I'm not crazy."

King leaned back in. "What's this about not putting his love on a shelf? What's that even mean?"

"Like, Miss Virgin is keeping him in limbo or something."

"It's lazy writing. I mean, he clearly just needed something to rhyme with 'yourself.' He's no Andrew Lloyd Webber."

KURT SCHLICHTER | 107

"Who?"

"Not a big show tunes guy, huh, Chris?"

"Don't put his love on a shelf, so defying it would mean...," Turnbull began. Then he went over to the shelves on the wall.

The shelves were wooden planks resting on brass fixtures screwed into the wall – Harvard might have been five hundred years old, but it shopped at Ikea before the People's Republic's branch of the chain voluntarily dissolved itself in recognition of its "legacy of exclusion of the contributions of peoples of color and non-cis gender identities in its presentations of Scandinavian culture." This university, however, had not taken the step that other schools took and inventoried its shelves, tables, and bookcases to find and dispose of racism-tainted assemble-it-yourself products.

"Nothing," King said, standing on a chair to look at the empty shelves from above. There was an outline of dust where the book spines had lined up before the tomes were unceremoniously tossed to the floor by whoever got there first. "Nice try."

"Take it off," Turnbull said.

"What?"

"Take the shelf off the metal things attached to the wall."

"The brackets?"

"I don't know what they're called. Take the wood board thing off it."

King lifted the shelf off of the supports. It was lighter than it looked, probably some cheap fiberboard, in keeping with the Ikea oeuvre. He put it under his arm and prepared to step down.

There was a metallic ping on the floor and something bounced around before settling at Turnbull's feet. He reached down.

"Bingo," he said, holding up the key.

"The professor cut a slot in the back of the shelf where it went against the wall," King said, examining the unpainted fiberboard of the back edge of the shelf.

"It says Boston Commercial Bank, number 533."

King put the shelf back where it had been and stepped off the chair as Turnbull continued to examine the key.

"So, now we go to the bank. Except you aren't Professor Strickland. They'll want ID."

"I have a Massachusetts driver's license for John Strickland with my picture."

"You guys thought ahead."

"I knew it would turn out complicated," Turnbull said. "It always turns out complicated."

"Well, let's go to the bank. The sooner we finish here, the sooner we get to the red and the sooner I get back here and back to work."

Turnbull did not respond. He stepped to the door and opened it.

Ross and Sorenson entered the Fauci Building lobby and the woman in red hair walked straight up to them.

"Your friends are all upstairs," she said.

"Friends?" Sorenson asked.

"Yes, you're obviously all cops."

"How many friends?"

"Well, the first two that I talked to," she said. "And then the second pair that I just saw go up a minute ago."

Ross and Sorenson looked at each other.

"I'll go see what's up," Sorenson said. Ross nodded. It was understood that he'd stake out the lobby in case Dr. Strickland was trying to flee whoever the two pairs that went upstairs – or to see what was up if they brought him down in custody.

Sorenson hit the call button, stepped into the car, and the doors closed. Ross moved across from, and offset to, the bank of three elevators and waited.

Two men in cheap suits were coming down the hall. Rough guys, out of place on this chestless campus.

"Hey!" one shouted as their eyes met, his hand going to his waist.

Turnbull drew as he leapt across the hall, but the man got his weapon out first and sent a round down the middle of the corridor from a Smith & Wesson M&P Shield M2.0 pistol.

Turnbull's Wilson was up, and he fired twice, hitting the second man in the upper shoulder. The wounded man spun, taking his partner off his game as he fell.

King pivoted out the doorway, opening up with his Smith & Wesson SD40 pistol. Turnbull kept firing. The wounded man staggered under the hail of gunfire, his suit a Jackson Pollock work in red.

At the far end of the hall, the doors of an elevator opened. Paul Sorenson was there, Glock 17 in hand, having heard the shooting. The uninjured intruder, surprised, shifted and shot him twice, once in the chest, once in the face. Sorenson went down.

Turnbull took aim and put a round through the temple of the man who was uninjured – at least until that moment. King put two more superfluous 9mm rounds into him as he fell.

The smoky hallway was silent, with only the ringing in their ears. Turnbull and King both reloaded.

As his magazine seated, Turnbull said, "Let's go!"

They tore off down the hallway in the opposite direction from the elevators, toward a sign that read "STAIRS."

Ross heard the shots even seven floors down, and his SIG P226 was in his hand, aimed at the elevator, even as he shouted to the red-haired administrator.

"Call for help now!"

The people in the lobby were vaguely curious about what was happening as the administrator got on a phone that sat on the desk.

He punched a call button and waited, taking deep breaths. The shooting upstairs intensified, then ceased.

"Come on," he whispered.

The light above the elevator went green and there was a ding. The door opened.

Over the gun sights, Johnny Ross saw Paul Sorenson lying on the floor of the car against the rear with a red splotch on his chest and much of his right cheek gone.

"Two down upstairs, Johnny. They shot me," he gasped, his words slurred. "Two more coming down." Sorenson spit out a wad of blood.

Ross turned back to the lobby, and across it, a door to the stairwell, opened.

A big guy and a little guy, with weapons – an M1911 and a Smith & Wesson automatic he noted. Neither looked like Strickland's photo.

Their eyes met.

Ross raised his pistol.

Turnbull saw the armed man at the elevator across the room and recognized his weapon as a SIG. The man looked different than the two coming down the hall – he was not a thug.

But he was going to try to kill Turnbull, and that was a no-go.

Someone screamed in the lobby, maybe seeing the armed men, maybe seeing Sorenson. But the high-pitched scream – it could have easily come from a male student – caused pandemonium. People began to run to and fro.

Ross clamped his free hand around his weapon as Turnbull and King raised theirs, but held fire. Too many civilians.

Turnbull drew a bead and instantly a pair of students flagged themselves running across his lane. He lifted the weapon and put three rounds into the drop-ceiling. The noise supercharged the chaos.

Ross could not get a shot, not without likely capping some civilian. The two men held their fire too – that struck Ross as odd – and they bolted for the front door.

Ross followed, pushing and shoving howling civilians out of his path.

"What the hell?" shouted King, panting as he followed.

"Run!" shouted Turnbull. In fact, he had no idea exactly what the hell was going on but apparently everyone was very interested in Strickland's MacGuffin.

They hauled ass across the courtyard and into the hobo encampment, disappearing inside the chaos.

When Ross finally came out the door, his SIG in the lead, they were gone. He holstered the weapon and walked back inside as the interpretive dancers/mathematicians stared at him.

8.

It was late, so Turnbull and King drove into Boston and took a hotel room at the Bel-Air, a mid-priced lodge in gentle decline with a breathtaking view of I-90. Like much of the city, the hotel lobby was decorated for the "Celebration of Independence from Racist Oppression Day" festivities set for July 4th, the coming Tuesday. Streamers of red, white, and blue, and orange, yellow, brown, magenta, taupe and several more hung in the lobby.

"A New Beginning That Decolonializes So-Called 'Independence'" read one banner. It occurred to Turnbull that decolonialization was the point of the old Independence Day.

There was plenty about the presidential election that was coming in six weeks too, on the road and in the city. The PR's election law decreed an eight-week campaign, the only reform enacted by the new country that Turnbull might consider getting behind.

The clerk had given them a single king bed and thanked them for their courage in rejecting the homophobia that apparently permeated the PR even though it was illegal. This arrangement was fine with Turnbull. King could sleep on the sofa. Or the floor. Or wherever. Just not the bed.

"What the hell was that back at Harvard? How did we go from giving a guy a ride to a campus firefight?" asked King once they were in their room and Turnbull had swept it for bugs. Outside the window, the traffic on the freeway was very light, a function of the carbon tax, and the reparations tax, on each gallon of gas.

KURT SCHLICHTER | 113

"They were looking for the key, too," Turnbull said. "And now they probably figure we have it."

"Great," King said. "I was better off in the Adirondacks."

"I didn't expect a shootout."

"You sure didn't hesitate to start it."

"I hesitated once," Turnbull said. "Never again."

"Yeah, well this Split has changed everything. Before this I could barely do a dozen push-ups and I'd never shot a gun. I had to learn a lot. Luckily, I had some good teachers."

"You did okay back on campus," Turnbull said. "You can shoot, which is handy. You're not much of a guerilla leader though."

"Well, the US of A thinks I am or else they wouldn't want me back."

"I long ago stopped trying to figure out why echelons above me do anything," Turnbull said.

"So, what do we do now?"

"We clean our weapons, one at a time with the other on security. And then tomorrow, bright and early, we go find the Boston Commercial Bank and then Professor Strickland opens his box and we get out of here."

"Where is it?"

Turnbull got on his iPhone and surfed for a moment.

"It isn't," he said. "At least not under that name. It's now the People's Collective Financial Institution."

"Catchy. That name will really lend itself to a jingle."

"It's downtown, on Franklin. Busy area, looks like. We'll be there at nine. Let's get cleaning, get some room service, and crash."

"I'm still unclear on that chop-socky at Harvard," King said.

Turnbull grunted. It was pretty obvious the four men they encountered were some sort of security service types, but why had one shot another one? Different agencies? The two in the hall looked like they could have been collecting for a loan shark. The other two were looked old school, detectives or even FBI.

Turnbull turned on the TV and ran through the channels until he found some news. Nothing about the shootout at Harvard.

Instead, after covering a demonstration by militant diabetics against "insulin privilege," they were reporting on how the poultry industry was racist for some reason.

"The chicken cartels erase the experience of Latinx and Blackx people," an overwrought man dressed in a skirt told the nodding reporter, who was also a man in a dress.

Turnbull clicked it off.

"What is it with these people adding 'x' to everything," he growled.

"Blackx is a thing, I think," King said. "It's new but catching on. There's this never-ending series of new terms they insist everyone use and new phobias and -isms they insist everyone fight. It's exhausting."

"You would think after getting rid of us racists in the red states it would be paradise here," Turnbull said.

"Oh no," King replied earnestly. "No, you don't get it, the genius of it. The struggle is the point. If the whole society is wrapped up in hunts for oppressive boogeymen and worrying about using the right words and avoiding the ever-increasing number of wrong ones, then people aren't worried about how they can't afford to drive anymore or how the grocery stores keep getting emptier. Plus, if you can't achieve something through actual performance, you can still get yourself some power by taking down others. And if the rules are uncertain and ever-changing, well, then it's a lot simpler to do."

"It's ridiculous," Turnbull said. "It's a joke."

"It's funny to you because you get to go home. To you it's a freak show, but to the people here, it's real. These people have to live with it. It's everywhere, and nonstop. It never ends. And when you have to live under it it's a lot less amusing."

Turnbull did not reply. He was looking out his window down at the freeway, and beyond to the huge tent city beneath one of the overpasses. A little farther away, a group of people marched down the street, blocking traffic, protesting something. It was unclear what.

"In under 48 hours, we'll be out of here," Turnbull said. "And that's nowhere near soon enough for me."

Ross knelt down by Sorenson's body. His partner had passed away while Ross was pursuing Turnbull and King out into the courtyard. There were dozens of FBI agents present now, documenting the scene, but no media – the media had been given a "no cover" order. And the media always obeyed.

"We're taking him now," said one of the coroner's staff. The stretcher was outside the elevator car and a black bag was unzipped on top. Ross wordlessly stood and walked out.

Colby was there. He held up his hands.

"I didn't know," he said.

"We walked into a trap!" Ross shouted. People paused and looked.

"Look, the job came down from the top. The very top. No one said it was dangerous. No one expected a threat."

"Paul's dead," Ross shouted. People paused and looked at them. Colby took him aside, the effort generating beads of sweat across his puffy forehead.

"Johnny, there's more information."

"Yeah?"

"The two stiffs upstairs we thought Paul got? Turns out he didn't. He never got off a shot."

"Paul told me the dead guys shot him," Ross said. "I don't understand this."

"The guys you saw leaving shot it out with the two dead guys and killed them. And there's more."

"Yeah?"

"They were Special Investigations Section of the Department of People's Justice."

"Who the hell is that?"

"Political. Very black," Colby said, pausing, trying to avoid a potentially criminal statement. "Dark. I mean, deep. Just, you know, bad news."

"So, who were the guys I chased who smoked the SIS agents?"

"No idea, but from the shell casings, one had a .45 and the other had a 9mm."

"The big one had a high-end 1911. I saw that from here," Ross said. "But why a shootout? And why would the SIS kill Paul?"

"Maybe he just walked into it," suggested Colby. "From what I hear, the SIS are not exactly ask questions first kind of guys."

Ross did not answer. His eyes were on a half-dozen men in awkward suits coming in the front door, rough-looking guys who did not look like suit aficionados. The senior one had wild eyes and a manbun, and it was clear to Ross the man had spent time in stir. Someone had cleaned them up and sent them here.

The leader walked over to them and stood there longer than one would expect without speaking.

"Yeah?" Ross finally asked.

"Well," Wayne Gruber said, inhaling air through his yellowed teeth. "You must be Special Agent Ross and Special Agent-in-Charge Colby, the head honcho. The big cheese. It seems we got ourselves a little problem here."

"This is a crime scene," Ross said. "Police only. Step back."

"Well," Gruber said, again drawing it out. "Turns out I am the po-lice." He exaggerated the "po" syllable. Gruber's hand went to his jacket and Ross's to his SIG. Gruber paused, smiled like an alligator, then slowly drew out and displayed his credentials.

After a moment, he put the ID away and Ross's hand relaxed.

"What was the SIS doing here?" Ross asked.

"Well," Gruber began. "That's what we call 'confidential.' Let's just say our comrades upstairs came here to do a little search and looks like someone started a to-do."

"Looks like your boys came out with the short end of the stick."

"Well," Gruber said. "Looks like one of yours got put down too."

"Yeah, and before he died, he said your shitheads did it."

Gruber was silent for a moment, grinning. And then there was a ruckus to the right. It was the red-haired woman.

"You all need to leave," she shrieked. "I am not answering any more questions. The unhoused persons who use this lobby have been disrupted enough!"

Gruber glanced at one of his men, who stepped forward and pushed the woman back hard.

"Sit your ass down, bitch!" he snarled.

"You can't..." she began. The man made a fist, and she realized this was something entirely new. This person was not playing by Harvard rules. She stepped back and sat down behind the desk.

Gruber turned back from the confrontation and addressed Ross.

"We have a mission. A mandate, if you will. And we aren't fitting to tolerate any interference."

"You saying my partner interfered and that's why your pals shot him?"

"Well," Gruber said. "I'm saying that bad things happen to people who get in our way."

"Am I in your way?"

"Well," Gruber said. "Not yet."

"So, what was so important that my partner and your two pals are dead?"

"Well," said Gruber. "Like I said, that's confidential."

"Well," said Ross, dragging it out. "Your boys were looking for something. The whole office was tossed. Maybe if you tell me what it is, we can cooperate."

Gruber pondered it for a long time, perhaps 45 seconds, though Ross never broke his lock on the SIS leader's dead eyes.

"Before Professor Strickland's unfortunate passing in custody," Gruber said. "We figured out that he might have a safe deposit box and a key. That key is crucial to national security. You would not have happened to find a key, would you?"

Ross considered. The redhead had said the two guys who escaped had been upstairs only a few minutes. The shootout was in the hall, so it was possible they were leaving when it started. And if they were leaving that soon after going up, maybe it meant that they had found what they were looking for. But there was another question gnawing at Ross.

"What's in the box?" Ross asked.

"A head," Gruber said. Ross did not react and continued staring. Gruber roared in laughter, too loudly, drawing looks from the others in the lobby.

"Like in that movie with that Brad Pitt guy and the black fellow? Ah, it's a good one."

"What's in the box, Gruber?"

"Something important. I take it you don't have the key."

"No."

"But maybe the pair that took out our guys does. And they'll be headed to a bank to use it."

"The banks are closing soon, so most likely they'll try tomorrow. And they'll need Strickland's ID."

"*If* it's under his name," Gruber said. "After chatting with the professor, he seemed to think of everything, you know?"

"I trust the SIS will keep the Bureau informed should it uncover anything, Agent Gruber. After all, this is an FBI investigation now."

"Well," Gruber said. "We kind of operate outside of channels."

"If you operate in my way, you will go down," Ross said. Beside him, Colby was visibly nervous.

"Well, there's a yin to that yang, Special Agent Ross. If you get in my way…"

Ross stepped closer. "What?" Colby put his hand on Ross's arm. Gruber grinned.

"You want to party with us, you better be prepared to pay the cover charge."

"I don't know if that bullshit is supposed to be a threat, but if it is, why wait, Gruber? I'm right here, right now."

"Come on, Johnny," Colby said, pulling Ross off. "This piece of shit's not worth it."

"Bye bye, F-B-I," Gruber said, still grinning, as Ross and Colby left them.

"What the hell are those psychos doing involved in this?" Ross asked.

"It's political," Colby said. "I told you, it came from DC, or whatever they're calling Washington now. Someone's pulling our strings, and someone else is pulling theirs."

"Who the hell is our Geppetto, chief?"

"I can't say," Colby replied tiredly. "But he's big."

"I need to meet him."

"I'll see, Johnny."

"And who is their puppet master?"

"That I don't know."

"If they have the key, the pair who walked out of here today is going to be at a bank at nine a.m. sharp tomorrow trying to get in. I want a bulletin out to every single bank in the Boston metro region to BOLO someone trying to say he's Strickland. You know, Gruber and his apes freaking killed him, right?"

"I know," Colby said. "And we'll tell the banks to be on the lookout for someone trying to pass as Strickland."

"I need a tac team on stand-by in case we get a call."

"You got it," Colby said.

"Now the next question is who the hell those two shooters were," said Ross. "They didn't hesitate to drop those SIS guys, so I guess we can't paint them all black. But are they on the job? Are they crooks?"

"I'll give you everything we find, Johnny."

"Shit," Ross said. "What the hell did we get dragged into?"

A dozen nude middle-aged women sat in the middle of Chauncey Street shrieking. It was not coordinated shrieking;

instead, each one was shrieking in her own way. And it was unclear why. They were just doing it, in the middle of rush hour. Cars were backed up in each direction, and a couple of bored People's Security Force officers ensured people stood back.

"I wonder what they're protesting?" King asked as he walked past them on the sidewalk.

"Conventional standards of beauty, probably," Turnbull speculated. "Why is it never the hot ones?"

"Stop eye-raping us!" one ancient, unclad crone shouted at a befuddled young man in a deliveryman's uniform who had glanced in their direction. The PSF officers converged on him.

Turnbull and King continued on toward downtown, glad they had left the car in the hotel garage and walked. Bike lanes, protestors, and random blockages that appeared to exist for no other reason than to make driving downtown even more agonizing than it already was, gridlocked the city's streets. And this was in addition to the fact that Boston was the home to North America's worst drivers.

Most people were masked; King and Turnbull were too, though not for fear of whatever the latest flu was. Cameras were mounted on poles along the streets, and in the event someone in the security services was actually monitoring things, face diapers would make it harder to ID them.

The bank itself was on Franklin, a street lined with high rises. The facade of the People's Collective Financial Institution – the word "bank" was being memory holed – was an elaborate silver and gold metal work. The windows were decorated with signage hailing the approaching holiday and advertising the institution's services.

"High Interest Rates Are Racist," one sign read.

The sidewalks had a few people on it, but it was not crowded. It was quiet, except for the howling nudists in the distance, and the pedestrians walked along as if in a funk.

"No one lurking out front," King observed. Turnbull was scanning the windows in the upper floors and rooflines on both sides of the road for observation posts.

"You stay out here and keep watch. Don't shoot anyone."

"I don't know why you're messing with me," King retorted. "You've been here like two days and killed like a half-dozen people."

"It's been slow," Turnbull conceded.

He stepped away, ignoring the many multi-colored People's Republic flags hanging from lampposts. Posters announced the big Celebration of Independence from Racist Oppression Day parade. The posters also noted that it was not actually a day off, in order to prevent "racists, wreckers, and traitors" from celebrating the Fourth of July.

Turnbull walked down the street, not making eye contact, but keeping situational awareness. There were bums every few yards, but they looked like real bums, not security forces in disguise. If they were, the one choking a grumpy outside the Starbucks was truly committed to his undercover gig.

Turnbull reached the door and pulled it open. The lobby was much bigger than it seemed from outside, and elaborately decorated. Sadly, the usual banners attesting to the bank's shame over its legacy of racism, sexism, fatphobia, and multitude of other sins took away from the impact, but in its day the place had been impressive.

The teller counters were old school and made of dark wood, but there were no cages or plexiglass shields – those had been taken out as "unwelcoming" and, of course, racist, and that consideration outweighed any pretense of viral paranoia. There were two security guards, both particularly unimpressive looking and both packing worn Beretta 92Fs. A dozen or so citizens lined up in the lobby; the shortest line was the one reserved for "Oppressed Peoples." The teller was heatedly arguing with a customer who, because he was Cuban, was "not legitimately Latinx enough to be considered 'oppressed.'"

Beyond them, in the rear, were a pair of passageways back into the recesses of the building. The vault would be back there, somewhere, as well as the safe deposit boxes. From the ceiling of each passage hung a chrome portcullis, a set of bars that could be dropped to keep robbers out or trap them inside.

There was a manager at a desk to the side, and Turnbull walked over. The manager looked up and Turnbull spoke.

"I need to access my safe deposit box," Turnbull said from behind the mask. The manager, bored, stood.

An older woman, a customer, stepped up and said, "Excuse me, I need to get into my safe deposit box."

"Follow me," the manager said and led them to a paneled cubicle with a computer and a monitor on a desk. From there, he could see past the side door that led behind the tellers' counter and back to a room lined with what had to be the bank's safe deposit boxes.

"Go ahead," Turnbull said to the woman when the manager turned to him. She was aghast.

"What, because I'm a woman?" she snapped.

"I'm a woman, too," Turnbull said, offended.

The woman blinked and turned to the manager and gave her name. The manager typed it into the computer as Turnbull peered over his shoulder.

A red banner read, "ALERT: REPORT ATTEMPTED ACCESS BY JOHN STRICKLAND TO FBI" and gave a phone number.

"You know," Turnbull said, turning to the woman. "Your hate crime has me literally shaking."

The manager turned back, concerned. The woman was mortified.

"Should I call the authorities?" the manager asked sternly.

"No, I'm just going to leave." Turnbull did an about face and walked out of the bank.

"Well?" King said when Turnbull joined him on the sidewalk.

"Keep walking," said Turnbull. They walked in silence for several blocks, using a different route that did not take them back past the nude protestors but did take them past a bunch of college students in Boston Common demanding that Biden invade Israel. Apparently, cutting off all of the Jewish state's access to weapons and intelligence was not enough.

When they were well away from the bank, they stopped by the new statue of Oprah Winfrey that had replaced the Robert Gould Shaw memorial – the colonel leading black union troops in the Civil War had been compared, unfavorably, to Hitler before the mayor presided over the prying of his bronze plaque off the stone monument. There, under Oprah's beatific face – she was now the honorary "Secretary of Caring" for the People's Republic – they paused.

"There's a 'be on the lookout' alert for Strickland," Turnbull said.

"Did they call the PSF?"

"No, not on me. But there was some obnoxious hag who might be getting jammed up for transphobia."

"So, they don't know you were making the attempt?"

"Nope. But one thing is clear. I'm not just walking in there to get into that box."

"Well, I guess that's just how it goes," King said. "So, we're off to Texas?"

"Oh, no," Turnbull said. "No, we need to look at Plan B."

"Do I want to even ask what Plan B is?"

"Probably not."

King sighed. "Okay, what's Plan B?"

"We're robbing that bank."

"I appreciate your partner's sacrifice," Senator Harrington said from where he stood near the window across the conference table. "I really do."

Johnny Ross looked back at the politician. They were alone in the law firm offices the senator had borrowed, except for Mx. Drysdale, who sat at the far end of the conference table waiting for xir boss to ask for something. The four security men were outside, and so was Special Agent-in-Charge Colby, who had gotten the summons and brought Ross along to the meeting.

"Why was he sacrificed?" Ross asked. Harrington arched his brow and Drysdale perked up, concerned – it had been a while since anyone had talked to the senator in any tone other than one of total deference. The last time had been in a hotel room in St. Louis in an encounter that had left someone dead.

"This has national security implications," Harrington said.

"What am I looking for? What's in this disc? Whatever it is is worth killing to get a hold of."

"That's true," Harrington said. "The others looking for it, the SIS men and women..."

"Just men," Ross said. Harrington did not bite and continued.

"The others from the SIS, you are sure they did not find what they are looking for?"

"I'm almost positive the two suspects that I saw leaving, who killed the SIS men, have whatever it is."

"You got a good look at them?"

"Good enough to recognize them if we cross paths again."

"Your report described one as big and one as small."

"That's right."

Harrington nodded to Mx. Drysdale, who was in gender fluid mode. Xe flipped through a folder and pulled out a photo, then slid it to Ross.

"Look familiar?" asked Harrington.

Ross examined the photo for a moment, but he knew instantly.

"The face is blurry, but that could be him. I do recognize the gun. A tricked out 1911." He dropped the photo back to the tabletop. "Where did you get it? And who is he?"

"That was taken at the scene of a firefight in upstate New York. That man – we believe he identifies as male – is a red operative. I've met him before. He used the name 'Chris.'"

Next, Mx. Drysdale produced a photo that was much clearer.

"This was taken at passport control in Montreal," xe said. "The individual entered Canada under the name 'Cristobal Ruben Sanchez,' a valued immigrant allegedly from New York. That's a false identity. His registered pronouns are he/his. He flew in from Dallas. We assume he entered the People's Republic via New York."

"That's our guy," Ross said. "A red operative."

"Precisely," Harrington said. "It seems everyone is taking an interest in the good doctor's project."

Mx. Drysdale slid a third photo to Ross, a publicity photo taken from the internet. "We think the smaller person, who also identifies as male, is this man."

"Don't know him," Ross said.

"Teddy King, a racist radio demagogue from before the Split," Harrington said. "He vanished during the Crisis after a warrant was issued for his arrest, evaded capture, and reappeared as the head of the guerilla band in the Adirondacks. He has a bit of a history, which is in his file. His bandit gang was mopped up or dispersed, and interrogations report that King and this Chris person departed together."

"Why are a red operative and talk show loudmouth after this item?" Ross asked. "I know it's in a safe deposit box somewhere in town. What is it?"

"National security." Harrington said, as if that answer should be sufficient.

"I expect I'm here because you want me to catch them," Ross replied. "I need to know what I am looking for."

Harrington considered. "It's a thumb drive. That's all you need to know."

"You know the SIS is looking for it too."

"They cannot find it first."

"I thought we were all on one team, everybody all in on blue."

"Don't pretend to be naïve, Special Agent Ross. It doesn't suit you. There is someone behind the SIS, controlling it and other levers of power. His name is Merrick Crane III. Do you know him?"

"I know he was listed as a terrorist for a while and then he was kind of – what's the word? – rehabilitated. I didn't do political cases, just regular crooks."

"That's actually what makes you useful. I think this will take real detective work."

"As for Crane, I don't know where he is now, or whose team he's playing for."

"His own, always. Crane is a very dangerous man. And if he gets that disc, he'll become very, very dangerous."

"But if you get it, whatever it is will be used for the common good?"

"Of course. It's all about the common good."

Ross eyed the senator. "I just want to know if I am working for the People's Republic of North America, or for Senator Harrington."

"Know that I am a powerful ally," Harrington said.

"And I assume the next thing you tell me is how bad of an enemy."

"Oh, I don't have to say it. You know. You're sharp. I've reviewed your record. Marines. The FBI with a stellar record of closing cases and a total refusal to be promoted into management. Wife dead of cancer. Not even a cat back at your apartment, just the job."

"You writing my biography?"

"I could write your ticket if you perform. Whatever you want."

"No offense, Senator. Okay, maybe some – you can't buy me."

"But I can have you pulled off the case. Your partner got killed. You have a score to settle. And you can settle it however you want, if you just get me that disc along the way."

"So, your threat is to pull me off the case you want me on if I won't play ball?"

"No, my threat is to have you fired from the FBI. Like you said, I can't buy you. But if I can't give you something, I can threaten to take away all you have left. You'll be out of the Bureau in 24 hours if you cross me."

Ross considered.

"These are criminals, Special Agent Ross," Harrington continued. "They led to your partner being murdered. I'm giving you carte blanche to find the people involved. And to do what you wish with them when you find them. I just want one little thing out of it."

"It's an offer I can't refuse."

"No, you really can't," Harrington replied. "Your superior will ensure that you have everything you need, including more personnel if you want them."

"I'll work alone," Ross said.

"Fine," Harrington said. "Where will you start?"

"We could tag this Chris trying to get access to the safety deposit box, but that's out of my hands. We have a warning out. We either catch him or not. But if he thinks he might get caught walking in peacefully, he might just decide to go the full Willy Sutton."

"One robs banks because that's where the disc is," said Harrington.

"I'll try to see if someone is setting up a score. Probably won't pan out, unless it does."

"You are the detective," Harrington said. "Go forth and detect."

"What about the SIS?" asked Ross.

"They and their patron are my problem."

"What if they get in my way?"

"I am distinctly unconcerned about them," Harrington said. "Do whatever you need to do to get that disc."

9.

"Kelly, you are many things, but you are not a professional bank robber," Clay Deeds said over the secure iPhone connection. Turnbull was back in the hotel room. Twenty-one seconds had ticked off already.

"Not yet," Turnbull said. "But how hard can it be? I mean, if I have what I need."

"And what's that?"

"I've been thinking about it. Boston is famous for bank robberies, right?"

"It is notorious for them."

"Well, then there have got to be some guys game for a score. They get me in, loot the place, and I go into the box room and unlock box number 533. Then we all clear out and go our separate ways."

"Do you know any bank robbers in Boston, Kelly?" Deeds asked.

"Not as such," conceded Turnbull. "But I bet your computer geeks can do some hacking and find me someone with that very particular set of skills."

"Why do you operatives always assume we can just *deus ex hackina* the answer to every tactical obstacle?" demanded Deeds.

"I have faith in you and your virgin computer dorks, Clay."

"Give me six hours," Deeds said, and the line went dead.

"You want them to find us a gang of bank robbers?" asked King.

"We could wander around the streets asking random passersby, but I figure that might take a while, and probably raise some suspicions."

"Maybe you should take me out of here and come back," King said. "The sooner I get to Texas, the sooner I can start up rebuilding."

"Why are you so fixated on igniting your own personal guerilla war?" Turnbull asked.

"Let's just say I owe some payback to the blues."

"Lot of that going around," Turnbull said.

"What did they do to you, beside wreck your country?" asked King.

"Let me put it this way. I've killed a lot of people for doing a lot less than what they did to me."

"I bet you have," King said. "You're some kind of operator guy. I know the type. And I bet your name is not really Chris."

"And to think you wasted those powers of deduction on talk radio."

"I would have been the number one conservative talker in America if this hadn't happened," King said. "I was better than all of them. O'Connor, Katz, Stigall, Gorka..."

"I know that guy. Good shot."

"Hewitt, Kelly, Levin, Shapiro, who I do *not* look like," continued King. "Buck Sexton..."

"The porn actor? I'm just assuming."

"I'm sure there's a porn actor named 'Buck Sexton," but no, the other one, the radio guy. I would have gone to top of the heap, but then the Split happened."

"I guess the country falling apart was a real inconvenience."

King got serious. "It's been a nightmare. I kind of thought, once, it might be the best thing, you know, to solve our problems. But the Split is a disaster."

"Especially here. Not so much in the red."

"I'm cleaning my pistol now," King said.

"At least someone taught you good habits."

While King disassembled his Smith & Wesson SD40, Turnbull stared out the window at the city and the multi-colored flags fluttering off the skyscrapers.

"Back my play," Turnbull told King. "Just don't shoot anybody."

"I'm not the one who shoots everybody," King muttered.

The Tangier was ahead at the end of the block. A couple of salty-looking dudes stood out front, smoking and joking, but they made Turnbull immediately and stink-eyed him as he approached.

"I don't think they like us," King observed.

Turnbull ignored him and locked stares with the one who seemed to be the dominant half of the pair. Turnbull glanced inside through the dirty windows as he passed to get a general idea of the layout.

"What?" the thug asked as Turnbull stopped in front of him.

"Looking for a Seamus McCloskey," Turnbull said.

"Get out of here," the thug snarled.

"Seamus," Turnbull said. "Now."

"Or what?" The thug's hand drifted toward his belt.

Turnbull stepped forward, bringing the Wilson Combat out and shoving it into the man's gut.

"If you want your liver made into pâté," Turnbull said, pressing the pistol barrel into the man's flab. "Keep reaching."

"I wouldn't," Teddy King warned the other one. "He's a real foodie." King had his own Smith & Wesson ready. The other guy just stared.

"I'm gonna take that piece and shove it up your...," the thug with the automatic against his abdomen began.

"Unlikely," Turnbull said. "We're going inside, you first." Turnbull used his left hand to relieve the man of his SIG 320.

"I'm going to kick your ass," the thug blustered.

"Move," Turnbull said, reorienting the thugs to walk inside through the door. The thug went and as he stepped inside,

Turnbull pushed him hard, sending him falling forward into the bar. Turnbull pivoted the .45 to cover the pair of gunsels at the side table.

"Don't," he said as they pondered going for their weapons. Behind him King pushed the other thug through the door and covered him with his own pistol. Their size differential amused Turnbull. He also noted that the sports memorabilia on the walls still referred to the old Red Sox, not the current club, now known as the Rainbow Sox.

Seamus McCloskey, iPad and Jameson's bottle before him on the bar, looked up.

"You Seamus?" Turnbull asked, his weapon never leaving the pair of seated bodyguards.

"And if I am?"

"Well, don't worry. If I was here to cap you, I'd have already smoked your minions. I want to talk."

"I don't know you," Seamus said.

"Yeah, you do," Turnbull replied. "I'm the guy with the gun who's going to make you a ton of money."

"Well, in that case, let's us get better acquainted. Would you like a snort?"

"I don't drink and deal. And we have a deal to make."

"Well, by all means come sit down."

"And your boys?" Turnbull asked, moving to the bar and depositing the liberated SIG there.

"Liam, Neal," he said to the men at the table. "Go back to what you were doing. And you two, get back to your post outside." The thugs who had been on the sidewalk sullenly stepped back out front.

"You know me," Seamus said as Turnbull slipped into a stool next to him. "But I don't know you or your friend."

"Call me Chris."

"Boss, I think his friend is that radio guy I used to listen to," either Neal or Liam said.

Teddy King smiled at Turnbull and nodded.

"Never thought I'd meet Ben Shapiro," either Neal or Liam said. "Could I get an autograph?"

Turnbull ignored King's glare and turned back to Seamus. He placed his Wilson Combat pistol on the bar.

"I have a business proposition."

"I don't do business with strangers."

"Well, think of me as an old friend you just met. You want $6.7 million in used US currency?"

"I'd not be averse to it," Seamus said guardedly. He was making calculations in his head. US dollars could be sold at better than street value, PR scrip being on par with Charmin – actually, it was worth less. He took a sip of whiskey.

"Well, that's the average cash on hand the first Tuesday of the month at a certain local bank," Turnbull said. "And that's just red dollars. There's more in blue."

"No one wants blue scrip."

"Suit yourself. I don't care about the money. I'm after something in a safe deposit box. I just need to get inside the bank for a few minutes. And I figure the king of Charlestown might know some enterprising boyos who would want to take advantage of this opportunity." In fact, it was Clay Deeds' analysts who had skimmed FBI reports then followed up with a former agent from the Boston office who retired just before the Split and moved to Houston. The consensus was that if there was something dirty going on in Charlestown, Seamus McCloskey was knee-deep in it. McCloskey was a hard case, suspected in but never charged with a number of premature demises. He cooperated with the feds when he needed to – he was, after all, a Boston mobster and his kind and the FBI had a long and sordid association.

Deeds passed on the info that the gangster operated out of a bar called the Tangier, along with details about the bank and its transactions that they had managed to pilfer across the web. Hence, Turnbull's visit.

"Well, Chris, no offense, but we don't need anyone to help us rob a bank," Seamus said. "And again, I don't know you."

"You know I got past four of your boys."

"That you did."

"And you know I seem to have some inside information. I have more, most everything a solid crew will need."

"*If* your info is good, Chris."

"How do I put this delicately? I work for … a governmental organization."

"Is that supposed to make me feel better?"

"Not this government," Turnbull said, and paused.

"Ah," Seamus said.

"We needed someone who could set us up with a crew, and here I am with you. We needed to know what was in the bank, and I do. And we have certain other resources we can put into play. But I need to hit that bank. And I need you to set me up with some pros who can do it and help with some of the prosaic logistics. I understand that backing scores is one of your many income streams."

"And the income?" Seamus said. "What about the money?"

"Like I said, I don't care about the money. It's all yours. Every red cent, if you pardon the expression. I need to get in and get out and then I am gone and you lucky Irishmen are rich."

"What's in the box?"

"None of your business. I'll worry about the box."

"Am I going to catch heat?"

"Probably. But six-point-seven mil is worth a little sweat."

"And how do I know it's not a trap?"

Turnbull snorted. "Do you think if I was People's Security Force, I'd go through all this to frame you, or would I just haul you away? You think the PR is concerned with things like guilt or innocence?"

"Good point. Let me make a call."

Turnbull read Danny Doyle as ex-military, and most definitely combat arms, right off, from his bearing to the way he chose a seat where he could watch the door.

"I'm not interested," Doyle said after hearing them out.

"Danny," Seamus said. "*I'm* interested."

Doyle exhaled slowly, weighing his options. They were weightless, since he had none.

"If it makes you feel any better," Turnbull said. "I don't trust you either."

"It doesn't," Doyle growled.

Turnbull assessed the young man. He was definitely smart and probably capable. According to Seamus, he and his crew could do the job. And according to Clay Deeds' internet sleuths, who had breached and pored through the JFCID, the Joint Federal Criminal Investigation Database, to find the players in the Boston crime scene, Seamus McCloskey would know who to pick.

"Danny," Seamus said. "Our new friend has sent me the schematics, the currency transfer documents, and everything else we would need. I don't know who he is, but he's no amateur, and he's backed by someone with resources."

"Who?" Doyle asked.

"I have my suspicions," Seamus replied.

"Not the PR. If the PR wanted you busted, it would just bust you, not set up an elaborate frame job," Turnbull said. "Evidence and stuff are racist to them anyway."

"He's got a point. The old school FBI made cases," Seamus said. "These blue bastards today start with you being guilty and work from there. The only thing keeping the PSF out of Charlestown is the chance we'd fight back."

"Even if I were to do it, we have a lot of planning to do."

"We've got until Tuesday."

"That's the Fourth of July," Doyle said. "It's a holiday."

"Not anymore. It's now sort of a holiday, America Sucks Day or whatever they call it now," Turnbull said.

"That's right," Seamus interjected. "You've seen the announcements on the tube. They outlawed fireworks as racist."

"Let's see how that goes for them," Doyle mused.

"It's not a holiday, so the bank is open," Turnbull said. "And there is a parade to celebrate how America is bad or something. Anyway, we can use that."

"It's not enough time."

"It's got to be," Turnbull responded. "There's a fuse burning. They might figure out where my box is. We have to move fast."

"There's a lot of specialized equipment we'll need."

"Seamus here can get us some of it."

"Time is tight and I may have some trouble with the guns we want for this," Seamus said. "I'll get you something."

"I might have the hook-up on the heat," Turnbull said. "That should convince you I'm for real if you still have doubts."

"I do. So, what's the plan?"

"Go in heavy. A sledgehammer. The civvies are too scared to interfere. You boys get the money. I get what's in the box. We exfil and go our separate ways."

"It can work," Seamus said. "Get Torrey working on the alarms. All the PSF will be at the parade when it goes down. It's simple."

"You really buying this, Seamus?" asked Doyle.

"It clears the Leprechauns' ledger. Even leaves you some cash for yourselves. Danny, I'm going to have to insist."

Doyle pivoted toward Turnbull. "Chain of command is me, then my XO, and then the rest of my lads. You are not in it. You are a passenger, and you do what I say. Clear?"

"You plan the heist. I'll do my part. Just get me inside and back out again."

"Okay, but for the next four days you stay with us. I got a room you can use."

"You want to keep me in sight, huh?" asked Turnbull.

"Damn straight. I do not know you, and I do not trust you."

Turnbull smiled – the man was smart all right. "Let's go plan this bank robbery," he said.

"First," Seamus said. "A toast." He pulled the bottle of Jameson's over and selected, then filled, two more glasses. "To six point seven million red dollars."

Turnbull and King followed Doyle home and parked out front of a run-down townhouse. In fact, every townhouse on the block was run-down – the gentrification that had hit Charlestown had stopped right at the time the country split in two before it had reached this deep into the old neighborhoods. When they stepped out, every eyeball on the block was on them. Turnbull got the tension vibe before his shoe hit the asphalt, the same vibe he had felt in Baghdad or Kandahar when an IED was about to pop.

"You seem tense," Doyle said, a sly smile on his face.

"Am I wrong?"

"Nah," Doyle said. "First Friday of the month. Basic Income Day. The money will hit their accounts and load their debit cards this afternoon. Tonight's going to be interesting. Like an infantry company coming back home from the field after a month on payday."

"Basic Income?"

"Nice way of saying welfare," Doyle replied. "Everyone gets $1,000 in blue bucks. Of course, the beer and booze prices get jacked up accordingly."

"Can't fight economics," King said. "Socialism's done a great job here."

"It's like Cuba," Turnbull muttered knowingly. "With redheads." He did not add that it was also hot and muggy; most of the locals were in t-shirts.

"Are we good with all these people knowing we're here?" King asked.

"You're safer than anywhere else," Doyle said. "No one gets in or out of the neighborhood without us knowing about it. And they won't say a damn thing to outsiders."

"And when the cash hits?" asked Turnbull.

"Chaos, but that's all internal. We handle our own."

"Oh yeah?" Turnbull said, pointing to the end of the block. "Look."

Doyle froze in place, looking up the street where he saw it, a single PSF patrol car turning onto the block. It was not speeding or doing anything other than patrolling – and it came under a hail of beer cans and rocks. It accelerated and drove past them, a chorus of obscenities in its wake.

"See," Doyle said.

"Maybe I can get a condo here," King said. "Can you hook me up with your wife beater guy so I can look the part?"

"I think they're called 'spouse beater' t-shirts now," Doyle replied. "And remember, you're the ones who needed us."

They went up the front steps and across the wooden porch, then inside through the screen door.

Turnbull froze. A German shepherd came bounding over to them and hopped up on Doyle.

"Her name's Clover," Doyle said, ruffling the canine's ears.

"I'm not a dog person," Turnbull said.

"He's not much of a people person either," King added.

"What kind of guy doesn't like dogs?" Doyle asked.

"I didn't say I didn't like dogs," Turnbull said testily. "I said I'm not a dog person."

"You got some damage, huh?" Doyle remarked.

The dog dropped back to the ratty living room carpet and Turnbull carefully came inside. The furniture was tired and there were some generic paintings of sailboats and the like, a few black and white pictures of long dead folks taken back in the old country, and a crucifix on the walls.

"Who are these two, Danny?" Katie McGowan asked, looking over Turnbull. "Did you just go for your piece?"

Turnbull realized his right hand was on the Wilson at his hip – he had not even thought about it when he heard her footsteps. He released his grip.

"Remind me not to sneak up on you," she said, and then she turned and kissed Danny.

"These are Chris and Teddy. They're working with us on a thing."

"Do you know them?" she asked, agitated.

"It's okay," Danny said.

"It's not okay to be bringing strangers around. No offense," she said to the guests.

"None taken," Turnbull said.

"I'm a little offended," King said. "You know, we're outlaws ourselves." Turnbull shoved him.

"This is Katie," Doyle said. He did not need to announce she was his moll. "She helps us sometimes."

"Where's the rest of the crew?"

"Coming."

"Oh, they should be in fine form," Katie said. "Tonight's Basic Income night. You better do your planning early."

The rest of the crew started trickling in around five. By then, out on the street, the sidewalks were packed with people coming home with cases of beer and bottles of booze. Everything else was in short supply in the PR, but not liquid anesthetics.

Katie greeted her brother Sean with a kiss; Turnbull picked up on the eagle, globe and anchor tatt on his bicep. Sean was bleeding from his lip.

"What happened to you?" Doyle asked, not particularly interested.

"Ah, Joey McCormick shot off his mouth and I had to sort him out." Doyle nodded, satisfied.

More lads climbed up the steps to the porch and came in through the screen door without bothering to knock.

The first there was Jimmy O'Connor, who Doyle introduced as their driver. A large guy arrived a few moments later with two more tough-looking guys following close behind. "This is Jimmy Sullivan," Doyle said. "Sully's a solid guy in a pinch. And these are Mikey and Torrey Sullivan.' He pointed to Torrey. "Sully here does our alarm work."

"Are these guys all brothers?" Turnbull asked.

"Nah, my brother's Pat," Jimmy said, offended. "Like I'd be Sully's brother."

"What's wrong with being my brother?" Mikey asked, indignant and standing up from the couch."

"Sit your ass down, Sully, you ain't doin' shit!" Jimmy said.

"Sully, shut up," Doyle said, annoyed. But Jimmy and Mikey were in each other's faces now and Torrey and Doyle had to pull them apart.

"I'm confused," Turnbull said to Katie, who did not seem to find any of this unusual. "Which one is Sully again?"

"All of them," she answered.

The beer came out immediately. There was no discussion – you planned the score and downed some brews doing it.

"You sure we ought to be drinking while we do this?" Turnbull asked Doyle as they hovered over schematics and maps Seamus had printed out for them. Doyle took a sip of Resistance Ale, the successor brand after Sam Adams had been canceled for its connection to colonialism, albeit it being on what one might think would have been the right side.

"You want to tell these goons they gotta go dry?"

Turnbull looked over to see Torrey and Mikey fall onto the couch punching each other.

"Knock it off, Sully!" Doyle shouted.

"Are they like this all the time?" King asked.

"Like what?" Doyle replied.

"I feel like I'm trapped in a Dropkick Murphys video," Turnbull muttered. "Let's focus."

"Torrey, stop playing grab ass with Sully and get over here," Doyle said, pointing to the map. "The People's Collective

Financial Institution is mid-way on this block. Lots of high rises. It'll take time to get out of there. It's the exfiltration part that's always the bitch."

"The parade is going to keep a lot of people out of downtown," Turnbull said. "The street should have light traffic."

Torrey joined them. "What?" he asked.

"How long can you give us?" Doyle asked.

"Hell, I can knock the whole alarm system off-line," Torrey said. "Since most of the companies beat feet to Texas after the Split, no one's really watching the store. Cells are the problem."

"We can deal with the customers and the employees," Jimmy Sullivan said. "It's people outside calling into the PSF that's the bitch."

"They won't know what's going on inside," King said.

"Yeah, well, sometimes that doesn't matter," Doyle replied.

"Response time will be down because of the parade," Turnbull observed."

"I'm still not going more than 180 seconds," Doyle said. "Three minutes in and out."

"I can do what I need to do in three mikes. Can you?" Turnbull asked.

"Three minutes is eternity," Doyle said. "We aren't messing around. We're going in heavy. No subtlety. We sledgehammer it."

"I like this," Jimmy Sullivan said, grinning.

"Sully and Sean take security, end of each block. Clear fields of fire in and outward. Jimmy drives, of course. Jimmy, me, and you two inside," Doyle said.

"Who does...wait, what?" asked King, but the Leprechauns were nodding along.

"I've been there," Turnbull said. "We're short. We need someone else inside."

"Don't have the manpower. But we do need five in the bank, including you off doing your thing with the boxes," Doyle said.

"How about me?" asked Katie.

"No," Doyle said.

"We need to circle back on that issue," Turnbull said. "Let's talk logistics," Turnbull said. Professionals always talked about logistics.

"Two rides. Hardware. Torrey, you got what you need to dope the alarm?"

"No, but I can make a list," Torrey said.

"Clothes, gear. Guns, of course," Mike said.

"Seamus is good for everything, except the guns," Doyle said. "It's short notice. Not sure we can get what we need from him."

"Your crime boss can't find guns?" asked Turnbull. "He hinted he could."

"Like I said, short notice is a problem. There are plenty of guns around. It's just people are holding onto them because the PR is cranking down on them. A .38 is a couple grand now, and in real money, not PR butt wipe."

"Expensive even before inflation," Turnbull said. "And we're not looking for some rusty .38 revolvers."

"No," Doyle said. "We need real heat."

"What did you like in the service?"

"Why do you think I was in the service?"

"Because you plan like a squad leader."

"I was one," Doyle said.

"Well, sergeant, what's your dream gun for this op?"

"You going to make my dream come true, Chris?"

"Never hurts to ask Santa."

"Okay," Doyle said. "Full auto, real military grade. The problem is fire superiority. We can have fire superiority at first, for a few minutes, but not forever. That's the thing – the PSF will keep coming and the enemy will always get stronger. We can't but get weaker. So, we gotta maintain fire superiority longer, until we can get out. We need something heavier."

"Heavier than 5.56mm?" Turnbull queried, liking what he was hearing.

"My M4 was okay, but they issued us HK417s in Afghanistan. I loved my 417."

"Good call. 7.62mm. A .308 round. Can't carry as much ammo though."

"If it goes to shit, we'll need to punch through cars and walls. A .308 will do the job, but where are we getting a bunch of high-speed assault rifles?"

"No promises, but let me show you what I can bring to the table," Turnbull said.

"Okay, you get the guns and ammo. We'll need pistols too. Seamus is good for the rest." The deal with Seamus was always that he set up logistics; his end more than compensated him.

"I'll get on the alarms," Torrey said. "I can do it Sunday night. It's an old Security One client and I still got the key to the office. What time's the hit?"

"Eleven hundred hours Tuesday," Doyle said.

"The alarm will be out starting at 1059," Torrey said, sipping his Resistance Ale. He made a face. "This is piss water."

"You can buy a brewery when we pull this off," his brother Sully said. "So, stop bitching."

"Recon?" asked King. Someone taught him right, Turnbull thought to himself.

"I'll run the routes tomorrow and then Monday with every swinging Richard," Jimmy O'Connor said. "Establish our infil and exfil, with alternates. They publish the parade road closures online, so unless they change up on us, we should be good to go."

"All of us need to make a pass through, but no stopping and no going in. Wear your damn masks too."

"I feel like a pussy in a mask," Mikey complained. "I had it, you know, and COVID-22 too. Kicked its virus ass."

"Yeah, cover your ugly mug, Sully," Jimmy Sullivan taunted, and they started pushing each other.

"Cut it the hell out!" shouted Danny. "Just wear it. I don't want photos of any of us in the AO." Turnbull knew the term "AO" – area of operations.

"I'll go inside Monday morning," Katie said. Inside recon was her gig; no one ever questioned a pretty girl, except in terms of her privilege.

Doyle nodded. Turnbull spoke.

"I made two security guards, not high speed, both with Beretta 92Fs. I'm very interested in whether they have any friends."

Katie nodded.

"Mask up," Doyle said, and Katie nodded again. The never-ending COVID panic was just about the best thing that ever happened to bank robbers.

Outside there was a brief cacophony of shouting and car horns. The various Sullys all looked toward the front door wistfully.

"Are we almost done here?" Mikey asked. The boys wanted to be out in the action of a Basic Income Friday.

"Tomorrow, noon, here," Doyle announced. The others scrambled to leave. "Be sober! Don't do anything stupid."

"Good luck with that," Katie said as the rest of the crew left.

"I gotta walk Clover," Doyle announced. The dog started wagging her tail upon hearing the magic word. "Chris, why don't you come with me?"

"Sure," Turnbull said. His shirt was untucked and it covered his piece. "We need to chat."

10.

"So, what's the deal?" Turnbull asked.

"The deal, Chris, like that's your real name?" replied Doyle.

"Your deal, Danny."

Doyle said nothing for a few steps. Clover led the way, straining a bit on the leash, and even drunks half-in-the-bag from the firewater their Basic Income deposits had just bought were wise enough to step off into the gutter to avoid the animal.

"Just trying to get by," Doyle finally said.

"From Army guy to bank robber," Turnbull said. "Quite a career trajectory."

"Just being all that I can be."

"You were in the 75th?" Turnbull asked. That was the Ranger regiment, the elite light infantry unit that frequently worked with Special Forces and other people whose background they were taught never to inquire into. Turnbull often grabbed platoons of Rangers for security for his operations – they were professional, tough, and they kept their mouths shut.

"Second Batt," Doyle answered. He had been in the 2nd Battalion, headquartered at Joint Base Lewis–McChord just south of Seattle when the unit wasn't off in some Third World hellhole killing bad guys.

"I probably worked with you."

"You got the vibe of one of those operator types," Doyle replied. "I have some ideas about where you came from."

"You have the operator vibe yourself. I could see you passing assessment. Why aren't you still in and wearing a Green Beret?"

"Woulda coulda shoulda."

"You get out when the Split happened?" Turnbull asked. Lots of soldiers did; the Split had sundered loyalties in the military just like the secessions had at the beginning of the Civil War.

Doyle did not answer because a pack of five young men were dragging another man out of an alley.

"Hey Bobby," Doyle said, as Clover watched the proceedings with rapt attention. "What gives?"

One of the pack turned around. "Hey Danny. This asshole knocked down Mrs. Dennehy and grabbed her purse when she was walking home from mass."

"Who is he?"

"I dunno. Not from here."

"Okay," Danny said, and the three of them proceeded on as the pack began pummeling the hapless purse snatcher.

"Not much on calling the cops, huh?" asked Turnbull, indifferent to the punk's fate. In a sense, the guy was lucky he was only getting the living snot punched out of him – in the red, a member of the armed populace probably would have capped him and the police investigation would have consisted of a local cop calling the meat wagon and shrugging.

"Even if the PSF would come if we called, and even if they still arrested street punks, we'd take care of our own. This is our neighborhood, Chris. And all this stuff about criminals being victims after the Split led some outsiders to think they could come in here and do the same shit here as they do in their own neighborhoods. Not on our watch."

"Aren't you a criminal?"

"I rob banks, not old ladies coming home from church."

The beating continued to the rear. The locals were not buying the PR's fashionable concept of restorative justice, nor its idea that theft was a victimless crime.

"I'm not a fan of the authorities in general," Doyle said.

"Anything to do with why you're out of the Army?"

"Well, I was dating this girl on base, you see," Doyle said. "This was before Katie and I were, you know, a thing. Her father was a colonel. And he thought his little girl was a virgin innocent."

"I take it she was not. Tell me she wasn't underage."

"Oh no, she was eighteen going on forty-five. Pretty teenager on an infantry base? Forget it. She was teaching me things I never even thought of."

"I'm guessing," Turnbull said, "that the O5 was less than pleased that little missy was tooling around with an 11B sergeant."

"I was a staff sergeant, and he was a full bird," Doyle said. "And yeah, he was pretty unhappy about it. Especially when he walked in on us."

"Yeah, that must have been awkward."

"It was extremely awkward," Doyle said. "There were words. He threw the first punch, and I threw the last."

"And I can guess how that went."

"My JAG got me a year in Leavenworth, a month per tooth as it were," Doyle said.

"Seems light for beating the shit out of a field grade."

"Part of the deal was I would delete all the photos she texted me and not call her to the stand at trial. Like you said, that would have been awkward."

"I'm guessing you don't like officers."

"Not a fan," Doyle said. "Are you one?"

"After that story, you think I'd tell you if I was?"

"Leavenworth was bad. Worse than any tour I did – at least over there I could shoot back. With all the racial bullshit going on, every day in there was a gladiator fight with other inmates and the guards."

He stopped and looked at Turnbull.

"I am never going back inside," Doyle said. "Not ever."

"Okay," Turnbull replied, not sure if he was expected to argue the point.

"If we're on the score and the PSF or anyone else gets in our way, it's on," Doyle said. "World War Three."

"I like the way you think," Turnbull said.

They got a table at Clancy's, a ratty locals-only bar where Doyle and Clover were apparently well-known enough that no one batted an eye when he brought the German shepherd inside with him. But Turnbull himself drew plenty of stares and low mutterings.

"Not really hospitable folks," Turnbull observed. A dark-haired young woman in an apron came over with two pints.

"Hi, Danny, hi Clover," she said, then turned and walked away. If Turnbull had feelings, they might have been hurt.

"We're a close-knit community," Doyle said, lifting his glass. "Tribal, almost, like back in Afghanistan."

"Not down with the *sharia* though," Turnbull replied, picking up his.

Doyle grimaced as the beer hit his palate.

"Everything's bad now," he said. "The beer, the food, the TV." He gestured at the dingy monitor hanging over the bar, sound off. It seemed to be a baseball game, but everyone on the field was a man made up as a woman. The chyron read "Tonight the Rainbow Sox celebrate the rejection of archaic gender presumptions."

"It never stops, does it?" Turnbull tipped his glass; it tasted vaguely of metal.

"No, the Split's always there. Everywhere you look, everything is different and worse," Doyle said, sipping some more of the noxious brew. "Is it that way in the red?"

"It's different than it was before the Split in the red," Turnbull said, his voice low. "For a long time, normal people never had to think about politics or war or whatever. And now they all do all the time. They have to."

"You really gotta be a vet to be a citizen?" asked Doyle.

Turnbull nodded. "Didn't want people who didn't have skin in the game, or blood, making decisions for the people who did."

"So, if I came down there, I'd be a citizen?"

"Yeah. But you'd have to be in the reserves."

"See, there's always a catch," Doyle said. Outside, there was a loud series of booms and pops. Turnbull realized his hand was on the Wilson .45.

"The townies love their fireworks, but they're illegal as hell now," Doyle said. "We're still patriotic, even though it's also illegal to celebrate the Fourth at all instead of whatever bullshit they're calling it now. Probably because we're sitting on the Bunker Hill battlefield."

"I saw the tower." The white monolith loomed over the peninsula.

"They're talking about tearing it down. Says it makes feminists literally shake because it reminds them of a penis. You got them in the red? I mean feminists."

"Not so much anymore. Most came up here. Lot of patriarchy and phallocentrism going on in the US of A. It's a free country, as in, you're free to go."

"You talk like those jerks on TV," Doyle replied.

"Gotta know your enemy, think like him. Or her. Or xir."

"Well, the penis tower is on Breed's Hill, where the real fighting was. Bunker Hill is to the northwest. The colonists – I guess that's a bad thing now – dug in here on the Charlestown peninsula, and that threatened Boston across the river. They sent a bunch of redcoat infantry, best in the world, over to clear it."

"And they met a bunch of farmers and other civilians with their own rifles," Turnbull said.

"Shot the shit out of the Brits," Doyle said. "Remember all that talk about armed citizens not being a threat? Civilians with rifles were a threat in 1775, just like in Afghanistan, just like during the Split."

"You see any fighting here?"

Doyle shook his head. "Nah. Massachusetts was always blue, mostly. We weren't really anything here in Charlestown. I think people just went along with it, celebrated it, thinking they were happy to be rid of all those Jesus people from the South and Midwest. But I knew those people, the reds, from the service. I did, Sean did – you met him, the Marine? He quit after the Split because they canceled "The Halls of Montezuma." Said it celebrated colonialism and the patriarchy and violence and aggression."

"It kind of does," Turnbull said.

"I know, right?" Doyle said. "But I don't think everyone else really thought the Split all the way through. Guess they forgot who fed them – you can't eat nothing but chowder."

"Most people never looked back at America from outside it and saw what a good thing we had going," Turnbull said. "Then we started hating each other. By the time the Split happened, we had ourselves irreconcilable differences, but we were still forced to live together relatively peacefully. But now that we're separated, but stuck on the same continent, there's nothing to stop us from going for each other's throats. Like these crocodiles I saw, both living in one swamp, fighting over scraps of..."

"Of what?" asked Doyle.

"Communists, but that's another story."

Doyle took another swig.

"Yeah, two big guys on one block. That's one too many. We'll probably screw with each other before it gets kinetic. You think the reds will cut off the food and the electricity too?"

"Probably," Turnbull said.

"I don't see lots of room for windmills. And when people get hungry – well, you know what desperate people do."

"Maybe you ought to go before they close the border," Turnbull said. "Take your girl and this dog, too."

"I think about it and then I remember the one and only time I left, it went bad, and I came back."

Turnbull finished the miserable pint. "This Split is all going to go bad. I can feel it, and I bet you can too. You ought to get out while the getting is good. You townies got no friends in the PR. You're too insular, you're too traditional, and you're too stubborn, and you're the perfect scapegoats for whatever is going wrong around here."

"Give us some credit, Chris," Doyle said, smiling a little. "We do cause some havoc. But remember what happened to the Brits. Three times they charged. We shot them down three times. The best infantry on the globe and we stopped them, right here."

"Then you ran out of ammunition and they drove you out."

Doyle shrugged. "But we showed those English bastards we could fight. And we showed the other twelve colonies too."

"A strategic victory, but a tactical defeat. Especially for all the guys those Brits bayoneted right here."

"We were in Afghanistan. We should be happy about whatever kind of victory we can get."

Clover had sat at Doyle's feet the entire time, watching the goings-on. No one came to pet her – they were well aware that she was very protective of Danny and Kate, and her snarl was fearsome. If they had been outside of the Town, like in Boston itself or Floyd, perhaps an animal rights activist would have confronted them for their speciesism. That would not have worked out so well.

Now the dog was attentive – a middle-aged man, definitely salty, was headed their way across the barroom floor, flanked by two toughs with blank stares and waist bulges.

Turnbull assessed the bodyguards as the premier threat, and the one to the left the more alert, and therefore, the more dangerous one.

Turnbull would kill him first, hopefully with a round to the forehead, then shift to the second bodyguard and put him away before finishing with the protectee. His tentative plan for killing them all made, he relaxed slightly.

Doyle, for his part, seemed mellow.

"Been looking for you, Danny," said the leader. "Katie said you were out walking the dog and I figured that meant you were in a bar drinking."

Doyle gestured to an empty chair and the man sat down and his crew maintained a respectful distance.

"Chris, this is Pat O'Brien, our neighborhood People's Council rep. He's also Seamus's right hand and his lawyer too.

"I have a very specialized practice," Pat said.

"You got a relative named Robert?" Turnbull asked.

"Yeah, a brother, and two – no, three – cousins," O'Brien said, a bit taken aback. "What of it?"

"I might have met one recently, but probably not."

Pat turned back to Doyle. "Tomorrow, fittings."

"Fittings?" asked Turnbull.

"Suits," Doyle explained. "We wear suits to look like Joe Businessman, but we need them cut right so we can hide our gear under the jackets without looking like we're hiding our gear."

"Got the bags, all the radios, which were a pain but we got 'em," Pat said. "Got you tactical rigs, like you asked for. No Kevlar plates, though. Looks too bulky even with the suits. Plus, speed is your best protection."

"If it goes right," Turnbull said. "We won't need them."

"Here's hoping for that," Pat replied. "Now, we figured out where to get the wheels. We got two nice newish Chrysler 300s spotted and ready to snatch the night before. Cloned the keys and made dupes. We have the plan for when you get back. I'll give all the wheres and hows for afterwards Sunday. I got everything squared away except the iron."

"The iron's kind of important, Pat," Doyle said with a hint of impatience.

"There isn't much out there, not what you have in mind. Right now, I got a gauge and a nine."

"Well," Turnbull said. "That's fine if we're rolling with Vanilla Ice and his crew, but we need something more…"

"More what?" Pat demanded.

"Potent," Turnbull said. He stood. "I'm making a call."

Turnbull came back in from outside on the sidewalk where he made his short call. There was a fresh pint before his empty chair. Doyle and Pat waited as Turnbull took a zinc-infused sip, then put the glass back down on the table.

"Well?" Pat asked.

"I'll be getting a call back soon," he finally said. "With a hook-up."

"Who do you know who deals guns that we don't?" Pat demanded.

"Don't know yet," Turnbull said.

"Who the hell is this enigma?" Pat asked Doyle.

"You learn that big word in law school, Pat?" Doyle asked, and Pat glared for a moment before dissolving into laughter.

"Asshole," he said, smiling. "Okay, I'll leave the bang sticks to your new pal here with the contacts. Everything else I'm getting squared away. Be at the tailor shop with your cronies, two at a time, starting at noon tomorrow. He needs time to work, so don't let those mutts of yours no-show. No offense, Clover."

The dog manifested no offense.

"We'll be there," Doyle said. Pat rose up out of his seat.

"The pieces are falling into place," he said. "See you around."

Pat and his two guards left.

"He's got a lot of heat out here," Doyle said. "He's the public face. The lawyer, on the neighborhood boards, deals with the PSF and the Equity Commission and all the rest. But he'll kill you. He knows where the bodies are buried because he's buried a lot of them."

There was more noise from outside, more fireworks. The stiffs across the water in Boston were probably furious because they could see the blooms over Charlestown, mocking their order to ignore Independence Day and quietly, nonpyrotechnically, celebrate whatever the holiday was that they sought to replace it with.

"So, you think you can get us the guns we need?" Doyle asked.

"If they can be got," Turnbull said. "My guys will get them."

11.

"It used to be called Franklin Park," Doyle said. "Now it's named for Teddy Kennedy."

"It does include a zoo," Turnbull mused.

It was now early Sunday morning. Saturday had been spent planning, testing the gear O'Brien delivered, and getting fitted for their suits. Several of the crew showed up Saturday morning hungover, while some of the rest of the guys were still buzzed. Clay Deeds had called at about 10 a.m.

"It's on," he said over the secure iPhone. "Everything you asked for."

Now Turnbull and Doyle sat in a parking lot in the middle of the 527-acre park, which the Google map had identified as "the Sausage Lot" for some reason. Maybe it was the shape – the lot resembled a bratwurst running parallel to Circuit Drive and bordered by tall, lush oaks and elms on the north. Past them somewhere was the Franklin Zoo – they did not change its name since to name a zoo after someone was a grievous insult, and they might as well leave it named after the notoriously cis-normative Benjamin. This served him right for failing to adhere to the esoteric mores in vogue about 250 years in the future.

Of course, the zoo was now closed to the public. Keeping animals was wrong, according to the PR's dogma. Also, embarrassingly, hungry locals kept trying to eat some of the less fearsome captives. A security staff remained to feed the remaining beasts and protect them from foragers until the powers that be could figure out what to do with them.

The former William J. Devine Golf Course was across Circuit Drive to the south. The 18 holes were no longer open to the public, but was instead a massive encampment of shanties, lean-tos and tents – occupied territory, the "Free Space of New Boston," according to the hand-painted sign along the road. There were shouts and yells from across the way, and numerous campfires.

No People's Security Force, of course. Being liberated territory, the PSF had gotten the orders to stay out of Ted Kennedy Park, and they gladly obeyed. Everyone else, besides the bums, derelict, lunatics, and criminals, stayed out too. The vast complex of trails and roads was given over to the freak show.

Making it perfect for the rendezvous.

Doyle was driving a Chevy Impala one of the myriad Sullys had lifted for them, and Turnbull was in the passenger seat next to him with his Wilson on his lap. Doyle had a .357 Smith & Wesson 626 revolver. Their headlights were off, and the lot's streetlamps were long ago broken out and abandoned, but the moon was up and casting enough to see with. Turnbull did a chamber check – the Hydra-Shok round was ready when needed.

Next to them, idling in the lot, was a beat-up plumbing company van that was likewise borrowed, this from its owner's company lot. It said "Turd Wranglers" on the side, and announced that their plumbers were "dedicated to reimagining plumbing in a non-sexist framework." Inside, the van reeked of dope, which was probably the best outcome possible under the circumstances.

Jimmy Sullivan was in the back of the empty van with a 12-gauge pump. O'Connor was at the wheel with an old M1911 .45 that Pat O'Brien had rustled up for him. It sat, loaded and cocked, on the fake leather passenger seat.

Sean McGowan, the Marine, was off in the tree line with a .30-30 deer rifle.

Doyle caught sight of something moving to his left and pushed the button to roll down the window.

"You," he shouted at a dirty man with crazy eyes. "I told you once to get the hell out of here. I'll break your damn arm next time I see your ass, you got it?"

The derelict swore at the interloper, but he wisely shuffled off.

"Where's our seller?" Doyle asked.

"The meet is at zero-one hours, and it's five minutes 'til then. I bet he's scoping us out," said Turnbull.

"Who is this guy of yours?"

"He's supposed to have the stuff we want."

"And he's taking it on credit?"

"Apparently, this Trevannian guy works for my friends often. He knows he'll get paid," Turnbull said. Clay Deeds had gotten back to him with a time and a place. Trevannian – no first name was provided by Deeds and Turnbull wasn't interested in the arms merchant's biography anyway – did a lot of work with the red and was a key part of Operation Gladius in the northeast People's Republic. Gladius was the initiative to create a network of arms caches throughout the split-off blue territories, just in case. Of course, when you were doing jobs like that, the folks you had to engage were often sub-savory types.

"He should come through, but don't get complacent," Deeds had warned him as the time on their call counted down.

"Has he screwed you before?" Turnbull asked.

"No, but there's always a first time."

Hence Sean in the woods with his scoped rifle. Trust, but verify, and if unverified, blow a huge hole in him with a .30-30 round.

"When he shows, we go out and meet him. The boys stay in the van until it's time to load up," Doyle said. "If nothing goes wrong, we should be done and out in five minutes."

"If," Turnbull said, watching for headlights.

Johnny Ross watched the Chevy and the plumber's van from his position in a clump of maple trees to the south. He got the tip through a colleague who had a confidential informant jammed up on a gun charge – one of the few crimes you actually went to jail for in the PR – and inside an arms dealer's organization. Ross had put out feelers about anyone with information on a gun buy of about half a dozen weapons. He investigated bank robberies; a robbery seemed like a possible solution to the safe deposit access problem. Earlier that day, the CI had mentioned a sale within those parameters would go down that evening, and Ross's colleague found him.

Now Ross was alone in the park, watching. He did not have the cavalry waiting – if it worked out as he hoped, he would follow the Leprechauns back to their lair, let them get comfy and fall asleep, or drunk off their asses – whatever. And then he would call in the tactical team and take them where they lay passed out – no drama, no trauma.

Colby had bought off on his plan; he had the tac squad on a 30-minute call. Now Ross waited in the warm summer air, the chirping of the crickets drowned out by the rumblings from the homeless encampment.

"Come on, Leprechauns, make your deal and lead me to your pot of gold," he said to himself. There was no reason this whole damn mission could not be finished up tonight, leaving only Wayne Gruber to be held to account.

But Gruber could wait.

"Lights," Doyle said, pointing southeast at the two pairs of headlamps approaching on Circuit Drive.

"Got them. Probably a sedan and a van for cargo," Turnbull assess.

"Great minds...," Doyle replied, not finishing his cliché. He keyed his mike on his Motorola.

"Two inbound. Get ready."

"Roger," Jimmy replied.

"On them," Sean answered.

The vehicles swung into the lot and approached cautiously. Turnbull was right – it was a Mercedes sedan and a Ford Econoline van, unmarked. They parked, on-line, about 25 meters to the front of the Impala and killed their lights.

"Slowly," Turnbull cautioned as he slipped the .45 back into its holster and carefully, very smoothly, opened the passenger side door.

"Stay in the van," Doyle said into his Motorola as he gingerly exited the van, his pistol wedged inside his belt at the small of his back.

The moonlight was still strong enough to illuminate the Sausage Lot even after the headlights crushed his night vision.

Three doors on the sedan opened, and from each a man stepped out. Turnbull assumed that number four was probably in the tree line with his crosshairs hovering over their faces.

No long weapons, at least not any visible. But who knew what they might lean back inside to grab and come out shooting with?

"Which one of you is Chris?"

The speaker was a tall, thin man with little hair and a face like a hatchet. He was in a suit with no tie, and looking a bit like his next stop was the Champagne Room at some pre-Split gentlemen's club had they still been allowed to exist – the tension between the PR faction advocating for the rights of sex workers had collided with the PR faction advocating against anything that cis-straight men might enjoy had been resolved in favor of neo-puritanism.

The speaker had come out of the rear passenger seat, and a beefy henchman was in front of him – should it all go bad, said henchmen would catch the lead.

Turnbull responded. "You Trevannian?"

"Let's talk. Just you."

"And just you. Meet ya in the middle."

Turnbull walked forward slowly, avoiding anything that smacked of a sudden movement. He did not bother to ask Doyle for cover; he knew he had it.

Trevannian, for his part, stepped around his henchman and approached. They halted about five feet apart in between the vehicles.

"You had quite a wish list," Trevannian said.

"I'm particular," Turnbull said. "Very particular."

"I feel like a sommelier when someone comes in and asks for a case of 1982 Lafite, and I just happen to have it in stock."

"I assume that's wine."

"Oh yes. I have a number of exotic interests," Trevannian assured him.

"I'm more of a Boone's Farm guy," Turnbull said. "But I do know my hardware."

"You certainly do. Do you want to take a look at the stock before you take delivery?"

"Yeah," Turnbull began, but there was shouting from Trevannian's men, and pistols came out.

The homeless man had wandered back and was babbling at them, and the henchmen were not having it.

"It's a disgrace what they have done to this city," Trevannian said, shaking his head. "But their fetish for disarming the population has certainly been a boon to my business."

One of the henchmen was hustling the angry bum away.

"Shall we?" Trevannian asked. Turnbull nodded. They walked toward the Ford Econoline.

"I do a lot of business with your people," Trevannian said. "Anyone else and I would demand cash up front."

"I'm sure my sponsors appreciate the vote of confidence."

"I don't wish to pry, and I would never think of doing so," Trevannian began as they approached the idling vehicle.

"Then don't," Turnbull said.

"But," he continued as if Turnbull had not spoken. "I do want to ensure that whatever happens with this arsenal does not blow back on me."

"Are all the serial numbers clean?"

"As far as anyone knows, they were all reported stolen from the federal government a while ago."

"Then you should be good to go."

They arrived at the rear and Trevannian rapped on the metal with the back of his hand. Both doors swung open. A pair of surly-looking gentlemen with AKs sat in the back. There were several long cases, each big enough for a number of long guns, and several canvas bags, probably holding the mags and ammo.

"Let's open them up," Turnbull said.

Trevannian sighed, and nodded at his minions. They began moving the top case toward the door.

"There was a time when people in this business trusted each other," he said mournfully.

"That was before my time," Turnbull replied. "Open it."

"That's him," Ross thought. The big guy with the big gun at Harvard. The man was making a deal all right, looking at something in the back of a van. Ross had a pretty good idea of what it was. But then he smiled. Mr. Big was never going to get a chance to use it. Within a few hours he'd be hooked up and behind bars, and Ross would deliver Harrington his disc, settle with Gruber, and he could get out of this political shit and go back to the kind of work where you could tell the good guys from the bad guys.

One of Trevannian's minions leaned over and flipped the clasps on the crate, then pulled back the top to reveal the contents.

"That's the stuff," Turnbull said, admiring the two HK417A5 Assaulters packed in foam cut-outs. They looked vaguely like

M4s, but a bit shorter. Their Trijicon optics were mounted above the actions.

"Six hundred rounds per minute, but the 7.62mm round means the mags are only 20 rounds each," Trevannian said.

"Eight per weapon?"

"Yes, and nine weapons total. And nine M1911s. I got Colts."

"Don't worry, I have my own."

"Eight mags for each of those too," Trevannian said. "The optics work, new batteries. We did a rough boresight zero on the optics with a laser. Can you do a real zero?"

"No time."

"It should be good enough then," Trevannian said. "Are you looking at long or close ranges?"

"Close to long, and everything in between," Turnbull replied.

"Then what you lack in finesse you can make up in firepower," Trevannian said.

There was one thing left, a canvas bag.

"I have no idea what you want these for," Trevannian said as Turnbull unzipped it and peered inside. He reached in and pulled out a hand-sized cylinder.

"I don't get many requests for thermite grenades," Trevannian said. The AN-M14 TH3 incendiary hand grenade was used primarily to destroy equipment thanks to the 4000 degrees generated by the oxidizing metals when the user pulled the pin. It would melt steel, which was what was required.

"How many?" asked Turnbull.

"I got three."

"Should be plenty," Turnbull said, closing the zipper. He kept one grenade out, sliding it into a pocket in his jacket, since he planned to test it later by frying the Chevy Impala he and Doyle were driving once they ditched it.

"Satisfied?"

"If I had some of that fancy wine of yours, I'd propose a toast."

"It's about five grand a bottle," Trevannian said. "Red cash, not that blue trash."

"Maybe I'll just have a beer later," Turnbull said.

"Your boys carry the product," Trevannian said. "Mine need to stay vigilant."

Turnbull stepped around the van and motioned to Doyle. Doyle spoke into his radio and both Jimmys came over to start carrying back the cargo.

"I had another buyer who is going to be greatly disappointed that your sponsor offered more," Trevannian said. "The unrest in Europe, especially in the British Isles, is a real boon to my business. Here, everyone has a gun already, so they don't think they need something special – present company accepted, of course. But overseas, they really appreciate the finer gear."

"I would think that being in Boston, you'd not help the Brits."

"Well, the EU occupation of Northern Ireland is controversial, and you know how our Emerald Isle brethren like to fight."

"Yeah, I've noticed that."

"Once you sold them an ArmaLite and you'd think you'd have given them a bottle of whiskey. But now they want premier brands, like HK."

"Glad business is booming for you."

"I've heard that joke before," Trevannian said. Turnbull thought for a moment.

"Right, I get it."

The boys made several trips, complaining a couple times about how they were not getting any help from the merchant's men. Finally, Jimmy Sullivan came and took the last two canvas bags.

"Get it loaded and go," Turnbull said. The plan had always been to leave separately. Turnbull turned back to Trevannian as Jimmy returned to the plumbing van.

"I'm going to stay with you until my guys are clear, if that's okay."

"What if it is not?" asked Trevannian, more curious about the response than anything else.

"Then I'll do it anyway and you'll be sad."

"Well, I don't want to be sad. I have a party to go to. A real one. With girls and cocaine, and music that is not government approved. I'd invite you, but I'm afraid they don't serve Boone's Farm."

"I never wanted to be in a club that would let me past the velvet rope," Turnbull said, making sure the Jimmys were set. The doors on the van slammed shut, and Jimmy O'Connor got in and pulled backwards, then turned and drove out toward the far west exit. When the vehicle got on the street and disappeared into the park, Turnbull pivoted back to Trevannian.

"We're done here," he said.

"A pleasure doing business with you," Trevannian said.

"Boss," said one of the gentlemen in the back of the van. "Headlights."

"Who the hell are they?" Ross muttered bitterly as three sedans came down Circuit Drive and turned into the Sausage Lot. There was nothing on his radio net, so it wasn't FBI.

"Oh shit," he said.

"If you set me up, I'm shooting you in the head," Turnbull said as he watched three vehicles – clearly government rides – turn into the parking lot.

"And that goes back the same to you," Trevannian hissed.

"If you didn't set us up, and I didn't set you up, who did?" Turnbull said as the vehicles came to a halt.

"Excellent question," Trevannian said, and then he addressed his men in a low whisper: "Get those weapons out of sight."

Wayne Gruber stepped out of the passenger side of his Ford without drawing his weapon. He had told his men the same – they had gotten the tip from their source and come directly here without grabbing their artillery from their trunks, as it was not clear what they were walking into.

For that reason, Gruber decided to go with fear. Fear was sometimes just as effective as bullets.

"Hey there!" he shouted in a friendly voice. His other eleven SIS men in their ill-fitted suits were lingering by their vehicles. No one had produced any iron – not yet.

Turnbull examined the grinning, manbunned thug approaching them. He knew the type. He had shot the type.

"That's close enough," Turnbull said when Gruber was about twenty steps away.

Gruber stopped and smiled broadly.

"Now, I'd like to introduce myself and my *hombres* here," Gruber said, pausing for a moment before continuing. "I am Chief Inspector Wayne Gruber, and we are with the Special Investigations Service of the Department of People's Justice."

"And I care why?" Turnbull said. Beside him, Trevannian was biting on his lip. Doyle was out of sight.

"Well," Gruber began. "We got us a tip from a very reliable source from a sister federal agency that there was some kind of illegal weapons deal going on right here in this parking lot tonight. And we come to see for ourselves, and here you are."

"We're just having a chat about wine. Turns out I have pretty bad taste."

"He really does," Trevannian added.

"I'd like to take a look, if you all don't mind."

"I kind of mind. You got a warrant?" asked Turnbull.

"I am not an attorney," said Trevannian. "But I believe unless you are investigating a hate crime, you need a warrant."

"Well, I am a federal officer and I think I know the law, and I think I need to come over there and check out what you all are up to."

"I think you'll just have to trust us," Turnbull said. Without even eye contact with Doyle, who he assumed would back whatever play he made.

"Well," Gruber said. "Call me skeptical, but my mom always said to trust but verify."

"Your mom was Reagan?" asked Turnbull.

"Don't talk about my mom," Gruber said, suddenly angry.

"Let's talk about this situation then," Turnbull said. "You got a bunch of guys, but you aren't making a move, and I don't see you as the kind of guy who hesitates when he smells weakness. In fact, I think you probably love it when you're facing someone weaker."

"You better watch your mouth, boy," Gruber growled.

"Here's what I think, *boy,*" Turnbull said. "I think you don't have your heavy weapons and you aren't sure that these guys don't outgun you. Plus, maybe you were smart enough to figure out that me and my pal here probably didn't trust each other, so I probably have a shooter in the tree line."

"I can't believe you are so suspicious," Trevannian said in a stage whisper.

"I bet you got one too," Turnbull replied.

"Of course, I do," Trevannian scoffed, louder now. "And if Chief Inspector Gruber gets cute, my man will splatter his head with that atrocious haircut all over this dismal parking lot."

"If my sniper doesn't do him first," Turnbull said.

Gruber licked his lips, and behind him his men were looking around uncertainly.

"We are the police!" Gruber said. "You need to give up. It'll go easier on you if you give up right now."

"Get out of here, right now," Turnbull replied. "You are just meat."

"You really should leave," Trevannian added. "While you can."

Gruber stood there, and Turnbull could see him assessing the variables. Were there really snipers? Did these guys – fewer in number – nevertheless outgun his men? And what would it look like if he backed down.

Turnbull could see it in the man's eyes. That last one was the key question to the bully with a badge standing in front of him.

Gruber began to open his mouth but Turnbull's .45 was out and aimed at his face.

"Don't even twitch," he said.

"It's going down here, right now," Ross said into his phone. Colby paused on the other end.

"Did you hear me? Those SIS assholes came in and there's a standoff about to become a damn firefight!"

"I know, Johnny."

"You know?"

"Johnny, I had to tell higher what was happening. I had to."

"And they alerted the SIS! Why did you screw me? And what about Sorenson?"

"I need to retire with a pension, Johnny. And you should be concerned about your future too. Let it go. Let it play out. It's out of our hands."

"Piece of shit," Ross said, hanging up.

Gruber put his hands up slowly. Besides Trevannian, he was the only one without a weapon out. The other three of Trevannian's men had various semiautomatics, while the two in the van had AK-74s. The SIS men had their Smith & Wesson M&P Shield M2.0 pistols. Dworkin, Gruber's second-in-command, shouted, "Just be cool!"

Everyone was aiming at everyone.

"I guess we got ourselves a Mexican standoff," Turnbull said. "And I'll shoot the first one to say that's a racist term."

"Well," Gruber began. "What do we do now?"

"You come over to me, very slow, without doing anything stupid. And you tell your people to be cool."

"Be cool, everybody," Gruber said as he stepped forward.

At about five feet, Turnbull ordered Gruber to turn around, which he did. Turnbull approached and pulled the Desert Eagle out of his shoulder holster and tossed it across the lot, then pulled Gruber back using his manbun as a handle and pressed the Wilson Combat into his right kidney.

The two sets of henchmen continued to cover each other. Turnbull grimaced as he caught a whiff of Gruber's breath.

"Listen up," Turnbull said loudly. "This is not going to be the day where some or all of you die. Here's how this goes. Chief Inspector Gruber's guys toss me the three keys for their rides. Then we're going to go, with Chief Inspector Gruber along for a short ride. We'll let him out down the road – you know I don't want his nasty halitosis in my car."

"I'm gonna kill you, Chris," Gruber said softly. "Yeah, I know you. The FBI knows your name, which means I do too. I mentioned you to my boss. He says you've met, that you ain't that good, and to waste you. But I ain't gonna do it until after I've taken you to see Merrick Crane the Third. You remember that."

"Shut up," Turnbull said, leaning in. "But after this is over, you go tell your pissant boss that I won't need an escort. I'm going to come for him myself."

"Mad cuz he killed your lady, huh?" Gruber asked innocently. Turnbull pulled his head back hard using the manbun and Gruber groaned.

"Tell your bitches to give up their keys, Gruber, before I lose patience and start shooting, with you the first to die."

"You gotta get off my parking lot, damnit!" someone screamed. Turnbull caught a glimpse over Gruber's shoulder – the hobo was back, staggering toward the confrontation. A panicked SIS man pivoted and shot him three times, and all hell broke loose.

The AKs behind Turnbull in the open back of the van were firing outward, and the SIS men were all unloading their pistols. An agent took aim at Turnbull from the flank, where Gruber's reeking body was not in the way, and Turnbull swung the gun his way. Gruber elbowed him hard and wrenched his head loose, leaving Turnbull with a hand full of greasy graying hairs.

Turnbull fired. The shooter flew back as if punched, first once, then again. With all the shooting, the booming reports of Doyle's .357 still sounded above the rest of the fury.

Gruber staggered forward toward his Desert Eagle and swooped it up. Turnbull engaged another SIS agent and put two shots into his solar plexus – he flew back across the hood of one of the government sedans.

"Come on!" yelled Doyle, but Turnbull paused to take aim at the Gruber, who was running in a crouch, looking to dodge behind a sedan. Trevannian ran past Turnbull from the left while making for his own sedan through the hail of bullets. Turnbull fired. Gruber shrieked and fell forward out of sight.

Gruber was on the pavement behind the sedan, his hands grasping his buttocks, blood seeping through them.

"He shot me in the ass!" he hissed at Dworkin, who was already there behind cover.

The SIS men were scattering, their wounded leader not able to organize them – in fact, he was busy spewing obscenities.

Turnbull switched the Wilson to his other hand and pulled out his thermite grenade, and then he grinned.

He tugged the pin out and threw it as hard as he could muster at the sedan Gruber had taken cover behind. The spoon clattered on the pavement as Turnbull watched it fly directly into the passenger side window.

There was a bright flash and a roar and the entire interior glowed and ignited. The SIS men were running about, and Turnbull transferred his .45 back to his dominant hand, hoping to get another shot at Gruber.

This time he'd finish it.

"Move!" Doyle said, putting another shot downrange without really aiming as he grabbed Turnbull by the arm.

Gruber was still hiding, and the bad guys were over the initial shock of the burning car.

A round cracked over their heads and another chipped the filthy pavement in front of them as they ran low around the side of the arms dealer's van.

Trevannian's sedan took off, peeling out across the parking lot past the Chevy toward the far exit at the end of the bratwurst. There was a burst of automatic weapons fire – an AK family rifle – and the van roared to life. The firing was intense now, with the van the target and Doyle and Turnbull using it for cover as they sprinted to their own vehicle. It leapt forward, looking to follow Trevannian's sedan, but the firing at it increased and it swerved, crashing head-on into the Impala and crushing the front end as it came to a stop.

"Shit," Turnbull hissed. He didn't have to tell Doyle what to do. He pivoted right, firing several unaimed rounds from his .45 and, with Doyle beside him, made hard for the tree line.

12.

Kelly Turnbull smashed through the brushes, Danny Doyle just behind him and a blizzard of lead clipping through the leaves.

"Where are we headed?" Doyle shouted as a branch slapped his face.

"Away," Turnbull said, nearly tripping on a log. The thermite grenade's detonation had screwed his night vision but good, and the moonlight dappling through the canopy was minimal.

Target ahead, long weapon.

Turnbull raised his Wilson Combat .45 center mass on the dark figure with some kind of rifle to his immediate front. Doyle pushed him.

"That's Sean," Doyle snapped as he took the lead.

It was Sean, his sniper rifle in hand, not realizing how close he had come to dying.

"What the hell?" he asked as the panting men ran by him.

"Where the hell were you?" Doyle demanded, not slowing down. Sean kept up, falling into the slot in front of Turnbull.

"I was shooting at them," he protested.

"Big help!"

"It's a bolt action rifle, not a 240-bravo," Sean said as they continued to beat feet through the brush. "You can't suppress with a shot at a time."

Turnbull, the rear guard, paused by a tree. There were occasional shots from the Sausage Lot, and he heard one round zing through the trees. The thermite grenade had gotten the sedan burning big time, and Turnbull could see the flames flickering through the undergrowth. There were yells, and the noise of people breaking track.

They were coming. Probably with the long guns in their trunks.

Turnbull spun about and ran after his companions.

"They're on our ass," Turnbull said. "Do you know where the hell we're going?"

"The Zoo," said Doyle, stopping. They all did. Ahead of them was a tall brick wall, crowned by barbed wire. It ran parallel to their route as far as they could see in both directions, disappearing into the woods.

Turnbull glanced back. More noise.

"I used to come here as a kid," Doyle said.

"That's fantastic. Any idea how to get over this wall?" asked Turnbull.

"Gotta be a door or a gate somewhere," Doyle said, and he turned left and started running along the wall.

They made their way alongside the barrier for at least 100 yards, their eyes gradually getting used to the dark again. Their pursuers were still back there, but they were slower and, from their shouts and profanities, they seemed to be confused.

The three stopped to catch their breath, panting as they leaned on the brick.

"They're going to call in the cavalry pretty soon and seal this whole place off," Turnbull said. "We need to get the hell out of this forest."

"You guys," Sean said, holding his .30-30 in one paw and pointing with the other. "Look at that."

The wall had collapsed a few yards down, though not naturally. It appeared as if someone had taken a sledgehammer to it and beaten a man-sized hole in through the bricks. They trotted over and looked though. It was dark beyond, with bricks scattered on the ground.

"Who breaks into a zoo?" asked Doyle.

There was more noise from the way they came. Turnbull lifted his weapon up.

"I guess we find out."

The Zoo was mostly quiet, but there were cries of various animals clearly not native to New England. That made Turnbull feel a little better – at least the place was not abandoned, because if it was, the new occupants were more likely to be savage than the original beasts.

They got on the concrete walkway and passed a large bird exhibit near the hole. There was a racket as the occupants screeched and yelled at the intruders. It died down as the trio passed out of sight.

They walked instead of ran, taking time to listen. There was still noise from the other side of the perimeter fence, and it was only a matter of minutes before the SIS men stumbled upon the hole in the wall.

Enclosures lined each side of the cement path, some of which seemed to hold creatures and others that were empty. The walkway itself was a mess, covered with leaves and sticks.

"Stop!"

It was a woman's voice from ahead of them. There were four figures abreast across the walkway, two smaller and two larger. Two held some sort of clubs, the other two some sort of firearm. Turnbull's instinct was to kill them all, but he suppressed it, first because he did not want to make noise, and then second when he realized the quartet were wearing khaki uniforms with cargo shorts.

They were being challenged by younger, thinner Steve Irwin clones.

"We don't want to hurt you," the woman began calmly. "We are sensitive to the needs of the housing-denied community, but this is a safe space for animals and we need to ask you to turn around and go."

"We're not bums," Sean said huffily.

"He's got a gun!" said a different female voice.

There was a pffft sound and Sean shouted, then dropped his rifle. Turnbull's weapon was up and at them.

"If you tranq me, I'll blow your heads off," he snarled as he approached them. The two carrying tranquilizer guns dropped them to the pavement, and the others released their makeshift clubs.

"Damn it!" Sean said, pulling the .50 caliber dart out of his thigh. "I'm going to kick your asses!" Except he tried to take a step and had to be caught by Doyle.

"What the hell did you hit him with?" Doyle demanded as Sean swayed.

"Ketamine," the woman replied. "Sometimes people come in to get shot on purpose."

"Unbelievable," Doyle said, holding up his writhing friend.

"I'm cool," Sean said, slurring.

"Who the hell are you people?" Turnbull asked, and not nicely. The two big ones were male, though one had long hair and lipstick, and the other two appeared to be female. They were clearly frightened. These were not the usual drunken derelicts who wandered inside the wall.

The leader spoke up. "We're the zookeepers," she said. "We stay here now, to protect the animals."

"Can't you just leave the lion cage open and let them do it themselves?"

"The lions are all dead," she said, with an inflection of sadness. "There's no real police anymore, and before we started staying here people would come in. Sometimes they wanted to let the animals out. Sometimes they'd hurt the animals."

"Assholes," Doyle said.

"No, it's our fault for not teaching them about the rights of animals," the lead zookeeper replied. "We try to confront our own human and other privilege, but it's hard when some people don't understand."

"No, they're assholes," Turnbull said. "Okay, we need you to walk us out of here. Take us to the front exit and we'll be gone. Fair enough?"

"Okay," the lead zookeeper said. "You aren't going to hurt us or the animals, right?"

"You get us out of here and you'll be fine," Doyle said. "But you big guys, since you doped him, you carry him."

"I identify as a woman," the one with lipstick began, but Turnbull interrupted.

"You better identify as carrying him." They complied, and Doyle picked up the .30-30 off the ground.

Their night vision was much improved now, and they moved along the walkway as fast as Sean would allow them.

"I can't believe you brought guns here," the zookeeper said to Turnbull as they went. "This is a sacred space."

"You remember you shot my guy, right? You had clubs."

"Yeah," she said, as if it was obvious. "We have to protect the animals."

"Everyone's conservative about what they care about," Turnbull said.

The zookeeper's mouth dropped. "I can't believe you called me that," she said. "It's offensive."

"Just keep walking."

Turnbull passed a large enclosure evocative of the Serengeti with a large sign posted there that read, "THE GNU: DECONSTRUCTING A LEGACY OF RESISTANCE TO COLONIALISM." There was more text – a lot more – and Turnbull could make out a few words, like "cis-normative" and "hyperdecontextualized" and several instances of "racist." He did not stop to read it more closely.

"An animal-human interaction facility is an opportunity to confront and reexamine power relationships that silence oppressed beings, including marginalized people, and to confront and dismantle the structures that promote speciesism," the zookeeper said.

"I thought a zoo was about looking at animals," Turnbull said.

"Don't call it that!" she replied, annoyed.

"What?"

"A zoo," she said quietly. "That's offensive."

"Is there anything that isn't offensive to you? I think the gnus will get over it."

They continued on. There were noises to their rear, including those bird calls again, and the zookeeper looked concerned.

"Are there more of you?" she demanded.

"We may have company. They'll leave you alone, maybe. But we're going to be gone soon."

To their left was a large open enclosure that dropped about twenty feet down to a large pool of dark water. To the rear of the pond were gray rocks and formations – maybe fiberglass but stone-colored. The sign read "*Caimánes de Cuba*: A gift of friendship from the Cuban people to the people of the People's Republic of North America." There was a little crocodile drawing, and the Cuban and an earlier version of the PR flag were crossed together on it.

"Those are pretty vicious reptiles," the zookeeper observed.

"Tell me about it," Turnbull said.

"We don't have enough meat for them. Sometimes they eat each other."

"Small pond, two big gators. Bound to go poorly."

"Crocodiles," she corrected him. "Not alligators."

"What if they identify as alligators?" Turnbull asked. "Isn't misreptiling a hate crime?"

The zookeeper was not amused and did an about face. Turnbull followed.

They caught up with the rest of the group in front of the offset enclosure on the other side. It was an open field with rocks and caves at the rear. Over the waist high wall, Turnbull saw movement inside.

Humanoid, mid-sized, hairy.

Gorilla? Turnbull's weapon was up.

"Put that away!" the zookeeper snapped. Then she turned to the figure materializing out of the dark. "We're sorry, Frankie."

Frankie approached; he was a young male with thick black glasses dressed in a ratty fox costume.

He hissed at Turnbull. Behind him were several more like him in similarly shaggy suits, watching from the shadows.

"We don't believe in guns," Frankie said.

"I don't believe in whatever the hell you are," Turnbull said.

"Frankie the Fox and his friends live here," the zookeeper explained. "As fox-identifying otherkin, they feel the environment here is more supportive of their needs than the outside environment. We support and cherish them."

"I have a right to a home where I am validated," Frankie announced.

"You know he's not a fox, right? Do you know that, Frankie?" asked Turnbull. Doyle had stepped over.

"What the hell is wrong with you?" he demanded. "Get a load of this guy."

Frankie was mortified. "Maureen, they are denying my existence!" he squealed.

"What kind of anti-furry bigots are you people?" the zookeeper said, horrified.

"Dress up like that in my neighborhood and you'll get your ass beat," Doyle said. "What the hell is wrong with you?"

Frankie's snout, which was held on by an elastic band, was quivering. He appeared on the verge of tears.

"It's okay, Frankie," Maureen said. "This is a safe place for you and your allies."

"You need to take us out of here," Turnbull said to Maureen the zookeeper. "Because it isn't going to be safe for long."

"Loser," Doyle said to Frankie.

"Why don't you try it?" Frankie snarled – literally snarled – back at Doyle. "Come on. You might like it. Some of us are feeling yiffy."

"I don't want to know what that is," Turnbull said, walking away. "And you better not tell us."

"Maybe you belong in the racist red states where furries are literally murdered every day," the zookeeper said. She was genuinely upset.

"Furries aren't murdered every day in the red because they ship those freaks to the Kentucky border and kick them over into the blue," Turnbull said. "Along with all the other weirdos."

"Just go," Maureen the zookeeper said. She was literally shaking.

But there were voices to the rear. All eyes looked back.

"How far to the front exit?" Turnbull asked.

"Not far," Maureen the zookeeper replied. She and the other three were visibly nervous.

"Hey Foxboy, the guys behind us will do more than talk smack about you," Turnbull said to Frankie.

"Frankie, you and your pack, you need to hide in your dens," Maureen told them.

Frankie nodded and turned to go join his pack.

"They're gaining, and our stoned buddy is slowing us down," Turnbull said. "You all go ahead and get him out of here. I'll see if I can delay them."

"We don't even know how we're getting back home from here," Doyle replied. "How will we link up?"

"I'll escape and evade. Just go. Get him back and don't worry about me."

Doyle nodded, and the little band moved off the way they had been going, moving as fast as Sean could stagger.

Turnbull hopped the wall into the furry exhibit. There were cigarette packets and Diet Pepsi cans in the dirt. Weirdos and slobs, he thought. How hard is it to pick up your yard? He moved along the wall back toward the way he came.

He did not draw his pistol, at least not yet. One shot and a whole world of assholes would be crashing down on top of his head. He considered screwing on the suppressor, but he did not have time.

There were several voices now, coming down different parallel paths.

Turnbull backed off into the shadows as he tried to make a plan.

The first one to come into sight was a weaselly-looking man in a bad suit with a reddish goatee. His M4 was hanging limply in his right hand as he walked nonchalantly down the concrete walkway, looking around.

Goatee stopped a few feet from Turnbull, and pivoted to the furry enclosure.

"Who's in there?" he demanded, his weapon up and approaching the stone wall.

"Just us foxes," replied Frankie's voice from the darkness.

"What the hell are –," Goatee demanded, but Turnbull had him by the front of his suit and pulled him face first into the top of the stone enclosure wall. He bounced off and collapsed to the ground, bloody and not moving.

"You're welcome," Frankie sneered, and he turned tail and ran back to the rocks. He literally had a tail, a plush white one.

Turnbull hopped over the low wall and bent over to pick up the unconscious SIS man. Then he dumped his victim over the wall into the furry exhibit.

"Well, well," began a deep voice close to him. Turnbull saw the moving shadow in the moonlight and turned suddenly and violently.

Another SIS man, a larger one with a gray suit and no tie, was leveling his M4 at Turnbull, but he was too close for his own good. Turnbull's hand slapped the weapon hard, and it went flying across the concrete as Turnbull launched himself at the man's chest.

They fell backwards, Turnbull and the SIS man tumbling on the cement as they grappled. Turnbull kneed him hard in the side. The man responded with a vicious right to Turnbull's ribs. They scrambled to their feet, and Turnbull saw the man was smiling.

The combatants squared off at about five feet, and Turnbull knew he would not get his gun out in time if he went for it. But the man did manage to pull his Fairbairn-Sykes dagger.

"Come on," he said, grinning. He wasn't calling out for help – he liked this.

Turnbull hated hand-to-hand.

He feinted, and his opponent lunged. Turnbull caught his forearm and spun him around, bringing the man's right hand with his knife to Turnbull's front. The man tried to pull away, and Turnbull elbowed him solidly in the mouth. He managed to break away, and stared, enraged, and spit out a tooth.

"I'm going to gut you," he promised.

Now the guy was grinning and swinging his knife at Turnbull, who backed up across the road. The guy with the blade was not totally unskilled, and Turnbull had only his bare hands. Turnbull again considered going for his pistol and ending the conversation with a 230-grain exclamation point, but the man would have been on him the second his guard was down as he drew, and besides, the noise of the gunshot would have alerted the other SIS punks. That was only marginally better than having his guts spilled out all over the concrete.

"I'm gonna split you from throat to nuts," the man said, almost giddy at the prospect. Blood was pouring from his lip and a front tooth was AWOL.

"You won't do shit," Turnbull replied. "Except die."

The guy was not used to victims resisting – that made it much less fun – and he decided to end this right then and there. He charged, his black Fairbairn-Sykes dagger leading.

Turnbull had backed up across the concrete walkway all the way to the low wall of the off-set enclosure, where he stopped.

The guy with the dagger was pissed off and not thinking about anything except plunging it handle-deep into Turnbull's liver, and Turnbull knew it.

He pivoted as the guy came at him, jagging left and grabbing the man's blade arm as he passed. The guy went off balance and Turnbull let his momentum carry him forward to catch on the enclosure's low wall. For a moment, the guy with the Fairbairn hung there, teetering, caught between falling back to the walkway and falling into the darkness of the enclosure. It looked like he might be coming back, so Turnbull decided to give him a little push – really, a hard shove – to his chest. The SIS man tumbled over the wall, and he realized what was happening too late as he fell into open space, down nearly 20 feet into the water. There was a huge splash.

Turnbull's weapon was out now and he looked down. The guy was floundering in the black water, shouting and swearing, and generally making a hell of a racket. Perfect. That would draw attention soon enough.

But not just of the other SIS men. Turnbull could see it in the water, the V-shaped series of waves heading towards the man struggling in the water, swearing at Turnbull and not yet realizing that he had fallen into the crocodile pool.

"I'm gonna kill you!" the man bellowed as he tried to find purchase on the slimy floor of the pond.

Turnbull peered down and smiled. "I am not sure it's gonna work out that way," he said.

The man sensed something behind him and whirled around in the water just as one of the giant reptiles lunged forward. The man swung his dagger wide and planted it inside the reptile's scaly hide. But it didn't stop the crocodile, or the second one either. Turnbull didn't bother watching after the first bite. He heard more than enough, both of the man's screams and of the wet tearing and crackling ripping sounds.

There was his distraction.

Turnbull sprinted off the way the rest of the group had gone. It was about another hundred yards to the front exit, and he found the zookeepers standing there, but no Danny and Sean. He holstered the Wilson and slowed to a walk.

"What's going on?" the one named Maureen asked.

"I think I solved your meat shortage problem," Turnbull replied. "At least temporarily."

Even in the dark, the woman looked pale.

"Listen," Turnbull continued. "There are a bunch of really bad guys coming. I don't think they want you but don't take a chance they don't want to take out their frustrations on the nearest civilians, which you are. You have time to get undercover – they're gonna be busy over by the alligators for a couple minutes."

"Crocodiles," Maureen corrected him.

"I'm not sure how relevant the nomenclature is to the guy they're currently gnawing on," Turnbull said. "Listen, you don't want to be around when these guys come by looking for me and my buddies, so get out of the way. Go hide somewhere. They're after us, not you and not the animals. Just get out of their way."

Maureen nodded and Turnbull pivoted, then went out the front entrance, hopping the turnstiles. There were no more screams from behind him anymore, but he could still hear faint splashing.

Turnbull stepped out into the front entrance area of the Franklin Zoo, a wide patio of asphalt flanked by large signs containing trigger warnings, disclaimers of prejudice, and apologies for the Zoo's long history of oppressing and marginalizing animals, humans, and otherkin. The Zoo also apologized for using the word "Zoo."

Turnbull was looking around for Danny and Sean, but what he saw was a man with a SIG handgun pointed at his face.

"Don't you freaking move," Johnny Ross said. After watching the fracas in the Sausage Lot from a distance, he had hopped into his G-ride and just arrived a moment ago to hopefully ambush the elusive Chris coming out the front. His plan had worked.

The guy was about 10 feet away, and Turnbull assessed his chances of charging him and not ending up with a slug through his face. They were low. This guy seemed like a pro, wearing a suit but not giving off the vibe of a Hells Angel who sprung for an outfit at Walmart to attend his civilian sister's wedding to an accountant like the SIS thugs did.

"You aren't one of those schmucks with that Gruber clown," Turnbull said.

"FBI," Ross said. "I'd show you my ID but then I have the gun so I really don't care if you believe me."

"FBI, huh? Gotta say, not a fan."

"Oh, we can chat about your feelings later. We have a lot to talk about."

Turnbull squinted. The man looked familiar.

"I know you," Turnbull sad. "You tried to shoot me at Harvard."

"Yeah, you got my friend killed." Ross replied.

"No, those assholes in the bad suits shot your friend. If it makes you feel any better, I smoked them both."

"I didn't say you shot him. I said you got him killed. But it does make me feel a little better," Ross replied. "I want you to turn around because I'm hooking you up and taking you in."

"This is not gonna work out that way," Turnbull said.

"Oh yeah?" said Ross. "How is this going to work out?"

"Badly for you, if you turn around," Danny Doyle said as he put the .357 to the back of the FBI agent's skull. "Put down the SIG or you are all over."

"You should probably do it." said Turnbull. "We're not here to hurt you, though we will if you make us."

Ross's weapon stayed on Turnbull. "Your problem is that a gunshot is going to bring Gruber's flunkies running."

"This is a problem for you," Doyle said, using his thumb to pull back the hammer on the wheel gun.

"Oh, I see you met the Gruber crew," Turnbull said. "Well, there are a few less than there were an hour ago. And a couple satisfied alligators."

"Are you giving up the piece or am I doing this?" Doyle asked. "Because I am getting bored."

"Give it up," Turnbull said. We won't do you. You got my word."

"I'm supposed to trust a red?"

Turnbull laughed. "Oh, you think you know me. Would you trust me if I told you I was from the blue?"

"No," Ross said.

"Then trust me when I say I'm about a second from shooting you," Doyle said.

"The gun," Turnbull said. "Put it down."

Ross considered for a few seconds, then pointed the handgun upward.

"I'm going to put this on the ground now."

"Good," Doyle replied. "But don't turn around because if you see my face, I'm gonna kill you, noise or not."

"I don't need to see you," Ross said, not looking. "Your voice is pure Charlestown."

Ross bent over and carefully put the pistol on the ground, then rose back up and stared hard at Turnbull. Behind him Danny kept the revolver leveled at the back of his head. Turnbull could see Sean was wandering about, and he stopped before a sign and squinted.

"Wow," Turnbull could hear him say as he read. "Zoos are racist too."

"So, you're after the disc?" said Ross, hands up.

"We need to go," Doyle said.

Turnbull ignored the bank robber, intrigued at what Ross knew. "Why not, everybody else is. You, Gruber, I'm guessing."

"You know he's Merrick Crane's catspaw, right?" asked Ross.

"Yeah, and if he hadn't beat feet, he'd be a smear all over that parking lot," Turnbull replied. "I think I shot him in the ass, though."

Ross chuckled and continued. "I'm impressed you got with this guy behind me with the gun. He's a Leprechaun, isn't he? You guys are gonna knock over a bank and find the safe deposit box."

Turnbull assessed. "That's an interesting theory," he said.

"Yeah, I think I've got it all figured out."

"Except you don't know which bank," Turnbull said.

"Come on, we need to haul ass," Doyle said. Behind him Sean was looking at his fingers and marveling. At least he could stand upright, which was an improvement.

"I'll just alert all the banks," Ross said.

"All 200 of them in Boston?" Turnbull asked. "Nah, you don't want anyone to know that we're coming for this disc. It's a secret. And you don't even know when we'd do it. I don't need to hit it Monday. Maybe Tuesday, maybe Wednesday or Thursday. You can't shut down all the banks and you can't guard them all, because you can't tell the whole world what you're actually guarding."

"Maybe I'll get lucky."

"Well, you're not lucky right now," said Turnbull. "Do you even know what's on the disc?"

"Not my job to know," Ross said. "I'm just a cop."

"No," Turnbull said. "No one in the PR is a cop. You're all political, especially on this case. Go ahead and tell me the FBI wasn't political long before the Split."

Ross did not reply; he was irritated because Turnbull was indisputably correct.

"Can we just get out of here?" Danny asked. "This gun is heavy."

"Maybe I'll find a record of you when I get back to the office," said Ross.

"Yeah, probably not," Turnbull replied.

"So, what happens now?"

"Step away from the gun."

Ross moved away, careful not to turn around and see Danny's face, and therefore cut the last thin thread keeping him alive.

Turnbull picked up the SIG, dropped the mag and kicked it away. He jacked out the hollowpoint in the chamber, then slipped the slide off and tossed it to the left while tossing the frame to the right.

"Making you report a stolen gun would be a super dick move," said Turnbull. He had his Wilson out now.

"You boys get moving," he said to Doyle.

Doyle nodded and stepped back slowly, eventually lowering the revolver, then taking Sean and moving off the patio and down the street into the dark.

"Who's got you hunting the disc?" asked Turnbull.

"Oh, I've been loaned out, seconded to somebody very powerful."

I'm guessing it's one of Crane's competitors."

"You know, I'm used to asking the questions," Ross said.

"Are you used to having people point .45s at you? Now, is it a certain senator?

Ross smiled. "My principal is aware of you, Chris. Apparently, you've met before."

"If it's who I think it is, he's an asshole."

"Yeah, then you've definitely met before," said Ross.

"I'm going to take off now," said Turnbull. "I don't think you ought to follow me. I don't wanna kill you because you seem like a guy just trying to do his job, but if you get in my way, I'm gonna put you in a grave. Got it?"

"Oh yeah," Ross said. "Won't stop me though. I will get you. That's a promise."

"Think that over," Turnbull said.

Turnbull was walking around him now, the gun still on him, moving towards the street.

"Can you tell Senator Harrington that I said 'Hi'?"

"Maybe you can tell him yourself. Can I give you something?" Ross asked.

"What, advice?"

"I'll give you that too. My advice would be to go back to the red, but that's not what I want to give you. I want to give you my card with my cell number on it just in case we need to talk."

"Why not?" Turnbull asked. "There's nothing I love more than sharing my feelings."

"Left hand going into right breast inside suit pocket, okay?"

"Good and slow."

Ross moved his hand very deliberately into the pocket and found one of his business cards, pulled it out, then carefully placed it on the ground and stepped backwards towards the entrance gate.

Turnbull approached, picked it up with his non-gun hand, glanced at it, and stuffed it into his pocket.

"Good to meet you, Special Agent John Ross," Turnbull said. "Now, from here on, stay the hell away from me."

"You know I can't do that," Ross replied.

"I know," said Turnbull, still carefully moving toward the street. "I'm going to do what I have to do, and if somebody tries to stop me it's going to be thermonuclear war. So, if you make your move, make it without a bunch of civilians around, for their sake."

"Noted, Chris."

"My love to the senator," Turnbull said before turning and running after Sean and Danny.

Ross sighed, and found that he was relieved. It hadn't occurred to him that he should have been killed, but now he realized that that was the most likely result and that he had gotten off very lucky. There was more noise from the SIS men inside the zoo. They were yelling and shouting, dealing with whatever the hell went on in there. At least the screaming had stopped. He started trotting across the cement, picking up the elements of his handgun. His suspicion was right. They were going to knock over a bank. Chris had a point, though.

Which one and when?

13.

Sean was coming down now off his ketamine high, and he was able to walk, generally, on his own. They ditched his .30-30, rifle because it wouldn't have done for three dudes being seen walking around with a gun. They weren't PSF, or People's Militia, or Antifa, or any of the people the People's Republic authorized to be armed.

They headed in a northwest direction, through Roxbury towards Brookline, an affluent town bordering Boston itself. They were hoping the pickings would be better there for a set of wheels.

The pickings were slim in Roxbury. It had never really recovered from the COVID panic of 2020, and got worse after the Split. There was trash in the gutters. There were few cars on the road. There were also few people out, and the ones who were out were unsavory. On the upside, there were few People's Security Force patrols, and when there were it was easy to dodge into the shadows since the majority of streetlamps were broken.

They kept walking down the streets, glaring at anyone who glanced their way. The message was "Don't screw with us." So far, everyone had gotten it.

At the corner of some of the streets, bolted to the street signs, were new panels. "People's Community Watch In Effect," they promised.

"Narcs," said Doyle. "They pick some reliable people on the block and make them the PSF spies."

"I didn't see any signs like that in Charlestown."

"We don't go for that bullshit. You'd get your teeth kicked in if you even thought of it."

"Guess you guys aren't very popular."

"We never have been," Doyle said. "We aren't rich and we aren't polite and we sure as hell aren't woke. But we're used to being the outsiders around here. Guess that's why we stick together."

"And why you ignore the law?"

Doyle smiled. "Ya gotta make a living."

It was nearing two o'clock, and occasionally, maybe once every ten minutes, some explosion would signal that someone lit off a firework.

"I can't deal with this no Fourth of July hate," Sean said. He was much more sober now, and not sure how he felt about that. "This is Boston, the home of the revolution."

"Not anymore," Turnbull said. "There's been another revolution."

"I didn't vote for it," Sean growled.

Turnbull gestured at some Elizabeth Warren campaign signs on the side of a closed down restaurant. "Strongly Progressive" was her motto.

"She's the fake Indian, right?" Sean said.

"You can get arrested for saying that," Doyle said, laughing.

"I didn't go to law school or anything, but aren't we supposed to have free speech?" Sean complained. "Did they forget that part when they rewrote the Constitution?"

"It's in there," Turnbull said. "But what's that matter?"

"It's always the same," Doyle said. "The rich people do what they want and we go to jail."

"You know you're a bank robber, right?"

"Yeah, but I only steal from big corporations," Doyle said, a bit offended.

"That makes it better," Turnbull said.

"You're one sarcastic son of a bitch," Doyle told Turnbull.

"No, really. That makes it better."

"So, what's it like in the red?"

"It's harder in some ways. You sit around on your ass here and someone gives you money. You do that in the red and you get hungry fast."

"No welfare, huh?"

"If you want handouts, go blue. If you want to support yourself, go red."

"Yeah, the red states are sending all their scumbags and losers north," Sean said. "They tried to resettle some in Charlestown. That went badly for them."

"You are just an uncooperative bunch, aren't you?" Turnbull observed.

"Wicked uncooperative," Doyle replied.

"Car," Sean said. It was up the street, coming their way. They backed up into the shadows. Turnbull had his .45 out. As he waited, he noticed his ears were still ringing from earlier in the evening.

It was a PSF cruiser, obviously a re-purposed Boston PD squad car, and it passed them without detecting them.

"That's two in the last ten minutes," Doyle said. "I think we're getting near Brookline."

At the outskirts of Brookline, they saw a checkpoint run by the PSF.

"I guess they're keeping out all the lowlifes," Doyle said.

"That's us," said Turnbull.

"You know, they told us this is all about equality and equity and whatever, but it always seems some people are more equitable than others."

"The guys behind those PSF are the ones who created the situation that requires them to have PSF guarding their town," said Sean.

"You sound like a revolutionary, Sean."

"Maybe we ought to start one," he replied.

.

"I'll be happy just pulling off this bank job," Doyle said.

They went up several blocks and turned into Brookline on a side street. It was residential, with nice homes, all of which seemed to have relatively new sets of bars on the first-floor windows. Many of these yards had "Defund the Police" signs.

At the same time, most had multiple other signs out front planted in their lawns.

"We Believe In Science."

"Gender Is A Construct."

"No Person Is Illegal."

"Black Lives Matter."

"Brown Lives Matter."

"Red Lives Matter." In one yard, that was next to a "Warren for President" sign.

"Yellow Lives Matter."

"You know," Sean said. "I was at my day job at the transit department and I said I liked Asian chicks and my supervisor said that was racist. Fired me. If I like Asian chicks, how does that make me racist?"

"That's the thing," Doyle said. "I'm not sure it's supposed to make sense. They gotta make new rules all the time, and change the old ones, so they can trip you up. If the rules were simple, like 'don't be an asshole,' then all you gotta do is not be an asshole and you're okay. But then they can't get you, right? They got nothing on you if you know the rules and can play the game."

"I played by the new rules when I kicked my supervisor's ass after he fired me," Sean said. "They called the PSF, but I told them I was a chick and my boss had laughed at me for being trans. They let me go free, and he got fired. True story. That's why I'm officially on disability. The mental trauma of it all."

"Another car," Turnbull said.

They ducked behind a hedge in the yard of a large house whose owners believed a wide variety of lives mattered. The PSF car passed them by.

"We never see this many at home," Sean said.

"Either they are looking for us, or this is the kind of security you get if you're rich," Doyle observed.

"I doubt they are looking for us," Turnbull said. "I think we just wandered into a rich neighborhood."

"We came out here on a field trip when we were in fourth or fifth grade, remember, Danny?" Sean said as they moved back to the sidewalk. "The JFK library or museum or something."

"Yeah, I got in trouble for asking Ms. Schneider if it was true that JFK tapped Marilyn Monroe."

"You know they closed it, right? JFK's a racist or something," Sean said.

"Car," Doyle said, and they were back behind another hedge as the PSF cruiser passed by.

"This isn't working," Turnbull said. "We can't duck every five minutes."

"There's an alternative," Doyle said. He turned and looked at the house whose yard they had taken cover in. These people also believed various lives matter, and another announced "Non-Reproduction Is The Responsible Choice." A campaign sign planted in the lawn by the driveway near the garage urged readers to "Kick Booty With Buttigieg." The sign had, in the lower left corner, the stamps attesting that the People's Election Misinformation Suppression Committee had approved the message.

Turnbull sprinted over to the window of the garage and peered inside.

"They got wheels," he announced after sprinting back to them.

"Okay, how do we get inside?" Sean asked.

"And how do we deal with the residents?" Turnbull asked.

"We just need their car, and only for maybe a half-hour before we ditch it. We can tie them up, not tight. They can wriggle out of it before dawn. We're home, PSF gives them back their car, no harm, no foul."

"Except for the whole home invasion part," Turnbull said. "But I can live with that. Here's the question – what's the chance they're packed? If we did this in Texas, we'd be in for a storm of hot lead."

"About zero," Doyle said, assessing the façade of the house. "These guys made a big show of turning in their grandpa's old hunting rifles or whatever they had. It was all over the news, them doing their civil duty right after the Split. You know these guys, if they ever had a piece, made a production number of turning it over to the PSF."

"How about an alarm?" Turnbull asked.

"Maybe," Doyle said. "But a lot of the alarm companies just sort of stopped caring after the Split."

"Fine, you guys know how to break and enter?"

"You kidding?" Sean said, looking at Turnbull like he was stupid. "We used to do that all the time as teenagers, especially when the outsiders started moving into the Town. But we never went in hot – we always watched until we knew everyone was out."

"Let's check the back door," Turnbull said. They went around through the side yard into the fenced backyard. Conveniently, none of the houses nearby overlooked it because of the trees and the generous set-back. There was a pair of French doors, unbarred, on a brick patio with white plastic furniture. They appeared to open into the kitchen.

Sean went up to examine the lock.

"You and I subdue the inhabitants," Turnbull said. He pulled out the suppressor and screwed it onto the end of his Wilson.

"Where can I get a piece like that?" Doyle asked, envious.

"You're in the wrong freaking country, Danny," Turnbull replied. There was the sound of breaking glass. Sean had wrapped his fist in his jacket and punched through one of the windowpanes, and was working the latch.

"Subtle," Turnbull said as Sean pulled the door open.

Turnbull went in first, followed by Doyle and then by Sean once he unwound his shirt. Doyle had his 626 revolver in hand.

It took a moment to fully orient themselves, but there was a first-floor light on in the hall and they could see. The kitchen was clean, and there was a half-empty off-brand bottle of Chardonnay with a screw-top standing on the counter.

They could also hear several sets of feet coming down the stairs.

Turnbull moved first and fast, out of the kitchen and into the hallway.

Rounding the corner from the stairway, the foot of which was across the entry hall behind the front door, were a man and a woman in pajamas. The man, tall, thin, and quite clearly terrified, led his oddly similar-looking wife. He held a golf club.

The man took a look at Turnbull, and his eyes popped wide. He dropped the club and turned, pushing past his wife to reach the front door.

"Get her!" Turnbull shouted, lunging after him. The man was out the door and running down the walkway as Turnbull pushed past the hysterical woman.

The running man got about half of his cry of "Help!" out before Turnbull tackled him. Turnbull turned him over on the cement and the man was blubbering. Turnbull pressed the silenced pistol into his forehead.

"Shut up," he hissed. The man did, and after checking to see if anyone noticed, he dragged the escapee to his feet and marched him back inside, closing the door behind him. The woman was in the living room on a chair. There was a dreamcatcher on the wall, and a painting of a rainbow. There were actual paper magazines on the coffee table, including the latest edition of the re-established *Weekly Standard*. The cover story was "Time to Disestablish the United States." In the corner, it announced the magazine's September cruise.

"Sit down, brave Sir Robin," Turnbull instructed, pushing the man toward the sofa where he took his place. The homeowners were shaking.

"You got kids upstairs?" Turnbull demanded.

"You think we would breed?" the woman said, seemingly more offended by that than by their invasion of their home. "We're responsible people."

"Check anyway," Turnbull told Sean. "And find their cells." Sean went upstairs.

"Where are the car keys?" Doyle demanded.

"The what?" asked the man, confused.

"Car keys!" Doyle repeated.

"Kitchen," the woman said. Doyle turned and left the room.

"I understand your pain," the woman assured Turnbull.

"My pain?"

"The structural pain you and your people face every day that forces you to take actions like this."

"Stop talking."

"I just want you to know that we are allies in the fight against the kind of oppression that you and your friends have suffered."

"If you want to suffer, keep talking."

"Got 'em," Doyle said, reentering the room and holding a key fob.

"Are you stealing my car?" the man asked, eyes wide.

"It's not stealing," the woman snapped.

"Yeah, it's redistribution of wealth," Turnbull said.

"You know that we're conservatives," the man said. "But true conservatives. Like Bill Kristol."

"Don't care," Turnbull replied.

Sean was coming down the stairs with their cell phones.

"These two have separate beds," he laughed.

"I respect her sexual autonomy," the man said.

"We are committed to zero population growth," the woman added. "We're serious about undoing the earthdamage that mankind has inflicted, but while there are still human beings, we support the struggle for social and economic justice."

"I'd hate to see liberals," Turnbull replied.

"They all talk like that," Sean said. "All the rich ones at least. It's weird."

"You need to educate yourself," the woman said.

"You need to stop talking," Turnbull replied.

"With two beds, all they probably do is talk," Sean said. "Weirdos."

"You're ignorant," the woman said peevishly. "You should go to the racist states where they welcome your kind."

"Find something to tie them up," Turnbull said.

"Homeboy here will probably get off on it," Sean sneered as he turned to go back upstairs to look for something to use. The male remained noncommittal.

"I want you to listen carefully," Turnbull said. "I'm guessing you don't believe in guns."

"We don't," the man responded, sitting up straighter in his pajamas.

"Your problem is that I do, and that I know where you live. We're going to tie you up, but you'll probably be able to wiggle out of it soon enough. Once you do, you can report your car stolen. We'll leave it somewhere and you'll get it back. But you never saw us. If I find out you told the PSF about us, I'll come back and I'll bring my gun. Deal?"

"Why tie us up?"

"Because you're stupid and we want a headstart in case you don't listen."

"Can you at least leave our phones?"

"No."

"Well, I got something to tie them up with," Sean said jauntily. He was coming down the stairs with a couple sets of fur-lined handcuffs.

"What the hell is it with you people?" Doyle said, shaking his head.

"We enjoy interrogating the boundaries of our gender identities," the woman said, with a hint of pride. "Arthur is not afraid to be submissive. He rejects traditional concepts of manhood."

"I noticed," Turnbull said. "Hook these freaks up hand to foot and let's go." Then he turned to the captives. "I'm putting the key on the floor in the kitchen. It'll take you a while to inchworm in there, but you will be able to unlock yourselves. Just remember that I remember where you live and if I have to come back, you'll both be identifying as dead. Got it?"

They both nodded.

"Weirdos," sneered Sean as he set to work.

Turnbull did not bother pointing out that post-Split, it was the folks in Charlestown who were the weirdos.

14.

They crossed the Charles River over what had been the Boston University Bridge until it was renamed for Vice President Kamala Harris after the Split, but that did not last. After the unpleasantness that led to her removal – the media never went into detail, but rumor held it had to do with some tainted ice cream she had sent to the president on his birthday – it was renamed again, this time for Hillary Clinton. Except Hillary Clinton was extremely white, while Kamala fell within the BIPOC rainbow, and the college students infesting the area were instructed to protest, which they did, occupying the span for several months until, finally, it was not named at all. The sign the trio crossed under read, simply, "BRIDGE."

It was nearly three a.m. as they turned up what had been Memorial Drive and was now called 1619 Boulevard. The wide road skirted MIT, which had also been renamed. It was now the Massachusetts Institute of Technology and Societal Change – MITSC. The road should have been deserted, but it wasn't. The southbound lanes, separated from the northbound lanes by a green median that was now a home-deficited persons' encampment, were packed with demonstrators using stacks of Marshall amps aimed at the dorms to broadcast their message: "No sleep while fatism exists!" chanted over and over again.

They had no trouble on the drive back to Charlestown. The Prius had a Buttigieg bumper sticker as well as one reading "We

Apologize To All BIPOC Peoples." It did not explain what for; apparently that was assumed.

Turnbull flipped on the radio, which was set to the NPR station. The segment was lauding the courage of trans-racial individuals who were transitioning into a different, and presumably more acceptable race. Since they were being celebrated in the media, it was unclear why this act required courage. Elizabeth Warren was briefly interviewed, and she explained why it required bravery. "When you transition, you will be subjected to denial, and that's actual violence," she explained. "I know that pain and fear."

The next segment was a report from the border, where red provocations were testing the patience of blue forces. Related was the news that the racist red states were cutting back on the food they shipped to the blue. "It's clear that the hunger in the People's Republic is a direct result of capitalist manipulation of agriculture by the racist states," the correspondent intoned.

Turnbull changed the channel on the hour, seeking local news in order to see if the incident at Franklin Park was getting covered. It was not. The announcer – the first thing he did was announce their pronouns ("He/their") – went right to a discussion of how the celebration of the Fourth of July was forbidden. "It has been officially listed as a hate holiday," he explained. "Our People's Security Forces are going to aggressively respond to the violence that this former holiday causes. And it remains against the law to use fireworks of any kind."

"Good luck with that," Doyle said, chuckling.

They ditched the ride on the edge of Charlestown and walked back to Kate's place, arriving a little before sun-up. It was dark, though – the power was out again. They saw no PSF cruisers, and received no flak from the locals.

"We got time to sleep before we get to work today," Doyle said. "Tomorrow is D-Day."

Turnbull got to his room, where Teddy King was lying in one of the beds.

"Where the hell were you?" he asked. "The guns showed up but you guys didn't. Thought you might have gotten rounded up."

"Just a firefight, then a close encounter of the woke pervert kind," Turnbull replied. "Oh, and I fed another guy to crocodiles."

"Fun," King said. "I tried to watch a baseball game on the television but they called it off in the fifth inning because the pitcher was throwing racist strikes. So, not quite as interesting as your night."

"I'm going to sleep," Turnbull said, putting the .45 on his nightstand.

The next day, Monday, was for recon and preparations. All the Leprechauns at least took a pass through the block containing the People's Collective Financial Institution, noting key locations and the general layout. They did it around zero hour, 11:00 a.m., to best match the conditions of 24 hours later when they would do it for real. Kate herself entered the bank, masked and sunglasses on, and got change for a blue $100 note. The bill with Barack Obama on it broke into five $20 notes with pictures of Chief Justice Sotomayor staring back. Kate carefully noted the guards, the layout, and the lackadaisical manner of the employees, as she scooped up her money and departed.

"Happy Celebration of Independence from Racist Oppression Day tomorrow," the bored teller told her.

Kate got in the backseat next to Doyle and removed her face-thong and shades.

"Two guards, not really observant, Beretta 92s," she said. "But a shit load of employees, at least a dozen. And about a dozen customers. You need another body inside."

"We don't have one," Doyle replied.

"Yeah, ya do," she answered. "Me."

"Kate, I don't want you in on this. They could make you. You already went in there once."

"Yeah," Turnbull interjected. "But she was practically in a hajib. You could see less of her face than some of those women back in Kandahar. Danny, if there are two dozen employees and civilians in there to cover, we'll need another body."

"It's settled," Kate said. "I'm coming."

"Shit," Doyle replied. "You take front security, then. Can you even handle a HK417?"

"If we all do our jobs, all I have to do is carry it and look scary, right?"

They ran the route in and the escape route out several times with everyone in the vehicles. That way, no matter who was driving, they would know the plan. Doyle knew without being told that everyone had to know everything; the unspoken rationale being if a driver got snuffed, anyone else could get behind the wheel and go.

They ate sandwiches with nearly-undrinkable Equity Ale back at Kate's place. Clover the dog was begging for the odd tasting turkey. Subway was gone, at least in the blue, and the new place – called "Sandwich Shop" as part of the emerging campaign against the waste inherent in branding – was government-owned and distinctly sub-par. Turnbull handed over a piece of the vile turkey, which Clover sniffed and rejected. He tossed the mushy bread and mystery meat in the bag it came in and tossed them out.

"What's the agenda?" Turnbull asked Doyle.

"Weapons checks, mag loading, running through immediate action drills," he replied. The weapons and the associated gear were all out on the family room floor. "I'm going to do some retraining on weapons handling. Wish we could hit a range and zero everything, but it is what it is."

"These are wicked badass gats," Mikey Sullivan said through a mouthful of rancid sandwich. Except for Teddy King, no one else seemed to mind the food.

"They see them and they'll wet their panties," Torrey added.

"That's the idea," Doyle said. "Intimidation. They're too scared to do anything stupid for the three minutes we're inside. We walk in, do our thing, walk out and no one gets hurt. If we shoot, we've lost."

"What if we have to shoot?" asked one of the Jimmys – Turnbull was unclear which.

"Then you go hard," Turnbull said. "Suppress. We want the PSF hitting the floor, not fighting back. These are heavy seven point six two rounds. They will punch through a car body and out the other side. They need to be hugging the pavement while we get out. That's the goal if it goes south – get out. Over time, more reinforcements come, so they always get stronger. We can only get weaker, whether because we run out of ammo or they drop some of us. So, this is not a head-on slugging match. We will always lose that because they can always feed in more cannon fodder to the fight. We gain fire superiority for long enough to get in the cars and get the hell out of Dodge."

"Fire supremacy," Doyle said. "We have better weapons than the PSF and we're better trained. But over time, they have numbers. So, if it goes down, lay down lead like it's a damn hurricane."

Turnbull joined in the practice Sean the Marine ran covering combat reloading. It was old stuff to him, but it never hurt to practice. There were more rehearsals of the job itself, not just each of the crew's own job but that of others.

Doyle sent pairs of the guys out to the tailor to get their robbery duds. It would have drawn too much attention if they all went in together. Doyle had Turnbull come with him when his turn arose, and they walked through the neighborhood toward the shop.

People were out and about in the sun, taking what was, in effect, a four-day holiday. And there were decorations, red, white, and blue banners and bunting, though it was worn and dirty, as it was being reused. It was also against the law to sell Fourth of July decorations.

There were no hanging Celebration of Independence from Racist Oppression Day banners in Charlestown, nor any version of the ever-morphing People's Republic flag. But Turnbull did see several American flags, albeit old ones that still had fifty stars.

"Kind of risky," Turnbull said. "You bait these blues enough and they will come down on you."

"Screw them," Doyle replied. "Nobody tells us what flags we can hang."

Pat O'Brien was there with a small crowd, talking to his constituents. Doyle and Turnbull caught his eye and he excused himself to join them.

"You boys ready for tomorrow?" he asked.

"All set," Doyle replied.

"You let me know if there's anything else. You'll have the cars tomorrow morning."

"What's all this," Turnbull asked, looking at the crates in the back of a city pick-up truck.

"We're getting ready for the Fourth. Big fireworks show tomorrow night."

"Won't that draw the PSF?" Turnbull replied.

"No one gets into the Town without our say so," O'Brien answered confidently. "Especially the People's Security Force. They tried coming in last night after some kids shot Roman candles out of the monument. We turned their asses around and sent them packing."

Turnbull grunted, and considered. The illegal celebration of the illegal holiday might just provide a useful diversion for when he and Teddy King blow town with the disc. O'Brien turned back to his townsfolk and Turnbull and Doyle continued to the tailor.

The gray suit was cut generously since Turnbull would be wearing a chest rig with his spare mags and thermite grenades. They were all going without Kevlar plates, which meant less bulk and more speed.

"And sunglasses," Doyle said, handing him a pair of deeply orange-tinted Oakleys with a sleek black frame. "I always wore dark glasses overseas. It's intimidating as shit when they can't see your eyes."

Turnbull modeled his suit with the shades in the tailor's mirror. On his feet were black running shoes.

It should work – on first glance he was just another businessman. Once the Assaulter came out, the illusion would be dispelled.

"I'm good to go," Turnbull announced.

"How is your ass?" Merrick Crane III politely asked Wayne Gruber. They were across the Charles River from Boston in a suite on the top floor of Le Méridien Boston Floyd, formerly Cambridge. Below, on Sidney Street, a band of about a hundred marchers were chanting and banging drums protesting systemic racism, transphobias, and "hygiene hate."

In fact, his ass ached and even the pills he was gobbling weren't helping. He was not going to some hospital and having to explain why a chunk of his left butt check was gone. They would want him admitted, probably hook him up to tubes to pump in antibiotics. He had no time for that. He had Dworkin pack the hole with gauze and tape it up, then gobbled some Bactrim one of his men was taking for chronic prostatitis – hopefully that was the right antibiotic. And then he took some Norco and answered Crane's summons to the hotel.

"Well, it's just a scratch," Gruber said.

"I don't care about your ass, Gruber," Crane said, letting his true feelings show. "I gave you an assignment. You've given me messes to clean up."

Gruber licked his lips. Crane was smaller and weaker and probably unarmed, and his security was in the other room, yet Gruber feared him. Gruber noted that the three dead SIS men, including the one fed to the alligators, plus the several more injured, including himself, were less important to Crane than the political capital he had been forced to expend to ensure media and political silence about the events of the prior evening.

"I did not want to have to come here personally," Crane said, returning to his conversational tone. "It's dangerous for me. This town is run by my opponents. Yet I felt I had to impress upon you just how important you not screwing this all up is to me."

"Well, boss," Gruber began.

"Stop. I don't want to hear another of your prison cornpone monologues that takes ten minutes to get to the point. What are you doing, exactly, right now, to find this Chris and get me my disc?"

"We think he's going to rob whatever bank has it tomorrow," Gruber said. "We just need to find which one."

"And how will you do that, Gruber? And how do you make sure the FBI doesn't get there first?"

"We use the FBI," Gruber said. "We let them go ahead and we follow. Then we catch up when the time is right."

"You have access to all their systems," Crane said. "That access cost me a great deal to obtain, so use it."

"I have something for you, boss," Gruber said a bit sheepishly.

"What?"

"This," Gruber said, handing his patron a sheathed Fairbairn-Sykes dagger. "We all carry one in the SIS. We, the men, wanted you to have one." In fact, Gruber, finding himself with several extra knives due to their owners' violent demises, decided on his own to make the offering.

Crane took it, then pulled it out of the sheath to look it over. He re-sheathed it and put it inside his jacket.

"I am touched," he said, not sounding touched. Gruber offered a meek smile.

"My competitors are closing in," Crane said evenly. "And I want that disc and I want Chris dead."

"You can count on me, boss."

"Good, because if you don't perform, I will use this on you." Crane dismissed him with a handwave. Gruber left without another word.

Crane watched the protest march disappear down Sidney Street and looked at the Monday afternoon traffic that had built up because of the disruption. Normally, this kind of chaos would have made him smile, but he was already out of sorts because he had been slighted.

He had found through his sources that the radical caucus would hold a short-notice strategy conference in upstate Michigan in a few days at Mackinac Island, where they hoped their opponents would not get wind of it. Buttigieg was going, Warren, veep frontrunner AOC, and the rest of the women of the Squad. He corrected himself – Rashida Tlaib had transitioned to Raymond Tlaib. Crane made a mental note to obtain her pronouns before referring to him – maybe "him," maybe something else – in public.

But there was no invitation to Merrick Crane III. The man they turned to for the dirty work, the man unafraid to get blood on his hands – he was to simply be tossed aside as too embarrassing by the so-called radicals?

They were not radical enough. This was their problem. This was why someone truly willing to do what must be done embarrassed them. They never hesitated to ask him for favors. Exposing the favors he had done for them would, if they would not have implicated himself as well, ruin them.

Need a mob to manifest out of the blue to wreck an opponent's campaign launch? Call Crane to turn out the rent-a-thugs.

Need compromising photos of an allegedly gay male politico in bed with a conventionally attractive female model? Call Crane to get the model, unemployed since being fired from Victoria's

Secret's stable in favor of a 238-pound fat activist, to hook up with the victim and expose his cisnormativity.

Need an inconvenient husband/brother to go poof and vanish? Call Crane and have him wave his magic wand.

How he hated them. And how he needed them. What was required was something big, something he could claim credit for. Then they would welcome him back into polite society.

After all, one non-gender-specified individual's terrorist is another non-gender-specified individual's socially-acceptable terrorist.

BOOK TWO

.

15.

"Rise and shine," Danny Doyle said to Teddy King, kicking the supine radio host lying on the worn couch in the living room. "Get up!"

"I am up," King replied, grumpy. "I've been up running through the plan in my head for the last hour."

"You're pretty high-speed for a Harvard guy," Doyle said, walking out of the living room as King shouted after him, "I'm not Ben Shapiro!"

Turnbull was already up and in the kitchen drinking some of the "Unexploited"-certified coffee that Katie had brewed up. The red can looked like Folger's, but wasn't. Proctor & Gamble, the megacorporation based in Cincinnati that had once owned the Folger's brand, had moved its operations to Omaha post-Split and a "worker's collective" had taken over what was left back in the blue. The brand name had been dropped because the original James Folger, while not owning slaves as he brewed his beans in San Francisco, had nonetheless "failed to demonstrate anti-racist allyship" back in the mid-1800s.

"You don't like it?" Katie asked as Turnbull grimaced on his initial sip. Clover the German shepherd was watching with great interest as Katie pet his head.

"It's...," he began, then stalled out as he attempted, for one of the first times in his life, not to give offense.

"Piss water?" Kate had replied. "I know. The PR screws up everything, even coffee. You know they closed down Dunkin' Donuts?"

"This being Boston, that might start a riot."

"It kind of did. Must have burned a dozen PSF cars. That's when the PR pigs stopped coming around, for the most part. You know donuts are racist, right?"

"I kind of assumed it." He had another sip and winced again. He'd had better joe out of a silver bullet at NTC. That was the National Training Center out at Fort Irwin, before the blues took over California and converted it to the Nancy Pelosi Desert Tortoise Sanctuary.

"The guys are on the way," Doyle announced, walking into the kitchen in his gray suit. "Jimmy and Sully are bringing the cars."

"Did you get what you wanted?" Turnbull asked.

"Oh yeah," Doyle said. "Chrysler 300s. Two each. Big, heavy, fast, just what we need. Seamus's boys had to go out to the suburbs to lift them."

There was a pop outside. Turnbull's hand was at his Wilson, but Doyle's reaction was a smile.

"It's already starting," he said. "Fireworks for the Fourth. Tonight's going to be wicked loud."

"The government won't like it."

"Screw them," Doyle said. Clover the dog walked over and sniffed Turnbull, who was not sure what to do about it. Doyle called the dog to him.

"I'm surprised anyone's up at eight in the morning," Turnbull said as he relaxed.

"They probably never went to sleep."

"By tonight, Teddy and I should be long gone."

"I expect we'll be celebrating. This score should wipe our ledgers, get us all clear."

"Let's not count our money before we steal it. I'm trying to think if we missed anything," Turnbull said. They had rehearsed their roles and movements on a diorama Teddy King had built out of cardboard and masking tape five times the night before, going through the plan again and again until the troops revolted and insisted on going out.

"It's the Fourth Eve," Mikey Sullivan had complained. "It's a big drinking night."

"Every Monday's a big drinking night for you, you falling-down drunk mick," Torrey Sullivan had scoffed, and they were at it.

"Careful of the diorama!" King shouted, but Mikey pushed his brother and Torrey's ass flattened the representation of the bank. Finally, Doyle told them all to get the hell out.

"And don't show up in the morning smellin' like a distillery," he yelled after them as the boys went out across the front porch. "We need to be STRAC!"

Only the former Marine, Kate's brother Sean, got the term and he didn't care. He was busy arguing with Jimmy O'Connor about some nonsense as they hit the sidewalk and headed off for a night on the town.

"You sure about these guys?" Turnbull asked, surveying the scene.

"Oh yeah, they like their beer and booze and their brawling, but the Irish are good at a few other things too. They drove the Brits out with some handguns and kept them hopping in Belfast with a few ArmaLites."

"Well, who didn't kick the Brits out?" Kelly asked.

"Us, apparently. They stopped teaching the revolution in school after the Split."

"Let me guess. Racist?"

"Yeah."

"Why do you stay?" Turnbull asked.

"I think about leaving and then I realize this is where I belong. Went away into the Army, ended up in Afghanistan and the stockade," Doyle replied. "Katie and I were thinking about New Mexico. Maybe we'll do that after today and I square everyone away. But can you imagine me with cactus?"

"I think that's Arizona," Turnbull said. "But both places beat the PR."

"Why are you here?" Doyle asked. "Orders?"

"I guess," Turnbull replied. He powered down the last few miserable drops in his mug.

"Nah," Doyle said, shaking his head. "It's the action. For you, the action is the juice. A little patriotism too. And lost causes are irresistible. You sure you aren't Irish?"

Turnbull shrugged.

"For me, there's nothing else I'd rather do. Nothing else I'm as good at," Doyle said. He opened the hall closet and took out his HK417 Assaulter, then locked in a magazine. "Let's get set."

Outside, the first of the two 300s that would carry them downtown pulled up.

It was on.

Wayne Gruber was first in the door of the Tangier, kicking it open and stepping through with his Desert Eagle up. He didn't mind going first, and not just because it impressed his boys in the SIS. No, it gave him the opportunity to do some shooting and working out the aggressions associated with his injured rear end.

One of Seamus's men made to grab his 12-gauge pump from where it was leaning against the bar, but he had not been expecting a bunch of thugs to break down the door. In fact, it was not much of a door at all, old and warped – it didn't need to be strong because its real strength was Seamus McCloskey's fearsome reputation.

But Wayne Gruber did not much care about that, and he lined up the front sight on the chest of the kingpin's henchman and blew a silver dollar-sized whole though the man's sternum before the Irish gangster even laid his hand on the scattergun. The unlucky crook spun into the bar and collapsed in a heap. The other two gangsters froze, and Seamus looked up from his plate of bacon and eggs and Guinness with a stare made of pure hate.

"Dayum," exalted Gruber as he swept his muzzle across the tableau and his dozen men filed in behind him. "Did you see that?"

The Irishmen stayed sullenly and stubbornly silent.

"I love this gun," Gruber announced, his joy overshadowing the pain in his ass. The body on the floor twitched and then stopped moving.

"Who the hell are you?" Seamus snarled.

"The Grim Reaper, man," Gruber said. "I guess you're the boss man because you're the only one who's talking."

"You're all dead," Seamus said. "You know that, right?"

"But I'm the law," Gruber said proudly. He pulled out his ID. "We are the Special Investigations Section, and we are here to investigate. Johnny FBI wrote down that he showed up to chat with you, and we figured you'd know what was going on with a certain upcoming bank robbery."

"No one knows anything about anything," Seamus said. "Now arrest us or piss off."

"Arrest you?" Gruber laughed a venomous little laugh and leaned forward on the bar. "Boyo, we ain't that kind of cops."

Turnbull did a chamber check on his .45. There was a round in it, of course. He slid it back into the holster under his suit coat. The 300 swerved to avoid a Camry with a 117-color rainbow sticker in the back window and he fell against Teddy King, who was cradling his weapon and was absorbed in thoughts of his own. The most dangerous part of this whole mission was surviving Boston traffic, Turnbull reflected, even on a day when there was hardly any.

Turnbull looked at the selector switch on his carbine. It was set to "Auto."

"Time to rock and roll," Jimmy Sullivan said to no one in particular from the front passenger's seat

Turnbull, running scenarios through his head, said nothing as they plunged deeper into the city.

Johnny Ross watched Gruber and the rest of the SIS thugs leaving the Tangier as rapidly as they had entered it. He was in his G-ride parked across the street a block up, having figured that the Fourth of July, or whatever it was called now, would be a great time to take a bank score and thinking maybe the crew might show up for some last-minute guidance from the local kingpin. It was his best and only shot. But he did not expect Crane's flunkies to have gotten there first.

"Must have got into my JFCID notes and found out about Seamus," Ross thought as he drummed his fingers on the steering wheel. The dash was littered with crumpled Equity Ale empties to give his car the lived-in look that would help ensure no one paid much attention to him as he surveilled the saloon. The hateful brew itself he had dumped in the gutter.

They were inside ten minutes, and Ross had run through his options. Instead of rushing inside, he decided to wait even after he heard a shot. There were a dozen SIS punks, and even if he could have counted on back-up it would take some time to get there.

The SIS cars peeled away – they must have gotten something out of Seamus that motivated them. He hit the gas and pulled his sedan up to the front door and exited.

His SIG was out as he went through the shattered front door. The air as thick with cordite and copper over the usual rank reek.

A dead man, capped in the chest, lay crumpled against the bar. That must have been the gunshot.

He was the lucky one. There were two dead Irish muscle boys on the floor, zip-tied with their throats freshly cut bleeding out on the creaking hardwood floor. Neither stiff was Seamus.

Ross moved though the dingy saloon, weapon leading. He peered over the bar – nothing. Then he came around the corner where a plate of bacon and eggs and a half-empty pint of stout waited on the dark bar top.

Seamus was on the floor, eyes half-open and short several fingers. They lay scattered on the floor – one was a thumb. He had several penetrating stab wounds, including to his neck, all oozing red, but he was moving a bit. When Ross came into view, he groaned a bit too.

Ross assured himself the wounded man had no weapon, then went to clear the back room. He returned to Seamus.

"I'll call a medic," Ross said, doubtful it would matter.

"That son of a bitch," Seamus said. Apparently, the throat wound was not deep enough to do the job, though the other wounds might be.

"I know who did it," Ross said. "Don't move. Hang on." He took out his cell.

"You gotta warn them," Seamus said, lifting his mutilated hand.

"Who?"

"The boys," Seamus said, his voice weaker. "I think I talked. I think."

"What did you tell Gruber?" Ross said.

"People's Collective on Franklin," he gasped. "Eleven. I set that bastard up for a surprise though."

"They're hitting the bank at 11:00 and Gruber and his assholes will be waiting?"

Seamus nodded, and spit up blood on his lips.

"Cut my fingers off, but I set him up," Seamus said, smiling a little.

"What do you mean?"

Seamus was fading. "You gotta warn them," he said. "You're from here. You gotta warn Danny."

"Shit," Ross said, turning and running out the door.

"My stop," Sean said, bailing out of the white Chrysler 300 at the west corner of the block on Franklin. "See ya, sis."

Katie, Doyle and Jimmy O'Connor, who was driving, were inside. The black 300 behind them was idling. Sean stepped out of the white sedan wearing a mask and blue coveralls that hid his chest rig. Sean was the only one not in a suit.

He carried a large green canvas bag, upon which he had stenciled "TOOLS" in black block letters. He started toward the entrance to the dual use business/apartment building at the end of the block. A bum lying against the façade said something to him which he ignored as he took up his position overlooking the Pearl Street intersection and Post Office Park.

Sean keyed his mic. "Southwest radio check, over."

Doyle came back. "Lima Charlie, out."

Franklin Street ran one-way, northeast to southwest, and they had to pull all the way around the block again. Traffic was light. When they completed the circuit, entering back onto Franklin up the road two blocks, Mikey Sullivan hopped out of the black 300 at the northeast corner, his suit covering his chest rig and his weapon up underneath. He took up his position by a streetlight pole, pretending to be focused on his phone, and completed his own radio check.

He was Lima Charlie too.

The white 300 started moving, and the black one with Jimmy Sullivan and Torrey Sullivan (who drove), Teddy King, and Kelly Turnbull pulled back into the street behind its companion. The two-car convoy approached the People's Collective Financial Institution like sharks closing in on their prey.

Turnbull's navy-blue suit fit perfectly, considering that Seamus's guy had cut it so that his Kevlar vest and multiple loaded 7.62mm magazines would not be readily apparent, at least on a cursory glance. He had an elastic balaclava around his neck to use as a flu mask and dark sunglasses. You had to look close to see the Motorola radio earpiece. His carbine was on his lap; it would hang under his jacket. His black briefcase carried his cutting tools. His shoes were black trainers. The rest of the entry team was done up the same way, with only the color of their suits different.

Nothing flashy. Unless you looked hard, they would seem like regular businessmen, definitely members of the patriarchy, but not exceptional. People who were part of the problem in general, according to the PR dogma, but not a problem in particular.

The two cars came to a stop in front of the People's Collective Financial Institution, knocking over the orange cones with signs on them that had reserved those spaces. The night before, one of O'Brien's men had dropped them there with handwritten signs reading "RESERVED FOR OPPRESSED DIFFERENTLY ABLED WOMXYN OF COLOR." People had obeyed the signs, not finding them unusual, preserving the open parking spaces for the bank robbers.

All but the drivers cleared the vehicles and marched toward the front doors of the bank. Jimmy and Torrey stayed at their places, engines idling, carbines next to them, monitoring the PSF band radios that Seamus had supplied. There was a call about a racist basset hound near what had been Faneuil Hall before its name was changed to "Equity Hall," but otherwise the radio traffic was mostly administrative minutiae regarding the parade. The march had just gotten underway and the only issue was some feminists who were lying down in front of the floats to protest something or other.

"This is Two-Charlene-Seven," one squad called. "We are moving to interface and hear their voices, over."

"Validate them and request to them if they would consider moving out of the parade path, Two-Charlene-Seven," the captain called back over the ops frequency. "One-Anna-Twelve, assist Two-Charlene-Seven. Over."

Two-Charlene-Seven called back to suggest this course of action might suggest an oppressive patriarchal power relationship, and the discussion continued as the parade apparently waited for a resolution so it could proceed.

Turnbull was first in through the front door, and he spotted guard one immediately. The guard was looking at his cell phone and apparently playing some new version of Candy Crush that integrated intersectional identifies into the game somehow. Turnbull went past him. Jimmy moved toward the guard and loitered nearby.

Doyle spotted the second guard, who was gender indeterminate with a blue pageboy. Xe was chatting up a young woman. A worn Beretta hung by xir side. Teddy stepped toward xir.

Turnbull continued forward through the dozen or so customers waiting in the various lines. At the head of one line, the hefty teller was accusing the baffled man at her window of "fatism" for expressing impatience as she finished chewing on the hash brown she had ordered at Burger Person of Royalty, formerly Burger King.

Doyle spotted the manager pacing back and forth on his phone, talking excitedly about some personnel issue. Satisfied the conversation was not about the pending bank robbery, Doyle waited patiently as Teddy took up position by the blue-haired guard and Katie stood off to the side of the front door.

Turnbull paused by the door to the back area and turned toward Doyle. The manager finally hung up.

With all eyes on him, Danny Doyle glanced at his Timex, then hit the countdown timer.

Ross drove like a madman through the streets into the city, offending even the notoriously awful Boston drivers. He had called an ambulance, but expected it to find Seamus bled out if it showed up at all. The dispatcher had asked him to confirm the address, as if it was somehow proscribed. He had also called Colby, who promised to mobilize the office. The FBI was not a first responder organization, and there was no way he was bringing the People's Security Force into this – that was an invitation to disaster. Ross hung up and punched it – he was maybe 60 seconds out. And he was on his own.

.

Danny Doyle nodded, and everyone nodded back.

Go time.

Jimmy Sullivan pulled out his M1911A1 and slammed the heavy butt into the back of the head of the guard playing his video game. The man went down, his phone skittering away.

The blue-haired sentry stopped flirting and turned, xir hand reaching to the Beretta, but Teddy King was there, carbine out and in xir face. Xe froze.

"Don't freaking do it!" Teddy shouted.

The guard looked at him with a hint of recognition, but King yelled "Get down!" and xe complied.

Turnbull's HK was out now, muzzle up, from under his coat too. Doyle nodded. At the door, Katie had produced her weapon as well, and she stood there, masked, covering the prisoners. The civilians, customers and workers, gasped as the reality of the takeover dawned on them.

"Down down down!" Doyle yelled. "Get the hell on the floor! Move!" The civilians began to comply, some sobbing, kneeling, and lying flat as the robbers' weapons swept over them.

Jimmy knelt and kicked away the guard's Beretta. He produced some zip ties and hooked up the semi-conscious guard.

King covered the nonbinary sentry as xe went to the floor, then rushed up and placed his knee on xir spine and the carbine muzzle to the back of xir head. With his left hand, he took the Beretta and tossed it aside, mumbling, "Stay cool, stay cool, no one gets hurt."

"You!" Doyle shouted, gesturing with his muzzle. "You're the manager?"

The man was too terrified to speak with the German assault rifle in his face. He nodded, fast.

"Come here." Doyle grabbed him by the collar of his cheap suit. His lapel bore a button, in the bank's colors, reading "We Apologize For Our Legacy Of Oppression." Doyle tossed him to Turnbull.

"Open the door," Turnbull said, dragging the man to the gate through the counter into the back. The man fumbled with his keys.

"Hurry," Turnbull snarled. The man kept fumbling.

"You want me to shoot him?" Teddy King asked. He was holding a briefcase.

"I don't want to shoot you, so I'll give you ten seconds to open it," Turnbull said. The manager found his key, slipped it into the lock and opened the door.

Teddy King and Jimmy followed, Jimmy with his own briefcase.

Inside the back area, they split up – Jimmy and King broke left toward the money. Turnbull, still holding the manager by the scruff of his collar, went right toward a barred grate – the metal door was open but the interior grate was closed. Beyond the bars were three walls of light-gold hued safe deposit boxes.

"Open it," Turnbull growled, his rifle prodding the supervisor as he stood before this next lock. The manager set to work finding the right key.

"Listen," Doyle said, having climbed up on the teller counter, where he was now walking. His HK417 was out in front of him in his right hand, and the black assault rifle served to silently punctuate his comments. "You tellers back here, come around, and get on the floor out front! Don't be stupid, don't be a hero. Everyone slide your cell phones to the far side of the lobby – go on! Do it!"

The tellers began to move out from under his cover on high. The customers began sliding their phones across the white granite floor. Out front, from her position by the front door, Katie covered them with her rifle.

"Don't look at me, look at the floor!" she shouted when she saw a face glance her way. Loud commands, no invitation for discussion, thorough fear – those were key to asserting and keeping control. Disorient and intimidate – it only needed to work for a few minutes, but done right it could keep any would-be intervenors from forming an action plan. Luckily, in the PR, it was safe to assume none of the hostages would be carrying concealed. If their crew had tried this in Dallas, the situation would have probably already devolved into a massive firefight.

"Do what we say and you get out of this alive!" Doyle said. "You go home to your families, your loved ones. Remember, this is not your money. It's the People's Republic's money! And it's fiat money. It doesn't really mean shit anyway."

"I love when he does that part," Jimmy said to King in the back in the vault as they stuffed one of the canvas duffels that had been packed inside his briefcase with stacks of United States currency.

"Yeah, it's classic," King replied, jamming in more stacks of hundreds.

Turnbull pushed the sweating manager through the now-open grate and then down onto the floor. The traumatized executive crawled into the corner.

"Keep your eyes shut and face the wall," he said to the manager, pulling out Strickland's key.

"Well," Wayne Gruber drawled into his phone. "It's going down now and it's going off. They'll bring it out of the bank right into our hands."

"Excellent," Merrick Crane III said. "Make a scene, Mr. Gruber. Make a point. Casualties are irrelevant, and we don't need any prisoners to talk about what we confiscate."

"Don't you worry about that part, Chief," Gruber replied, grinning.

"Call me when you have it," Crane said and disconnected.

Gruber did not put down his phone quite yet. He made another call, to the People's Security Force headquarters.

"Lemme talk to the captain," he said. "This is Special Inspector Wayne Gruber of the Special Investigations Section of the

Department of People's Justice, so you might want to do that right this minute."

There was a pause until the captain came on the line.

"Now captain, I'm going to need you and your boys to back us up on a little op we're pulling at the People's Collective Financial Institution on Franklin. Some mean hombres are walking out of there in a couple minutes and me and my boys mean to take them. So, you set up a perimeter..."

The captain began talking and Gruber gritted his teeth.

"Now listen you dumb son of a bitch. I told you who I am and I told you what to do and I don't care about your parade or any other damn thing. If you don't do it but quick, I will tear your fingers and toes off one at a time with a pair of pliers. Do you read me?"

The response was satisfactory. Gruber hung up and looked at the phone mounted on a holder on the dash – ETA was one minute.

"We're going to get it on," Gruber said cheerfully, despite his buttock throbbing.

"What are there – four of them?" asked Dworkin.

"That's what Seamus said. "With handguns."

He had a G36 rifle on his lap – his men had M4s. The robbers were outnumbered and outgunned. Gruber smiled. Seamus was neither as tough nor as smart as he had thought he was.

Gruber pulled out his Desert Eagle and confirmed there was a round in the chamber, then slipped it back into its holster. Behind him, Dworkin and another of his thugs were readying their rifles.

"Boys," Gruber said. "This is gonna be fun."

Turnbull's key unlocked safety deposit box number 533's aluminum door with no trouble at all. There was a separate grey steel insert inside that held the goods. Turnbull pulled out the 18" metal insert and carried it to the table in the center of the room.

"Eyes to the wall," he snapped at the prone manager. He put his rifle on the table too.

There was a lid on the box with a metal clasp, but no additional lock. Turnbull opened it and pulled up the lid.

The box contained a piece of paper that read "IF YOU ARE READING THIS I AM DEAD. I TOLD YOU THERE WAS A CONSPIRACY AGAINST ME. CONGRATULATIONS!" Turnbull put the note aside on the table.

There were some insurance papers, an antique watch, and an old-style DVD with the handwritten label "MATHEMATICAL PROOF OF EXTRATERRESTRIAL EXPEDITIONS TO EARTH." And there was also a thumb drive with a piece of paper taped to it. On it was the word "KRAKEN."

"Bingo," Turnbull whispered to himself. The drive went into a pouch over in the front of his chest rig between a couple of his dozen 7.62mm mags.

Turnbull put the other contents back into the metal insert and took out one of his thermite grenades. Turnbull did an about face and walked to the slot, pausing to use his feet to push the briefcase and tools right underneath box 533. Then he pulled the pin on the grenade, dropped it inside the insert and slid the insert back into the slot.

"Come on, get up," Turnbull said, roughly taking hold of the shaking manager and pulling him to his feet.

Grabbing his HK417, he walked out the doorway, pushing the manager through and shutting the solid door behind them. The PR authorities would eventually figure out what box he was after, but by melting most of the boxes along that wall into one glob of metal he could at least be sure that it would happen long after he was back in the US of A.

"Ninety seconds!" shouted Doyle. Turnbull moved out toward the front of the bank, passing Mikey and Jimmy packing wads of American cash into the duffels inside the vault.

Ross knew every street in Boston, and more importantly, he knew which to avoid when he wanted to get through town fast. He parked and was out of his car, which he left across from Post Office Square, and took off running northeast toward the bank.

A man in a suit ran past Sean as he stood by the building at the southwest corner. That was weird, but not worth calling in. Maybe he was late for a massage. Sean kept watching outward. Two PSF cruisers rolled up by the square and stopped in the intersection. There were a couple of unmarked cars arriving too, and lots of guys getting out, guys in suits.

With M4s.

"Ah, shit," Sean hissed, keying his mic.

Nothing but static.

"Sixty seconds!" Doyle yelled. He scanned the hostages – they were properly cowed and submissive. Turnbull appeared and gave a thumbs up. Back in the rear, there was a low roar – probably the thermite grenade taking out the safe deposit boxes. But where were King and Jimmy?

But a moment later they appeared, each weighted down with two duffels and their rifles. King's duffels seemed almost as big as he was, but the erstwhile radio host would be damned if he let anyone else see him struggling under the weight of a few million dollars in US scrip.

They dumped the duffels on the white granite floor before Jimmy turned and rushed back into the vault for the last one.

There was no need to explain what to do. Turnbull took up one, easily hefting it over his shoulder. Doyle nodded at Katie, who trotted through the hostages to pick up hers, then returned slowly to the door position just as Jimmy came out with his duffel.

"Hey Chris," King said, handing Turnbull an ample stack of bills. "Just in case. For our trip." Turnbull stuffed it in his pocket. Cash was always useful.

"Keep down, keep quiet, keep alive!" Doyle shouted to the hostages as he hopped from the teller counter down to the floor and picked up his duffel.

Then he took out a playing card and lay it on the teller's counter. The spunky leprechaun smiled, as did Danny Doyle.

This was a score to be proud of.

Gruber had split his 15 other men and four cars into two teams, one to come from the northeast, the other from the southwest. The PSF would hold the perimeter – he did not need any wannabe cops getting in their way during the action, or especially in the aftermath.

"Now, I need you to hit the jammer," he told Dworkin, who was in the backseat, his M4 locked and loaded.

"That will take down our cell and radio comms too," Dworkin said. "You sure?"

"Oh, I am sure," Gruber said, smiling. "We wait until they get in their cars. We take 'em there cuz it's harder to fight from inside a ride."

"What about civilians?" asked Dworkin.

Gruber laughed, as he popped open his door. "Ain't no civilians, boy."

16.

Turnbull was at the front door of the bank, with Katie still watching the prostrate prisoners. He had his duffel over his back just like the other four did. Turnbull scanned the street through the smudgy glass – lots of civvies walking by, but none seemed to notice what was happening inside the branch. The two Chrysler 300s were out front idling – he could see their exhaust.

"Black and white, we're coming out. Pop the trunks. Northeast, southwest, we clear? Over." Doyle said into his mic.

Nothing. Dead air.

"Where are your boys?" Turnbull said, cradling his HK417. His earpiece had emitted a low hum and nothing more.

"Comms are down, but the cars are right there," Doyle said, looking through the window.

"I didn't hear you over the air," Turnbull said. "Why are the comms down?"

"Comms go down," Doyle said.

"We need to go," King said urgently.

"What are we doing?" Katie asked, still watching the hostages.

Turnbull took charge. "Teddy, Katie, out to the cars. Get them to pop the trunks. Go!"

Jimmy and Katie each pulled down their masks and hid their weapons under their suit jackets. They pulled open the front doors and stepped out onto the sunlit sidewalk.

No one, except for a bum sitting on the sidewalk with his back against the façade, noticed the two figures in suits with duffels over their shoulders walking across the wide sidewalk to the waiting Chrysler 300s. The hobo amiably wished them "Merry Christmas!"

The sedan windows were all down and, as Katie approached the passenger side, Jimmy O'Connor asked, "Why didn't you call on the radio?"

"We tried. Pop the trunk!"

"I don't like this!" Jimmy said. His weapon was across his lap.

"They're coming out," Dworkin panted as he, Gruber and another two SIS men ran toward the northeast up the opposite sidewalk from the People's Collective Financial Institution branch. "I see two on foot, no visible weapons but a couple duffel bags. And they got two cars!'

Gruber and the rest were using the parked cars and trucks as cover during their approach. The leader knelt behind an elderly Buick. This did not square with the info they had forced out of Seamus. But the SIS crew was committed now regardless.

"Let them get in the cars," Gruber said, grinning. He still had the element of surprise. "Make sure we wait until they are in the cars."

"The jammer's on," Dworkin said. "I can't call the other guys." Another team was heading northeast on the bank's side of the street. The other two sets of four were moving southwest on opposite sidewalks to converge on the bank from the far intersection.

"Let's get closer," Gruber said, sprinting toward a Ford panel van parked a few meters ahead.

Four guys in suits rushed past Mikey Sullivan on his side of the street, and there were four more across the way. They paid him no heed, as his automatic rifle was hidden under his jacket. Their M4s, in contrast, were out, and civilians were starting to notice and to scatter.

"Entry team, entry team, we got cops or something coming, over," he said into the mic as he watched the eight SIS men heading toward the bank.

Nothing. Dead air.

Mikey keyed the mic again.

"Damn it, they're coming!"

Ross was about four storefronts from the bank when two of the robbery crew appeared, a male and a female. Each hefted a duffel and, after a brief exchange with the respective drivers, dumped their bags in the trunks and went and got into the respective backseats. He had not seen weapons, but that didn't mean anything.

He drew his SIG 226, keeping it low by his side, but one pistol against at least four robbers, probably with superior firepower, was a NO GO at this station. Moreover, there were dozens of civilians walking along the sidewalks, oblivious to the threat.

"Go on," he said to himself. "Go, go, get the hell out of here!"

Then he saw movement on the other side of the street. There was a group moving in, and they had rifles. They were wearing suits, but not looking like guys who normally wore suits.

SIS.

"No, no, no!" he said to himself. "Not here. *Not here.*"

Sean McGowan watched the eight guys in two groups pass him heading toward the bank. It was clear comms were down, whether by malfunction or because someone was jamming it, and it was also clear that his sister Katie, Danny, and the rest were walking out of the score and into an ambush. He looked over at the PSF cruisers, now numbering four, blocking the intersection at the far end of Post Office Square to his west.

Franklin Street was one-way running toward him at the southwest. That roadblock had to come down if the crew was to have any chance of fighting its way out.

He knelt down and opened his tool bag. The HK417 inside had a grenade launcher slung under the barrel, and he had ten 40mm grenades.

Teddy King slipped into the backseat of the black 300.

"We get the money?" Torrey asked.

"We got a shit ton of money," Teddy King said, his black HK417 out and on his lap.

Torrey laughed. "Walk in the park. Where's Mikey? He's supposed to come down to us."

Teddy King twisted around to see.

"Oh shit," he blurted out.

"Okay," Doyle said. "Let's go."

Jimmy nodded, pulled down his mask and stepped out first, heading to the back 300, duffle over his back, rifle concealed.

"You next," Turnbull said, his HK417 still out and the duffel over his shoulder. Doyle nodded.

Doyle stepped into the sun, and took a couple steps forward to the white 300. Katie was in the backseat. He'd take shotgun, and he placed his hand on the door latch.

Turnbull pulled down his bandana and went out the door. The sunlight did not much affect him since he still had his sunglasses on. He was riding in the rear car, the black 300, and he pivoted toward it. Teddy was in the back, moving around, more agitated than usual.

Why?

He spotted them as a Blue Cab – Yellow Cab had changed its name because that color had been declared "racist" – moved forward. The ad board on the roof, for a local "Non-Cis Gentlebeings Club" called "Fluid" had blocked his view. Now, as the taxi pulled away, it exposed the four men in suits moving down the opposite side of Franklin Street with M4s.

Turnbull dropped the duffel and whipped up his HK417 from under his jacket to his shoulder.

The selector switch was still on "Auto."

Turnbull's first burst was long and sustained. The fine German engineering worked as promised – the extra-large gas ports ensured that there was plenty of pressure to cycle the heavy .308 rounds through the system. The roar from the short 12" barrel was incredible, like a jet engine echoing between the tall buildings. This had the salutary effect of driving the terrified civilians filling the sidewalks to scream and take cover.

The Trijicon ACOG optic worked well, though his sight picture disintegrated into a useless shaky blur by the time Turnbull finished his initial ten-round burst. Three to five round bursts were standard, but Turnbull wanted to make a statement.

He did.

The first part of the statement consisted of three heavy rifle rounds tearing into the torso of the lead SIS man. The first bullet hit dead on his Kevlar chest plate, and he might have survived that, albeit with a shattered breastbone. But the second bullet hit above the plate and vaporized the top of his sternum and everything through to the spine. The next round sliced through his throat, severing his esophagus and blowing out his C-6 and C-7 vertebrae before passing through and into the face of the guy behind him. The round did not punch through the back of the second man's skull, having dumped most of its energy into the first guy's bones and in the frontal skull of the second. The round pinged around the man's brain pan even as he fell dead on top of his comrade.

Two SIS thugs to the northeast dived as their friends were shot to bits, and Turnbull's remaining rounds shattered the windshield and ripped apart the hood of a Ford Taurus next to them.

One of the SIS men on the bank side of the street to the southwest, a thick and tall one, raised his carbine and began squeezing off shots down the street at the shooter. Turnbull heard the crack over his head – the 5.56mm rounds were going high – and he pivoted. He squeezed off a three-round burst, then another. The first trio of bullets hit the shooter, but he was still standing – unsteadily – when the last three killed him. Turnbull fired off the remainder of his HK proprietary 20-round polymer mag, then dropped to his knee behind the cars for a combat mag change as the street erupted in a hurricane of lead.

Ross watched as a very big robber opened up with some sort of automatic rifle – it looked like an M4/M16 platform but that sound said it was not spraying any puny 5.56mm rounds. He blinked, and it seemed to him he had seen the man before.

Chris.

His 226 felt both heavy and useless.

There were still civilians in the area, lots in fact, and they were scattering or dropping to the pavement. The smart ones were taking cover inside doorways or behind anything solid. The dumb ones were running scared.

Across the street, Ross saw that some SIS men were opening up – one of them was Gruber, and the headman had a distinctive German G36 rifle. There were a couple of women in between them and the bank robbers, and first one of the women went down, and then the other, as Gruber sprayed.

Ross considered trying to drop the SIS man, a long shot and a hard one to make, but there was a crack by his head and he turned. More SIS thugs were advancing behind him on his side of the street, and they were firing at the Chryslers and not caring much that he and other civvies were in the way.

Ross pulled back into a doorway as the rounds flew past, holding his SIG, trapped.

A few feet away, a young couple cowered using the steps up to the front door of a coffee shop as inadequate cover.

"Get down, get down!" Ross yelled. The terrified young woman was staring at him as a burst from Ross's rear took off the top of her boyfriend's head. He sprawled and she stood and shrieked. A flurry of shots from the SIS men spun her around and flung her to the sidewalk in a marsh of scarlet.

There were at least a half dozen civilians trapped between Ross and the robbers.

Ross turned back to the advancing SIS thugs. The lead shooter was moving fast, weapon at his shoulder ready to fire, heedless of the background civilians.

Ross pointed his SIG. "Don't you shoot!"

The SIS man saw the target with the gun and swung the muzzle in Ross's direction. The maneuver ended abruptly as Ross fired twice into his forehead.

The SIS man dropped, and the façade of the building above Ross's head exploded in dust and paint chips as more rounds slammed into it.

A trio of PSF cruisers arrived and blocked the northeast intersection as Mikey Sullivan produced his HK417 and left his corner to move southwest, following behind the SIS men. A round flew at him from behind – the PSF officers had seen his weapon and opened up. Bad training and lack of communication were the reason – he looked similar to an SIS man wearing a suit and with a weapon that looked a lot like an M4 and they should have not engaged for that reason. But there was another, more critical reason they should have left him be.

Mikey turned around and opened up on the PSF cars with suppressive fire, unleashing all 20 rounds of .308 in about three seconds. One cruiser's tires blew out and all its windows shattered. The officers were sufficiently suppressed, or worse – the bullets sliced through the sheet metal and took down the PSF personnel trying to use the vehicles as cover unless they were smart enough to get behind the engine blocks.

Most weren't. They died.

Mikey lowered the empty carbine, his ears ringing, but over the tinnitus he could hear sirens in the distance. He executed a combat reload, just as Sean had drilled him.

Doyle looked left as Turnbull opened fire and dumped his duffel on the sidewalk. His HK417 was up and, using the roof of the white Chrysler 300 for stability, he engaged the surviving SIS men across the street with short, controlled bursts, tearing the sheet metal body of the Camry that had been unlucky enough to have them hide behind it into jagged aluminum shreds.

Was that a manbun? Gruber?

Turnbull slipped in another mag from his rig and the bolt slammed forward. He rose to engage northeast, but a round tore into the door in front of him from the southwest. He pivoted and spotted more shooters down the sidewalk on the bank side. The civilians in the way were dropping – he hoped it was to take cover. Doyle was close to his line of fire, but not quite in it. Turnbull stepped back to get clear, acquired one of the SIS men, and squeezed the trigger.

Four rounds flew down the sidewalk and one snapped the femur of the SIS shooter, who sprawled on the sidewalk in agony.

Doyle pivoted and joined in the fire down their sidewalk to the southeast. But on his left, he saw movement – more men with rifles advancing and firing.

"Get in!" Jimmy yelled as the white Chrysler's windshield erupted with a string of white geysers of vaporized safety glass. Three of the rounds passed thorough harmlessly. The fourth round came through the windshield and punched into Jimmy O'Connor's forehead, blowing his brain matter all over Katie as she fired northeast from the backseat.

Gruber smiled. He got the driver. To his immediate right, Dworkin was firing. Gruber took a knee to reload behind the front of a 530i. The valley between the high rises sounded like it contained a raging thunderstorm, echoing with the automatic rifle fire. The BMW he was hiding behind shook and glass sprayed over him. He snapped the fresh mag into his weapon.

"Holy shit," Dworkin sputtered and bullets tore up the vehicle he was hiding behind. "That mick bastard set us up!"

Gruber grinned. "He sure as shit did." One of the tires on the vehicle popped.

"But there's still more of us," Gruber said, rising up to return fire. "Time to die, boys!"

"Where's Mikey?" Torrey yelled. Bullets slammed into the side windows of the black 300, shattered glass cascading down on the occupants of the car.

"I don't know!" Teddy King yelled. He raised his carbine and fired off a series of controlled bursts at the enemy across the street to his rear. "We need to get the hell out of here!"

Outside the car, on the sidewalk, Turnbull was engaging southeast, and then he swung around and engaged northeast until he went dry and reloaded.

He locked in another mag and sent the bolt forward, but instead of immediately returning fire he shouted to Doyle, who was also reloading.

"We need to drive!"

"Jimmy's dead. Jimmy the driver!" Doyle said, qualifying it for clarity. He got up to window level. Katie was in the backseat, red splatters and gore across her face, the muzzle of her HK417 sticking through the open window and firing out a long burst.

She went dry.

"Katie, you drive, you drive!" Doyle shouted while she changed mags. Katie nodded and opened the door. Immediately, bullets punched through it, narrowly missing her. Doyle rose and suppressed Gruber and his shooters with several short bursts.

Katie rolled out onto the street, but the enemy was not suppressed long. They returned fire and the front tire of the 300 blew out. She dived back inside the vehicle as more bullets punctured the door and front quarter panels. A wisp of white steam escaped from under the hood.

"Danny, this car's not going anywhere!" she yelled.

Mikey was running fast toward the southeast now, even as more PSF were arriving behind him. To his front, it was a war zone, and the noise as deafening. One of the SIS men was reloading behind a Chevy truck as he approached. The thug looked up just as Mikey put a burst into him, and the bank robber kept running toward the getaway cars.

Turnbull sprinted the few feet to Doyle, noting that an SIS shooter ahead of them to the southeast was lying dead on the ground near the wounded one even though neither he nor Doyle was shooting at the moment. Turnbull put it out of his head. He grabbed Doyle as Doyle reloaded.

"This has gone to shit," Turnbull shouted. He had to shout to be heard. "We need to get out now!"

"This car's wasted," Doyle said.

"Mine's still good," Turnbull said. "Get Katie!"

"The money..." Doyle said.

"Your money or your life?" Turnbull said.

Doyle nodded. "I ain't going back inside, man," he said.

Turnbull sprinted back, bullets crackling over his head. At the black 300, he paused to fire two short bursts at the SIS men firing from up the street, then leaned into the 300. King just finished off a mag and was reloading smoothly. Torrey fired a burst out the window. Rounds punched into the side panels.

"This is the escape car, the other's dust," Turnbull said. He pointed at Torrey. "You, get ready to punch it!'

"Where's Mikey?" Torrey shouted. "I ain't leaving without Mikey!"

"We need to go! He'll escape and evade! Katie and Danny are coming. Get ready!" Turnbull rose and used the roof as a firing support to unload on the remaining SIS up the street.

The PSF were pursuing him now, pinning Mikey down for a moment until he suppressed them with a full mag dump that bought him enough time to move down the road to another vehicle. He felt a round pass through his suit at his side, but he kept moving. As he did, he reloaded and dropped two PSF uniforms who got caught in the open.

The bank and the getaway cars were only 100 meters, and a few remaining SIS men, ahead.

Ross emptied his SIG mag at the car 15 meters away. The SIS man behind it had tried to kill him, but in fairness, Ross had just blown his friend's brains out. The FBI agent was unsure whether he had hit the guy, but he hoped he had. The mag he was inserting was his last one.

"Mikey!"

Torrey bailed out of the black 300 with his rifle, spraying a long burst from the hip. He then sprinted northeast toward his brother.

"Shit!" Turnbull said.

"What the hell?" Teddy King said.

"Get in the driver's seat!" Turnbull said. Several rounds hit the vehicle's hood. Inside, Teddy King started climbing between the seats into the driver's slot.

Turnbull searched for targets as Torrey ran forward. In the distance were PSF running toward them, but Turnbull didn't engage. They were far off and he'd need his ammo.

Doyle arrived beside him as Turnbull scanned for targets. Katie and Jimmy Sullivan were with him.

"Get in!" Doyle said. "Let's go!"

"Your boy Sully ran off!" As Turnbull spoke, there was more fire and they watched as Torrey staggered and fell in the street.

"He took the remote!" Teddy King shouted from inside. "No key!'

"Shit!" Doyle said.

"We gotta fight our way out, and northeast isn't going to work," Turnbull said, gesturing toward the approaching enemy.

"Sean's down the other way," Katie said.

Teddy King scrambled out of the car onto the sidewalk.

"Bounding," Turnbull said, and Doyle nodded. "I'll take rearguard."

Turnbull nodded, and looked at Teddy King.

"Let's see how good they trained you. Go on!"

King nodded and sprinted southeast, spraying controlled bursts at the SIS men now to his front.

"You next," Turnbull said, pausing to fire several aimed shots at the SIS men. Doyle was still there.

"What the hell are you waiting for?" Turnbull said.

"You make sure Katie's taken care of," Doyle said, weapon ready. "You promise?"

"Yeah, yeah, now get going!" Turnbull snapped.

Doyle smiled. "Moving!" he yelled as he bolted to the southwest, firing as he ran.

Mikey saw Torrey stagger and fall in the middle of Franklin Street. He sprinted toward his brother, pivoting as he ran to shoot an SIS man crouching by a blue Mazda. Rounds were flying all around him now, most from the PSF following behind him. He reached Torrey, who had dropped his rifle as he stumbled, and who now had his .45 M1911A1 out. Blood oozed from his gut and his left arm.

"You dumb mick!" Mikey shouted.

"Shut your damn mouth, I can still kick your ass!"

Mikey slapped in another mag – he was running low –and turned toward the pursuing PSF. One fired a shotgun, but from too far away. Several double-aught pellets hit his legs and Mikey paid him back with a burst of 7.62mm before falling to his good knee.

Torrey was firing from his pistol, blowing off a mag and painfully reloading as Mikey fired off the rest of his rounds and dropped the mag.

The PSF were firing faster now, and there was a red eruption on Torrey's leg. It didn't stop him from reloading or firing off the rounds.

"I'll carry you!" Mikey said as he reloaded. He stood and turned but a 9mm round went into his kidney. He fell back to his knees.

"I ain't running," Torrey said, dropping the empty magazine out of the well. "Not from these pussies."

Mikey nodded and turned back to the enemy, opening up with a full mag dump. Two PSF dropped, one minus most of his skull.

Torrey locked in another mag and began firing his M1911A1. A round hit Mikey's HK417 and knocked it out of his hands. Mikey shook off the sting in his paw even as rounds swept past him, and drew his own .45.

"Hey Mikey –" Torrey began but a round went into his temple and his pistol arm dropped as his body went slack.

Another pistol round slammed into Mikey's left shoulder as he looked down. The shooting stopped.

"You, racist criminal! Throw down your weapon!"

Mikey was not sure who was yelling at him – there were so many uniforms arrayed against him up the street. One thing was for sure – they were all pointing weapons at him.

"Kiss my green Irish ass," Mikey said, lifting the up the .45 and firing until they shot him to pieces.

Teddy King and Doyle got to a Cadillac that was already riddled with holes and began suppressing the surviving SIS men on both sides of the street. The heavy rounds were just too much – the thugs took cover while King and Doyle ripped the cars they cowered behind to jagged metal shreds.

As they fired, Turnbull slapped Jimmy Sullivan on the back and Katie followed him a few steps behind. Turnbull pivoted to spray some suppression to the northeast then lunged after his companions. Bullets flew overhead from behind them as they bounded past King and Doyle.

"Moving!" Turnbull yelled, lunging forward, weapon scanning for targets.

There was a man in a suit ahead, crouching in a doorway, but with no visible weapon. Turnbull vaguely thought he looked familiar but ran past him.

There were two SIS men on the ground immediately to his front, one alive with a huge hole in his thigh and writhing on the ground. As he sprinted, Turnbull raised his rifle to finish him, but Gruber with his G36 across the street rose up to fire and Turnbull suppressed him with two short, sharp bursts. He ducked and Turnbull was past the wounded thug and taking cover behind the rear of a riddled Ford sedan. It bore bumper stickers reading "I SUPPORT LBGTQAI&% RIGHTS" and "DON'T ASSUME MY GENDER."

Katie and Jimmy knelt beside him. Another dead SIS man lay in the street in front of them.

There was movement to his front – an SIS man stood up and fired a series of shots in his direction. They were high. Turnbull's return fire wasn't – he put a five-round burst into the man's torso. The Kevlar plate stopped the first and the second, but the other three smashed through. The M4 clattered across the asphalt as the SIS man fell back dead.

Turnbull lowered his rifle and looked back to Doyle.

"Move!" Turnbull yelled.

"Moving!" Doyle yelled, and slapped Teddy King's back. King was up and sprinting, and immediately sprayed rounds toward the SIS thugs across the street as he bounded forward.

Doyle glanced to the rear, to the northeast, and saw the Sully brothers were both down. He unloaded the rest of his mag at the PSF officers surrounding the prone brothers' bodies, dropping two and scattering the rest. Doyle executed a flawless combat mag reload and stood up as his bolt drove forward, ready to sprint southwest to the next position.

Teddy King bounded past them toward the next position. Turnbull looked to the rear to see Doyle following. Turnbull fired two short bursts at the SIS men across the street and Doyle passed them, following King.

Then there was an explosion ahead of them to the southwest.

Sean McGowan knew what his task would be; it was simply a matter of deciding when to start. Without comms, he was forced to look up the street at the firefight and guess about his timing. And now it was clear that their vehicles were wasted because the rest of the crew was approaching on foot. He could not help them during their bounding movements – his friends would have to fight their way to him on their own. But he could make damn sure the uniformed hacks of the People's Security Force manning – personing – the perimeter could not stop their egress.

Sean had chosen to dress like a workman because his HK417 was just too bulky to hide under a suit coat with the Trijicon optic and the under-barrel grenade launcher. The PSF officers personing the row of cruisers blocking Franklin Street at the southwest corner of the next block paid him no mind. This was why, as World War III was going on behind him up the street by the bank, they did not notice when he reached into his tool bag, and proceeded to take one of the 40mm grenades on the chest rig in the bag and slip it into the launcher's breach.

He stood up, partially shielded by an ornate art deco steel lamppost, and took aim at the center PSF sedan in the row of them blocking off the street. He did not have a launcher sight affixed, but he knew similar weapons systems from the Marine Corps and went with his gut as he fired the shell.

The solid but relatively light recoil was familiar, as was the "PLOOT" sound of the grenade firing from the launcher. He could actually see it in the air, a black blur that lazily rose then dropped, breaking the driver's side window of the perpendicular patrol car and detonating inside.

The vehicle jolted and shuddered as the windows blew out and flame and black smoke erupted. The PSF officers took cover and Sean further incentivized them further by opening up with his HK417, putting a burst into each vehicle, seeking to blow out tires and shatter windshields in an effort to disincentivize any of them from interfering.

His mag went dry and he dropped it and smoothly slipped in another, and began suppressing again. One PSF officer stood up with a shotgun and Sean acquired him and riddled his torso with 7.62mm rounds. He fell backwards, clearly dead. Maybe the rest of his buddies would take the hint. At least one did – he was running away full speed toward Congress Street.

Sean dropped the empty mag and picked up his chest rig from the bag. It was heavy as he slipped it on, and after he buckled it into place, he took one of the spare mags off and reloaded his carbine.

Behind him, up the street toward the bank, the shooting was getting closer. But Sean was focused on the PSF thugs and waited to take the head off the first one to raise it over the smoking rim of the cruisers that made up the perimeter roadblock.

Gruber lay back against the front end of a BMW beside Dworkin as broken glass rained down on them from the suppressive fire from the bank robbers. He was not grinning anymore. They were outgunned, and his ass hurt.

"We're pinned!" Dworkin said, clutching his own M4. Gruber slapped another mag into his G36.

"Them PSF boys better be calling in the cavalry," Gruber said, raising his head just a hair above the edge to look over the hood at the enemy.

The escape vehicles were riddled hulks, so his quarry was going to try to escape and evade on foot. But if they got through his SIS men, then how would the uniformed amateurs of the PSF who were manning the perimeter fare?

Just before he pulled his head down in response to a hail of 7.62mm rounds slamming into the German sedan, Gruber saw that the two robbers remaining by the escape cars were moving. No, they could not get away. He darted around the back of the sedan, keeping low, and brought up his G36.

There was one taking up the rearguard. Gruber took aim.

Doyle was going full speed now even as he assessed the situation to his front. There was a line of PSF patrol cars sealing off Franklin at the intersection the next block to the southwest. One PSF vehicle was on fire – actually two were. Another detonated even as he ran. That would be Sean, Doyle told himself, clearing their path for them.

Semper fi.

Ahead of him, Katie and Jimmy were crouching, while Turnbull fired off a burst at the SIS guys behind now to Doyle's rear. Further up, at the next position, Teddy King had slid in behind a blue Dodge Caravan and was changing mags.

Doyle smiled and his legs pumped, gripping his rifle.

Not far now.

Gruber exhaled, took aim, and squeezed off a single shot.

The round hit Doyle low, in the right iliac of his pelvis, shattering it. He stumbled and fell, his HK417 clattering away across the street as he went face forward into the pavement.

Turnbull saw Doyle hit, as did Katie, who shrieked. Turnbull raised his rifle, but Dworkin was suppressing with his M4 and Turnbull had to crouch back down as the 5.56mm bullets punctured the sheet metal of the Ford.

Doyle groaned, lightning bolts of pain coursing through him, his right side, rendering it useless and unresponsive. The gunfire around him went silent – where was his rifle?

Doyle saw it was out of reach.

His pistol.

He reached his right hand back and took hold of the holstered M1911. He pulled, and the pain doubled. But it did not stop him – the automatic was out and then it was gone, flying across the street.

His fingers hurt now, and he realized someone had kicked the gun out of his hand.

"I got you, boy," Gruber said, proud and eager, standing behind his prey. "You gonna tell me everything I want to know."

Gruber was grinning again.

The suppression stopped and Turnbull grabbed Katie as she stood to charge back for Danny Doyle.

"Take her!" he told Jimmy. Jimmy hesitated.

"Do it now!" Turnbull shouted. Jimmy moved forward.

"No, we gotta get Danny!" she howled.

"Come on, Katie!" Jimmy said as he lifted her and pushed her in front of him, moving to the southwest.

Turnbull rose up, weapon ready.

Gruber was standing, triumphant over the prone, wounded Doyle, an enormous rictus of a smile on his weathered visage. His G36 was at Doyle's face.

Behind him, Dworkin was reloading his M4.

Doyle twisted and his eyes met Turnbull's. He nodded.

Turnbull hesitated. From the northwest, a swarm of PSF were advancing toward Gruber and his prisoner. Turnbull did not have enough rounds to kill them all.

"Do it!" Doyle shouted and Gruber kicked him savagely in his shattered hip.

Doyle groaned. Turnbull paused, and flipped his selector switch to "SEMI."

"You gonna wish you were dead," Gruber said.

Doyle twisted back to lock eyes with Turnbull. But Turnbull's eye was peering through the optic, with the red dot on Doyle's forehead.

"Sorry, Danny," Turnbull whispered as he squeezed the trigger.

The round hit Doyle's forehead dead center, and he fell face forward onto the street.

Gruber was stunned for a moment as he saw his victim's head lurch and drop, not exactly sure what had happened for a moment. There was a woman's scream, and Gruber lifted his eyes.

The big bank robber was standing now, his thumb flicking the selector switch back to "AUTO."

Gruber pitched left as Turnbull fired, diving back to cover under the BMW. A tire blew and the car dropped several inches and .308 rounds lanced though the sedan's body. Dworkin, howling, was flat on his face as the sheet metal above him erupted in a line of punctures.

Gruber was in agony as the impact from his dive had torn open his wound. He scrunched up into a fetal position behind the wheel – the disc brakes saved him – and waited out the tsunami of gunfire.

He missed Gruber – the bastard had jumped behind the BMW and Turnbull dumped the whole mag into it. Some of the PSF officers approaching from the northwest were firing on him now, mostly with pistols, but a couple had shotguns.

Turnbull dropped the mag and inserted another – he had only a couple left. He took aim, the hot barrel burning his left hand. He ignored the pain and sighted in on the PSF. He fired. One with a pistol dropped, then another, and he put a third burst into a shotgunner as the officer moved to cover.

Most of the PSF officers were scattering and going to ground. But some were returning fire with their Berettas and Remington

870s. Rounds buzzed by him and one connected. It hit right on his chest rig, but at a broad angle and into a mag so it did not dump all its energy into Turnbull's chest.

Turnbull staggered back, the frayed ballistic webbing of the chest rig flapping where the round had grazed it. He felt like someone had punched him in the chest, but that was it – he was grateful not to be dead.

Turnbull caught his breath, pivoted back and dumped the rest of his magazine into the BMW, then bolted, dropping the empty and slipping in one of his last 7.62mm magazines as he ran.

Katie's face was streaked with tears as Jimmy Sullivan hustled her to Teddy King's position. King had seen Doyle, and seen him drop dead as the SIS thug hovered over him. But there was no time to talk about it.

"Take her forward!" Teddy King shouted. "Go!"

"Moving!" Jimmy yelled, hustling Katie along with him.

Teddy turned and raised his rifle to the northwest, firing a few bursts past the running Turnbull at the BMW and the PSF pursuers.

Turnbull slid in next to him.

"Let's go," he said. Teddy nodded, rose, and sprayed off three bursts as Turnbull rose and rushed forward shouting "Moving!"

King then lowered his rifle and ran along behind. The fire from behind them rose up again into a storm of lead.

"Come on, Katie!" Jimmy Sullivan said, pushing her along.

"They killed Danny!" she said, not really knowing what else to say.

Jimmy didn't reply. His hand on her shoulder went limp and he staggered three stepped before falling on his face. The back of his head was a red mess, staining the collar of his gray suit coat. He twitched once and was still.

Katie stood staring numb as bullets zipped around her.

"Jimmy?" she asked, unbelieving, as the 9mm round coming from behind entered her scapula and shattered it.

Turnbull caught her in his left arm as she wavered and pushed her forward, the HK417 in his right hand. He turned, bringing it up and dumping off bursts on full auto to scatter the pursing PSF.

"Keep going!" he shouted as Teddy King approached. King assessed the scene – Jimmy lay dead and Katie was wounded – and obeyed. King kept running forward as Turnbull's mag went dry.

Now, Teddy King stopped and turned back, kneeling and bringing his rifle up to suppress the enemy to their rear as Turnbull dragged Katie forward.

The bank robbers, led by the elusive Chris, had executed a pretty skillful bounding overwatch maneuver to the southwest right past his position in the doorway. Packing a SIG pistol and with a single mag holding a couple bullets left, Ross was not going to engage a band of criminals who showed no hesitation in engaging in a full-auto war on a city street.

Chris had glanced his way as he moved by, but there was no recognition – luckily for Ross. The man would have certainly shot him to bits with his assault rifle.

The PSF and the surviving SIS men had followed, fighting their way south toward the Pearl Street intersection. Incredibly, the battle had intensified. Apparently, one of the Leprechauns had a grenade launcher and zero compunction about using it.

Who the hell were these guys?

PSF officers rushed past him, firing at the fleeing robbers. Ross pressed himself back in the alcove, concealing his piece. No sense in getting shot by those nominally on his own side.

He had seen the woman get hit and the Leprechauns carry her off. They were now down by the intersection, giving the pursuers hell. Ross waited until the bulk of the PSF passed him and then headed up to the bank, carefully avoiding the bodies and blood puddles in the way. The hobo, miraculously unscathed, was disclaiming loudly about the Apocalypse.

The ex-hostages were milling about inside the bank lobby, uncertain and scared.

"I'm FBI," Ross announced. They looked at him and stood there, staring blankly. "Stay inside – it's not safe out there."

The ex-hostages did not move. The noise of the gunfight continued.

Ross crossed the white marble floor to the teller counter. The Leprechaun card was right there, mocking him.

Another PSF cruiser arrived and Sean greeted it with a grenade. It exploded on the street about a meter in front of the driver's door, and no one got out. The other vehicles of the roadblock were smoking hulks, glass shattered, tires flat, and those not blown apart by the fragmentation grenades were riddled with the heavy 7.62mm rounds from Sean's rifle. If any of the PSF were alive, they were taking cover or pretending not to be.

Sean popped the breech of the launcher open, then slipped another 40mm shell from his chest rig inside and snapped it shut again. He glanced back and saw Teddy King running towards him. Behind him, Turnbull and Katie were coming – he seemed to be helping Katie.

"Katie?"

"Hit – Chris has her," King said, scanning for targets among the wrecked roadblock vehicles. He could hear sirens.

Turnbull hustled the limp Katie to their position by the light post at the corner of Franklin and Pearl Streets.

"Where are the rest?" Sean asked as Teddy reached him.

Teddy paused, panting. "Gone, they're gone!"

It was a lot to process.

"We gotta go," Turnbull said, breathing heavily. He handed Katie to Sean, who held her up, and changed out his empty mag.

Teddy King had turned and was now firing on the dozen or so PSF pursuing from the northeast.

"You okay?" Sean asked his sister.

"Danny's dead," she said. Her face was pale. "He's dead, Sean."

"You need a medic," said Sean.

She groaned. Teddy stopped firing and looked up at Turnbull and his frayed webbing.

"You hit too?" he asked.

"I'm okay," Turnbull said, surveying the situation. "We can cut through Post Office Park." The urban greenspace lay to their right off Franklin, and it appeared to be clear of enemy. But the enemy was coming. And the sirens were getting louder.

"We'll grab a car on the other side, if we can," he said. There was still, oddly, traffic on the streets moving across on Congress Street on the far side of the greenspace despite the pitched battle going on one block over.

Sean pushed his sister to Turnbull, who caught her.

"You take her. Somebody's got to hold them off," he said.

Turnbull hesitated, but remembered his mission. Still…

"And I got the grenade launcher," Sean said, grinning.

"You Irish and your lost causes," Turnbull said, holding up Katie.

"Sean, no…," she said.

"Get going. I'll hold them until you get clear and then escape and evade back to the Town," Sean replied.

Turnbull nodded and pulled Katie along with him as they ran across Pearl Street towards the park.

Sean watched them go, catching one last glance from Katie, then turned to engage the pursing PSF officers and surviving SIS men.

"Come on!" Gruber said, waving the PSF survivors forward. The roadblock just past Pearl was a ruin of twisted metal, and he was damned if he was going to let his quarry blast their way out of his trap.

Dworkin ran beside Gruber as he painfully loped forward, Dworkin's M4 with a fresh mag in the well. It was one of his last. There were some dead civilians in the street, and some SIS men, and some of the bank robbers too. They would need to be searched for his prize. But he ignored them for now as he and his forces charged ahead.

A Volkswagen to his left exploded, the fragments shredding a pair of PSF officers unlucky enough to be running beside it when Sean's grenade hit. Gruber took cover, as did the rest of them, and shook his head. These boys sure had some firepower.

He raised his rifle. There was one of them at the corner of Franklin and Pearl behind a lamppost. Where were the rest?

Gone. This was the rearguard.

He took aim and fired, and saw the bullet impact on the metal. The bank robber responded with automatic rifle fire, and one of the rounds took down a 300-pound PSF officer who was already heaving and pale from being out of breath.

Dworkin knelt next to Gruber and opened up with his M4. The robber pulled back behind the metal lamppost.

"Go on, now!" Gruber yelled to the unsteady, hesitant PSF around him. "You dumb sons of bitches wanna live forever?"

There were many civilians in the park, most taking cover but a couple filming with their cell phones. One seemed to be narrating the firefight live on Facebook. The trio ignored them, making their way through the concrete paths to the other side where traffic was still, incongruously, continuing as usual in the midst of an urban war.

At Congress Street, where there was traffic, they exited the park and were greeted by two PSF cruisers that were weaving through cars, the vanguard of the relief force. Turnbull dropped Katie roughly, but there was no time to let her down easy. He raised the rifle to his shoulder, sighted in on the first driver and pulled the trigger.

The windshield broke apart in white splotches blooming across it as the 7.62mm rounds punched through the glass and the PSF officer driving the vehicle. Turnbull pivoted the weapon a bit and emptied the mag into the passenger even as the vehicle swerved up onto the sidewalk and narrowly missed them.

The second vehicle stopped, but Teddy King was on it, drilling the passenger in his seat and shooting the pink-haired driver as xe opened the door to get out with xis 12-gauge.

They stood, panting. Turnbull was out of mags, and he tossed his HK417 and drew his Wilson Combat .45.

"Get her!" he ordered Teddy and stepped into the road. He ignored the latest explosion in the distance, and the continuing gunfire.

There was a white Volvo in the closest lane with a driver staring slack-jawed at the carnage in front of him. Turnbull jogged to his side window and leveled the pistol at him.

"Open the door," he snarled. "Or I will blow your brains out."

The man, who had a little goatee, and a tight t-shirt that read "SOME FATHERS ARE WOMEN," hastily stepped out.

"My car," he mumbled.

"*My* car," Turnbull corrected him as he snatched the key. "Teddy!'

The man just stood there.

"You better run," Turnbull said, the big gun hovering in the man's face. The man turned and ran away toward the park.

Teddy carried Katie over and slid her into the backseat, then went around to get in on the passenger side.

Turnbull was looking across the park. Sean was on the ground, and the PSF were approaching him.

"Shit," he hissed, and then he slid into the driver's seat and hit the gas.

Sean nearly emptied his .45 before they got him.

17.

Johnny Ross was out on the Franklin Street sidewalk, staring at the carnage. He had been extremely lucky that the firefight had passed him by without him having been swept away with it.

It was over now. The shooting had stopped and the echoes from the high-rises had faded away. His ears were still ringing, though. That would take longer to fade away.

Wounded and dead civilians littered the sidewalk and Franklin Street. There were dead SIS men too, including the ones he had shot – that was going to take some explaining. And there was a wounded one, blood spurting from a massive hit in the thigh.

Ross walked southwest past his old position and stood over him as the man moaned and tried to staunch his arterial bleeding.

"Why the hell did you do this?" Ross demanded. "You started a war in the middle of a city."

"Get me some help, man," the wounded agent sputtered.

"You didn't have to take them here," Ross hissed. A few feet away a young man in a blue t-shirt lay dead, cut down in the crossfire.

"Orders, man," the agent blurted. "Please, help me! I'm bleeding out."

"Whose orders?"

The man shook his head, apparently more scared of talking than of dying of blood loss.

"Then bleed," Ross said.

"Okay, okay," the man said. "It was Crane. He wanted to send a message."

"Merrick Crane?"

The man nodded intensely, blood oozing out between his fingers. His face was very pale.

"Thanks for your help," Ross said, walking away and taking out his phone as, down the street, the shooting petered out. He ignored the dying man calling after him.

Gruber walked among the wreckage and the bodies, directing his reinforced SIS men to check the bodies of the criminals very, very carefully. But he had a feeling that what he really sought had gotten away.

Some fresh SIS men had arrived. They had entered the bank and brought Gruber out a playing card with a Celtics leprechaun on it. He had crumpled it up in his hand.

His cell phone rang. He sighed.

"Hey there, boss," he said to Merrick Crane III.

"Did you get it?" Crane demanded.

"Well, we're looking for it among the casualties. Got five of them."

"I only care about the drive," Crane said. "Did you get the drive?"

"No, chief, but we will.

"Why do you think that?"

"I know where they came from, and where they'll go."

There was a pause. "Are you going to make me ask?" demanded Crane.

"Charlestown."

Now Crane paused. "Charlestown," he repeated. He knew about that place – a no-go area for PSF and People's Militia, a defiant rogue backwater that, had the current so-called leadership in Boston been properly aggressive, would have been dealt with long ago. This refuge for misfits and racist criminals had been a thorn in the side of progress for far too long.

"We will damn sure get that disc," Gruber promised.

"You damn well better," Crane said, hanging up.

A swarm of PSF vehicles passed him by heading downtown, lights and sirens going off. Turnbull gripped the leather wheel of the Volvo and suppressed the desire to punch it. Draw attention and you draw fire.

"She's bleeding bad," Teddy said from the backseat, putting pressure on the wound. Katie moaned. "This is beyond me."

"She needs a medic," Turnbull said. His mind considered the situation. The smart move would be to drop Katie at a hospital and let her take her chances explaining her 9mm kiss, then for both of them to get out of town now and off to the red. But if he was smart, Turnbull reflected, he wouldn't have taken this job in the first place.

Crane lowered his iPhone from his ear and considered. When one door closes, another opens, though the door on the mad scientist's disc drive was not actually closed. They could still get the drive, perhaps, but this other opportunity was simply too good to pass up. Merrick Crane III had scrolled down his iPhone 15's contact list to the name "Travis Lumumba-Zapata," the former Boston College sociology grad student who had dropped out to join, and subsequently rise to the top of, the local People's Militia.

Actually, "dropping out" was not quite the correct term – Lumumba-Zapata had shown up at the college after a year of unexcused absences with a dozen armed militia members in tow and demanded his diploma right then and there. Denying him a master's degree merely because he failed to attend class, complete assignments, and pass the tests, he informed the dean, was more proof that the college was part of the systemic patriarchal racism infecting every part of society. The dean agreed and apologized profusely for this grave failure of vision and called down to administration to prepare a diploma right then and there. Unfortunately, the clerk who rushed it to the dean's office failed to proofread it. Had she done so, she would have seen that the computer system had made it out to "Theresa Hofsteder," the government name imposed upon Travis Lumumba-Zapata by his parents back in the Connecticut suburbs, where he had been cruelly raised as a female by a hedge fund manager father and a psychiatrist mother merely because he had been born with a vagina.

After Lumumba-Zapata had the other militia members beat the dean to a pulp for deadnaming him, another diploma with the correct name *du jour* was prepared, though the dean had to repeat his instructions several times to the terrified clerks because most of his teeth were broken out.

As they left his office, the dean thanked Travis Lumumba-Zapata for his lesson in the importance of intersectional awareness.

Lumumba-Zapata answered his phone within one ring.

"Comrade Crane," he said, a frisson of fear at the edge of his voice. Despite the hormones, provided to him for free pursuant the People's Republic's CXXXVIIth amendment, "The Right to Funding and Validation of Gender Affirmation," his voice sometimes broke high when he was stressed.

"How many personnel are ready to mobilize in the next five hours?" Crane asked, dispensing with formalities.

"Ten thousand," Lumumba-Zapata replied, hoping both that this was what Crane wanted to hear and that he could round up that many troops from their crash pads, dorm rooms, and parents' basements.

Crane doubted the estimate, but if his minion managed half that many it should be sufficient for his purposes.

"You no doubt know about the terrorist attack in downtown Boston today," Crane said. "The perpetrators were racist insurrectionists from Charlestown."

"I understand," said Lumumba-Zapata. Though he didn't.

"By six tonight you will move into Charlestown and suppress the right-wing revanchists there," Crane instructed his subordinate. "Occupy the area. Eliminate the criminal element."

"Invade Charlestown?" Lumumba-Zapata said, not quite believing what he was hearing.

"You are to use all force necessary to suppress these rebels and secure the area. I will be sending you some additional individuals to assist you. They have a special mission and I expect you to provide them your full and unstinting cooperation. Are you clear?"

"I am," Lumumba-Zapata said, though he was not very clear at all. He made a mental note to use some of the left-wing veterans of the old United States forces who were sprinkled throughout the Militia to help him plan how to do this. He was smart enough to realize that this operation was far over his head – this operation was far more than just intimidating a bunch of civilians.

"Good," Crane said pleasantly. "Remember that your predecessor in command, Venus DiPaulo, failed me and..."

Crane let his voice trail off. He did not need to finish the sentence.

"Did you get it?" the senator demanded.

"I guess you hadn't heard yet," Ross replied into his Android phone. "But World War III just played out in downtown Boston. It's a massacre."

"Did you get it?" Senator Harrington repeated.

"No." Ross said. "Do you want to hear about the dozen dead civilians all over Franklin Street, not to mention the dead PSF?" His omission of the SIS men was deliberate, since their deaths were, at best, immaterial to him.

"I expect that it will make for a bad visual."

"Yeah, Senator, you could say that. Poor optics," he spat. "The SIS punks tried to take them coming out of the bank. But the

Leprechauns were not prepared to be taken. I got caught in the middle, if that matters."

"Are you damaged?"

"Not physically. I did get an interesting tidbit of info from one of the SIS guys before he bled out."

"Yes?"

"Merrick Crane ordered them to do it. He told them to fight it out here. He wanted to send a message."

"A message," Harrington repeated blankly, his mind already assessing the byzantine motivations behind the bloodbath on the streets of Boston.

"Why would he do that, Senator?" Ross demanded. "What message was he sending?"

Harrington ignored him. "Where is the drive? Did Gruber get it?"

"I expect it's with our friend Chris. He was leading the crew, it seemed, and last I saw he was shooting his way out of the ambush with the survivors."

"Where will they go?"

"Back to Charlestown."

"You need to go get him."

"In Charlestown? Crane's flunkies wasted Seamus McCloskey, the Irish godfather in there. After this, the natives are going to be restless and angry. You'd need an army."

"There will be one," Harrington said. "My sources tell me the Boston People's Militia is mobilizing."

"What the hell does that mean?" asked Ross.

"It means that Merrick Crane is making a bigger play than just our thumb drive," Harrington said, beginning to appreciate what was happening. He actually felt some grudging respect for his opponent's cunning. But he returned to focus on the problem at hand.

"It will take them a few hours to mobilize. Go there, find this Chris, and get me the drive," Harrington said.

"What about Crane?" asked Ross. "He needs to pay for what he did here, and his lackey Gruber too."

"Special Agent Ross," Harrington said pleasantly. "If you happen to come across them while accomplishing your assignment, you're free to kill them both."

Turnbull went through the intersection, running a red light that appeared with no intervening yellow, right in front of a PSF cruiser. The officers did nothing. Traffic stops had been banned as racist soon after the Split, accomplishing the nearly impossible – making Boston drivers drive even worse.

"How is she?" Turnbull asked over his shoulder. He was taking her to Charlestown; he would drop her with friends and then he and Teddy King would boogie. If she chose to go to a hospital and its attendant risks, that was on her.

"I have pressure on the wound," King said. He was using a QuikClot pad to stop the bleeding, and it had slowed the flow to a trickle.

"Where's Sean?" Katie asked between groans.

"I'm sorry," Turnbull said. Bad news did not get better with age, or with ambiguity. "He's gone."

Katie breathed out hard, but she was done crying.

"They ambushed us," she managed to say. "Somebody talked."

"Who?" Turnbull asked.

"Who else knew?" asked Teddy, but he knew the answer.

"Seamus," Katie said. "He's the only one who knew the time and place."

"The curse of the Irish was always the supergrasses," Teddy King said. "Let's go kill him, Chris."

"You read my mind," Turnbull said.

CNN was already showing footage of the brave resistance by the People's Security Force to the right-wing terrorist attack in Boston today. "Those who would undermine the security of the People's Republic will be punished harshly!" Don Lemon informed the viewers, pounding on the table in front of him. He was wearing his olive drab uniform and cap, which he tended to do when calling for the destruction of the red states and red people. "The People's Militia is being readied to take action to quell the insurrectionists in Charlestown. This is the greatest treason since January 6th, 2021!" He paused for effect. That date was now a People's Republic holiday.

Lemon was reading a statement, but he sincerely wanted vengeance. So did the rest of them. The other meat puppets braying on the other two licensed news channels were saying precisely the same thing, figuratively and literally reading off the same script regardless of network. Maddow was in tears. Colbert was literally shaking.

Harrington clicked off the monitor and again felt a grudging appreciation for his opponent. Crane had gotten to the media first, spinning the story to allow himself to arrive and save the day from the dreaded insurrectionists. The underlying narrative was that the leadership of Boston had lost control of its streets, requiring that the People's Militia step in. Harrington's allies ran the city, but Crane owned the Militia. And its guns trumped everything else.

Crane's hunt for the drive would take place under cover of a major operation to suppress the uppity proles of Charlestown, an operation that would allow Crane back into polite society as the man who stamped out the insurrectionists in Boston.

"You are very good, Crane, very good," Harrington conceded aloud. "But I am better."

There were no roadblocks up yet, and most of the traffic was disrupted by the parade, which actually made the drive back to Charlestown faster than it would have otherwise been. Turnbull pulled the Volvo up in front of the Tangier. There were no sentries out front.

"We'll be right back," he told Katie as he got out. Teddy King bailed from the other side, his pistol by his side.

The front door was open, mostly because it was knocked off its hinges. Turnbull drew his piece and went inside into the dark, with only a flickering TV for light.

Patrick O'Brien was behind the bar and three others were standing in front of it, and they froze with the Wilson Combat CQB in their faces.

"Don't even twitch," Turnbull said. It took a moment for his eyes to get accustomed to the dark, but the smells of cordite and copper – blood – were hanging in the fetid air.

"Shit," Teddy said, his weapon on the trio but his eyes peering into the dank.

Four trussed up bodies – it was clear they were bodies – lay on the floor in a row, wrapped up in black plastic sheeting.

"Talk," Turnbull said to O'Brien.

"That one there on the end is Seamus," he said. "We put the fingertips they cut off of him in there with him."

"Where are the cops?" Teddy asked.

Malloy snorted. "If the ambulances won't come, why would the PSF?"

"So, you're just cleaning up the mess yourself," Turnbull said. "And taking over."

"Somebody has to."

"Your boy Seamus talked before they offed him," Turnbull said, lowering his piece. "We walked out of the score into an ambush."

O'Brien sighed. He had seen Seamus's body, so he understood. "Danny?" he asked.

"Dead. All of them dead, except Katie. She's hit. You need to take her."

"Take her to the doctor."

"You got a doctor?"

O'Brien nodded. "Doc Farnham. He's been stitching up players around here since my granddad was in the life. He can take care of her."

"What are you going to do with those?" Turnbull said, gesturing with his .45 at the bodies.

"Disposal's always a problem," O'Brien said. "But we have techniques."

"You've got a bigger problem," Teddy said, looking at the TV screen. There was footage of People's Militia members gathering in some shopping center parking lot – lots of them. The CNN chyron read "People's Militia Mobilizes To Crush Right Wing Charlestown Terrorists."

"They're coming here?" O'Brien said, not quite believing it. "Fine. Let them come. Won't be the first time."

"Write down this quack's address. I've got no intention of being here when Task Force Asshole show up."

"They really ought to rethink this idea," O'Brien said, taking a pen and a paper napkin from under the bar. "If not, they better bring body bags."

"Bunker Hill II," Teddy King said. "Maybe we should stick around for the party."

"We've got other plans," Turnbull said. "It'll take that cluster a few hours to get organized. When they do, it'll be a lot of drugged-up scumbags with AKs. I dealt with their comrades at Cajon Pass. I want to be gone before they get here."

"The Brits thought they could come in here too," O'Brien observed. "That went badly."

"Save your ammo by letting them get close," Turnbull suggested. "Don't shoot until you see the bloodshots of their eyes."

"Good idea. Here's Doc's address," O'Brien said, handing over the napkin. "I need to spread the word and get things organized." Outside, a round of firecrackers went off.

"Happy Fourth of July," Turnbull said as he turned and left.

"She's resting. Her scapula is shattered. I dug out the bullet and the fiber from her suit the round pushed into the wound.

She's still looking at a bad infection," Doc said, washing his wrinkled hands in his sink. The water falling away was pink.

He was a pediatrician, taking care of kids during the day and their hoodlum parents at night. This was not his first gunshot wound. It was not even his first gunshot wound this month, and it was only the Fourth.

"We need to move," Turnbull said.

"I bet you do," the elderly doctor replied, drying his hands. The office was Spartan and spare, and the walls were covered with government-mandated warnings about how every patient had a right to be treated for free, and that the higher the privilege level the higher the priority for treatment. It also warned parents that "The childrenx assigned to you by birth have a right to obtain the gender-based health care necessary to validate their true identities regardless of transphobic objections."

Doc left the posters up on the wall for the benefit of the frequent inspectors from the Massachusetts Department of Medical Equity, then did the best he could to do for his patients as he saw fit. Medical care was free in the People's Republic, of course – the problem was the shortages of medicine and years-long waits for any kind of medical procedure except for gender validation surgeries, which got priority. Unlike many of his fellow pediatricians, Doc had yet to recommend that any child be castrated, surgically or chemically – something that the inspectors always noted with concern when auditing his records, as they did frequently.

The doctor finished washing up. Turnbull loosened his tie. Teddy King was standing by the office door, on guard. He still had his HK417. Outside, there were firecrackers going off.

"Can I leave her with you?" Turnbull said.

"Hell no you can't," the physician replied. "I'm a mob doctor, not a mob hospital. Besides, if the rumors are true and the damn blues are going to try to come into Charlestown in force tonight, I'll be busy. Really busy."

"Looks like they're coming. Maybe I can drop her with some family."

Doc shook his head. "Her mom died a year ago," he said. "It was back before the Split just after the Medical Equity Act put her at the back of the line for heart surgery. She was privileged, you know, just like all those other rich housekeepers. Funny, all these rules and regulations about medical equity never seem to stop the Brookline set from getting the meds and surgeries they need."

"Lot of privilege happening around here in Charlestown," Turnbull observed sourly. "Does she have anyone else?"

"Nope. Her pa got knifed in a bar a decade ago. And now you say Sean's gone."

"He went down fighting," Turnbull said.

"Good," the doctor said. "I hope he took a pack of those blue bastards with him to hell. But there's no other blood relations I know of, and I've treated the McGowans for better than forty years. Thought I'd be treating her and Danny's kids too. Damn shame."

"Can't take her to a hospital," Turnbull said.

"No, not even claiming it was an accident or a robbery. They'd report her gunshot wound and then the PSF would probably figure out she was in on the bank job with all the news coverage. Besides, she doesn't have the privilege level to get into a good hospital anyway, and the low privilege hospitals are worse than they were even before the Split. No medicine, few doctors, just chaos."

There were more firecrackers going off, and then some small explosions what did not quite sound like firecrackers."

"That's gunfire," Teddy King observed, cradling his rifle.

"It's starting," Turnbull said. "I need options, Doc."

"I don't have any good ones. She's strong and as tough as rebar, but if she doesn't get some real care, she may well die."

"Chris, we need to make a call," King said and the noise outside increased. "Are we getting out of here or what?"

.

"Shit," Turnbull swore. He had made a promise to Doyle. "Look Doc, can she travel if there's medical care at the end of the trip?"

"I wouldn't recommend it. And I know a bit about gunshot wounds. I was a medic as a kid at the end of the Vietnam War."

"Well, would you recommend she stay here in Charlestown instead without any?"

"No," Doc said.

"She might die if I take her out," Turnbull said. "But it sounds like she will die if I leave her here."

"Probably. But where the hell would you take her?"

"That's my business, Doc."

"You're talking about taking her to the red."

"And if I am?"

"Well, maybe she can hold on for 24 hours, and if you get her some real care in the USA, where I hear they still have it, she just might make it."

"That's what I needed to know."

"Look, I have my secret stash of painkillers and antibiotics for my special patients. I can give her some injections and give you some pills, but she really needs rest and maybe even blood."

"Okay," Turnbull said. "Can you at least hold her here for an hour? I gotta get a new ride and a change of clothes."

"Damn right," King said from the door. There were rips and flecks of blood on his suitcoat and slacks. "We look like we manage hedge funds in Mogadishu."

"Yeah, she can stay here for an hour," the Doc said. "One hour. I gotta go though. I'll shoot her up and give you her meds."

"Let me talk to her," Turnbull said. He went into the exam room, where Katie lay on an examination table. Next to her was a steel tray with bloody instruments and heaps of moist, scarlet gauze.

"Hey," she said weakly.

"Hey," he replied.

"So, am I gonna die?"

"Eventually," Turnbull said. "But probably not of this. That is, if we get you out of here."

"I don't want to go to a hospital, Chris," she said, rising up.

"No, not one of those butcher shops. A real hospital. On the other side."

"The other side?" she asked, puzzled. "The other side of what?"

"In the red," Turnbull said. "That's where we're going, Katie. The United States. There's no one to leave you with here, and if you don't get real treatment, you will die. So, I'm taking you with me."

"I'm not going anywhere," she said.

"Katie, this town is about to become a war zone. If the blues don't kill you, gangrene will. And I promised Danny I'd take care of you."

"Who the hell are you?" she asked.

"I'm the only chance for you to get out of this alive."

"You're some kind of secret agent," she said as it became clear to her. "And you used Danny and Sean and the rest for your mission."

"They were big boys. They knew the risks," Turnbull said.

Katie paused. "Yeah," she said. "It still makes you a bastard though."

"Hate me when we're in Kentucky," Turnbull said. "You and Teddy wait here for an hour. I need to get us new clothes and a car for the trip. Doc will give you some medicine. Rest."

"Get Clover," Katie said firmly.

"What, the dog? No," Turnbull said.

"My brother's dead. I got no one else. And neither does she."

"I'm not going out there and getting you a damn dog."

"Then I'm not going," Katie said. It was clear that was final.

"Can't you get another dog in the USA?" Turnbull said.

"You don't know how dogs work, do you?" she said, grimacing. "I go with the dog or not at all."

"I'll try to get the dog," Turnbull said.

"There is no try," Katie said. "Do. And between Sean's and my dad's stuff at the house, you can find clothes to travel in. You remember where it is?"

"Yeah," Turnbull said. "You sure about the damn dog?"

"Positive." She winced.

Turnbull left the room. Doc was prepping a syringe. Teddy King was still by the door.

"I have to go get her dog," Turnbull said.

"She can't leave her dog," King said, amazed he had to point this out.

"Why not?" Turnbull asked.

"Were you damaged as a child or something?"

"Stay here and watch her," Turnbull said. "Don't leave. I'll be back in an hour."

"Don't forget the dog," King said.

"Stop talking," Turnbull said over his right shoulder as he left the office.

18.

He could feel the hostile energy on the streets of Charlestown as Turnbull hit the sidewalk and began walking past the row houses and businesses. Packs of kids ran everywhere, back and forth, shouting and firing off bottle rockets. The adults were different, less exuberant, more focused. And they were armed. Danny had complained about how hard it was to get firearms, but that was not a function of there not being any guns in the town. Far from it. Rather, as during the great ammo shortage of 2020-2021, it was a matter of people sitting on their stockpiles until they needed them. And they needed them now.

There was clearly some organization to what was happening – the adults were moving toward the edges of the neighborhood in packs, but as an outsider, Turnbull could not see exactly who was in charge. They all just sort of knew that the People's Militia was coming, and they all just sort of knew where they should go.

Walking past the famously phallic Bunker Hill Monument on Breed's Hill, it was clear that this was being converted into some sort of redoubt, just like old times. In 1775, it took several charges by various groups of fusiliers, grenadiers, and infantrymen to absorb all the rebel rounds so that the final bayonet charge at the out-of-ammo Yankees allowed them to finally overrun the last position. Now, several trucks were there with salty-looking dudes carrying an array of rifles and shotguns. The monument door was open and locals were going inside, probably to get a better view of the area from the top of the 221-foot obelisk.

There was no violence on the block outside of Doc Farnham's office, but a couple blocks on that changed. Along Main Street, gentrified and filled with shops that most of the locals could not afford to patronize even if they were welcomed in by the newcomers, the crowd was taking its revenge. Most of the proprietors had cleared out earlier, when it became obvious that the situation was going to deteriorate fast. They locked their doors, but that didn't help. One gigantic youth, to the cheers of his running buddies, picked up a garbage can off the sidewalk that was overflowing with trash – the sanitation workers had chosen to skip this week's pick-up – and tossed it through a Starbucks plate glass window. The sheet of glass collapsed on the sidewalk and inside the vestibule. The rest of them climbed into the hole and began to pilfer the shelves of coffee mugs, travel cups, and Enya CDs.

Turnbull moved through the chaos in his tattered suit, attracting no attention at all. Most of the youths were interested in looting the hated interlopers' stores and liberating the consumer goods reserved for the affluent new residents.

Those residents still remaining were not faring well. For the most part, they huddled inside their townhouses and condos as toughs shouted obscenities and hucked the occasional rock through their windows. One scared, goateed man in an ironic Porsche had a couple locals jumping up and down on his hood as others pointed and jeered. The victim was screaming into his phone to no avail, his enthusiasm for defunding the police having dramatically waned in the last few minutes. One guy smashed his side window with a tire iron, dropped it, and reached inside, tossing out the man's cell phone and pulling the screaming hipster out over the glass and dropping him on the street, where the crowd proceeded to kick and punch him as he vainly tried to ward off the blows.

Turnbull watched the beating as he passed, torn. He sighed.

"Hey, get off him," he said, loudly and without allowing any ambiguity about his order.

Most of the mob looked up, puzzled, then complied – the youths generally understood the chain of command between obviously tough older men and callow younger ones. In the real Charlestown, people got punched, as the bleeding, sobbing hipster was discovering to his chagrin. And people did not mess with guys who seemed like they meant business.

But one guy looked at Turnbull, assessed him, then resumed pummeling his quaking victim. The crowd looked at Turnbull to see what he was going to do about this defiance.

Turnbull sighed again, mostly at annoyance with himself for getting into a situation where he could easily become a target himself if he showed weakness.

"I said to lay off him," Turnbull said.

The puncher paused, looked at Turnbull, and suggested he perform an anatomically challenging act. Then he resumed slugging the hipster. The mob looked as one to Turnbull to see what was going to happen next.

Turnbull walked over and the guy again stopped slugging his victim, then turned to square off, and was promptly stunned at the speed and ferocity of Turnbull's attack. The youth was a peacock – his fights on the streets were often more of a show of strength than a true battle, not really designed to cause serious injury but to signal his fortitude to his peers.

Turnbull, in contrast, was dead serious about violence. His first blow shattered the young man's nose and threw him back against the Porsche. He then drove his meaty paws into the target's sternum and gut in quick succession, leaving his prey on his knees, gasping for air.

There was no need for Turnbull to address the other members of the mob – they understood. As his target gulped oxygen and hacked on the pavement, Turnbull reached down and pulled up the battered hipster, who stood unsteadily on his feet.

"Get in your car," Turnbull said. "You need to go."

Turnbull was sideswiped by the young man, who had been tougher than he looked. Turnbull reeled back a few steps as the young man stooped and picked up the tire iron.

The Wilson was out and in his face before Turnbull even consciously thought to draw it, the safety clicking off as it swung up.

The young man paused, the .45 adding a new element to the scenario, and one whose game-changing nature penetrated even his thick skull. He stood there, pondering his options. The muzzle of the handgun seemed to get wider as he stared.

Turnbull said nothing for a moment, then he spoke to the victim.

"Go on, get in your car and get out of town."

"Is that a gun?" the man asked.

"If you tell me you don't believe in guns, I swear I will leave you to them," Turnbull said.

"Shoot them," the hipster said. "Shoot them all!"

"Get in your car," Turnbull said, loudly. "Last chance."

The youth squaring off with him stared back, uncertain, tire iron in his hand. The Wilson was still in his face, unmoving.

The hipster slid into the battered coupe, turned over the engine, and then pulled away. If he didn't stop, and if the locals hadn't sealed off the town yet, he might get out damaged, but in one piece.

Tire Iron Boy made no move, and after a moment, Turnbull lowered the pistol and walked away – listening for the sound of feet behind him in the event the young man decided to try his luck. Tire Iron Boy wisely did not.

The Whole Foods was being looted, with people pushing out carts heaped with lentil pasta and exotic cheeses. Most of the delicacies they were liberating were foreign to the Charlestown townies' customary diet, but with food expensive when it wasn't scarce, they could find something to do with a free quarter wheel of Manchego or a bag of fresh kale.

Turnbull continued past, pausing to let the women – most of the looters by now were female, as the men were assembling on the border of the town to await the invaders – maneuver their heaping shopping carts past.

"I don't know what salted caramel ice cream is, but it sounds wicked good," one mommy said to her friend. Each had a cart with a couple kids on it in addition to a pile of extremely discounted groceries.

"Sounds like ass," her pal replied, unconvinced. She had found a bottle of Enfield Foot Tread rosé on the shelf and was looking forward to getting it home and mixing it with some of the 7UP she had been lucky enough to find and buy with her EBT card.

The ladies pushed by and Turnbull continued past, moving quickly and with a purpose. There was a fire in a townhouse off to his left. It would probably burn up the whole block, since there was no chance of a fire truck showing up. He kept to the opposite sidewalk and watched as a dozen men with long guns – shotguns, bolt-action deer hunting .30-06s, and a couple of modern sporting rifles that hadn't been legal in Massachusetts even before the Split – passed by in a rough approximation of an informal formation. There were still bottle rockets going off, and firecrackers, but there were more actual gunshots than before.

The leader of the squad had a Motorola radio and Turnbull saw him put it to his ear, then yell into it. He turned to his guys.

"We gotta go the other way. The bastards are coming in boats now, too. We gotta meet them at the waterfront!"

The rough formation did a 180-degree turn and they began to jog toward the water. They were eager for a fight.

Overhead was a PSF helicopter. The fact that it was well out of range did not stop several locals from taking shots at it.

"Outstanding," Turnbull muttered bitterly, the possibility of getting struck by a falling round some knucklehead had shot at the clouds adding to his extensive and growing list of short-term hazards.

He was getting close to Katie's house now, recognizing the area from his walk with Danny. The morale of the locals was high, but he knew that would change once the fighters started seeing their buddies drop. The Leprechauns were committed criminals; fighting was their life. But most of these people were regular folks, albeit inspired by their predecessors who had fought on this same ground against a different tyrant about two-and-a-half centuries ago.

Once again, the local militia was being called up, and once again, the people were answering. Except this time the enemy wasn't just firing iron cannonballs and fiery, sulphur-laden carcass shells at them from ships. The enemy had planes, and artillery, and drones – that is, if they used the actual PR Army. In a closed area against concentrated rebels, those assets would be deadly and determinative even if they would not be so effective against a dispersed and decentralized insurrection out in the sticks. But if they just sent in the fodder, the People's Militia, into Charlestown, then it would be rifleman against rifleman, and the townies stood a chance.

But only for a while. It wasn't a fight the locals could ever win in the long run. It was a whole country – really, a half of a country – against one neighborhood. But unfortunately for the invaders, Turnbull noted, the Irish were as good at embracing lost causes as they were at drinking whiskey.

The gunfire was increasing as Turnbull stepped up onto the porch of Katie's house. Some of it was automatic now, and it was unclear whose. But it was still sporadic, the relative calm before the storm.

Inside the house, Clover was barking, driven wild by the noise from fireworks and firearms. Out on the street a truck trundled past, filled with shouting and packing locals.

Turnbull opened up the unlocked front door. Clover growled at him, but he stepped inside anyway and shut the door behind him.

He ignored the dog and went upstairs. It took him a few minutes to find a bag and pack it with clothes. Sean's duds seemed like a reasonable fit for him. The father's smaller clothes were probably okay for Teddy King. He selected jeans, polo shirts, and jackets. The Red Sox jackets both men had he rejected – they would draw attention for being racist somehow.

He changed, dropping the chest rig but retrieving the disc. It was in one piece. He found a small gym bag and stuffed Teddy King's clothes into it.

Going back downstairs, he looked around and found Clover's leash, then hooked her up.

"Come on, dog," he said, opening the door. There was a pack of teens running down the street. He pulled the German shepherd down the steps and started back to Doc Farnham's clinic.

The People's Militia command post was set up in a Hampton Inn conference room in what had been Cambridge and was now known as Floyd. The militia fighters, most carrying Chinese AKs, milled about as their senior leaders – they would not have called themselves that, as they publicly eschewed concepts like "hierarchy" even as they rigorously embraced them – gathered to plan the coming assault on Charlestown.

Travis Lumumba-Zapata was doing his best, considering his limited experience in military operations. He had several veterans among the People's Militia force of 6,500 that he had assembled, and together they looked at an old AAA map and tried to figure out how to proceed. It was a similar problem to that of General Howe during the old Revolution – how to isolate and eliminate the threat on the peninsula that stabbed out into the water north of Boston proper.

The smaller Alford Street Bridge and the larger Tobin Bridge over the Mystic River were sealed off, as was the North

Washington Street Bridge to the Southwest. Charlestown's neck from the mainland had been quite narrow in June 1775; over the centuries, it had been widened with fill. Now, there was no easy way to seal off the Town on the western side. The Northern Expressway, I-93, wound around the west side as an informal border. The ugly, elevated eyesore would be the front line of troops and act as the perimeter line. The Militia was already engaging in limited firefights with bands of locals, who somehow had a lot more weapons than anyone expected.

The forces, they decided, would advance down axes from the northwest at Bunker Hill Drive and southwest from Austin Street. There were not enough boats to make a major landing from the water, but there were a few police boats and requisitioned watercraft to make a feint and draw some of the locals to the waterfront.

The idea was to make a significant show of force and convince the locals to retreat into their homes. Then the troublemakers could be tracked and arrested at the People's Militia's leisure. Lumumba-Zapata had already arranged to use Fenway Park to hold prisoners. And along with the People's Militia would go the SIS men led by Gruber, who stood to the side with a disconcerting grin. Lumumba-Zapata had no idea what the man's mission was, and he did not want to.

"Okay," Lumumba-Zapata told the assembled Militia officers. "Time to attack."

Clover jumped up on the bed and began licking Katie's face.

"Get that dog away from her!" Doc Farnham shouted. "She's got enough to worry about without getting an infection from its filthy mouth."

"Change," Turnbull said, throwing the gym bag containing Katie's father's clothes to Teddy King. King began pulling off his bloody suit as Turnbull took up security.

"She ready to move?" Turnbull asked.

"As ready as she's going to be," Doc replied. "Which is not very."

"If you have an alternative course of action, I'm open to it."

"Well, I don't," the doctor replied. There was a lot of gunfire now, still sporadic. The actual assault was not quite here yet, just skirmishing. It was still fun and games. But soon it would get real. "Of course, it's only a matter of time before they overrun us. But like the last time, I bet we'll make them pay for every foot of dirt. My relative Ralph Farnham was here in 1775. The colonials killed a couple hundred redcoats and only withdrew when they ran out of powder."

"A tactical victory for the British," Turnbull observed.

"A pyrrhic one," replied the doctor.

"Next question," Turnbull said. "How do we get out?"

"That's your challenge," Doc Farnham said. "The bridges are no doubt blocked. I expect they are patrolling the Mystic, so you aren't sailing out. You have to break through their perimeter to the west."

"I've dealt with militia before," Turnbull said. "I was at Cajon Pass. They aren't exactly disciplined."

"You mean there'll be holes in their lines?"

"I hope so," Turnbull said. "Maybe we can find a sector where they all decided to walk off their posts and get high."

"I wouldn't put it past those militia dirtbags," Doc said. "About one notch above a mob, if you ask me."

"Yeah, but they do have one important advantage."

"What's that?"

"There's a shit ton of them."

19.

"It hurts to walk," Katie said. "Even with all the drugs."

"I bet it does," Turnbull said, holding her up with one arm and holding Clover's leash with the other. "You know what hurts more? Getting caught trying to drive out of here."

Teddy King was walking ahead of them down the street, his HK417 out. It was drawing admiring looks from the toughs passing by on the way to the fight at the outskirts. Those looks, in turn, drew the stink-eye from Turnbull.

They were moving west, toward the mainland, the tower on Breed's Hill visible over the rows of buildings. There were a lot of gunshots now, and in all directions, including from the waterfront. Overhead were helicopters, still drawing fire even though they were far too high to hit.

"We'll find their perimeter, then try to figure out where we can pass through," Turnbull said.

"How will we know?" King asked.

"It'll be the part of the line that no one's shooting at us from."

They kept moving. Turnbull felt the urge to check – again – that the disc was there in his front pocket, but his hands were full.

The dog was alerting left and right and straining at the leash, over-stimulated by the sights and sounds. Katie was doing better than he expected, needing only a bit of help. Doc Farnham had given her a bag of saline and a pint of O+ – who knows where he had gotten that. At least she had some color again and no longer looked like Charlestown's biggest Cure fan.

There was firing up ahead, a lot of it. Some locals had put a couple vehicles, a mail truck and a bread delivery truck, across the street and were in position behind it firing at something. And that something was shooting back.

"AKs," Turnbull said, knowing the sound from experience. "Let's go north."

They peeled off left at the next corner. A dead woman in expensive clothes lay in the gutter, bruised and bloody.

"She probably mouthed off," Katie said. "Should have kept her trap shut."

"Come on," Turnbull said. They moved on down the street. About one in five townhouses, inevitably the nice ones owned by the gentrifiers, were trashed, with broken windows and their doors hanging off their hinges. Looted goods the thieves dropped and trash filled the street. A broken, $500 juicer from Williams-Sonoma lay forlornly in the gutter.

The firing was getting heavier. The first push was underway, and it was running into a wall of lead.

But Turnbull was focused on trying to figure out just how he was going to get them out of there.

Travis Lumumba-Zapata was frightened, even though he was far from the shooting. The initial reports back from the first attempt to force their way into Charlestown were in, and they were ugly. The locals had erected roadblocks on all the main thoroughfares, and they were defending them with guns. Lots of guns.

"Where did they get so many guns?" he asked his subordinates.

"Gun ownership was a result of systemic white supremacy," one lieutenant said, remembering what xir professor had taught xir at Wellesley. The others gathered around the old Triple-A map on the conference room table nodded. It was so obviously true.

"It's an honor to be in the vanguard of fighting the racist paradigm of privilege represented by this enclave of insurrectionists," xe continued. There was more muttered approval, including by Lumumba-Zapata. He realized that all this talk was adding nothing toward solving the problem at hand, but he certainly could not say so – the entire enterprise would then degenerate into a witch hunt for internal heretics. He understood that – he had led such degenerations in the past when it suited his own interests, but it did not suit them now. He had a mission to accomplish, and if the command group spun off into a tangent of rooting out the insufficiently woke, it would fail. And with Merrick Crane III, failure was terminal.

"Yes, we are fortunate to have this opportunity to strike a blow against systemic prejudice," Lumumba-Zapata said. "Comrade Gerkin is correct to validate our shared allyship in that initiative. We must redouble our efforts. We must attack again."

"My troops were slaughtered. I lost at least a dozen," said a lieutenant near the back. He was bandaged and an AK hung off his shoulder. He was one of the vets; he had been an infantryman in the Massachusetts National Guard before the Split. "We need a better plan than just march forward and get shot."

Lumumba-Zapata sensed the danger he presented. He waited a moment, to let the tension build.

"What are your pronouns?" Lumumba-Zapata asked.

"He/him," the lieutenant said. "Look, we need to…"

"Of course," Lumumba-Zapata said. "I'm not surprised, considering your linear worldview, your focus on so-called accomplishments, your refusal to acknowledge the existence of other ways of seeing and knowing."

The lieutenant knew the game too, and realized he was out-maneuvered. "You're a he/him too!"

"I accepted my male identity, not the male gaze. Get this transphobe out!"

Several Militia members piled onto the lieutenant, relieving him of his rifle and hustling him outside as he shrieked and struggled.

Lumumba-Zapata did not show his relief at having resolved this challenge. He simply ordered another attack. Perhaps the veteran was right tactically, but he had been wrong in all the ways that actually mattered.

The shooting intensified to their left, the west, as they headed north parallel to the perimeter cutting off Charlestown. So far, no luck. There was no way out, and the enemy was coming.

More men and vehicles passed them, moving toward the sound of the guns. A white pick-up full of men screeched to a stop beside them. Pat O'Brien stepped out, with an AR-15 in his hands.

"Where the hell are you going?" he asked.

"Out," Turnbull said.

"Good luck. They got the Neck sealed off tight. I tried to get some boys through so they could come around and hit them from behind. They got waxed."

"What do you suggest?" Teddy King said. Several of O'Brien's cronies were eye-balling his sweet, sweet HK417.

"I suggest you come fight with us. Put Katie in her house with her mutt and join the party."

"I got a job to do," Turnbull said in a manner that excluded the possibility of debate.

"Yeah, well the fight may come to you. They're trying to break through northwest and southwest. We beat them back the first time, and we'll beat them back the second. I don't know about the third time. We are running low on ammo."

"You know how to remedy that, right?" Turnbull asked.

"We all grew up hearing about not shooting 'til you see the whites of their eyes," O'Brien said. "We know."

"Eventually, they'll get through. Then what?" asked Turnbull.

"Then I guess we're screwed. Nothing new about that." O'Brien got back in the passenger seat of the truck.

"Good luck," Turnbull said, meaning it.

"Yeah, the luck of the Irish," O'Brien said. "If we didn't have bad luck, we'd have no luck at all."

He pulled his door shut, and the truck pulled away.

Turnbull looked up and down the street. There were more trashed townhouses, some with people still looting. The shooting got much louder.

"I have an idea," Turnbull said.

Johnny Ross walked through the streets of Charlestown avoiding eye contact except where necessary to dissuade young men considering whether he might be a potential victim. He did not have that look, and a hard-eyed glance was enough to get the predators looking for sheep instead of taking the risk that they were rousting a sheepdog.

He had worked his way into Charlestown just as the People's Militia was setting up a perimeter around the Neck. The Militia members were not as clued in as their bosses about who was playing for what team in the Machiavellian world of People's Republic politics, and his FBI credentials served to get him the deference he needed to infiltrate the besieged town.

He kept his SIG under wraps, having restocked on loaded mags before coming. People were running about, many armed, and there was shooting in the distance.

The People's Militia was coming. He had to act fast.

The dead robbers were all local. He had gotten some fingerprint identifications back. One was Danny Doyle, the rest his running buddies. But who were the others? Chris, of course, yet who the hell was he?

But he did have one piece of information. The girl – she was shot.

He called Colby and had his boss set some techs to work at the Joint Federal Criminal Investigation Database terminal and start looking through records and confidential informant reports for names of mob doctors in Charlestown. The first one that came up was a guy who had died a couple years ago, throat slit in an alley. According to the CI's information, the sawbones had botched fixing a mobster's ankle wound. It got infected, he got gangrene, and the patient's buddies had settled the score. They took malpractice seriously in Charlestown.

The other reputed mob doctor, never arrested or charged, but popping up in a number of informant statements, was one Dr. James Farnham. And he was alive and well and still practicing as a pediatrician.

Ross made for his clinic.

The mob on the street was half preparing for the invasion and half dedicated to looting the nicer shops and houses in the neighborhood. The few gentrifiers who had not hopped in their Priuses and gotten the hell outta Dodge were getting beaten up in the streets.

Ross arrived at the clinic and the front door was open. He went inside the waiting room and a man who was obviously Dr. Farnham came out an interior door. He carried a medium-sized duffel bag and wore an old red cross brassard over his civilian clothes.

"We're closed," he snapped.

"You're open for me," Ross said, raising his FBI ID. "And for others, I expect."

"A fed in here right now? Are you crazy brave or just really stupid?"

"I can take care of myself," Ross said. "I'm interested in who you've been taking care of."

"Well, Special Agent, maybe you don't hear Khe Sanh II going on outside, but I figure I'll be taking care of a lot of people tonight."

"I'm interested in only one," Ross said. "Back inside."

Doc Farnham turned around and they went back through the door into the treatment area.

"Empty saline drip, bloody gauze," Ross said, surveying the room. "I guess my hunch was right."

"My nurses went home before cleaning up," Dr. Farnham said. "Couple mugs got in a fight. Happens. Now, if you don't mind, I have patients out there who need me."

"If I dig around here, I'm going to find a bloody bullet from a PSF weapon," Ross said. "So, let's just cut to the chase. Who's the girl?"

"What girl?"

"You're starting to piss me off, Doc," Ross said.

"What are you going to do? Arrest me? I think you might find carrying me out of here in cuffs draws some attention you don't want. Why don't you do yourself a favor and get out while the getting's good?"

"I'm guessing the girl is a local. You gotta be loyal to her. I get that. But the big guy with her, calls himself 'Chris.' He's not. And you don't owe him anything."

"I didn't get to be 74 grassing on folks, Special Agent."

"I don't even want him. He's got something I need. Tell me where she's holed up and I'll go get it. I'll leave her be."

"I ain't helping you."

Ross looked around the clinic and drummed his fingers on his thigh.

"She isn't here. You couldn't send her to a hospital," Ross said. He walked over to the needle box and peeked inside, then to the bio waste box. He looked inside that too.

"You gave her blood," Ross said. "You're a full-service mob doctor. I'm impressed. And antibiotics. Painkillers too."

"Oh, you're a trauma surgeon now, are you?"

"She's not holed up somewhere, is she?" Ross said. "You got her ready to move. He's taking her out, isn't he?"

"Like I said, I ain't helping you."

"You already have."

"Chris, we need to keep moving," Teddy King told Turnbull. "We need to get out through the perimeter."

"No," Turnbull said. "We need the perimeter to come to us."

He surveyed the street and saw a particularly nice townhouse, its front door hanging off its hinges and a trail of furniture and knick-knacks leading down the stoop and along the sidewalk where the looters had dropped it.

"Come on," Turnbull said. "Inside."

The people on the street paid them no mind as they stood at top of the short stairway that led up to the front door, staring at the façade.

"Here," Turnbull said, handing Katie over to Teddy King. "Come on, dog. Make yourself useful."

Turnbull drew the Wilson Combat CQB with his right hand and held the leash with his left as he carefully walked up the steps. It was dark inside – the blues had cut the power a few minutes before – and Turnbull let the dog go first. She growled and strained forward as they entered the front hallway.

Clover exploded into a spasm of barking and jumping. There were three teens in the front living room enjoying what was probably a very, very good bottle of cabernet while sitting on the sofa.

They were displeased by the agitated German shepherd and very, very displeased by the big, unsmiling man with the gun.

"Get out," Turnbull said.

They did, fast, rushing outside and down the stoop past King and Katie and then disappearing into the street.

"Come on in," Turnbull said.

King helped Katie up the steps and followed Turnbull. He was looking in doors on the first floor, opening several until he found one with stairs leading down.

"Wait," he said, disappearing into the kitchen. After a couple minutes he reappeared with a flashlight and a Whole Foods rustic ciabatta, plus some cheese.

Turnbull left the dog, bread, and brie, with King, then turned on the flashlight and went down the stairs, gun ready. In less than a minute he returned, and together they descended into the wine cellar.

"He knows his stuff," King said, examining a bottle of 2013 Jamie Slone Duo cabernet. Nearby, Katie lay, resting with the dog beside her.

"Put it away," Turnbull said. "This is a hideout, not a wine bar."

King reluctantly complied as Turnbull went up the steps, shut the door, and came back down again. After hours of hearing fireworks and gunfire, the silence was eerie.

"Okay, why are we in a wine cellar?" asked King.

"We're going to wait for the perimeter to come to us," Turnbull said. "They've attacked twice already. The locals are not exactly conserving their ammo. If the Militia doesn't break through the third time, they will the fourth or fifth."

"And you want them to push past us."

"Not want. That's just what's going to happen. Pretty soon we'll be to their rear instead of to their front. Then we move."

"But there'll be Militia all over."

"I have a plan for that too. Rest up. I'll take the first watch."

Turnbull woke up Teddy King with an ungentle kick to the thigh.

"My turn?" he mumbled.

"It sounds like it's going off," Turnbull said. And it did. There was shooting, close by, lots of it. The front line had moved inwards and they were on it.

Glass shattered upstairs, which was surprising since much of it had been broken out.

King picked up the HK417 and aimed at the door. Turnbull handed him a wad of what looked like tissue paper.

"If you pull that trigger in this wine cellar, we all go deaf. So jam some of this in your ears."

King nodded; Turnbull had a suppressor screwed onto the end of his Wilson .45.

There was a burst of fire nearby, probably out front, and voices. Clover growled. Katie, who was awake by now, whispered for her to be quiet and put her hand on the dog's snout.

Something crashed up, and there were more voices. It was confused and undisciplined, and there were footsteps. Turnbull took aim at the door. He turned off the flashlight.

"Don't do nothing unless I tell you to," he whispered. King didn't hear him clearly with the tissue paper in his ears.

More footsteps, then nothing but some shooting.

"Were they good guys or bad guys?" King asked softly.

"Maybe it was Militia clearing the townhouse," Turnbull whispered. "If it was, they did a shit job."

"What next?" Katie asked, holding the dog.

"We wait. Let them move on," Turnbull said, relaxing a little. There was now definitely less shooting than before.

"How long?" she asked.

"Long enough to let the Militia get comfortable," Turnbull said.

Lumumba-Zapata's forces had finally pushed back the locals on their fourth advance, the volume of return fire having slackened off dramatically. It was now a question of clearing the holdouts, locking down the population, and finding the individuals who needed to be dragged to Fenway Park for interrogation and eventual punishment. That several hundred people were dead or wounded was an afterthought.

"There's an FBI agent to see you," one of Lumumba-Zapata's lieutenants said.

"I thought I just dealt with them," the commander said, annoyed and frazzled. "Send them in."

Johnny Ross was led inside the command post by the lieutenant. Lumumba-Zapata turned to assess him.

"Your pronouns?" he asked.

Ross paused. He was tired and had almost gotten shot at the roadblock on the North Washington Street Bridge where he had slowly approached the jump Militia troops manning it holding his FBI credentials high. He did not have time for nonsense, but also no time for an unnecessary fight.

"He/him," Ross replied.

"I just gave your people a Humvee to go inside the perimeter," he said. "What do you want now?"

"My people? FBI?"

"Whatever they were. Look, I'm busy here."

"Big guy, bun in his hair, crazy eyes?"

"That's a bit stereotyped."

"I'm busy, too. Was it him?"

"Yes," Lumumba-Zapata said. "I'm supposed to lend you feds all assistance possible, so what do you want?"

Ross silently gave thanks for the inability of this jumped-up grad student to distinguish between the types of feds and what team each was playing for.

"I need to know if your people picked up this guy coming out of the perimeter. He'll be with a man and a woman. The woman is wounded."

"How the hell would I know?" Lumumba-Zapata said. "We've arrested a lot of rebels tonight, men, women, non-binary, and genderqueer. Killed a bunch too."

Ross sighed. Maybe he could go to Fenway Park and walk the holding pens and hope to get lucky. But then this Chris didn't seem the type to accept captivity.

"The other agent, the one with the hair."

"What about him?" asked Lumumba-Zapata.

"'Where was he going in this Humvee?"

Wayne Gruber drove into a dark and smoky Charlestown with three of his surviving men in a hummer he requisitioned from Travis Lumumba-Zapata. The People's Militia commander did not need to be intimidated by the SIS boss; he was pre-intimidated by his chat with Merrick Crane III and whatever this manbunned sociopath – Lumumba-Zapata kept his biased reaction to this manifestly differently mentalitied individual to himself – wanted, Crane's catspaw got.

Gruber ignored the bodies in the streets – there were lots. The Militia was not removing the civilian dead and wounded. If someone got shot, they were a combatant, and the Militia forces were content to let them lie there bleeding. Gruber's driver took it a step farther – he ran over the legs of one young man who was crawling, gut shot, to the sidewalk. The hummer jolted and Gruber chuckled, then he turned back to his cell phone – the cellular service was back on now that the battle was simmering down – and checked the address.

"Turn here," he grunted, and his driver made a left.

"You think they are in there?" Dworkin asked from the backseat.

"We know there was a girl there," Gruber said. They had identifications on all the bodies. "And we know that Sean McGowan's sister has a record. So, it's an educated guess."

"But there's only four of us," Dworkin said. He left unspoken the fate of most of the SIS men they had brought to the bank.

"Then we better be really sneaky," Gruber replied. He pulled the G36 up as they came to a halt in front of Katie's house. Perhaps a dozen People's Militia milled about on the block. There were a couple dead guys at the far end.

Gruber was out and running, ignoring his anal injury, intent on making up through aggression and speed what he lacked in numbers. He hit the door hard and it flew open. He swept the front room with his muzzle, and, seeing nothing, moved into the kitchen in the back. His compadres fanned out, and there were several shouts of "Clear!" before he relaxed and the team met up in the living room.

"Nothing," Dworkin said. "Empty. But they were here." He held out Turnbull's discarded chest rig.

"Where's the puppy?" asked Gruber.

"The what?"

"The dog. Look, there's a couple bowls. I don't think the McGowans were eating out of them."

"Maybe he ran out during the fighting, scared or something."

"No, the door was shut and I don't see a leash by the door. That's where I'd keep a leash if I had a dog." Gruber was grinning now, mighty pleased with his powers of deduction.

"They're on the run."

"With this big guy from the red, I bet," Gruber said. "I have a personal beef with him and I would like to resolve it. *Mano a mano.*"

Gruber thought for a moment.

"Grab me some neighbors. Bet they have an idea what's up. And I bet they'd be happy to tell me with some proper incentives."

"Stay here," Turnbull said. He got up off the concrete floor and moved slowly to the stairway up into the townhouse. There was some little bit of light streaming in from the doorframe, enough for him to feel his way upward without falling.

His Wilson automatic was in his hands, suppressed, ready.

Turnbull paused and listened at the door for a full two minutes. The dog's panting seemed like the roar of an engine in the silence. Then he leaned forward and put his ear on the door and listened for another full minute.

Satisfied, he pulled it open.

The power was back on, and all the light was artificial since it was dark outside. There were occasional yells and the odd gunshot, but the most prominent noise was from big military diesels, five-tons and Humvees, out on the streets.

Carefully, he picked his way down the hall to the front room and, keeping low, peeked out the shattered front window.

The street out front was a mess, illuminated by the unbroken streetlamps and the orange glare from the flickering fires. A silver Ford F-150 smoldered across the road. Several People's Militia military vehicles – mostly liberated from old National Guard units – were parked in no particular order at various angles. Several Militia troops milled about. And a few wounded were moaning.

And there were bodies, at least eight or nine, depending on how the pieces added up. Most were civilian. There were a couple dead Militia too.

A Humvee crackerbox ambulance, so named for the large square structure that carried patients, was parked just outside the townhouse, the back doors spread wide open but no passengers. The woodland camouflage paint scheme included a large white square on the side, and inside that used to have a red cross indicating its non-combatant status. The red cross was sloppily painted-over with flat brown paint, leaving a large smudge in its place. It had been decided that the cross was offensive to people of other faiths or none, which was preferred. Besides, such petty blasphemy was always fun and served to let the believers still remaining in the blue understand exactly where they and their beliefs stood in the new order.

Most of the Militia troops moved out, the street being secure. Left behind were two Militia members in camouflage uniforms checking the bodies of the Militia casualties in the eerie light. They ignored the dead civilians, and the wounded ones too. A woman in bloodied blue jeans asked them for water and they found it hilarious to spit at her.

Turnbull waited until they returned to the ambulance carrying one of the dead Militia fighters, who they unceremoniously heaved into the back of the crackerbox. The dead fighter landed with a thud.

Turnbull scowled. In the real military, ambulances carried the living, not the dead. And you treated the fallen with respect. But then, the dead of the People's Militia deserved none.

"I hate this job," one of them said.

"Could be worse," the other replied as they walked over and picked up the second camo-clad corpse. "You could have had to be out in the fighting."

"I wouldn't mind that," his partner replied as they carried the dead female to the ambulance. "I like killing racists and transphobes."

"Yeah, well, I bet she did too, until one of them shot her. I'm just fine doing this."

Turnbull looked up and down the street. Empty, except for the dead and wounded. The two ambulance attendants were unarmed, or rather, their weapons were probably still in the vehicle. A rookie mistake, and a costly one.

"Hey asswipes," Turnbull said, walking down the stairs out onto the dark sidewalk in front of the townhouse, his Wilson .45 up with the suppressor jutting out. They looked up at him slack-jawed, and Turnbull could see them both think the same thought: "Where is my AK?"

Their weapons were too far away.

"Get in the house," Turnbull directed. They dropped the stiff and stood there, just staring.

"Okay," Turnbull said. "Have it your way."

He shot the first, then the second through the forehead, the suppressor keeping the sound of the shoots below the background noise. Both dropped to the street. Turnbull walked down and dragged both bodies up onto the sidewalk, leaving their heads in the gutter to drain. That way, their uniforms would be less of a mess.

"Just the jackets," Turnbull instructed King, and he took the camo uniform off one of the dead medics. "The pants don't matter. If we have to get out of the ambulance we're going to be rocking and rolling anyway."

Katie was in the back of the ambulance on a stretcher with the dog, and the doors were closed. Turnbull had gone and brought them up after securing their ride.

"You can be pretty cold," King had observed looking at the two dead medics laid out on the pavement.

Turnbull didn't respond. He had hesitated once before, and he was not going to make that mistake again.

They dumped the dead Militia fighters out of the meat wagon into a heap on the street. Then, wearing the Operational Camouflage Pattern top, Turnbull walked over to the wounded woman with a canteen he had liberated from the back of the ambulance.

"Here," he said, kneeling and handing it to her. He could see, in the light of the streetlamps, that she was wounded badly in the legs. The woman took it as eagerly as she could and drank.

"Thanks," she gasped. "And thanks for shooting those pieces of shit."

Turnbull nodded and walked back to King as he was finishing putting on his top.

"Get in," Turnbull said. "I'll drive."

20.

Merrick Crane III was greatly pleased. It appeared Travis Lumumba-Zapata had managed to complete the mission of subduing the riotous neighborhood of Charlestown. He did not bother with the details like the list of people to be detained. It was enough for everyone to know that the enemies of the People's Republic were being dealt with.

By him.

And while the People's Militia had suffered several hundred casualties, this was no pyrrhic victory like the first Battle of Bunker Hill – which like this one, had really taken place largely around the nearby Breed's Hill. The casualties among the Militia were immaterial in the sense that there was a bottomless well of disaffected young cannon fodder to draw from within the PR. During Bunker Hill 1.0, highly-trained and storied British regiments were decimated, and the British reinforcements had to come from across the ocean. But 2.0 was different. To get more warm bodies for the security apparatus, Merrick Crane's subordinates would merely have to troll among the poor, hungry, and vicious here at home. The lure of money and the ability to hurt others under the color of law was irresistibly attractive to a certain demographic of sociopaths.

So, it was not the tactical result that mattered to him. He would have been just as pleased at five times the casualties. It was the strategic result, and the message it sent.

"Congratulations on an excellent job rooting out these racist criminals," Eric Swalwell had said during a short telephone call. The former congressman had been named to a post in the security services, and he had seen to the hate crime prosecution of several people for joking about his legendary flatulence on social media. But he was not entirely in the clear. There were still very serious questions about his alleged cis-hetero fetishization of Asian womxn and the complicity with white supremacy it supported. But the slimy politician might survive that, so Crane opted to be polite.

"I aim to serve the People's Republic," Crane had replied without emotion. In the background, there were the sounds of several young womxn giggling and speaking in what Crane recognized as Mandarin.

"I need to go," Swalwell said and hung up. Crane found it amusing that this mediocrity would hang up on him, but this was not the time to deal with petty slights.

There were more calls offering accolades, calls from people who had lost his number when he was on the outs and who had now found it again when his star rose once more. And it was not merely the radicals; progressive figures were calling him too, including one from the formerly-White House thanking him on behalf of President Biden, who was no doubt unaware of what had happened in Boston. According to rumors and sources that Crane believed, the president-in-name was interested only in his daily gruel and Angela Lansbury's investigation of the murder mystery *du jour* in Cabot Cove.

What pleased Crane most was the invitation.

Of course, he needed to come.

Of course, he needed to attend the Mackinac Island retreat for the leaders of the radical faction of the People's Republic.

Of course, it was all some grievous oversight that no one had extended an invitation before now.

He smiled thinly. From terrorist leader to legitimate political power player, all accomplished through one evening of bloodshed.

Oh, he would be going to Mackinac Island. And he would happily be welcomed into the fold as he mixed and mingled with some of the most powerful people in the People's Republic. And soon he would take the leadership of the radical faction from those same powerful people, people who talked about blood but never actually shed it. And then he would use the ultra-radical faction to take power from the merely-radical.

Sooner or later, Merrick Crane III would be the most powerful man in the People's Republic.

And it would be sooner if Wayne Gruber and his men found Chris and that disc.

Gruber wiped the blood off his hands. Katie's home was a wreck.

"Let's review," Gruber said to Dworkin, who was having trouble hiding his distaste. "The big guy and the little guy were here for the last few days. The big guy came back earlier today, changed, and left with the dog and a bag. Sounds like a trip. But the big news is he was an outsider – no one ever saw him before."

"You think he's headed out? I mean, out of the country?"

"I would be," Gruber said, holding his rifle in one hand pointed at the ceiling. "I'd be high-tailin' my ass to the red right about now."

"Well, what do we do?"

"Well," said Gruber, as if he was talking to a village idiot. "We tell our Militia friends to keep their perimeter up and to look for a dog, and if he gets out, we chase him."

Now that the shooting had stopped, there was light Militia traffic on the streets of Charlestown, and no civilian traffic. After a few refugees trying to escape in their over-loaded SUVs got lit up by trigger-happy militiapeople, the rest of the civilians wisely chose to wait it out inside their homes.

It was not an organized operation. Clumps of militia stood milling about at intersections and in parks, usually under the few unbroken streetlamps that still cast their pale light, not really sure what to do. The buildings near the perimeter were heavily damaged, the lucky ones with their front-facing windows shot or blown out. The unlucky ones were on fire, and the fire department was nowhere in sight. Whole blocks smoldered.

And there were the dead.

The Militia had not even picked up all of its own bodies. They lay intermingled with dead civilians where they fell, on sidewalks, in alleys, even in the street where trucks did not seem to even swerve away.

"It's like a war zone," King said. He had one of the AKs in his lap. It was filthy and beaten up, a gift of the Chinese government from some ancient stockpile. The other weapon, equally poorly maintained, rested next to the driver's seat, where Turnbull sat.

"It was a war zone," Turnbull said. Unlike other drivers, he turned slightly to avoid flattening a woman lying face down in the street.

"It smells like smoke and gunpowder," King said.

"It'll smell worse tomorrow when it gets hot."

"What's happening out there?" Kate shouted from the back.

"Rest," Turnbull ordered.

He continued driving, the headlamps illuminating the occasional body he had to swerve to avoid, or the clump of fighters he had to stop to allow to cross the road. Sometimes they had prisoners, civilians with hands either up or zip-tied, going off to who-knows-where and probably some unpleasant fate.

Crime was not criminal here, except for the unforgivable crime of resisting the People's Republic.

Near the Schrafft's City Center, a high-rise business tower with many of its windows shot out, they found themselves in a line of vehicles at a checkpoint.

"Go time," Turnbull said. The Militia at the checkpoint appeared to be waving military vehicles through after a cursory check, but something like this could go south in a heartbeat.

"Will they make us get out?" asked King, clutching the rifle.

"If they do, we shoot our way out," Turnbull said.

"That's pretty much your answer to everything," King replied sullenly.

"Waiting on a better plan," Turnbull said. "None? Okay, then we'll go with mine."

Immediately ahead of them was a five-ton truck painted in OD green. Whoever was driving was now in a beef with the checkpoint militiaman, who was shouting something indecipherable back into the cab. There were maybe two dozen militia milling about the area, most not paying much attention to the fracas. They carried their AKs as if they were a burden instead of their premier piece of equipment.

And none paid any attention to the ambulance.

A shaved head militia fighter leaning on his rifle as if it was a cane was cackling at the confrontation along with three others. Another of the quartet must have been 300 pounds. They were a few feet off from Turnbull's driver's side window, and he marked them as targets if this all went to hell.

The chaos began with the bald fighter's head exploding in a pink mist and chunks spraying his chunky pal. The report of the rifle shot came just a beat after.

Baldy dropped dead and the other three scattered, the splattered heavy one doing his best to sprint after his comrades.

The guy at the checkpoint stopped yelling, and a moment later there was another shot and one of his companions at the roadblock clutched his gut and sat back, shrieking.

Turnbull followed the sound back to the Schrafft's building looming above them.

"Sniper!" he shouted. "Get down!"

King hunkered low in the seat, realizing that a passenger in a vehicle would be easy pickings for the marksman high above them.

The militia fighters were scrambling and taking cover now, with another shot echoing through the intersection. If it hit someone, Turnbull didn't see it.

The five-ton wasn't moving.

"Come on!" Turnbull shouted.

"He can't hear you!" King exclaimed, trying to make himself as small as he could. "Go!"

But the truck was not going anywhere.

Turnbull hit the horn – it was thin and weak, more like a car horn than a truck's air horn, and it did nothing to encourage the driver blocking their way.

Another shot.

"He's going to get to us eventually," Teddy King shouted.

"Shit," Turnbull hissed. He hit the gas and the Humvee ambulance lurched forward five feet and slammed into the rear of the truck, then bounced back several feet. The five-ton shook, but did not move.

"Did we crash?" Kate shouted from the back.

Turnbull ignored her and hit the gas.

Once again, the hummer ambulance lurched forward into the rear of the five-ton. The impact jolted them in their seats and drew a long string of obscenities from Kate in the back.

But the truck moved, slowly at first, and then it picked up speed. Turnbull followed, accelerating as the truck did. There was a loud ping, and an eruption on the fiberglass hood.

Behind them as they pulled away from the Schrafft's checkpoint, the militia fighters had begun firing back at the building. They probably had no idea which of the hundreds of windows the shooter was in, but that didn't matter.

Halfway down the block, Turnbull pulled left and accelerated around the five-ton.

"That worked out well," King observed.

"Let's hope our luck holds out," Turnbull said as he drove to the northwest. "Such as it is."

Senator Harrington hated chess. Not because he was bad at it. He was actually quite good at it. But he was not the best, and he hated any game where his victory was not assured.

He was beginning to hate politics, though he was sure that would not last.

Crane's coup had been brilliant, and it had worked out perfectly. The People's Militia had gone into Charlestown and suppressed the reactionaries, demonstrating the kind of strength his progressive allies who ran Boston had been unable to muster. There was some number of Militia dead, and civilians. Neither mattered. What mattered was the boldness, and the ruthlessness. Crane had not asked permission. He simply acted, and Harrington understood that deep within the hearts of leftists was an infatuation with the daring and the brutal. It was almost erotic – the sexy iconography of Che Guevara was what they remembered, not his cowardly whimpering before the Bolivians shot him.

It was a function of a cis paradigm, utterly and completely cis, Harrington realized without judgment. It was almost primitive, though he knew enough not to use that term aloud – in fact, he would never speak any of these forbidden truths aloud. But, he understood, there was nothing that those who mouthed hatred of traditional sex roles loved more than a fellow leftist whose toxic masculinity was aimed at their enemies.

Crane was the man, very specifically a man, of the hour.

Everyone was talking about it; Harrington's own phone had been ringing incessantly with allies – some wavering – autopsying the implications of Crane's political resurrection.

It was clear that Merrick Crane III would be moving into the front rank of radical leaders, up from the underground. And any notion of the People's Militia coming under the sway of progressive leaders was now a non-starter. Harrington's plan to absorb them into the establishment was now, at best, on hold and probably doomed.

He found it very annoying that his progressives were now the establishment, and that the radicals were attacking them from the left. That had been his move throughout his career, to take positions to the left and pull the Overton window open for his own advancement. Now he was firmly within the camp of the status quo, and it felt both unfamiliar and unwelcome.

"Mx. Drysdale!" he shouted, pronouncing it as "mix." Mx. Drysdale was feminine today, to the point that she had announced earlier that her pronouns for this evening would be "she" and "her."

She entered his suite, perched high above Boston in a luxury hotel penthouse. Outside were four security men with assault rifles – after that incident with Crane in St. Louis, Harrington was taking no chances with his personal well-being.

Through the window, he could see the fires burning in Charlestown. It appeared that the shooting had stopped.

"Senator?" she asked.

"We have work to do," Harrington replied. "Listen carefully. I want you to reach out to all our media friends. Let them know that this Charlestown situation was badly handled, that the casualties were unnecessary. And pass the word that the People's Militia command was all white male with no input from BIPOC or LGBTQ!%, etcetera."

"The media is cheering it on," Mx. Drysdale replied. "I'm not sure that will help us."

"It probably won't, but we should try. I'll also call for an investigation in the Senate," he said. "And I want you to watch our friends very carefully. Tell me about anyone wavering."

Mx. Drysdale nodded and left the room. Harrington turned back to watch the fire across the water.

She was right, of course. These were Band-Aids being applied to an arterial spray. They were merely time-killing chess moves, not killshots, a mere simulacrum of power. They were not power itself.

That mad scientist's disc, now if that was what it was rumored to be, would be real power.

Johnny Ross had better come through. For both their sakes.

They were on Mystic Avenue to the northwest, which was mostly empty, when Turnbull noticed the temperature gauge rising.

"You know there's steam coming from the engine?" King asked.

"I can see that. The steam coming out from under the hood gave it away."

"The sniper's deer rifle must have hit something important," King replied.

A one bullet kill on a military vehicle – all hail the tyranny of the low-bidder!" Turnbull growled.

There was a large parking lot in front of what had been a Home Depot ahead. Home Depot had had its name changed a few months ago, as the whole concept was intensely insulting to those who were differently housed. Moreover, the whole "home improvement" idea smacked of the kind of traditionally patriarchal vision of men as doers of manual labor. The renamed "Domestic Task Depot" survived a few weeks and then simply ceased operations. The management of the chain had fled south, and simply abandoned the stores still in the blue. There were felony warrants issued on the operators, enforceable in the unlikely event any ever returned to the PR, for "refusal to furnish jobs" and "unlawful cessation of business."

The parking lot was dark, but not entirely empty. The store itself had been broken into by the housing-deficited and the pharmaceutically-inclined, and the lot had its share of shanties, lean-tos and tents pitched on the filthy cement. There had been some pleasant trees on the perimeter and in some of the islands in the lot, but most were dead, having been used as latrines and for the dumping of even more unsavory things. And the denizens were wandering about, wraiths in rags staggering through the night.

The hummer slowed dramatically in the middle of the lot – the engine locked and refused to continue. Turnbull was displeased – he had hoped to get off to the side of the lot behind the building so he would be out of sight.

No luck. The engine wheezed and died.

"Well, that sucks," King observed.

"Where are we?" Katie called from the back.

"Looks like that shopping mall in *Dawn of the Dead*," Turnbull said.

"Which one?" King said. "There's two."

"I don't know. I hate zombie movies," Turnbull said, getting out with the AK. He left his thermite grenade on the console. One of the locals was staggering toward the ambulance.

"You!" Turnbull shouted, pointing. "Turn around, walk away."

The wretch stopped there, stared for a moment, then turned and walked off aimlessly.

King got out from his side.

"Any chance we can fix it?" he asked.

"Do I look like a mechanic?" snapped Turnbull.

"Lighten up. I didn't shoot it."

"We need another ride," Turnbull said.

"Hey," King said, his voice serious. "Who are they?"

Turnbull pivoted. From the other end of the lot were two pairs of headlights coming in through the entrance they had used. One was a hummer, one seemed civilian.

"Militia?" King asked.

"Maybe," Turnbull said. "But does it matter?"

"Nope," King said.

"Pop the hood," Turnbull said. "Fast."

"What's happening?" Kate shouted from inside.

"Guests," Turnbull said as loud as he dared, while pulling off the rubber latch that held the hood down. "Stay quiet. And shut that dog up."

They lifted the hood, which pivoted at the front of the engine compartment, not the back. They lay their AKs on the steaming engine block. It was dark, and Turnbull hoped it obscured the fact they were not wearing OCP trousers.

The hummer pulled up behind the crackerbox and stopped. The civilian vehicle was a white SUV.

Turnbull pretended to ignore them.

A woman stepped out of the hummer's shotgun seat, evidently the one in charge. She had a large black nose stud and purple bangs. The other three got out too, all armed with AKs.

Men in suits stepped out of the SUV, two of them, hard-looking men. One had an M4.

Definitely SIS.

"Are you kidding me," King whispered.

"Just be nice," Turnbull said. "Until it's time to not be nice."

"Did you just quote *Roadhouse* at me?"

"What's *Roadhouse*?" Turnbull muttered as Nose Stud advanced.

"You break down?" she asked, squinting in the dark.

"Yeah," Turnbull said. "Some hose or something."

"You got wounded in there or what?"

"Yeah, but we got this."

"You need a wrecker or a tow?" Nose Ring asked, approaching without any evident hesitation or concern.

"Yeah, we called it in already," Turnbull said. The woman stopped beside the crackerbox, watching the men bent over the engine.

On King's side, two males stepped forward, watching. King eyed them, then his weapon.

"Be nice," whispered Turnbull.

The SIS men were bored and they stepped forward toward the ambulance. They figured they had pissed off Gruber somehow and gotten the perimeter gig instead of getting to go into Charlestown and kick in doors. They had missed the fight downtown this morning, but they didn't regret that. Most of the guys in on that were lying on slabs.

There was a bark from inside the crackerbox.

The SIS men looked at each other.

"Didn't Gruber say something about a dog?" the one with the M4 asked.

"You got a dog in there?" asked Nose Stud.

"It's a service dog," Turnbull said. "Some fascist shot it. We're taking it to a vet."

"I want to see the dog," the SIS man with the M4 said to the other, stepping forward toward the double doors.

"You put a dog in an ambulance? This should be for comrades," Nose Ring said.

"I'm not much on dogs either," Turnbull said. "Orders."

"I think she's a little humancentric," King said to the two on his side of the ambulance. They looked uncomfortable, as if their leader's statement might be a serious issue with significant repercussions.

"Be nice," Turnbull repeated.

The SIS man put his hand on the steel door latch at the back of the crackerbox and pulled it, the unlubricated steel hinges squealing in protest. The door would not move.

"What are you doing?" Nose Stud said, turning around to look toward the SIS man who was trying to get inside the ambulance.

The other SIS man, half-visible behind the ambulance replied.

"He just wants to see the dog."

His partner was pulling on the door, which was resisting, as if someone inside was holding it closed.

Nose Ring, and the other militia fighter with her on that side, turned back to Turnbull. Then she squinted again.

"Where are your uniform pants, comrade?" she asked.

Behind the ambulance, the door gave way, just like that, so the SIS man pulled it wide open and sixty pounds of snarling German shepherd sprung out at his throat. He shrieked.

"Shit!" the other SIS man shouted, grabbing for his pistol.

"Be not so nice," Turnbull said to King, picking up the AK.

Seeing Turnbull move, Nose Ring and her accomplice moved too, bringing up their weapons. Turnbull was faster, and set to full auto.

King lurched backwards with his own weapon up. The two on his side were stunned, giving him the drop. King squeezed the trigger.

Turnbull's first burst ripped into Nose Ring's chest, throwing her and her weapon backwards against the side of the ambulance and leaving a bloody splotch across the paint even as she spun and fell.

King shot the first one on his side of the ambulance before the man could get his weapon up. As the first target collapsed on the filthy parking lot asphalt, the other turned and ran.

Clover was tearing into the SIS man's face, his rifle having gone clattering across the parking lot, and he desperately used both hands to fight off the animal. His buddy finally managed to draw his pistol when he heard the bursts of fire from the front of the ambulance. Whoever these people were, the buddy decided, they were dead men.

He'd do the dog first, then the shooters. He aimed the Smith & Wesson M&P Shield M2.0 automatic at Clover while his buddy screamed as much as he could manage without lips or most of his tongue.

Turnbull pivoted to the other militia fighter who was standing over his ventilated boss's corpse, not sure what to do with the weapon in his hand.

Turnbull suffered no such confusion. He aimed center mass with the dirty AK and squeezed.

Nothing.

He squeezed the trigger again. Not even the click of a hammer fall. Jammed.

The militia fighter smiled and began to lift his own weapon, determined to take full advantage of this serendipitous turn of events that converted him from prey to predator in an instant.

Turnbull threw the weapon at his face hard, and the man's reflex was to block it. Turnbull's reflex was to draw the .45 and put three 230-grain Hydra-Shok hollow points into his thorax.

The SIS man saw movement to his left in the doorway of the ambulance just as he took aim at the dog devouring the soft parts of his partner's face. It was a woman, of all things.

A woman standing unsteadily in the elevated doorway of the ambulance, with a red bandage around her upper chest, and a HK417 rifle held at her waist level, meaning it was pointed directly at his face.

He thought it was a M4, because that weapon looked similar, and he died wrong. The 7.62mm x 54mm round that entered his left eye punched right out the back of his skull, taking a good chuck of it along as it exited.

King took careful aim at the escaping man's back as he ran and put two bullets in him. The militia fighter dropped to the concrete. King exhaled. He realized he was getting as cold as his companion.

The SIS with the dog gnawing on him was screaming hysterically as Turnbull came around back.

King appeared from the other side, looking with horror at the bloody scene.

"Clear the vehicles," Turnbull said. King nodded and went off, AK up.

Kate was leaning heavily against the door that was still closed. She let the HK drop to the metal floor of the crackerbox.

"Can you call off Cujo?" Turnbull asked. The dog was extremely enthusiastic.

"Clover!" Kate shouted. "Clover, off!"

The dog reluctantly pulled back, but the man kept screaming and locked his hands around his shredded face.

Turnbull did him a favor with a slug through his forehead. Disappointed, Clover walked off to take a leak on one of the barren parking islands.

"Piece of shit was going to hurt my dog," Kate said.

"A lot of creatures are eating my enemies lately," Turnbull observed. "Oh, well."

King trotted back.

"Both clear. We should probably go."

Turnbull surveyed the carnage, then looked around the lot. There were shapes on the fringe of the dark, staring at them.

"Keys for the SUV?" Turnbull asked.

"In the ignition."

"Pick up the M4," Turnbull instructed King. "Kate, come down. Let me help."

Carefully, she lowered herself and Turnbull took her to the ground, where she stood shakily. King helped her to the SUV.

Turnbull hopped up into the back of the ambulance and gathered up Clover's leash and what few medical supplies he could stuff into an OD green aid bag, mostly some bandages, a little saline, and some medicine Doc Farnham had supplied. He hopped down off the back and took the HK and its three remaining mags, then trotted to the SUV. King was sitting in the driver's seat and it was running.

"I'll drive," Turnbull said.

"No, I'll drive," King answered. "Every time you drive people start shooting at us."

"I don't think driving is the common denominator," Turnbull said. "I am."

"Get in," King said.

"Pop the hood."

"What, is this one broke too?"

"Pop it!"

King looked under the dash until he figured out the right latch, then pulled it. The hood released and Turnbull pushed it up and bent over inside. Under a minute later, he shut the hood and came around to the passenger seat with a handful of wires.

"GPS system," he said. "Now we're offline." He tossed the mechanism away.

"Okay, can we roll now?" King asked when Turnbull failed to hop in.

"Wait a sec," Turnbull replied as he put the HK inside with the two M4s from the SIS man. "I forgot something."

He jogged back to the driver's compartment of the ambulance and grabbed his thermite grenade.

21.

Gruber surveyed the six bodies on the pavement around the ambulance and shook his head. It was a mess. Yet he felt a sort of respect for his quarry for pulling it off.

"What the hell happened to Charlie?" Dworkin asked, nauseous. This was worse than what the gators did because the reptiles finished most of their entrée off. Charlie was a mess.

"Remember the doggie bowls?" Gruber said, grinning over the growing pain in his tush. "Got us a mighty hungry puppy."

"Damn," Dworkin responded. He did not know what more to say.

"Forty-five shells, and a 7.62mm NATO," Gruber said. "You know who likes his .45, and we saw plenty of those 7.62s this morning downtown. We are on the right track."

"The bums say there were three of them, and one was hurt. They took our SUV, so they should be easy to find," Dworkin observed.

"Unless I am mistaken, and I am not, that's the GPS system," Gruber said, pointing to a collection of wires and fuses lying forlornly on the pavement," Gruber said. "Our friend Chris is a professional."

"Well, let's see if our professional can get far with a nationwide BOLO out on his ass."

The mention of the word "ass" reminded Gruber of how much his hurt where Turnbull had winged him. In fact, he was beginning to feel sick. But he dare not show it.

"Well," said Gruber slowly, like he was explaining something to a slow nine-year-old. "If we ask every agency in the PR to be on the lookout for our friends, then every agency in the PR will be on the lookout for our friends and we won't get them first. We can't roll those dice. No, we gotta do the dirty deed when it comes."

"So how do we do it?" asked Dworkin.

"There are lots of cameras and plate scanners between here and the red, which is where they gotta be going. You get them to ping us every time that plate shows up."

"Unless they change plates."

Gruber scowled. "How about you just get your ass on what I told you to do?"

Dworkin licked his lips nervously and nodded his head before taking off. Gruber grimaced. Just saying the word reminded him about his wounded ass.

Dworkin was right, of course. But what else did he have? He couldn't allow some deputy sheriff in Pudpull, Pennsylvania, to take his target, or risk that the disc might fall into someone else's hands. He would call Crane in a few moments and give him the good news. They had something. The chase was on.

Gruber stared down at his dead men and felt nothing like sadness, only anger at the insult. This guy was killing his men, disrespecting him, and that could not be tolerated. Sure, the boss wanted what the boss wanted, and his little disc was no doubt very important. But to Wayne Gruber, this Chris had insulted him by refusing to die like all the others had. And he was determined that he and Chris would meet up again and settle this once and for all before the intruder got his ass over that border into the red.

Ass again. Gruber gritted his teeth and got to work.

Johnny Ross watched the doings in the former Home Depot parking lot from his car back up the road, careful not to alert the SIS men to his presence. There had been some kind of massacre in that lot, and that meant the elusive Chris. The SIS thugs were no geniuses, but they might find something of use to track him down. He would call into Colby and pull more favors – the SIS would be using the system to track whatever vehicle Chris and his compatriots fled the scene in, and by following Gruber and his punks, Ross would be led right to Chris.

He hoped.

But it would make it very convenient if he came on Chris and Gruber together. Then he could take care of all his unfinished business at once.

"We're heading for Kentucky," Turnbull said as King pulled them onto the freeway heading west.

"Why Kentucky?" asked Kate. "Canada's right there."

"Because he came in from Canada," Teddy King said. "You don't go out the way you came in."

"We'll take I-90 west," Turnbull said. "Albany, Buffalo, skirt Lake Erie, get to Toledo and head south down I-75 to Kentucky."

King was looking at the Google map on his phone even as he drove. "That's about twelve hours to Toledo," he said. "Then another five or six south to Kentucky. That's a lot of time with no sleep."

"You drive, I'll sleep, then we'll switch."

"There's also the matter of the ride. GPS or not, these plates are going to get read."

"Then we need to switch them out."

They pulled off in Framingham and found a Sheraton with several vehicles in the lot. Turnbull used King's Swiss Army knife to liberate a set from a black Ford Escalade with tacky rims, then stick his own plates on it. The owner was almost certain not to notice the switch before he got scanned and the PSF swarmed him, and by the time they figured out who to look for, the trio would probably be in Louisville.

Stealing another vehicle was not an option – too much attention. If it is merely missing, it gets reported. If it gets jacked, best case is some citizens reporting it and worst case another shootout.

They got back on the road and headed west.

Ross decided to head west. Chris came in from Canada and even though it was close, he would probably not try to leave that way. The route straight south went through New York City. A lot of things could go wrong. But there was also west, and then cutting south. They could still keep the Canada option open since they'd be skirting it.

It was about two hours before he got it confirmed.

"I figure I owe you," Colby told him over the phone.

"Yeah," Ross said. "You do."

"They got them going west on I-90. No BOLO, nothing publicized. Just the SIS using our damn techs to figure things out. They lifted some plates in Massachusetts and they got scanned heading through New York State.

"Text me the plate they're using."

"Should be coming through."

Ross's phone pinged. He laughed. "You're kidding," he said.

"Nope. No wonder the owner noticed the switch. Update me whenever they get scanned."

"In the system already. Last we saw they are heading toward Utica."

"I'm leaving Albany," Ross said. "Not too far behind. Any word on how Gruber's bunch is going to try to take them?"

"No, nothing. I think they are waiting for the right time and place," Colby said. "Listen, Johnny…"

Ross hung up. He was getting tired, but he had loaded up with a giant coffee when he put $213 of his own money into filling the tank a few miles back. The coffee was advertised as "cruelty, racism, capitalism-free." It costs him twelve dollars.

The trio refueled the Chevy for nearly $300 cash at a People's Energy station outside of Utica, and then Turnbull took the wheel. Kate was sleeping fitfully, and the dog was resting beside her. Teddy King did his best to sleep, but he could only manage the half-asleep fugue state often associated with trying to catch z's in a passenger seat.

The M4 they had taken back at the Home Depot parking lot was beside him in the well next to his legs.

"I need you here," Crane said firmly.

"Boss, I want to be there when we take them," Gruber explained. "I owe this Chris and a Gruber always pays his debts."

"You come to Detroit, next flight, and you will lead my security team at the Mackinac Hotel. I want the rest of the SIS here with you. Your Dworkin can take seven others and intercept a single car, a few people and a dog. At least I hope he can."

"Yes, boss," Gruber said.

"You can have him after I'm done, if that makes you feel better."

"It will, it most certainly will." But Gruber felt anything but better.

Crane hung up and Gruber licked his lips, but then realized that the flight to Detroit would mean sitting on his posterior wound for several hours. At least in a car he could lie face down in the backseat.

It hurt, a lot, and when Dworkin had changed out the gauze it was ugly. But Crane did not want to hear about his problems, and Gruber did not want to give up the best job he was ever likely to have.

"We're all flying to Motown," he announced to the remaining two dozen SIS men. He turned to Dworkin. "Once we get to Detroit" – Gruber drew out the first syllable – "you take seven bodies and go make the stop before he gets to Toledo. That's where he goes north or south and we might lose him. The rest of us have a special mission with the boss. Get your shit. We're moving out pronto."

They started moving. Gruber leaned against a wall, shutting his eyes.

"You need a doctor, Chief," Dworkin said.

"I need to skin that son of a bitch Chris alive," Gruber said.

"I figure you're about thirty miles behind him," Colby said. "I can get field agents on it for you."

"No," Ross replied, exhausted. "This has to be me alone. You got a location on Gruber?"

"Johnny, I can't..."

"You won't."

"I'm doing too much already," Colby pleaded. Ross hung up, then hit another number.

Harrington picked up on the second ring.

"I hope you are calling with good news," the senator said, not fully expecting any.

"I'm in Ohio about a half hour behind them on the interstate. We're tracking their stolen plates. But so are Gruber and his people. "

"My sources tell me that all of the SIS is flying to Detroit as we speak," Harrington replied. "The plane holds forty."

"Why would they do that? Unless they are planning on stopping our boy somewhere nearby," said Ross.

"No," Harrington said. "They might want to grab him, but they have another reason to be in Michigan. One that might just be more important in the overall scheme of things."

"I better get Chris first."

"Yes, do that." Harrington hung up.

The senator's mind was churning. And then it all became clear.

"Oh Merrick, you naughty boy," he said aloud, drawing a confused glance from Mx. Drysdale. "You really are quite clever. But not clever enough."

Crane was at the private aviation hangar to meet up with the SIS jet. He had arrived in Detroit earlier, having stopped by to terminate – in every sense of the word – the low-performing head of the local People's Militia force. Now he would hitch a ride with his SIS force the three hundred miles north to Mackinac Island.

The ground crewman had protested that he was on his meal break when the jet had landed and that they would have to wait for him to finish before he drove the stairs over. Several vicious punches later, delivered by Crane's bodyguards, and the man was hopping to it.

Dworkin came down first with the seven others getting off there in Motor City, each carrying their gear and weapons.

Dworkin looked concerned.

"Where's Gruber," Crane said, scanning the sullen faces.

"He's sick," Dworkin said. "Bad. That bullet wound in his..."

"Ass?" inquired Crane. Dworkin nodded.

"He needs a doctor, a hospital doctor."

Crane sighed. "You should probably call an ambulance. And send five bodies with him to ensure he's not bothered."

Dworkin nodded. It would not do to have anyone else get access to Gruber, considering the secret he held in that broken brain of his.

But it was probably moot, Crane reasoned. Considering the quality of the nationalized hospitals of Detroit, Gruber was probably going to die anyway.

Too bad. Gruber would have been extremely useful for what he planned to do up at the retreat on Mackinac Island.

Turnbull was driving and he did not notice the two generic blue Ford Taurus sedans slip onto I-90 westbound behind them from the service plaza at Vickery, Ohio. He had noticed the sign that apologized for the "earthdamage" the fossil fuels they sold did.

It was early afternoon, and both hot and humid. The AC was cranked, and Teddy King and Katie McGowan were asleep. Turnbull had been listening to the radio, just in case they had been declared public enemies. They had not, at least not yet. But for that reassurance, Turnbull had to endure a long farm report that spent considerably less time talking about sorghum crops than interrogating the racist legacy of northern Ohio agriculture.

Toledo was ahead maybe 10 or 30 miles, along with I-75, which they would use to head south to the United States and leave the People's Republic forever. The ground was flat, and I-90 was set down with three lanes and ample shoulders on both sides in each direction. The eastbound-westbound lanes were together with no median; instead, a Jersey barrier-shaped wall of ugly asphalt divided them. There was less graffiti out here in the country – it was flat farmland with occasional stands of trees as far as one could see in any direction – but various slogans still flashed by. Having legalized graffiti, the People's Republic was thrilled that most of it was defiantly pro-regime.

"Crush the racist state menace" one wrote in red along the median. "Fat BIPOC trans lives matter," added another.

Turnbull was doing about 55, the new national speed limit, with the cruise control on. The last thing they needed was to be pulled over by some PSF cruiser or, more likely, by a deputy in one of the jurisdictions whose law enforcement had not yet been assimilated into the People's Security Force Borg collective.

"That's them," Dworkin said, confirming the license plate from his vantage point in the lead sedan's front passenger seat. "Get ready."

The traffic was light. That was good. He had his M&P Shield 2.0 automatic out and on his lap as he watched the white Chevy ahead of them moving at about 55 in the center lane. The two SIS men in back were checking their M4s. The driver used his console to drop all the windows. A hurricane of hot, wet farm air hit them.

"Okay," Dworkin said into the radio mike. "We PIT them and then we swarm them when they stop." The other car acknowledged. It was behind Dworkin in the right lane.

Dworkin had learned the pursuit intervention technique maneuver back when he was a cop, a job that lasted a couple years until the prostitutes he shook down for trade in exchange for not running them in told a do-gooder from a church who was trying to save their souls. The DA refused to prosecute – it was a young cop's word against that of a half-dozen whores – but his chief knew the score. Dworkin was fired, which left him to pursue his real avocation, committing crimes instead of solving them.

"Just like I told you," Dworkin instructed his driver. "Ease up to him on his left, match his speed, gently tap it with your bumper right behind the rear wheel and then accelerate. He'll spin, and maybe flip. You get control of our car and stop, and out we go. We want them alive if possible. Got it?"

The driver nodded. He was not nervous. Doing things like crashing into other cars was exactly the kind of thing he had joined the SIS to do. It sure beat breaking arms for bookies.

He slid into the left lane and slowly accelerated toward Turnbull's SUV.

"Who wears suits in this heat?" Turnbull wondered as he glanced in his driver's side mirror. "And who has all the windows down?"

The Taurus behind them speeded up in the lane over.

"Shit!" Turnbull yelled, and he put both feet on the brake.

Dworkin's car shot past the SUV and he made eye contact with Turnbull.

"Stop!" he shouted. The driver hit the brakes.

Teddy King was roused out of his sleep and held back from slamming into the dash by his seat belt, while the dog in the backseat yipped as it was thrown forward. Katie moaned, but Turnbull ignored it.

He was now behind the second Taurus, and he hit the gas.

Turnbull's SUV accelerated – as a government law enforcement vehicle, it had no governor that sapped its power like civilian vehicles were now mandated to use.

Turnbull had graduated a course in tactical driving while in the Special Forces, and unlike the SIS driver, this was not his first PIT maneuver.

Turnbull made contact with the passenger side of his front bumper on the rear quarter panel of the second Taurus and punched it. The driver was unprepared, and tried to compensate and hold his course instead of steering into the skid, which might have given him at least some control.

The Taurus went left, utterly unstable, and then lost it completely, flipping over three times and tossing out two of the occupants who had prepared for a quick exit by unbuckling their seatbelts. They came to rest in crumpled heaps in the road, while the Taurus rested on its roof.

Dworkin watched as the second Taurus tumbled down the freeway. It was a miracle it barely missed them as they skidded to a stop. The Chevy SUV pulled up thirty feet to their rear.

"Go, go!" Dworkin yelled. He meant "Drive," but the driver thought he meant to exit and engage.

Turnbull undid his seatbelt with his left hand while he pulled the HK417 out of the backseat with his right.

"Toss me the extra mags!" he ordered Katie as he popped the door and stepped out of the SUV onto the freeway.

One of the shooters in the backseat got a round off, high and to the right, before Turnbull opened fire and blew him off his feet. The other was bringing up his M4 when Turnbull stitched him across the chest, and he spun and splattered against the median, leaving a scarlet brushstroke across its concrete face.

He emptied the rest of the mag into the idling Taurus, then dropped the empty and reloaded with one of the mags Katie had tossed onto the driver's seat. The rear window exploded in shards of glass, while the trunk was peppered with rounds and a rear tire exploded.

Turnbull, empty, dropped the mag and reloaded, then sent the bolt forward. Two left. He pumped all twenty shots into the sedan. There was no movement, except a sliver of glass where the front windshield used to be dropped into the car with a crash.

He reloaded and blew off the entire mag into the shredded Taurus.

Turnbull ejected the empty and reloaded the final mag, not paying attention to Teddy King's firing at the flipped-over second Taurus.

Walking forward, he sprayed the remaining twenty rounds into the passenger compartment, tossed away the Assaulter, and drew his Wilson Combat CQB.

Gun up, he approached the shredded automobile. Incredibly, the engine was still on even though fluids were spilling on the cement and steam was curling up from under the hood.

The first man he had engaged groaned and Turnbull shot him in the head, then trained the barrel back onto the Taurus, approaching from the rear passenger side.

He let the weapon go a bit slack when he saw what was in the front seat. Dworkin and his driver had gone to their reward; there was no need for a confirming headshot on either one.

Turnbull reached into the window, trying to avoid the goo, and pulled open Dworkin's suit. His cell phone was there. Turnbull pulled it out. Luckily it unlocked on a thumbprint instead of using facial recognition, as even Dworkin's mother would not have recognized him after the storm of 7.62mm rounds hit him.

Teddy King jogged up, M4 in hand. Behind them, traffic was piling up.

"They're all dead," King said.

"Good."

"And Chris, I think I figured out how they found us. Just a pro tip from me to you, but don't steal a personalized license plate next time. It's easy for the owner to tell that it's been switched."

"I didn't," Turnbull said, confused. Teddy sighed and pointed at the Chevy.

Turnbull looked at the Massachusetts plate.

"So?"

Teddy sighed again. "I8URM0M," he said, pronouncing each digit and letter.

"Oh," Turnbull said after a moment.

"Can you get your linear-thinking ass in our ride? We have got to get gone."

Ross flashed his ID and the local Sandusky County Sheriff's deputies on the scene let him past. Eight dead bodies on the freeway, and now the feds were here. Whatever the hell was going on was far above their pay grade.

Ross noted the dead men who had been ejected from the first of the two sedans. The bad suits and the headshots that finished them off told him what had happened. The HK417 lying on the deck, surrounded by spent casings, confirmed what he already knew.

The white SUV was gone. Would they ditch it? And where would they go if they did. Ross sighed and pulled out his phone as he walked back to his car.

They parked behind a closed transmission shop in Fremont, a few miles off the interstate. The tall brick smokestack of the Heinz plant on the north side of the small town peeked over the shop's weathered roof. From here, it would be an easy drive on back roads southwest to hook up with I-75 south and head on to Kentucky.

"I gotta make a call," Turnbull said. He had spent the last thirty minutes tapping Dworkin's phone to keep it from locking again. Now he went down the contacts and hit the one that said "MC3." MC3 picked up.

"Do you have it?"

"I recognize your voice," Turnbull said. "Do you recognize mine?"

There was silence on the other end.

"I take it my man Dworkin is no more."

"Yeah, he ran into a bunch of bullets, so he's out of the picture for good. So are the rest of your assholes."

"You killed eight of my men?" Crane said. "You know, if you ever wanted to come over to my way of thinking, I expect we would make an incredibly effective team."

"Sure, tell me where you are and we can discuss it face-to-face."

Crane chuckled mirthlessly. "No, I don't think I have time for a visit from you, Chris. What is your real name anyway?"

"I'm the Grim Reaper, as far as you're concerned."

"Oh, now you're sounding like Gruber. You know, you shot him in the ass?"

"I do always aim for vital organs. Don't worry, I will finish what I started with Gruber. And I'm counting the hours until I finish with you."

"You are a very angry man, Chris."

"You killed my friend, and I'm going to kill everyone who gets between me and you, and then I'm going to kill you."

"Yes, very angry," Crane taunted. He paused, then spoke again. "Well, I am not going to indulge your thirst for revenge over, I guess, that tramp from Fox News. I don't even remember her name, to be honest."

"It was Avery. That's going to be the last word you ever hear."

"Chris, you really are committed to your bit. Look, I won't tell you where I am, but how about I tell you where our mutual friend Mr. Gruber is?"

"You don't sound like a very good friend."

"Quite the contrary. He expressed to me how excited he would be to see you again. I'm just helping make the arrangements for your reunion."

"So where is he?"

"He's getting treatment for his infected ass at what used to be Henry Ford Hospital in Detroit. But Henry Ford was a racist, so it's not called that anymore. It's now called the People's Medical Facility No. 3. See, here in the blue states, we have a system of free healthcare for the people, although I heard the standards have fallen there a bit."

"You're going to die, Crane."

"Eventually, but not by you. Good-bye, Chris." He hung up.

Turnbull returned to the SUV. King was on his knees in front of the bumper, replacing the plates with new Ohio ones he had borrowed off a pick-up truck parked around the corner.

"You want this?" he said, handing back the front "I8URM0M" plate. "Like, as a keepsake? You are not going to ever live this down, well, for at least the five or six hours we're still together on our way to Kentucky."

"I'm not going," Turnbull said.

"I don't understand," King said, standing up. "We're five hours from being out of this shithole country."

"I have something to do. You go. By the time anyone figures out your new plate, you'll be over the line and in the US."

"Wait, Chris," King said. "What is this thing you've got to do?"

"Not a thing. A person. Gruber."

"You're going to go kill Gruber?"

"Pretty much. He's at a hospital in Detroit. That's the wrong direction from America."

"How do you even know he's there?"

"His boss told me."

"Crane?"

"Yeah."

"It's a trap!" King exclaimed.

"Thanks, Admiral Ackbar," Turnbull said. "I figured that out all by myself."

"You don't have to do this," King said.

"But I want to. Cross over into the red. I'll give you the number to call when you get there. They'll debrief you and set you up. Someone will ask you if I have the disc. Tell him I do, and I'll see him soon."

"You could give it to me."

Turnbull shook his head. "This is my mission. I'll finish it. How's Katie?"

"Asleep. Doing worse, of course. We don't have a lot of time. She needs a real doctor."

"Then you should stop arguing with me and get going. Just drop me at the bus station. These blue people love their public transportation."

"Sure," King said. "But can I ask you one thing?"

"Probably not."

"What's your real name?" asked King.

Turnbull smiled. "Ben Shapiro."

22.

People's Bus route number AZ621 was surprisingly crowded. Gas at over $10 a gallon would do that. Turnbull found a seat and resolved to make the transition to route number BF221 in Toledo. It would take him to Detroit. His big problem was getting comfortable with a M1911A1 and a thermite grenade under his light jacket.

The Toledo bus station was what he expected, full of low-lifes and bums hassling the normal folks forced to use the intercity shuttles. But the denizens took a look at Turnbull and understood he was not to be messed with. Turnbull made his transfer without incident.

The man sitting next to him on the last leg began watching loud and bizarre pornography on his phone. Behind them were a single mom and her kids. Turnbull asked the voyeur politely not to do so once. And when the perv did it again, Turnbull asked not so politely. The single mom then told Turnbull she did not need a white knight rescuing her and told the viewer to continue his viewing because she would never, ever judge another's erotic preferences. The man looked at Turnbull, who looked back hard even as the woman harangued him for helping her, and the pervert then began watching some relatively non-freaky anime.

What had been the Henry Ford Hospital near downtown Detroit was now People's Medical Facility No. 3 was a sprawling red and white brick complex with only about half the building lit in the darkness. Whether the power was out, or the vast swaths of the buildings were abandoned, Turnbull did not know. It was clear, though, that the tragedy of the commons was in full effect.

The high-rise buildings were surrounded by green open space and wide lawns out front. They were now inhabited by derelicts and hobos, with tents, shanties and lean-to set up in the mud where the grass had been. A military surplus water tanker truck painted with the black words "CITY OF DETROT" – the "i" was aptly missing – was parked near the front and government workers were using a hose to service a line of local residents holding old bottles, cans, and buckets. Nearby, another batch of workers handed out ladles of what appeared to be gruel.

He passed the parking lot, where the employees left their vehicles – at least the ones who could afford the gas. The cement floor of the lot was covered with broken glass; none of the savvier workers kept anything they wanted to keep inside their vehicles. The smartest ones posted signs that read "NOTHING OF VALUE IN HERE PLEASE DON'T BREAK IN."

Turnbull went through the lot and approached the front entrance, past the signage apologizing for the hospital's legacy of complicity with systemic racism, its association with the Fords (especially since the company had been the only one of the Big Three manufacturers to pick up and jump to the red after the Split), and for having stolen the land from some Indian tribe a couple centuries before. There was a statue pedestal out front, but no statue. Henry Ford had fallen, but not as far as his massive charity project.

It was filthy, with the front pavilion covered in trash and the walls showing evidence of use as a urinal. The acrid smell was overwhelming. Inside did not seem much better. The main entrance opened into a lobby, which had a wide ground floor level and a second-level balcony. It was a fine place for a shooter – good fields of fire looking down, and it was harder to spot the sniper.

Turnbull watched it for a while. Nothing unusual, just people going in and out – the ones going in often seemed to be carrying food with them.

There was a non-zero chance that Crane had called his boys here with Gruber and told them that he was coming. And while they were not criminal geniuses by any stretch, it was reasonable to assume that they would be watching the front door. Turnbull turned away and proceeded around the vast complex on foot.

"Nothing?" Gruber asked his man. The SIS agent shook his head.

"No sign. We got the entrance and we are watching the monitors from the security station." He did not mention that most of the cameras were out, as Gruber was already upset. His dinner had consisted of a baloney sandwich – one slice of baloney on one slice of wheat bread – and an off-brand single-serving bag of tasteless potato chips.

"Well," Gruber said, sitting up. "I think he's coming. And I want to bring him to the boss, so you be gentle. We only kill him if we gotta. You understand, Joe?"

The SIS man nodded, but he was nervous. This guy had put a lot of SIS boys in slots over the last couple days. He was glad he had his M4, even if it did freak out the nurses.

Gruber's arm was tethered to an IV drip, pumping in saline and antibiotics, the right ones this time. He had demanded it, brandishing his Desert Eagle, and they complied. It had helped – he was vastly improved over how he was at the airport, though the nurses debriding the wound on his posterior had not been particularly gentle.

But he was no longer dying. Maybe he might even get out of this hellhole soon enough that he could join his boss on Mackinac Island and not have to miss all the fun.

The door pushed open, displaying the number 533. It was the head nurse, who took on Gruber herself after the others had protested having to be in a room with him.

"You do a bowel movement yet?" she demanded.

"Woman," Gruber said. "You don't tell me nothing. You don't even know who you are dealing with."

"You're Wayne Gruber," she replied, pronouncing it "grubber." "You got shot in the ass and now you're a pain in mine."

"Joe," Gruber said to the SIS man. "If she disrespects me again, you take that rifle off your shoulder and you shoot her in the face."

Joe said nothing, but the woman went pale.

"Now you get out of here, woman. I will shit on my own schedule, thank you very much, and next time send that pretty little Oriental girl," Gruber said, only vaguely aware that he had committed a hate felony. "She can watch me take a dump anytime."

He grinned broadly. The head nurse left without a word and the door shut behind her.

"Like I was saying," Gruber continued. "He's coming. I can feel it. And the boss wants me to finish this, right here."

Joe nodded, but thought better of observing that Merrick Crane III was obviously using Gruber as bait. He also decided not to reveal his misgivings about having only four other SIS agents to provide security for Gruber with the infamous Chris perhaps on the way. He resolved to stay on the fifth floor with Gruber and send the others out hunting.

"Yep," Gruber said, lifting up his pillow and revealing the Desert Eagle underneath. "We finish this right here once and for all."

He paused in thought for a moment. "And order me a pepperoni pizza."

It was a relatively slow evening, though the ER was still overflowing. Old people sat and stared at the walls, waiting, while kids screamed and the homeless took up many of the dirty chairs to escape the humid night air outside. Many wore masks, and many of those wore them wrong. The staff was half inert, some playing solitaire on the computers, and half frenetic, doctors and nurses trying to actually help the mass of humanity inside the waiting area.

The linoleum floor was scuffed and stained. The chairs were a hodgepodge of various types and styles. Many had signs on them reading "DO NOT USE SOCIAL DISTANCING IN EFFECT," but no one was paying attention and most of the seats were taken. Underneath a sign announcing how the new constitution of the People's Republic, Articles 17 and 206, guaranteed "free, quality healthcare to all men, women, and others within the People's Republic," sat a middle-aged lady coughing up a lung. There was graffiti on the sign, an approximation of male genitalia. It was unclear what the pictogram was commenting on precisely, or if the artist was simply inspired to share his vision with the sick and the dying.

Turnbull surveyed the ceiling before stepping inside. He had found a mask on the ground outside and was prepared to take his chances wearing it if it looked like there was effective surveillance inside. It did not come to that. There were several camera mounts bereft of cameras – maybe they had been stolen, but they were gone. In the far corner, there was one left, but its wires hung down forlornly. Turnbull stepped into the chaos and observed.

There was a little waist-high swinging door through which the nurses summoned patients into the back after their lengthy waits. A formidable male nurse – maybe male, for at that distance Turnbull could not make out the pronouns on his name badge – was the gatekeeper. Every few minutes, the gatekeeper would call a number – he was up to 461 – over the scratchy loudspeaker. He would carefully scrutinize whoever showed up for admittance. Turnbull watched him turn around and send away a derelict who sought to stumble through. There was no way Turnbull was getting past him without a confrontation.

He needed another way in.

At the far end of the waiting room there was a janitor mopping. He had not been there a moment ago, and he did not come through the swinging gate. Turnbull headed over to him. There was another door out of sight of the front, with a sign reading "EMPLOYEES ONLY NO ACCESS IF YOU ARE TRIGGERED BY THIS SIGN PLEASE SEE THE NURSES."

It was propped open with a broom handle.

Turnbull, head down and not making eye contact, worked his way towards the portal, past the mopper and the moaning and hacking people waiting to be called. Standing beside it, he confirmed the mopper was engaged in his work facing the opposite direction, but seated directly across from him in a red plastic chair like one Turnbull had sat in in middle school, was a young man with glassy, sunken eyes looking at him. After a moment, the boy turned his attention back to his Android phone, and Turnbull quietly slipped inside.

The backstage, administrative portion of the hospital included laundry facilities as well as kitchens, lockers, storage areas and everything else behind the scenes necessary to run a medical center. People were working, most of them, though not particularly actively.

Turnbull grabbed a white coat from the rack near the dryers. Too small. He flipped through them until he found one big enough and slipped it on, then kept walking.

There was a door reading "DOCTOR'S LOUNGE," and no apology for its exclusivity. The ones at the top of the pyramid never apologized. He pushed open the door and it was dark. The light illuminated a white coat draped over a chair and, beyond it, a snoring male on an institutional bed. Turnbull quietly liberated his ID card from the coat, and the keyring in the pocket, and slipped back out again.

The photo was not a great match, or even a good one, but the picture would suffice for the "passing in the hall" test, especially when he pinned it so his lapel partially covered it. Turnbull noted that his pronouns were "he/them."

He also noted that Doctor Singh drove a Hyundai and the keyring held a master emergency elevator key. That meant he was probably a surgeon with the capacity to take over an elevator and go directly to his destination. He pocketed the keyring and moved out.

The next exit from the backstage area led into the lower level of the front lobby, which was not what Turnbull was expecting. He went with it – doing an immediate U-turn would draw more attention than some doctor passing through. It was about five seconds before he spotted the two SIS men, with their M4s slung, walking through the lobby, their attention outside toward the pavilion.

It looked like Crane had gone ahead and spoiled the surprise.

The pair did not seem particularly engaged, or particularly careful not to be seen. The other people in the lobby saw them, and avoided them. This seemed to make the agents happy. They were the toughest guys in the whole of People's Medical Facility No. 3.

Or so they thought.

The pair turned and strolled to the elevators, hitting the button and waiting. Turnbull surmised they would be taking it up to the balcony, a better position. He made his move.

The door opened and the two stepped inside, bored, and one hit the "2" button. A big doctor stepped inside and immediately faced the control panel. It looked like he was sticking a key in the emergency slot.

"Sorry," the big doc said. "Got a Code Orange in the basement."

The "2" light extinguished and the doors shut, then they began descending.

"We were going up to two," one of them complained.

"No, see he's got a key to take over the elevator when they have a Code Orange," the other explained.

"What's a Code Orange?"

Turnbull's elbow slammed into his face at the moment he finished pronouncing "orange." He fell back, his mouth a cauldron of blood and teeth.

Turnbull spun and the other was attempting to unlimber his M4. Turnbull charged, his forearm catching the man under the chin and crushing his larynx. He gasped, or tried to – no air was going in or out. As he fell to the floor of the cab, Turnbull went at the other man, who was drawing his pistol. Turnbull got him around the neck and viciously pumped his legs. There was an audible crack and the man went limp.

The car stopped and the door opened to a darkened, industrial-looking hallway. A sign with an arrow pointing right read "MORGUE."

"Perfect," Turnbull whispered aloud. The man with the crushed throat was ashen and suddenly went limp.

Turnbull's pistol was out, and he looked both ways. Satisfied, he took a moment to screw on his suppressor.

The morgue was unattended, and Turnbull stowed the dead SIS men in a couple empty freezer drawers. He tossed in their M4s as well. This would require subtlety.

The third floor was labeled "REPRODUCTIVE CHOICE/PREGNANCY TERMINATION SERVICES ALSO OBSTETRICS," recognizing the two specialties' relative priority in the People's Republic. Turnbull figured that he if had guessed right and Doctor Singh was a surgeon, the folks manning – personing, he reminded himself – this floor would have less of a chance of recognizing him as not Dr. Singh.

The elevator opened and he stepped out. Even though it was night, the terminations suite was packed with sad-looking women, a sharp contrast to the colorful poster of smiling women in the sunshine, often surrounded by flowers, with slogans like

330 | THE SPLIT

"ABORTION ALLOWS YOU TO KEEP BEING YOU!," "SAY YES TO FREEDOM!" and "DOES THE EARTH REALLY NEED ANOTHER BABY?"

He headed toward the quiet obstetrics wing. A single nurse was at the front desk. The dry erase board had patients in five of the twenty or so rooms.

"Hi," Turnbull said. "I'm Dr. Singh. I'm looking for a patient."

The nurse paused. When Turnbull did not react, she spoke.

"Uh, she/her?" she said, the up-talk making it into a query.

"Oh yeah, he/them," Turnbull said.

"What's the name?"

"Gruber."

She punched the name into her computer. "There's a Wayne Gruber in 533," she said, puzzled. "But that's not part of the obstetrics department, and plus, he identifies as a man. Of course, some men do get pregnant, but –"

Turnbull was already gone, heading for the elevators.

"Where are Jody and Mark?" Joe asked into his cell phone. "They should have checked in."

The voice on the other end answered. "I don't know. You want one of us should go look for them?"

"No," Joe replied. "I want one of you should get his ass up here with me. I want the other watching those cameras. And where the hell is Gruber's pizza?"

Turnbull carefully stepped off the seventh-floor elevator, head down and his Wilson under wraps. It was an administrative floor, and most of the administrators had gone home well before five. But the security folks would still be there.

He walked down the hall, face to the dirty linoleum, toward the door at the far end. It read "SURVEILLANCE CONTROL ROOM."

It opened when he was ten feet away, a man in a bad suit opened the door, saying, "You can't be up here..." pulling the handle. His eyes got enormous – this was not some lost doctor. He pushed the door closed.

Turnbull drew and fired three times through the wood. There was a groan, and a sound like a bag of moist chicken parts plopping onto the floor.

Turnbull aimed two more shots downwards, then carefully pushed the door open.

The SIS man was all gone, one of the rounds having passed through his forehead and out the back, saving him the necessity of a coup de grâce.

The wall inside was covered with video monitors, but most were blank. It would have taken two or three security men to effectively observe them had the system been up and running right.

Turnbull released the half-empty mag and reloaded a fresh one, then pocketed the partial one. He put his pistol on the console and looked for the fifth floor. There was one view, outside in the hallway, covering the nurses' station. There were a couple nurses and … there was the money shot. An SIS man with a M4 walking about like he was guarding something.

Wait, now there were two SIS men.

Turnbull considered his options. It occurred to him he could go to room 633, uncork the thermite grenade and hope it dropped right down on his pal Gruber.

Tempting, but Turnbull wanted certainty. He took his weapon and left the guard station.

"He's not answering," Joe told the other SIS agent, who had just joined him from the monitoring room.

"Maybe he's out taking a whizz. I don't know. Simmer down."

"You don't get it," Joe said. "This Chris guy is an animal."

"I thought we were the predators."

"Just go watch the elevators. And don't shoot the delivery guy."

The SIS man stood by the elevator bank in the center of the fifth floor. There were four of them, but one was out of service. The one on the end rang, and his M4 came up.

Nothing. The doors swung open to reveal an empty car. He relaxed.

The one on the other end dinged, and he was there with his weapon up.

Zip. Empty again.

He relaxed, but this was getting old.

A minute later the middle opened up. He covered it with the M4 as it revealed a family, dad, mom, a couple kids. They did not exit – the door shut.

"Shit," the SIS agent swore. Another ding.

Nothing.

"I think there's something wrong with the elevators," he yelled back up the hall at Joe, who was near the nurse's station covering the stairwell door.

"Shhhh," the head nurse hissed back.

"Bitch."

Another ding. The door opened to nothing and he relaxed as Turnbull spun out with the suppressed .45 and drilled him through the mouth. It severed his spine at the C1 vertebra, and he collapsed to the floor, his M4 clattering on the linoleum.

Turnbull sliced the pie covering the hallway outside the elevator. It was clear, but there was one more around and he probably heard his buddy flop onto the deck. Cautiously, he stepped out, his Wilson Combat CQB high and suppressed.

Nothing.

Turnbull slowly worked over to the hallway, covering to his front after clearing the rear. He began moving down the hall.

No movement.

He kept going, passing Room 533 on the left. It occurred to him that was a weird coincidence, considering it was the safe deposit box number. No noise from inside, not even the television.

He kept going. He needed to eliminate the M4 threat before he dealt with Gruber.

The nurse's station came into view, and the head nurse sat nervously in the seat. The other nurses were gone.

She knew.

Turnbull's eyes met hers. Slowly, they went to her right and down, then back to Turnbull.

He fired twice through the desk to her right, and there was a groan. Turnbull came over the top and Joe was there, bleeding from the side. He finished him with a headshot and turned back to Room 533.

The nurse would call in the cavalry, so he needed to be quick.

Turnbull stood in front of the door to 533, thinking of how to solve the tactical problem when Gruber did it for him by opening up the door as he hollered, "Where the hell is my pizza?"

Turnbull smashed the butt of the weapon down on his nose, shattering it and sending him staggering back. The Desert Eagle clanged as it hit the floor, and Gruber was against his bed, his gown flapping, his IV drip tower toppled over onto the floor.

"Look at me!" Turnbull commanded.

Gruber groaned, and his face contorted. He whimpered.

"Where's Crane?" Turnbull demanded.

Gruber's mouth moved, but it was dry as a sun-bleached bone as the big pistol hovered in his face.

"Please," he managed to stammer. "Please, man."

There was a noise like the tinkling of a garden waterfall. Gruber was pissing himself.

"Crane," Turnbull repeated, his weapon ready, his finger light on the custom trigger.

There was a ding. The elevator.

Out of time.

Turnbull put two rounds in Gruber's sternum. Gruber wheezed hard, his eyes doubling in size as the pain of his pulped heart washed over him.

Turnbull lifted the weapon and fired again. The manbun flopped over a ragged hole where the 230-grain hollow point round exploded out of Wayne Gruber's skull.

He slid to the floor in a heap, his face still in a twisted rictus.

Movement to Turnbull's rear.

He spun, gun up, prepped to engage. The front sight post was on the face of the head nurse. A couple others were behind her, looking in.

"We didn't see shit," the head nurse said.

Turnbull walked out, weapon up to engage the target who got off the elevators. It was a kid in a red polyester shirt with a flat box.

"Hey man, just take it," he said. "It's pepperoni."

Turnbull lowered his weapon and passed the delivery boy on his way to the elevators.

"It's for the ladies."

Turnbull had Dr. Singh's Hyundai Elantra and nowhere to go, at least not in Detroit. He needed a plan, a new way out. But first, he needed to make a call. He pulled out Ross's card.

"Ross."

"Thought you might want to know," Turnbull said. "I just visited your pal Gruber at Public Medical Facility No. 3 in Detroit."

"I take it he's left this mortal coil."

"Yeah, he died badly."

"Oh well," Ross said. "How did you find him?"

"That's the interesting part, Agent Ross. Merrick Crane himself told me. I think he was hoping our little close encounter would be of a different kind."

"With you on a slab."

"Didn't work out that way. Unfortunately, I had to remove the back of Gruber's skull before I could get him to tell me where his boss is. You got any ideas?"

"If I did, I'd take that piece of shit out myself."

"Too bad," Turnbull said. "I'm going now."

"We still have unfinished business, Chris."

"Go back to Boston. Bye."

The line went dead. Ross considered, then dialed.

Harrington answered.

"What do you have for me?"

"It's over," Ross said. "Our Chris just capped Crane's sociopath right hand and since he can't find Crane he's heading home."

"You know this how?"

"He just called me."

"So, you have his phone number?"

Ross snorted. "I have a number, but it's gotta be spoofed. He's a lot of things, but not dumb."

"You text me that spoofed number," Harrington directed. "And you get on the road.

Turnbull decided to get out of town into rural Michigan and then contact Clay Deeds and figure out his next move. He was actually reaching for his phone when it rang. It was a strange phone number, a dozen nines.

"Yeah?"

"Am I speaking to Chris?"

"Harrington?"

"Senator Harrington. I guess I'm impressed you remembered my voice."

"I'm impressed you got my number."

"You know the FBI is intermittently competent," Harrington said. "Or People's Bureau of Investigation. Whatever they are changing the name to."

"I do appreciate your cynicism, Senator Harrington."

"And I do appreciate your effectiveness, Mr. Chris. So, I'm going to share something with you. A bit of information you might find useful."

"Tell me quick. I'm not staying on the line long enough for you to fix my location."

"I know where Merrick Crane is."

Turnbull paused.

"Where?"

"He's at a conference of all the members of his political faction. It's supposed to be a secret, but I know about it and now so do you. It's in the Grand Hotel on Mackinac Island. That's north of you, conveniently near Canada by the way."

"What do you expect me to do? Go kill him for you?"

"Remember, Chris, I was there when he murdered your friend, the beautiful Ms. Barnes. I expect you to go kill him for *you*."

Turnbull hung up and tossed his compromised phone out the window, where it shattered on the freeway asphalt.

There would be no calling Deeds for a new out. He was all on his own. And he would not have it any other way.

23.

The view from the lengthy veranda was gorgeous – the lake glistened and there was not a cloud in the sky. Flanked by four of his SIS men, Merrick Crane III worked the attendees, up from the underground and unashamed. Technically, the retreat had an agenda and presentations, but they were for the third-tier saps. This was where the action at the radical retreat was, right there and then, and Crane was the person of the hour, the toast of the radical, the bane of the merely progressive.

Of course, both factions were Democrats – though other parties were allowed and, once registered and approved, they were required to abide by a set of guidelines and mandatory positions provided by the People's Electoral Justice Committee. What it meant is that the battle for supreme power in the People's Republic was being waged within a very narrow ideological band on the far-left side of the spectrum.

The radical leading lights gathered there were eager to greet him as if they were old allies, and as if they hadn't shunned him when the blood he spilled in the pursuit of their shared radical agenda threatened to splash on them too. But Crane's masterful suppression of the right-wing terrorist cabal in Charlestown had legitimized his view that real progress was colored red. There was no talk of the casualty numbers, the hundreds of civilian corpses and the hundreds of People's Militia fighters who died as well. The dead were both abstract and expendable and, in fact, inevitable and acceptable.

"Senator Blumenthal, I appreciate your support," Crane said, shaking the old man's hand. The politician had been known as a moderate, relatively speaking, but after the Split he had read the writing on the wall. It was literal writing, the slogan "Kill the moderate traitors" that was spray-painted all over his state.

"You have to be firm with insurrectionists and extremists," the senator said. "As a military man myself, I approve of your strategy."

"That means a great deal coming from a veteran of the Tet Offensive," Crane said, smiling politely.

"Yes, I, uh, I believe I'll get another soda pop," Blumenthal said, excusing himself.

"Very good to see you again, Senator," Crane said. He smiled even as he mentally added the Connecticut senator to his list of dead wood to be cut away.

That's why he had offered to supply security for the radical retreat with his own men. The purpose of the conference was to chart a way forward for the radical faction against the progressive faction nominally in control of the People's Republic. And tonight, through an instructive exercise in raw power, Merrick Crane III intended to demonstrate conclusively that he was the way forward.

The mad doctor's disc would have been nice to have, but now it was no longer necessary.

Turnbull left the stolen Hyundai Elantra in a parking lot in Mackinaw City by a seafood restaurant with a sign that had a cartoon chef in a floppy white chef hat reeling in a trout. A sign attached to the pole beneath it issued an apology for the trauma inflicted upon those people who saw the sign and somehow convinced themselves the chef hat was a Ku Klux Klan hood.

He had caught some sleep off Interstate 75 on the long drive north from Detroit. It was early afternoon now, and Turnbull had no idea how he was going to get to the gorgeous island several miles north out at the far western tip of Lake Huron.

The ferries were shut down and tied up at the island, though no one knew why. He had heard some rumors when he went to grab lunch at a local diner. There were private jets at the island airfield. Some kind of conference, people heard. The locals who worked there were saying there was to be a big to-do tonight. The painful part is all boat traffic near the island was banned as a security measure. That was pretty painful in the middle of summer, especially when they were already being told all the boats needed to be electric within two years because of climate change.

Turnbull saw something familiar through the window facing the sidewalk. Two guys in mediocre suits, dark glasses, and a thug vibe.

"Excuse me," he said to his waitress. "You got any place around here that sells suits?"

"Yeah," she said. "You looking for something really nice for this big party?"

Turnbull smiled.

"Well, not too nice."

Ross had never heard of Pellston Regional Airport before he bought a ticket to fly into it. The small Embraer jet headed north toward the regional airport, about 15 miles south of Mackinaw City. As they came in on approach, the stewardess – who had earlier identified herself (she gave her pronouns before her safety briefing) as a "flight facilitator" – welcomed the passengers to the northern tip of Michigan's Lower Peninsula.

The flight facilitator also apologized for the area's legacy of white supremacy.

Crane handed his list to his new senior SIS agent, a man whose name he had forgotten. It would have been awkward had he cared.

There were nine names on the list. Some who were competitors. Some who had become inconvenient. Some who he merely found annoying.

"Those are the people. Do it tonight, after the party. Get their room numbers, assign your people, and take them out," he said.

The agent scanned the list.

"It can be quick," Crane added. "The act itself makes the point. No need to embellish."

"There are going to be repercussions," the agent said, scanning the names.

"Are you under the impression that I am asking you for advice?" Crane said. "I am well aware of what I am doing and why, and the potential consequences. It will be attributed to right-wing extremists – you brought the red ball caps to leave as the killers' calling cards, correct?"

"We have them. It's hard to find them, because they're illegal. We had to take them from the evidence lockers at the DOPJ." He was referring to the Department of People's Justice.

"And if someday the truth comes out that it was not die-hard insurrectionists following Q's orders – I still find it remarkable that Q was Ben Sasse – so be it. I *want* them to know it was me."

His men departed, and Crane smiled. Hummingbird II was a go.

"Pretty slow today," Turnbull said, staring down from the dock at the two middle-aged men in their small fishing boat.

"Yep," one answered, his eyes suspicious. Who was this fellow in a gray suit and what did he want?

"Kind of unfair, a bunch of rich jerks holding a conference, and you guys getting screwed."

"What do you want?"

"I want you to take me over to the island when it gets dark."

"We can't. No one is allowed within two miles of the island until day after tomorrow."

"Then I guess I'm going to have to give someone else five thousand dollars." Turnbull held up the bills. The men gaped.

"Five thousand *American*," Turnbull clarified. The stack had come from the robbery.

"Who are you?" the fisherman demanded.

"I'm a journalist," Turnbull replied.

"I don't know," the man replied. "Ya look like an asshole, but not that big of an asshole."

Turnbull smiled. "We're gonna get along just fine."

The Mackinac Island Grand Hotel would seem to be everything the radicals hated, and yet they adored it. Opened in 1887 after just three months of construction, it had become a legend in terms of its old-fashioned luxury and the eminence of its guests. There had been some updates to its stodgy customs – the dress code was first rendered gender neutral, then eliminated entirely after an unfortunate incident involving allegations of discrimination by a group of visitors who insisted that requiring any clothing at all was an act of violence against them.

Planted on the heights at the south end of the island, most of which was a wooded state park, the Grand Hotel was a throwback to another age, and the radicals delighted in it, whether being served drinks on the 660-foot-long veranda or swimming in the gigantic pool. It had long catered to presidents and other political figures, and even featured a number of suites designed by and named in honor of first ladies from Jackie Kennedy to Laura Bush. There had never been any question of one done by Melania Trump.

Of course, most of these did not last long after the Split. Except for the Rosalynn Carter room, the others were redone and renamed because the related presidents were all racist or worse. However, the hotel did add a suite nominally designed by Michelle Obama. It featured a socialist realist motif, and AOC swooped it up for the conference.

Crane watched the sun going down from the magnificent patio and took a flute of Taittinger Blanc de Blancs from a silver tray held by a passing waiter. If he had not seen the bottles, he would not have risked being served swill. His radical comrades may have had class consciousness, but not class.

Crane had grown up in this world and slipped easily back into this life, but some of the other attendees had not had the benefit of his upbringing. They drank too much, or talked too much, or dressed like hoodoos. His own dark suit was exquisite, and he had left his Walther in his room because it broke the coat's perfect lines. But what none of them ever did was doubt their own entitlement to live like French aristocrats before anyone in Paris thought of storming the Bastille.

"Great party, huh?" Gavin Newsom asked, swaying a bit. Crane noted that the former governor had disappeared for eight minutes after chatting up a thin blonde refreshment facilitation person. His breath smelled like he had been into a bottle of the tacky wine his minions produced back in Napa.

"It's good to work together to forge an initiative for true change," Crane replied. Newsom nodded enthusiastically, and then another waitress caught his eye. He mumbled something about their faction being on the right side of history and drifted off after her. Crane sighed and wished he were able to add a tenth name to his list.

Johnny Ross pounded on the door of the police station in Mackinaw City. The deputy opened it.

"Yeah, what?" he asked.

Ross flashed his credentials and the deputy's jaw dropped.

"Your department have a boat?" he demanded.

The deputy nodded, baffled.

"Let's go."

Turnbull made the jump to the rocks without falling in. The small fishing boat puttered away. There at the northern tip of

Mackinac Island, it was mostly trees. He drew out his Wilson and did a chamber check. There was a round seated. He wished that carrying it with the suppressor affixed was not so awkward, but it was. He did a final check, confirming he had both the disc and the last thermite grenade. He did, but he briefly considered ditching the bulky canister before rejecting that idea.

No one ever had too much ordnance.

"Do you want to dance?" AOC asked Crane, smiling her distinctive smile and pulling him toward the ballroom. They're playing disco! I *love* disco!"

He smiled coldly, for her up-talking grated on him and he disliked the Bee Gees intensely.

"I am sure I will see you in there," he said, which made her frown. But sometimes you had to disappoint even a rumored vice-presidential nominee.

Turnbull found a path that took him toward the hotel. It was more exposure, but it beat breaking brush and the resulting damage to his duds.

There were shapes ahead, a giggling woman in a hotel white uniform and a man with pretty amazing hair peeling off into the woods together. Turnbull pressed on, heading toward the sound of the music ahead. Was that Anita Ward singing about getting her bell rung?

Ahead on the path was a bored SIS man, in a distinctively mediocre suit, cradling his M4. It was too dark to make out his face.

"Hey," the man said.

"You see those two?" Turnbull said.

"Bangin' in the woods. That brings back memories," the agent replied.

Turnbull stepped up close and the man squinted. "Do I know...," he began, but Turnbull kneed him in the groin and he bent forward. Turnbull locked his right arm around the man's neck and squeezed.

The guy was not giving up. He had dropped the carbine, but he still had his Fairbairn-Sykes dagger. Unfortunately for him, while he could draw it from his scabbard, he could not whip it around and into Turnbull.

Instead, Turnbull grabbed the hand with the knife and forced it up, into the man's neck. He dropped to the cement path dead, and Turnbull barely escaped being splashed with a wave of blood.

Turnbull dragged him off of the path and into the brush. He considered taking the M4, but decided against it. He headed toward the pounding bass.

"How do I get to the Grand Hotel?" Ross asked the deputy as the lights of the island docks loomed ahead. A half-dozen ferries were tied up there, waiting in case any of the guests wished to leave. And also ensuring that there would be no unwanted visitors.

"You walk. There are no cars allowed on the island. But the Hotel itself is right there," the deputy said, pointing at a large shape on the heights with flickering lights.

Ross swore he could hear someone playing "Boogie Wonderland."

Turnbull stepped up onto the patio, and realized he did not have much of a plan for getting out. He figured that at some point, all hell was going to break loose, and when it did the guests would hightail it to the ferries that he had seen tied up down at the Marina. He had a general notion of fading in with the flow back to the mainland.

If he lived.

Merrick Crane III stood alone in the center of the dance floor. One of his security men stood at each of the two entrances, no long guns so as not to frighten the squeamish. A third had gone to the DJ and asked nicely for silence the first time, and then, when rebuffed, not so nicely. Crane got his silence.

"Someday," Crane said, his voice loud and crisp. "History will write about this retreat. About how what some call radicals came together to forge a bond to bring true change to the People's Republic of North America."

He paused for effect before continuing. "I know that some of you fear me, and some of you wanted nothing to do with me before I showed what we can achieve in Charlestown when we put aside childish notions of tolerance and mercy for the fascists."

The crowd watched and listened, and none of them dared speak.

"You!"

There were three SIS men and their leader at the far end of the main hallway. Turnbull was lurking in the dark by a door to the patio. At the far end was the ballroom, but the doors were shut and the music had been turned off. Someone was talking, but it was muffled.

"Come on. Boss wants us in the ballroom. He wants to send a message, you know. That's why he offered to provide all the security."

They started heading toward the ballroom. One of them had an M4.

Turnbull reached down and confirmed the hammer was back on his Wilson. Then he followed, trotting behind them, trying to keep his face down. The longer he could put off the inevitable, the better.

"We will take power," Crane said. "We will prevail and impose the justice we deserve. Even the People's Republic is built on a legacy of systemic racism, of patriarchy, of transphobia and other pathologies that come from being part of the old United

346 | THE SPLIT

States. We cannot just pretend that the People's Republic is immune to white supremacy and anti-otherkin hate. The evil must be vanquished and I showed you in Charlestown what that requires. We will do what it requires here in the People's Republic until we see the evil of right-wing extremism of the kind we now see in the White House and in traitors like Senator Harrington and others, purged and punished. Then we will destroy the racist red states and wipe out the cancer that is the United States of America and its fascist Constitution forever."

The crowd paused, unsure of what to do. This irritated Crane, but so did the tardiness of his men. It would have been perfect to emphasize his own power to have some more of his SIS men step inside just as he hit his high note.

The crowd was still for a moment, and then there was a clap, and then another and another and finally the round of applause he had expected, along with some cheers as well.

Merrick Crane beamed.

"To paraphrase what an American fascist once said, not understanding that he had the right sentiment in service of the wrong cause, extremism – what the revanchists call our dedication to comprehensive change – is no vice, and moderation is no virtue!"

Smiling broadly at the applause, he briefly considered adding his thoughts on how Pol Pot demonstrated the kind of stern commitment called for today, but he left that insight for another time and contended himself with basking in their adulation.

The lead SIS man got to the ballroom door as the second round of applause hit. He turned back to his men to tell them something, but his face scrunched up, and he looked at Turnbull and spoke.

"Who the hell are you?"

"Enough politics," Crane said as the applause died. "Let's resume the festivities. Music!"

The SIS men all turned as one on Turnbull, confused. Turnbull wasn't. He drew and immediately put two into the leader, who flew against the ballroom door and splashed it with crimson.

Turnbull pivoted to the guy with the M4, blasting him twice in the chest. He flew against an antique chair set up under a gold-framed mirror.

The other two were drawing, and the ballroom door was opening. Turnbull went for two headshots, getting one through the nose but taking out most of the right cheek of the other. He pivoted back to the ballroom and another SIS man was coming through, his automatic out. Turnbull shot him twice in the chest, but he stayed on his feet until Turnbull completed the failure drill with a final shot through the forehead.

The slide locked back and Turnbull instinctively dropped the dry mag.

His ears were ringing and the acrid smoke was burning his ears. Then he saw movement down the hall, two more SIS sprinting his way.

Dropping his .45 on the long rug that ran the length of the hall – and which was in the process of being ruined by the crimson leaking from his victims – Turnbull dove for the M4 and opened up on the approaching agents from his knee with two long bursts even as they fired their pistols his way.

Both caught rounds and dropped. Turnbull stood and put a burst into three of the SIS men around him, then tossed away the empty carbine and retrieved his Wilson from the floor.

There was chaos in the ballroom, with the two remaining SIS men closed on Crane, pistols out. They had just seen their buddy's head nearly blown off as he tried to go out into the hallway, where there was a firefight going on. They were advising evacuation.

"I can't run!" Crane said. "We fight. You fight!"

Turnbull slapped in the fresh mag and kicked in the door. It was pandemonium, with people running in every direction, most not having figured out that the far exit led to the outdoors and safety. There were screams and the music was pumping. Turnbull felt, not heard the spray of wood chips on him as a bullet slammed into the door over his head. Then a tall woman in a black cocktail dress running immediately in front of his front right to left caught a round in the head and sprawled. Her male-identifying companion looked back and kept running.

Turnbull advanced, and acquired a target, who also acquired him. They fired at the same time. Turnbull felt the crack by his ear as the bullet tore past. The SIS agent felt the bullet punch a hole through his heart.

He spotted them, Crane and the last SIS man dragging him through the crowd. Turnbull took aim on Crane, the sight picture absolutely terminal, right on his smug face, and if a panicking Ted Lieu had not tripped and fell on him, Crane would have been gone.

But the impact knocked the weapon out of his hands and broke the aim of the shot he was firing when the congressman ran into him. The round flew off target, and into the agent's chest. Turnbull looked for his pistol, but all he saw was Lieu's eyes grow wide as he picked himself up off the floor and took off running.

Crane was there, looking at the bodies, and at their guns.

Turnbull charged, pushing past the panicked Senator Mazie Hirono, who had been running in a circle making a noise like an angry chicken, as Crane bent to retrieve one of the Smith & Wesson M&P Shield M2.0s that his dead bodyguards would no longer be needing.

Crane was no match for Turnbull's tackle, and the gun went flying as they sprawled on the floor. Turnbull recovered faster. He was on his feet as Crane got to his, and delivered a smash to his mouth with his meaty paw.

Crane was staggered by the blow, and blood poured from the hole where an incisor had once lived. Turnbull grabbed him by the lapels and punched him twice more in the face.

He was not so pretty anymore.

Crane struck a glancing blow to Turnbull's side, more effective because it was unexpected.

He backed up and squared off.

"I told you I'd kill you." Turnbull said, breathing hard. Around them, some of the people were slowing to watch the fight.

"My guys are converging and you aren't armed," Crane said, smiling his bloody smile.

"You think your little bitches would have learned their lesson about trying to kill me," Turnbull shouted over the disco music.

"Oh, they aren't going to kill you, Chris," Crane hissed. "I am."

Crane charged with his Fairbairn-Sykes stiletto out and high. He was bringing it down to plant in Turnbull's chest, but Turnbull's beefy left hand caught it. Turnbull launched forward powered by his legs, the crest of his skull impacting Crane's nose and dazing him for a moment.

With his right hand, Turnbull ripped a green canister out of his jacket and clenched the metal ring between his teeth, then pulled it out. The thermite grenade's spoon dropped to the floor and clattered on the hardwood dance floor.

He let loose of Crane's knife hand, taking the calculated risk that stabbing would be the last item on Crane's priority list in a few seconds.

Turnbull's left hand took hold of Crane's belt and pulled it out, opening a gap that was just big enough for Turnbull to drive the smoking canister downward and inside. He let go, and Crane stumbled backwards.

"For Avery," Turnbull snarled, loud enough for Crane to hear it over the music and the screaming and shouting of his fans.

Smoke started coming out of his pants, and for a split-second Crane wondered which was worse, the indignity of it or the 4,000 degrees the grenade would generate.

The grenade detonated, and Crane knew the answer.

The burning was much, much worse.

The light from Crane's melting abdomen was too bright to look at, as much as Turnbull wanted to stare and enjoy it. After just a few moments, Crane's molten pelvis collapsed and he fell to the floor, his arms still flailing.

Reluctantly, Turnbull joined the exodus and left the ballroom. The sound of the lyrics "Burn, baby, burn" was pretty loud, but not loud enough to drown out the sound of Crane's screaming.

24.

The crowd was pouring down the Grand Hotel's long driveway down to the town and the docks, the partygoers staggering and stumbling as they rushed to safety. The women in heels ditched them on the road, as did the males wearing heels, of which there were many – it was easier to run in bare feet.

The screaming behind him stopped by the time Turnbull was 100 yards away. He was a bit disappointed, as he had hoped that the human inferno would have gone on a bit longer. Now Turnbull flowed with the crowd, and if any of the refugees recognized him from the battle in the ballroom, they wisely held their tongues. If this man would publicly melt the notorious Merrick Crane III into a puddle of molten fat and charred bone, only Gaia knew what he would do to them.

Turnbull felt naked without his Wilson, and toyed with the idea of going back to find it. He pivoted to glance back at the white façade of the hotel, with its windows illuminated by flames and thick, acrid smoke pouring out, and accepted the fact that his beloved piece was lost in the chaos. He hoped it burned rather than was picked up by some leftist; he couldn't bear the thought of his beloved weapon in the soft paw of some blue.

But in keeping with his firm conviction that a man without a gun was no man at all, he resolved to indulge his toxic masculinity. The opportunity presented itself as he noticed an SIS agent in uniform, M4 at low-ready and an S&W M&P Shield M2.0 automatic in his holster going against the flow of the

352 | THE SPLIT

fleeing leftists like a blue salmon. He had probably been pulling security down by the docks and decided to respond to the desperate radio calls of his comrades.

Turnbull pivoted and vectored in on the man, who was straining to see past the surging wall of bodies to figure out just what was happening at the hotel up ahead. Turnbull intercepted the thug next to a high hedge that would serve his purpose well.

"Hey," Turnbull shouted when he got within arms-length. "There's a racist up there!"

"Where?" shouted the SIS agent, his eyes locked onto Turnbull's. It was therefore a surprise when Turnbull's fist pile-drove into his liver, causing him to bend forward with a loud "Ooof."

Turnbull manhandled him into the hedge and out of sight, asking loudly "Hey, are you all right?" and adding "Here, sit down." None of the escapees running past spared an iota of attention to their injured protector – he was mere human wallpaper to the people he was about to die for.

After a few steps, the SIS agent stumbled and tried to recover, but once behind the foliage Turnbull wrapped his arm around the man's neck and used his legs to jerk hard. The snap was audible, and the thug went instantly limp. Turnbull let him drop onto the leaves and bent down and relieved him of his Smith & Wesson and his three spare mags. Shoving them into his belt under his jacket, he stepped back out to the driveway and joined the lemmings in their gambol down the hill to the ferry.

A crowd was formed on the dock around a hundred-foot blue and white catamaran. A sign said "Saint Ignace," a town across the water and also across the water to the north from Mackinaw City. The fare was free for the highest privileged levels; the rest of the levels paid graduated amounts up to $120 a ride. Many of the Gucci-clad escapees were arguing with the beleaguered woman in the sales booth that they were actually oppressed and should not have to pay.

The ferry had two decks, and it was filling up fast. Turnbull forced his way through the tightly packed bodies at the gangway, not hesitating to deliver an occasional kidney punch to secure the cooperation of a blue blocking his way in getting the hell out of it. It took a few moments, but he shoved his way to the beleaguered clerk, squeezing out a bitter-looking crone with a necklace of pearls around her wattled neck.

"That man pushed a woman out of his way," she howled, and Turnbull faced her.

Instead of offering his opinion that leftist women did not count as women, he said, "I cannot believe that you just imposed a gender on me!"

The woman turned paler than she was before, and mumbled about how sorry she was. The crowd was aghast, and when Turnbull handed his money to the clerk, the woman in the booth returned it.

"Hate has no home here," she said, and the crone was roundly jeered and harassed as Turnbull made his way onto the boat and around to the other side, where he found a space on the deck along the railing and looked out over the water as it finished loading.

Johnny Ross's SIG P226 led the way as he entered the Grand Hotel from the long porch. There was smoke, but the flames were out. A few people ran back and forth, guests and employees still panicking. A weird, foul smell like burned hair hung in the hallway air.

The music had stopped inside the ballroom, and some of the drapes along the windows were charred and covered with foam. It was largely empty now, with many of the tables overturned and several bodies on the ground. Plainclothes SIS agents, he figured, most with a couple holes near vital organs. There were shell casings on the hardwood floor, along with debris left behind from the fleeing blue revelers and substantial blood.

His weapon was hanging downward now, still in two hands, as Ross surveyed the ruins. No SIS meant they likely hustled Merrick Crane III away. And the lack of the carcass of the elusive Chris meant he was probably right behind his quarry.

Movement right.

His SIG was up and on the target, a man in a tux hiding under a buffet table. Ross moved over carefully, the weapon locked on its target, and then he pulled back the white tablecloth.

The youngish man underneath turned his head and put up his hands. Even Ross recognized him, and he tried very hard to ignore politicians.

"No, no, please," he begged. "Please don't hurt me."

Ross sighed, reaching down and grabbing the spindly arm of the cowering man.

"Stand up, Mr. Secretary," he said. This blubbering schmuck must have gone over great in Afghanistan back in the day.

"I'm okay," he said, shaking.

"There was a man," Ross said. "He did this. Where is he?"

"He, he left. Went out with everyone else."

"And Crane?" asked Ross. The lip of the man who had once been spoken of as a potential president began to quiver, and he pointed a bony finger out toward the dance floor. Ross followed it, and saw the black, smoking pile on the floor. He turned back to the shaking man.

"Get out of here," he said. "And change your pants."

The man scurried away, and Ross stalked out across the floor. The black mess had been a human being, though you could only tell because what remained above the shoulders remained intact enough to identify it as such. The rest was charred and melted.

Ross looked at the face, and recognized it. He holstered the SIG; the SIS guys were no doubt long gone since their boss had met his incendiary doom.

"You got off easy," Ross said, and then he began trotting downhill toward town.

Ross forced his way to the front of the line at the dock. The ferry was packed and the flustered crew was trying to push off. At least 200 more people were ashore clamoring and demanding passage to Saint Ignace. There was a lot of "Don't you know who I am?" going on, and the crew largely had no idea who any of them were.

Ross, however, had ID, and he flashed it to the officer at the bottom of the gangplank.

"I'm FBI," he said. "Let me aboard."

"We're overloaded as it is," the sailor complained.

Ross produced his SIG and pointed it at the crewman.

"Maybe this ID is good enough?"

The crewman nodded and Ross clambered aboard, the last passenger to do so before they shoved off.

Turnbull leaned on the wood railing and looked out over the placid black water of what had been Lake Huron. It was a warm summer night, and except for the overdressed blues surrounding him crying about the racist right-wing militia attack they had just witnessed, it was a pleasant evening. Most of the lights on the mainland were off – it must have been another "power usage conservation celebration." The Grand Hotel back on the island seemed calm. They must have put Crane out. He smiled.

A cold metal ring enclosed his right wrist, and Turnbull pivoted with the M2.0 up and against the gut of Johnny Ross.

The other end of the handcuff was locked on Ross's left wrist. The SIG was in his right, and pressed against Turnbull.

"If I have to dig out a key and unlock myself, you'll be sorry," Turnbull said quietly. "Unlock me. Now."

"I promised I'd catch up to you," Ross said, also quietly.

"And I promise that if I'm still hooked up to you in five seconds, I'm splattering your liver all over that gender fluid being with a leopard skin skirt and blue hair that's standing right behind you."

"I got who I was really after," Ross said, holstering his pistol and producing a handcuff key. "Or, rather, you did."

Turnbull smiled. "Oh, I guess you found Crane. How's he doing?"

"Well done," Ross said.

"From asshole to ash-hole," Turnbull said, smirking.

"Karma's a bitch."

"And Crane was mine."

Ross looked around to see if any other passengers were paying attention. They were all in their own little worlds. He stuck the key in the lock on the cuff around Turnbull's wrist.

"You're really letting me go without a fight?" Turnbull said. "I'm the Swayze to your Keanu?"

"I hate that movie," Johnny Ross said, almost under his breath, clicking the lock and taking back the cuff. Only then did Turnbull replace his pistol in his holster. "If I tried to take you in, who knows how many of these nice people would have been caught in the crossfire?"

"True," Turnbull said. "Probably would have made Boston look like teatime."

"Boston was on Crane. If not for him and his pack of psychos, you boys would have walked in, walked out, and no one would have been hurt. My only regret is you got to pull the pin."

"Crane and I had a personal issue. I think I resolved it tonight."

"Remind me not to have any issue with you."

"Just as long as when we get to shore you go the opposite of where I do. I got something I have to deliver."

"So, do you still have the disc?"

"Yeah," Turnbull said. "In all the shooting, I kind of forgot about the MacGuffin."

"What does it actually do?" asked Ross.

"They never told you?" Turnbull laughed. "Typical. In the end, does it even matter?"

"Probably not," Ross said. "Still, my principal is going to be mighty disappointed."

"Tell him it fell in the lake. Tell him I did, too."

"I'll give you thirty minutes before I call it in," Ross said.

"Thirty minutes is an eternity in my business."

"And what is your business?" Ross asked. "Who are you, Chris?"

"I'm not Chris."

"No shit. But you are red."

"I am."

"I liked being a cop better when it was about the crime, not the politics."

"Then why were you in the FBI?" asked Turnbull. "Whatever. Anyway, I liked America better when it wasn't split in two. When it wasn't two crocs fighting to the death in one little pond."

"What the hell are you talking about?" Ross asked.

"Just something I've been thinking a lot about lately."

They both looked out on the water as the catamaran gently slid over the waves. It wasn't far to Saint Ignace now. In the distance, the Mackinac Bridge spanned the Straits of Mackinac, connecting Upper and Lower Michigan peninsulas. The span was unlit, with little traffic. Before the Split, it was both beautiful and busy.

"You can come with me. A guy like you could do okay in the red," Turnbull said.

Ross shook his head.

"A lot of good folks are making the move," Turnbull said.

"And if all the good folks leave the PR, what then?"

"Then it hits bottom that much faster and this insanity ends. You've seen what's happening. This isn't sustainable. It's just a question of time and how many people have to die first."

"I'll stick around," Ross said. "I'll do my job. Someone has to."

"The door is always open," Turnbull said.

"It's nice out here," Ross said. The sound of the water was relaxing, and the wind cool on his face. "We should enjoy this quiet before the storm."

"Yeah, we should," Turnbull replied. "So, stop talking."

AUTHOR'S NOTE

I hope all the technical stuff seemed plausible because I invented it. Even if I knew that stuff, I would never disclose it!

After *The Split* and its predecessor *Crisis* have covered the beginning of the Kelly Turnbull saga, I may hop back to the future, so to speak, for Novel No. 7. Or not – there are a lot of stories to be told about the future that lies just over the horizon and they may not all be just about Kelly Turnbull, though he's not going anywhere (except back into enemy territory)!

People seem to love these novels, and I don't think I could quit writing them even if I wanted to – and I have no intention of doing so until I have nothing more to say. The response to these novels has been hugely gratifying. I never really expected them to take off to the point I was selling more of them than whoever wrote *Fifty Shades of Grey* was selling of her suburban mommy porn epics. But that's exactly what happened.

By the way, I sketched most of this out listening to '80s alternative music. I don't know if that means anything, but there it is.

I am still struggling with the fact that the present is almost crazier than any future I can imaging. Our struggle to reimpose sanity is not going to end anytime soon. And as always, these books remain a warning, not a goal or objective. As I write in every single one of these books, don't let this work of fiction become nonfiction.

KAS, July 2021

Kelly Turnbull will return in…

*Inferno**

*At least that's the plan right now, but plans often change upon contact with the enemy!

ABOUT THE AUTHOR

Kurt Schlichter is a senior columnist for *Townhall.com*. He is also a Los Angeles trial lawyer admitted in California, Texas, and Washington, DC, and a retired Army Infantry colonel.

A Twitter activist (@KurtSchlichter) with over 325,000 followers, Kurt was personally recruited by Andrew Breitbart. His writings on political and cultural issues have also been published in *The Federalist*, the *New York Post*, the *Washington Examiner*, the *Los Angeles Times*, the *Boston Globe*, the *Washington Times*, *Army Times*, the *San Francisco Examiner*, and elsewhere.

Kurt serves as a news source, an on-screen commentator, and a guest and a guest host on nationally syndicated radio programs regarding political, military, and legal issues, on Fox News, Fox Business News, CNN, NewsMax, One America Network, The Blaze, and with hosts such as Hugh Hewitt, Larry O'Connor, Cam Edwards, Chris Stigall, Dennis Prager, Tony Katz, John Cardillo, Dana Loesch, and Derek Hunter, among others.

Kurt was a stand-up comic for several years, which led him to write three e-books that each reached number one on the Amazon Kindle "Political Humor" bestsellers list: *I Am a Conservative: Uncensored, Undiluted, and Absolutely Un-PC*, *I Am a Liberal: A Conservative's Guide to Dealing with Nature's Most Irritating Mistake*, and *Fetch My Latte: Sharing Feelings with Stupid People*.

In 2014, his book *Conservative Insurgency: The Struggle to Take America Back 2013-2041* was published by Post Hill Press.

His 2016 novel *People's Republic* and its 2017 prequel *Indian Country* reached No. 1 and No. 2 on the Amazon Kindle "Political Thriller" bestsellers list. *Wildfire*, the third book in the series, hit

No. 1 on the Amazon "Thrillers – Espionage" bestsellers list and No. 122 in all Amazon Kindle books. *Collapse*, the fourth book, hit 121.

His Kindle book of his fifth Kelly Turnbull novel, 2020's *Crisis*, hit No. 29 on all of Amazon and was No. 1 on the Amazon "Political Fiction" bestseller list.

His non-fiction book *Militant Normals: How Regular Americans Are Rebelling Against the Elite to Reclaim Our Democracy* was published by Center Street Books in October 2018. It made the USA Today Best Selling Books List.

His Regnery book *The 21 Biggest Lies About Donald Trump (and You)* was released in 2020 and hit No. 1 on an Amazon list.

Kurt is a successful trial lawyer and name partner in a Los Angeles law firm representing Fortune 500 companies and individuals in matters ranging from routine business cases to confidential Hollywood disputes and political controversies. A member of the Million Dollar Advocates Forum, which recognizes attorneys who have won trial verdicts in excess of $1 million, his litigation strategy and legal analysis articles have been published in legal publications such as the *Los Angeles Daily Journal* and *California Lawyer*.

He is frequently engaged by noted conservatives in need of legal representation, and he was counsel for political commentator and author Ben Shapiro in the widely publicized "Clock Boy" defamation lawsuit, which resulted in the case being dismissed and the victory being upheld on appeal.

Kurt is a 1994 graduate of Loyola Law School, where he was a law review editor. He majored in communications and political science as an undergraduate at the University of California, San Diego, co-editing the conservative student paper *California Review* while also writing a regular column in the student humor paper *The Koala*.

Kurt served as a US Army infantry officer on active duty and in the California Army National Guard, retiring at the rank of full colonel. He wears the silver "jump wings" of a paratrooper and commanded the 1st Squadron, 18th Cavalry Regiment (Reconnaissance-Surveillance-Target Acquisition). A veteran of both the Persian Gulf War and Operation Enduring Freedom (Kosovo), he is a graduate of the Army's Combined Arms and Services Staff School, the Command and General Staff College, and the United States Army War College, where he received a master's degree in strategic studies.

He lives with his wife Irina and their monstrous dogs Bitey and Barkey in the Los Angeles area, and he enjoys sarcasm and red meat.

His favorite caliber is .45.

The Kelly Turnbull Novels

People's Republic (2016)

Indian Country (2017)

Wildfire (2018)

Collapse (2019)

Crisis (2020)

The Split (2021)

Also By Kurt Schlichter

Conservative Insurgency: The Struggle to Take America Back 2013-2041 (Post Hill Press, 2014)

Militant Normals: How Regular Americans Are Rebelling Against the Elite to Reclaim Our Democracy (Center Street Books, 2018)

The 21 Biggest Lies About Donald Trump (and You) (Regnery, 2020)

Made in the USA
Columbia, SC
27 August 2023

22184663R00204